The AMISH
Millionaire

A 6-in-1 Series from Holmes County

The AMISH *Millionaire*

WANDA E. BRUNSTETTER

& JEAN BRUNSTETTER

BARBOUR
PUBLISHING

The English Son © 2016 by Wanda E. Brunstetter and Jean Brunstetter
The Stubborn Father © 2016 by Wanda E. Brunstetter and Jean Brunstetter
The Betrayed Fiancée © 2016 by Wanda E. Brunstetter and Jean Brunstetter
The Missing Will © 2016 by Wanda E. Brunstetter and Jean Brunstetter
The Divided Family © 2016 by Wanda E. Brunstetter and Jean Brunstetter
The Selfless Act © 2016 by Wanda E. Brunstetter and Jean Brunstetter

Print ISBN 978-1- 64352-870-0

eBook Editions:
Adobe Digital Edition (.epub) 978-1-68322-241-5
Kindle and MobiPocket Edition (.prc) 978-1-68322-240-8

All scripture quotations are taken from the King James Version of the Bible.

This book is a work of fiction. Names, characters, places, and incidents are either products of the author's imagination or used fictitiously. Any similarity to actual people, organizations, and/or events is purely coincidental.

Cover design: Müllerhaus Publishing Arts Inc., www.mullerhaus.net
Cover photography: Richard Brunstetter III, RB III Studios

Published by Barbour Publishing, Inc., 1810 Barbour Drive, Uhrichsville, Ohio 44683, www.barbourbooks.com

Our mission is to inspire the world with the life-changing message of the Bible.

Member of the
Evangelical Christian
Publishers Association

Printed in the United States of America.

BYLER FAMILY TREE

Eustace and Effie (deceased) Byler's Children

Elsie (Byler) Troyer
(m) to John Troyer

- Glen
- Mary
- Blaine
- Hope

Doris (Byler) Schrock
(m) to Brian Schrock.

Arlene (Byler) Miller
(m) to Larry Miller

- Doug
- Martha
- Lillian
- Scott
- Samuel

Joel Byler

The ENGLISH SON

CHAPTER 1

Akron, Ohio

One thing Joel Byler couldn't stand was a dirty car. While the vehicle he'd bought today might be a classic, the exterior needed some help.

Joel was thankful his girlfriend, Kristi Palmer, had gone shopping in Holmes County with her mother and wouldn't be back until Sunday evening. That would give him all weekend to spend with his new car. As soon as he got it washed, he might see if Tom Hunter was free to take a test drive with him.

Joel leaned against his work truck and stared at the tuxedo-black 1967 Corvette Stingray convertible. What a beaut! Even with a layer of dust, it was any man's dream. Well, Joel's anyway. He'd wanted a car like this for a long time and had been watching the ads, as well as going to classic car auctions every chance he got. The sale he'd attended this morning had been surprisingly successful. When this gem came up for auction, Joel couldn't resist. A few others apparently wanted the Corvette as badly as he did, because the bidding shot up quickly. Before Joel realized it, the highest bid was $200,000. In desperation, he upped the bid by $50,000 and won. The only downside was he'd gone way over his budget to get the car, even though with its 435-horsepower engine, the model in this good condition usually sold for more than $300,000.

As a general contractor, cash availability was often feast or famine. Before the most recent job—a big office complex—Joel's cash flow had been on the meager side. Now, after using more than half the money he'd earned from that job to buy the car, the amount left over was not enough to pay all his subcontractors. But Joel felt certain his bid on a huge upcoming job would be chosen and the advance from that would get him out of the jam he'd put himself in. Once he got paid, he'd have money to spare, even after he paid everyone else. And he would finally be able to get the engagement ring Kristi deserved. Joel had already proposed, and she'd said yes, but he didn't have the funds for a ring yet—at least not one big enough to prove his love for her. Kristi had assured Joel she didn't need a fancy ring, but Joel wanted her to have the best. They'd both been saving money for their future together and would eventually use it on a down payment for a house.

Joel turned his attention to the Corvette again. The first order of business was to wash the outside. He paused a minute to study himself in the side mirror, realizing he, too, needed some sprucing up. Besides the streaks of dirt on his face, his thick, dark hair could use a trim. He'd have to get it done before seeing Kristi—and even-up his short beard. As a business owner, he needed to make a good impression on his customers, but he didn't care about his appearance when he was at home.

Joel turned on the outdoor faucet, but before he could grab the end of the hose, it started twirling around under the water pressure, and a blast of chilly water hit Joel square in the face. It also gave his clothes a good soaking, especially the T-shirt, now sticking to him like glue.

He jumped back and wiped his eyes, then grabbed the flailing hose and pointed it at the

Corvette. This was not the way he'd planned to take a bath, even though the cool water felt good.

It took Joel almost an hour to get the car clean and dry. He used a sponge to clean off a smudge he'd missed and then rubbed the spot shiny clean with a chamois. About to go inside his single-wide mobile home, Joel paused, watching his friend Tom pull up. *Perfect timing*. Joel grinned.

Tom got out of his SUV and sauntered up the driveway, where Joel's new car was parked. "Wow! Where'd ya get the good-looking Vette?" Tom let out a low whistle while checking it out.

"Got it at a car auction this morning." Joel pointed to the shiny black hood. "What do you think?"

Tom blew out his breath. "You've either come into a large sum of money, or you're deep in debt. She's sweet all right. Bet this classic had to be expensive."

"It was," Joel admitted.

"So how'd ya swing it?"

"I recently got paid for a big job I completed, so I had the money to pay cash." He chuckled, pulling his fingers through his scruffy short beard. "Well, to be honest, I actually wrote a check."

Tom continued to eyeball the car, walking all around it and then opening the passenger door. "Why don't ya take me for a spin? I bet this Vette has got some get-up-and-go."

"You read my mind. I was planning to drive over to your place to show it to you." Joel tugged on his wet shirttail, wringing out the moisture still left. "Give me a few minutes to get cleaned up, and then we'll take a ride."

"Sounds good." Tom followed Joel up to his single-wide. "Mind telling me what you paid for the car?"

Joel hesitated a few seconds. "Umm. . .got it for $250,000."

Tom's mouth dropped open, and he blinked his pale blue eyes a couple of times. "You're kidding, right?"

"Nope. It was my final bid."

"Wow, at this rate you'll be living in a mobile home the rest of your life and never get your dream house built, let alone marry your girlfriend. When Kristi sees your new purchase, I wonder what she'll have to say."

Joel cringed. "I don't plan on letting her see it. At least not right away. So please don't say anything, okay?"

Tom slid his fingers across his lips. "She won't hear it from me. That's a promise." Pointing to the Corvette, Tom's eyes darkened. "How you gonna keep something like this baby hidden from her, Joel? Doesn't Kristi ever go in your garage?"

"I'm not keeping it there. I'm gonna put the Vette in my shop, under a tarp." Joel's deceit didn't bother him that much. He figured he'd tell Kristi about the car when the time was right—maybe after he'd given her a ring and a wedding date had been set. They could go out to dinner in the Corvette to celebrate.

❧

Berlin, Ohio

"Sure wish I had enough money saved up to buy an Amish quilt," Kristi commented as she and her mother entered a quilt shop on Main Street. "All the extra money I make goes into the joint account Joel and I opened eight months ago. I won't touch that—not without Joel's permission. We made an agreement when we first opened the account not to take out a penny of the money unless an emergency arose, and then, only with the other person's approval."

Mom tipped her head. "What is this savings account for?"

"Our future—together."

"Has he asked you to marry him?"

Kristi nodded.

Mom took hold of Kristi's left hand. "I don't see a diamond sparkling back at me."

"He hasn't bought me an engagement ring yet, but I'm sure I'll be wearing one soon."

Deep wrinkles formed across Mom's forehead. Her blue eyes, mirroring Kristi's, had lost their sparkle. "I'm sure you're aware of what the Bible says about being unequally yoked with unbelievers."

"Yes, Mom, I'm aware of what the Bible says, plus you have mentioned it often enough."

"But you're not listening. If you were, you would have broken up with Joel by now."

"I love him, Mom. Besides, he's gone to church with me every Sunday for the past two months."

"Going to church and becoming a believer are two different things. Has Joel told you he's become a Christian?"

Kristi shook her head. "Not in so many words, but—"

"He might only be going to church for your sake—to make you believe he's something he's not.

Joel seems to be nice enough, but from what I can tell, he's not spiritually grounded."

Irritation welled in Kristi's soul. She wished her mother would stop harping on this. Mom didn't realize how much Kristi loved Joel. She apparently didn't see the good in him either. "I doubt Joel's only going to church for my sake, Mom. He promised he'd go to church tomorrow, even though I won't be with him because you and I will be worshipping at the Mennonite church we saw near our hotel in Walnut Creek."

Mom didn't say anything as she moved to the next aisle full of more quilts, but Kristi was fully aware of her mother's reservations about Joel. Kristi pursed her lips. *Aren't we supposed to look for the good in others? How come Mom can't do that with Joel?*

She rummaged through her purse to find her cell phone. When she touched the smooth object with her fingers, Kristi clenched the phone and took it out of her bag. *Maybe I ought to call Joel and remind him about going to church. No!* She immediately dropped the phone back in. *He might think I was treating him like a child. He told me he would go, and I believe him.*

Kristi had learned many things about Joel in the year and a half they'd been dating. One thing stood out more than the rest: He didn't like to be told what to do. When she'd first met him, he wasn't willing to attend church at all. At least he went with her now, and that's what mattered. While Joel didn't talk about spiritual things, Kristi had noticed how easily he could find scripture passages when the pastor preached his messages. When she'd asked Joel about this, he'd merely explained he'd grown up going to church and the Bible had been crammed down his throat. When she'd asked for more details, he'd said he didn't want to talk about it.

Joel never spoke of his family. Kristi couldn't help wondering why. Since he had asked her to marry him, she figured it was time to meet his folks. When she'd brought up the topic, Joel informed her that his family was different, and Kristi wouldn't have anything in common with them; then he'd quickly changed the subject. Kristi realized it was best not to press the issue and hadn't brought it up again. But it didn't keep her from wondering what Joel's family was like and how they would be different from her. Someday, when Joel was in the right mood, she would broach the subject again. It wouldn't be right to marry Joel when she had no knowledge of his family other than being told they were different. Surely, Joel would want to invite them to the wedding.

Shaking her thoughts aside, Kristi moved to the next aisle, where Mom stood, studying a quilted wall hanging. Her mother had recently gotten her auburn hair cut in a shorter style. It made her look younger than her fifty years. "Goodness gracious, even this quilted piece is expensive," Mom commented when Kristi joined her.

"The price is a shocker, but it's worth every penny." Kristi pointed to the nearly invisible hand stitching. "A lot of work goes into making one of these."

"I can see that." Mom shook her head, clicking her tongue. "I can sew a straight seam, but I might not have the patience to make a quilt, or even a hanging such as this."

"If I wasn't working long hours at the nursing home, I'd try making a quilt." Kristi smiled. "Of course, someone would have to teach me, because even with a quilt pattern, I would have no idea where to begin."

"It's apparent how important nursing is to you. Honestly, though, Kristi, you need to make time to do some fun things for yourself."

"I do," Kristi was quick to respond. "In fact, Joel and I are going out for supper one evening next week."

Mom's lips compressed. "I wasn't talking about going on dates. I meant doing something creative just for you. They give quilting lessons here in the store. Maybe the two of us could sign up for one."

Kristi mulled over her mother's suggestion. "It's a nice idea, but I'd have to attend on a Saturday, and I like to keep my weekends free to spend with Joel."

"You're here now, and he didn't object." Her brows furrowed. "Or did he?"

Kristi shook her head. "A quilt class would probably mean coming here several Saturdays in a row in order to complete the quilt. Besides, it's a bit of a drive from Akron down here to Holmes County, and as I said, Joel and I usually do something together on Saturdays."

Mom held up her hand. "I understand. You want a quilt, but you can't afford to buy one, and you don't want to be away from Joel long enough to make one."

Kristi cringed. The curt tone of her mother's voice was all she needed as a reminder of how much Mom disapproved of Joel. *She and Dad don't know Joel as well as I do. He's smart, good-looking, and a successful businessman. Once he's fully committed to the Lord, he will make a great husband.*

"Why don't we get some lunch?" Kristi suggested, realizing she needed to change the subject. "There's a restaurant next to our hotel in Walnut Creek we should try."

"Since you mentioned it, I am kind of hungry." Mom moved up the aisle, and Kristi followed. After lunch she hoped to check out a few of the Amish-owned businesses in the area.

Kristi wasn't sure why, but she was fascinated with the Amish culture and wanted to learn as much as possible about it.

❧

Walnut Creek, Ohio

"How's your meal?" Mom asked as she and Kristi sat at a table near a window in Der Dutchman Restaurant.

Kristi licked her lips. "The chicken is delicious—crispy on the outside and tender inside. I'm glad we chose this place to have lunch."

"Yes, and our waitress has been so attentive." Mom motioned to the young Amish woman who had left their table after filling the glasses with fresh iced tea. "I'll make sure to leave her a nice tip."

Kristi smiled. Mom had always been good about leaving generous tips when she'd had exceptional service. It was a good example for Kristi, and she remembered to do the same.

As they continued eating their meal, Mom mentioned the beautiful weather. "We picked the perfect time for this weekend getaway—nice even temperature and not much humidity, which is unusual for August."

"I agree." Kristi blotted her lips with a napkin. "Some summers it's been so hot and humid it was hard to be outdoors." She glanced out the window at a passing horse and buggy, wondering how it would feel to ride in one of them. She'd seen an Amish man across the street from the hotel offering rides for a reasonable price. Maybe after lunch, before they got back in Kristi's car, she would suggest they take a buggy ride.

Before taking a sip of iced tea, Kristi looked out another window, where the horse and buggies were parked. She watched in awe as an elderly couple was about to leave. The Amish woman held the reins of the horse while her husband, a bit shaky on his feet, got in. Once he was settled in the buggy, she handed him the reins. Keeping her eyes peeled to the window, Kristi watched as he backed the horse up and guided their buggy toward the road.

"Is there anything else I can bring for you?" their waitress asked, stepping up to the table. "A piece of pie or some ice cream?"

"Both sound good, Doris, but I'm too full." Mom nudged Kristi's arm. "How about you? Do you have room for dessert?"

Kristi placed both hands on her stomach, glancing one last time out the window. "As good at it sounds, I don't have space for another bite."

When the waitress smiled, Kristi noticed her flawless complexion, offset by dark brown eyes with long lashes. Not much of her hair showed under her stiff white head covering, but what did show was a dark brown color.

I wonder how it would feel to dress in plain clothes.

Kristi looked down at her pale green blouse and darker green capris. She was tempted to ask the young woman if she wore the white cap all the time or only when she was in public. Mom would have been embarrassed by her blunt question, and the Amish woman might think she was rude.

"Thank you for coming in. You can pay your bill up front." The young woman placed the piece of paper on the table beside Mom's plate. Apparently she assumed Mom would be the one paying the bill.

After the waitress walked away, Kristi leaned closer to Mom and whispered, "How come you called her Doris? I don't believe she ever told us her name."

"She was wearing a name tag—Doris Schrock. Didn't you see it?"

"I guess not. I did notice her pretty brown eyes though. They're almost the same color as Joel's."

Mom quirked an eyebrow. "You're comparing the Amish woman to Joel? Is he all you have on your mind today, Kristi?"

"Of course not. I thought of Joel when I saw her pretty brown eyes."

"Maybe they're related. He does have an Amish-sounding last name."

"But you said her last name was Schrock, not Byler."

Mom heaved a sigh. "I was only teasing, Kristi. Joel is obviously not Amish. He drives a car, uses electricity in his mobile home, and dresses like other non-Amish men do."

Kristi crossed her arms. "I know Joel pretty well, Mom, and besides, this is a silly discussion." She reached for the check. "Lunch is on me, and when we leave here, I want to go on a buggy ride."

Mom's forehead wrinkled. "I thought we were going to do some more shopping. Didn't you say you wanted to check out a few of the Amish-owned businesses in the area?"

"Yes, I do, but we can do it after the buggy ride."

"You go ahead if you want to. I'm not interested in going for a ride. I'll sit on the bench in front of the hotel and wait for you."

"Never mind. If you're not going to do it, then neither am I." Kristi pushed away from the table. "Let's head for Charm. I hear there's a cheese shop there. I may pick some up to take home."

"Good idea. I'll buy some cheese, too. Your dad would be happy if I came home with a brick of Colby."

As Kristi made her way to the front of the restaurant, a vision of Joel flashed across her mind. *I wonder if he'd like to make a trip to Holmes County with me sometime. When I see him next week, I'll ask.*

CHAPTER 2

Akron

Stretching his arms behind his back to massage the knots, Joel ambled into the kitchen. He'd spent all weekend joyriding in his new Corvette and had gone to bed late last night. Joel had been with Tom most of Saturday. On Sunday, he'd gone to Cleveland to see an old friend. When he returned home, he was tired and hadn't taken the time to check his voice mail. He'd had his cell phone with him all weekend, of course, but didn't want to be disturbed with any work-related calls, so he'd kept it muted.

Joel picked up his phone from the kitchen counter, where he'd plugged it in to charge before going to bed. *Guess I'd better see if I have any messages. Kristi may have called.*

Scrolling through his phone with his index finger, Joel saw that Kristi had called. He typed in the password and pressed the phone against his ear to hear the message she'd left on his voicemail. Apparently, she had tried calling him when she got home last evening and couldn't wait to tell him about the fun she'd had in Amish country.

Joel grimaced. The last time he'd paid a visit to Holmes County, he'd come away appreciating his truck and mid-sized car. Now Joel had another vehicle to brag about. He hoped the Corvette would be the first of many classic cars he'd own. Of course, he'd have to make a lot more money for his dream to become reality.

Joel had prepared for getting more cars by building a spacious five-car garage. The added space at the back of his shop would also be utilized when his collection grew. Since Joel owned two acres of land, he had the option of building another garage or additional shop, if and when it became necessary. His dream was to keep some cars for show and to ride around in, but some he would fix up and sell for a tidy profit. He planned to keep the Corvette, however, since he had dreamed for a long time of owning one.

Joel's passion for cars began when he was a teenager. After he'd gotten his first job and saved enough money, he'd bought a classy-looking red convertible. His family hadn't approved, but it had turned many other heads. Eventually, he'd been forced to sell it. That was another story, but Joel didn't want to dwell on the details. He had better things to do today, starting with checking the rest of his messages.

He found a few work-related calls—some from subcontractors with questions about a small job he was supposed to do later this week. Another was from Carl and Mary Blankenship, an elderly couple who wanted Joel to give them a bid on a partial bathroom remodel. The things the Blankenships wanted done wouldn't take long, nor bring in much money, so Joel would handle the job himself. He hoped to hear something soon about the bigger job he'd bid on. Once he got the go-ahead, he'd get his subcontractors started on it right away.

One thing was for sure; he wouldn't tell Kristi about the car. She might think he was never going to buy her a ring and would probably say he'd been foolish for spending so much money on a car he would drive occasionally. Good thing she never had any reason to snoop around in his shop, and he'd make sure she never did. At least not until they were married.

Joel glanced at the clock above his refrigerator. Kristi had probably left for work already, so he would wait and call her back sometime this evening. Right now, he needed to eat breakfast and head out the door.

❧

As Joel drove his pickup toward the Blankenships', he decided to take a side road. It wouldn't hurt to check out the jobsite he figured he would be starting soon. His bid had been reasonable, and Joel felt sure he'd been chosen to do the job. He saw right away that the land had been fenced, in readiness for the project to begin. If by some chance the owner was there, Joel could ask when he wanted him to begin the building process. Once everything had been finalized, he would request half the money now and the rest when the job was complete. Even the first half would be a nice chunk, allowing Joel to pay all his subcontractors what he owed from the last job he'd done, with some left over for expenses and Kristi's ring.

When Joel approached the jobsite, already cleared and excavated, he drew in a sharp breath unable to believe his eyes. Tacked to the fence closest to the road was another general contractor's construction sign.

"This better not mean what it looks like," Joel muttered. He pulled over and grabbed his cell phone, hurriedly making the call. "Hey, Andy, it's Joel Byler. I'm sitting in front of the property you bought for your new business and am wondering why another contractor's sign is tacked to the fence."

"Didn't my secretary call you, Joel?"

"No, she did not. What was she supposed to tell me?"

"I gave the job to Martin's Construction. He came in with a lower bid and is able to start working on the project right away."

Joel clenched his teeth so hard he felt it all the way to his head. "But you promised me the job, and I'm able to start on it now, too."

"I made no promises, Joel. Only said it sounded like a fair bid and I'd get back to you."

Joel's hand shook as he switched his cell phone to the other ear. He couldn't lose this job; he had too much at stake. "Listen, Andy, why don't you let me refigure things a bit; I'm sure I can knock some off my original figures."

"Sorry, but I've already accepted Jim Martin's bid. The contract is signed, and he'll be starting the job tomorrow morning."

"Are you sure? I mean—"

"I have to go now, Joel. Another call's coming in." The phone clicked off before Joel could say another word.

Pounding his fist on the truck's dash, Joel shouted, "What am I gonna do now? All I have scheduled are a few small jobs. Those won't earn enough money to pay even half what I owe. How am I going to get any of my subs to work for me if I can't pay 'em what they've got coming?"

Joel would have to figure out a solution to this problem soon, or he'd really be in a pickle. The only sensible thing would be to sell the new car, but it might take awhile to find someone willing to pay what it was worth. Besides, Joel didn't want to part with the Vette. No, there had to be some other way.

~∽~

Kristi smiled as she put her grocery items away, reliving the past weekend with her mother. Shopping was something she and Mom had always enjoyed doing together. Even when Kristi was a child, she'd liked to shop. Every time Mom put on her coat, Kristi would ask, "Are we going shopping, Mom?"

Chuckling, Kristi checked her phone messages. She'd been running late this morning and, in her haste, had left her cell phone on the kitchen table.

Yesterday evening, when she'd returned from Holmes County, Kristi had called Joel and left a message, so she was eager to see if he had responded.

Disappointment flooded over her when she saw no message. Hadn't he checked his voice mail since last night? If he had, surely he would have returned her call. This wasn't like Joel at all.

Kristi punched in Joel's number, feeling relief when he answered.

"Hey, Joel, it's me. Did you get my message from last night?"

"Uh. . .yeah, I did. Sorry for not responding. I've. . .uh. . .been kinda busy."

"That's okay. I was wondering if you were free to have supper with me tonight. On my way home, I picked up a couple of steaks and some baking potatoes; so, instead of going out, I thought we could eat here."

"Not tonight, Kristi. I've got a bunch of paperwork I need to get done."

"Paperwork? I thought you were going to work on it over the weekend." She couldn't hide her disappointment. Joel had previously said they would get together one night this week, and she was anxious to tell him about her trip to Holmes County.

"I. . .umm. . .had a lot to go over, but unfortunately, I didn't get it all done."

"How about tomorrow night? The steaks will keep till then."

Silence on the other end.

"Joel, are you still there? Did you hear what I said?"

"Yeah, I'm thinking is all."

Kristi reached up and released her hair from the ponytail she'd worn to work today. "Are you thinking about whether you want to come for supper?" She couldn't imagine he wouldn't. Joel always seemed to enjoy her home-cooked meals.

"No. . .uh. . .I have a few other things on my mind right now."

"Want to talk about it?" Kristi felt concern. It wasn't like Joel to be so distant or evasive. She wondered if he was irritated because she'd spent the weekend with her mother instead of him. She was about to ask when he spoke again.

"There's nothing to talk about, Kristi. I had a rough day, but I'll be okay." Joel cleared his throat. "Tomorrow evening for supper is fine with me. What time do you want me to come over?"

"Is five thirty too early, or would you rather make it six?"

"Let's shoot for six. Is there anything I can bring?"

"A hearty appetite. I bought some whoopie pies

at the bakery outside of Berlin, so we'll have those for dessert."

"Okay. See you then." Joel hung up before Kristi had the chance to say goodbye. Something was definitely wrong, but if Joel didn't want to talk about it, there wasn't much she could do. Kristi felt hurt because Joel hadn't even said he loved her, which he usually did before they hung up. Could the thrill of their romance be fading? *Maybe I'm overly sensitive today.*

"I hope Joel's willing to talk about this when he comes here tomorrow night," Kristi murmured. She didn't want to make any assumptions that may not even be true.

Feeling uptight, Kristi decided to go for a run. Physical activity usually helped whenever she was stressed. She quickly changed into her jogging clothes, put her hair back in a ponytail, and headed out the door.

Kristi had only run a few blocks when she saw her friend Sandy Clemons running in the opposite direction. Sandy was into fitness even more than Kristi, and they sometimes ran together. When the young woman drew closer, they both stopped running and stood on the corner to talk.

"How's it going?" Sandy asked, pushing a strand of her chin-length, naturally blond hair behind her ear. "I missed seeing you in church yesterday."

"I went shopping in Holmes County with my mom on Saturday. After spending the night in Walnut Creek, we attended a Mennonite church near our hotel."

"Sounds like a fun outing."

Kristi nodded. "We had such a good time. I'm

anxious to go there again—maybe next time with Joel."

"Where was Joel yesterday? I didn't see him at church."

Kristi bent her knee back to rub the calf of her leg, where a muscle had begun to spasm. The cramp was her fault. The weather had turned a lot warmer from the past weekend, and she was sorry she'd left her condo in a rush, forgetting her water bottle. "Are you sure Joel wasn't there, Sandy? When I told him I was going away for the weekend, he said he wouldn't skip church."

"If he was there, I didn't see him. But even though I'm up front leading the worship team, I don't always notice everyone in the congregation. When I get into a worshipful mood, I focus on God, not on the crowd."

"That's where it should be, alright." Kristi didn't voice her concerns, but she had a feeling Joel hadn't gone to church. When they'd talked on the phone, he'd said he had done paperwork, so there was a good chance he'd spent Saturday and Sunday working on it. Of course, it was no excuse. Kristi had been brought up to believe in the importance of going to church. Unless she was sick or something unexpected came up, she made an effort to be there.

"Guess I'd better finish my jogging session so I can go home and start supper before my hubby gets home from work." Sandy gave Kristi a hug and started running again.

As Kristi continued her run, she made a decision. Tomorrow night when Joel came for supper, she would ask if he'd gone to church. Surely he would tell her the truth.

CHAPTER 3

Kristi glanced at the clock and frowned. It was six thirty. Joel was supposed to be here thirty minutes ago. The yummy smell of baked potatoes coming from the oven made her stomach growl. She was eager to eat. The potatoes would stay warm in the oven. Fortunately, she hadn't put the steaks on the grill yet, thinking it would be best to wait until Joel arrived.

Kristi left the kitchen and peeked out the living room window. No sign of Joel's car or work truck in her condo driveway. She looked at her wristwatch and groaned. *I hope he didn't forget. Wonder if I should call him.*

She reached for her cell phone and was about to make the call when Joel pulled in. She hurried to the deck at the back of her condo and turned on the gas grill, which would give it time to warm up before Joel came in.

"Sorry I'm late," Joel apologized when she let him inside. "I had to make a few phone calls after work and time got away from me." He leaned down and gave her a kiss.

"It's okay." She smiled up at him, reminded once again what an attractive man he was. His thick, dark hair with eyebrows to match and those expressive chocolate-brown eyes were enough to turn any woman's head. Of course, his good looks weren't the only reason Kristi had fallen in love with Joel. He was intelligent, a hard worker, had a good business head, and his attentiveness made her feel good about herself. Joel also enjoyed jogging, which was one of Kristi's passions. She'd always believed in being physically fit—ate healthy foods and exercised regularly. The day she'd first met Joel at a fitness center in Akron, Kristi wanted to get to know him better. After a few more visits, Joel had asked her out.

"Umm. . .guess I'd better put the steaks on the grill." Pushing her dreamy thoughts aside, Kristi headed for the kitchen, and Joel followed.

"If there's something else you need to do, I can put the steaks on for you," he offered.

Kristi smiled. "You can if you want to, but the salad is in the refrigerator, the potatoes are in the oven, and the table's set, so I don't have anything else to do. Why don't we both go on the deck and watch the steaks? It'll give us a chance to visit while they're cooking. In fact, I'll get some iced tea to drink while we're sitting outside."

"Sounds good to me." Joel took the steaks out to the deck, and when Kristi showed up with their drinks a few minutes later, the meat was sizzling on the grill. She placed their glasses on the small table then took a seat in one of the wicker chairs she'd recently purchased.

Shielding her eyes from the setting sun, Kristi smiled at Joel. "I'm anxious to tell you about my weekend and hear about yours."

Holding his glass against his flushed face, Joel sat in the chair beside her. "There's not much to tell about my weekend. It was basically pretty boring."

"What about church? Did you go there Sunday morning?" Kristi already suspected the answer, but wanted to give him a chance to explain.

Joel shook his head.

"How come?" Feeling the heat and humidity of the summer evening, Kristie fanned her face with her hand.

"I had planned to go, but I had too much paperwork."

"I realize your work is important, but couldn't you have taken an hour out to attend church? You promised you would go, remember?" Despite her irritation, Kristi appreciated the fact that Joel hadn't lied about not going. If there was one thing she wouldn't tolerate, it was someone lying to her.

Frowning, his tone quickly sharpened. "Don't start nagging me, Kristi. I get enough of it from my customers." He stood abruptly and went over to the grill to check the meat.

She flinched. Joel had never talked to her so harshly before. It took her by surprise.

After he added some seasoning to the steaks, Joel stood quietly, looking out behind her place. Kristi wondered what thoughts were rolling around in his head. Even after he took a seat beside her again, he said nothing.

"I–I'm sorry, Joel." She placed her hand gently on his arm. "I didn't mean to sound bossy."

"No problem."

Kristi got up to flip the steaks, and as the flames shot upward, a piece of hot gristle popped out. "Ouch!" She jumped back when a tiny piece landed on her arm.

"Are you okay?" Joel bolted out of his chair.

"I'm alright—just startled is all." Kristi felt reassured, seeing the depth of worry in his expression and knowing he really cared. This was the Joel she'd come to know and love.

"I'll be right back." Joel rushed inside and returned with an ice cube wrapped in a napkin. "Here, sit down and put this on the red mark. I'll tend to the steaks." His face softened. "I'm sorry I barked at you before. Guess I'm kinda testy tonight."

"Bad day at work?"

He gave a nod. "Thought I'd landed a pretty big job, but another contractor came in with a lower bid."

"I suppose it happens sometimes. Do you have other jobs lined up?"

"A few, but nothing big." The worry lines on his forehead returned, causing Kristi concern.

"Let's pray about this, should we?" she asked.

"You mean right now?"

"Yes. There's no time like the present." Kristi reached for Joel's hand and bowed her head. "Heavenly Father, Joel is disappointed because he didn't get that job, but we're trusting You to bring an even bigger job along for him. Thank You for hearing our prayer and for all You do on our behalf. Amen."

Kristi opened her eyes and smiled at Joel. He smiled back, but it appeared to be forced. Didn't he realize no matter how big the problem seemed, God could take care of it and provide for his needs? She hated to admit it, but this was an indication of Joel not having a strong faith in God. Perhaps it would come in time.

⁕

Berlin

Doris Schrock stepped from her kitchen to the back porch, hoping to find some cool air. Not a single leaf in the yard moved. As far as she could see, everything was still. The stifling heat and humidity felt like thick fog. The restaurant where she worked in Walnut Creek had air-conditioning, so she'd been comfortable all day. But after putting a roast in her oven for supper here at home, the already warm kitchen had become almost unbearable. If the weather was cooler, she and her husband, Brian, could eat outside. But unless a sudden breeze came up, it would be as bad as eating in the house.

She sighed deeply and stepped back inside. Brian should be in from his chores soon, and then they could eat.

While Doris waited, she filled their glasses with iced tea and placed them on the table beside their plates—plates that used to belong to her mother.

Unexpectedly, she thought of her brother, wondering what he was doing for dinner this evening. *I wonder if he would come if I invited him here for a meal. It's been awhile since any of the family has seen him. Does he miss us at all?*

Using a potholder, she opened the oven door to check on the roast. A wave of hot air hit her in the face. She waved the worst of it away, then poked the potatoes and carrots with a fork. They were done, and so was the meat. The supper she'd planned was probably not the best choice on an uncomfortable evening like this. Using the oven made the kitchen even more stifling. BLT's would have been easier, but since the meat had already thawed, Doris didn't have much choice. There wasn't anything to do now except wait for Brian.

She took a seat at the table to read the latest edition of *The Bargain Hunter*. It seemed like there were more ads than usual from people wanting to sell baby items. Several advertisements were for cribs, strollers, and high chairs.

Tears pooled in her eyes. Short of a miracle, she would never own any of those things. Doris and Brian had been married six years, but God had not blessed them with children. It didn't seem fair that Arlene, who was thirty-two, recently had a baby. Arlene's pregnancy had been a surprise, since her youngest child, Scott, was eight years old.

"But God knows best," she murmured. "At least that's what Mama used to say."

Doris's tears dripped onto her cheeks. Her mother had died two years ago, but she still missed her so much. Dad missed her, too. The last time Doris went to his house, she'd caught him sitting on the sofa in the living room, looking at Mama's rocking chair while talking to her as if she was still there.

She and her sisters had tried talking their father into selling his house and moving in with one of them. But Dad insisted on staying in the home he and Mama had lived in since they first got married. Doris couldn't really blame him. If something were to happen to Brian, she wouldn't want to leave this house, either, even though it was small and needed a lot of repairs. They'd planned to add on, but with Brian so busy working for a local carpenter and completing all his chores at home, he hadn't had time to build an addition. Still, this little house held memories, making her understand how Dad felt.

I suppose it doesn't matter. Since we have no children, we don't really need a bigger place. Doris reached for a napkin and wiped her damp cheeks. *I will not give in to self-pity. At least Brian and I both have jobs. A lot of people in our community are struggling financially, so I'm grateful.*

Hearing her husband's footsteps on the stairs outside, Doris got up from the table and collected herself. She would not let Brian see her tears. She'd done too much crying already.

～

Akron

As the evening wore on, Joel became antsy. He wanted to be with Kristi and have a nice evening, but right now, he couldn't deal with her questions. Before their meal, she'd questioned him about going to church. During the meal, she'd asked not once, but several times, if everything was alright between them, saying he seemed kind of sullen this evening. As they sat eating their dessert, Joel had assured her everything was fine, but not more than five minutes had passed, and she'd begun firing questions again.

"I told you before, nothing is wrong. Now can we talk about something else?" he snapped, a bit too harshly. Truth was, Joel was worried about his financial situation, and talking about it only made him feel worse. What he wanted to do was go home, hop in the Corvette, and leave his troubles behind on the open road.

"You haven't asked about my weekend." Kristi looked at him with misty eyes. "Don't you want to hear about the shopping trip I took with my mom to Holmes County?"

Not wanting to hurt her feelings, Joel nodded. He was drawn in by her eyes, which suddenly looked three shades bluer. "Sure, honey. Tell me what you bought." He fingered her beautiful auburn hair.

"Actually, I didn't buy much. What I really wanted was an Amish-made quilt, but the ones Mom and I looked at were too expensive." She paused to take a bite of her whoopie pie. "But I did buy a few quilted potholders. Those will look nice in our kitchen someday."

Our kitchen. Joel groaned inwardly, taking a toothpick from his shirt pocket. With his current financial situation, it could be some time before he had enough money to buy Kristi an engagement ring, let alone set a wedding date. *If Mom were still alive, she'd say I was foolhardy for buying the Corvette. Maybe I was, but I couldn't pass up the opportunity to own something I'd been wanting for a long time. Besides, how was I to know my bid on that job wasn't the lowest? Thought it was a sure thing.* Joel clenched his teeth until his jaw ached. *Guess it's what I get for not looking before I leaped. I need to figure a way out of this jam. Once I get some good money coming in, I'll be fine again.*

CHAPTER 4

Millersburg, Ohio

"I can't believe how much produce my garden has yielded this summer," Elsie Troyer commented as she stood at her kitchen sink, washing beets.

Elsie's sister, Arlene Miller, had been helping her can some of the bounty all morning. Tomorrow they would go to Arlene's home in Farmerstown and do the same with her crop.

The skin around Arlene's blue eyes crinkled. "I am ever so thankful my older girls are willing to watch the *boppli*, or I'd never get anything done at home, much less be able to help you. Of course, once Martha and Lillian start back to school, I'll be on my own with the baby and most household chores."

"If Mary didn't have a job cleaning house, I'm sure she'd be willing to watch little Samuel, and so would Hope." Elsie glanced out the kitchen window, where eleven-year-old Hope was busy pulling weeds in the garden. "If Hope came into the kitchen with the smell of pickled beets cooking, she'd plug her nose and say, 'Eww. . .those are *ekelhaft!*'"

"Oh, that's right; your youngest daughter has never liked beets. It's no wonder she thinks the odor is disgusting."

"I'd thought about bringing Samuel with me today, but Martha and Lillian needed to clean their rooms, so they'll take turns minding the baby."

Elsie washed another beet and placed it in the bowl for Arlene to cut. "Yesterday I went over to Dad's to clean his house."

"How's he doing?"

"He left a few minutes after I got there. Said he had an auction to go to." Elsie wrinkled her nose. "I can't believe how much junk Dad keeps on buying. He seems to have gotten worse since Mama died."

"He took her death pretty hard." Arlene slowly shook her head. "Dad's always been a hoarder, but I believe he has more collections now than ever before. Larry says Dad has so many old milk cans sitting around the place he could start his own dairy. I enjoy going to yard sales, but only to look for practical things."

"And what about his collection of pens? I discovered two drawers in the kitchen desk, full of pens with different logos on them." Elsie rolled her eyes. "It's probably not the only place he's stashed his collection of pens either. Due to the money Dad's gotten from the oil wells on his land, some people in our community have begun teasing him about being 'The Amish Millionaire.' Pretty soon, they'll be calling him 'The Eccentric Millionaire.'"

Arlene chuckled. "Guess what Aunt Verna told me once?"

"About Dad?"

"*Jah*. She said even when he was a little guy he hoarded things. Since she's ten years older than Dad, I'm sure she remembers many of the things he did as a child."

"Did she say what kind of things he hoarded?"

"Not really. But she explained how he used to cry whenever their *mamm* threw anything out. He wanted to save everything."

"That's interesting. I'll have to ask Aunt Verna for more details the next time she comes for a visit."

Arlene's lips compressed. "Please don't ask her in front of Dad. He wouldn't take too kindly to us talking about his strange habits."

"You're right, but then maybe he thinks there's nothing odd about his habits. He might believe his actions are normal and we're being too scrutinizing of his ways. Anyway, while we're on the subject of our *daed*, what would you think about the two of us taking him out for lunch sometime soon? He enjoys eating at Der Dutchman in Walnut Creek, and we'll make sure Doris is working the day we go, so we can say hello to her, too."

Arlene nodded. "Good idea. Whoever sees Dad first can ask if he'd like to go."

❧

Farmerstown, Ohio

"How's our little fellow doing?" Arlene asked her twelve-year-old daughter, Martha, when she returned home later in the afternoon.

Martha motioned to her four-month-old brother sleeping contentedly in his crib. "Samuel did well. When I was busy doing other things, Lillian kept him entertained." She spoke softly.

"Good to hear," Arlene whispered. "Did you both get your rooms cleaned like I asked?"

"Mine's all done. Lillian's upstairs finishing hers."

"I'm glad, because it'll be time to start supper soon, and I'll need both of you in the kitchen to help."

"How'd it go at Aunt Elsie's?" Martha asked after they'd left the baby's room.

"It went well. We got lots of beets canned, and

some corn frozen, too. Elsie will be coming to help me tomorrow."

"Do English people help their family members as much as we Amish do?" Martha blinked her brown eyes.

Arlene shrugged. "I'm sure many of them do."

Martha gave her mother a hug. "I'm glad to be part of a family that cares about each other."

She gently patted her daughter's back. *Unfortunately, one of our family members doesn't seem to care much about anyone but himself.* Arlene did not voice her thought.

The distinctive *clip-clop* of horse's hooves coming up the driveway could be heard. Martha rushed to the kitchen window. "It's Grandpa's rig, Mom. Is he comin' for supper?"

"I wasn't expecting him," Arlene replied, "but he's always welcome, so we'll invite him to stay."

"I'll go help him put his horse away." Martha hurried out the door.

Arlene smiled. Her oldest daughter had always been helpful. Martha was also quite fond of her grandfather. Perhaps it was because they had something in common. Like him, Martha enjoyed collecting unusual things. Since Arlene's father lived nearby, they got to see him fairly often; whereas her husband, Larry's, parents lived in Wisconsin and the children weren't able to see them as much.

Arlene opened the refrigerator and took out the chicken she planned to fix for supper. She'd finished cutting it up when Dad entered the house with Martha.

"I have something for the boppli," he announced, grinning. "It's a wooden rocking horse I got at the auction today. I left it sitting in the utility room." He removed his straw hat, revealing a crop of thick brown hair with a few streaks of gray. If it weren't for Dad's full gray beard, no one would have guessed he was sixty-five years old.

"*Danki*. I appreciate the gift for the baby." Arlene moved toward him. "Where's the greeting you give whenever we see each other?"

Dad held out his arms. Arlene dried her hands on a paper towel and stepped into his embrace. It felt good to be hugged by her father. Dad's hugs were sincere, and Arlene always felt she was loved. She was certain he loved all four of his children, but Dad often said he felt closer to his three girls. Most likely it was because they all lived close, and he got to see them on a regular basis. Their brother, on the other hand, rarely came around.

Smiling, Arlene clutched Dad's arm. "I saw Elsie earlier today. We were wondering if you'd like to go out to lunch with us—maybe one day next week."

"Sounds good to me." He hung his hat on the wall peg nearest him. "Where do ya want to go?"

"How about Der Dutchman? Since Doris works there, we'll get to see her, too—at least for a little while."

"Name the day. I'll be ready to go." Dad turned and tweaked Martha's upturned nose. "I'll bet you'd like to go, too, wouldn't ya?"

Martha nodded. "But someone will have to babysit Samuel, so I'll probably stay home. Besides, you and your *dochders* deserve some time together without the grandkids hanging around."

Dad peered at Arlene over the top of his glasses.

"This girl's a *schmaert* one, just like her mamm."

Arlene smiled in response. "I'm frying chicken for supper, Dad. Would you like to stay and eat with us?"

"Sure would." Dad shuffled across the room and took a seat at the table. "Mind if I sit here and watch you cook? When your mamm was alive I used to keep her company in the kitchen whenever I could." He thumped his belly a couple of times. "Smellin' all the good food helped me work up a voracious appetite."

"What's that word mean?" Martha asked.

"It means 'greedy or ravenous.'"

Martha snickered, draping her arms around his chest from behind the chair he sat on. "I love you, Grandpa."

"That goes double for me." Grinning, he reached up and patted her hand.

"Would you like something to drink, Dad?" Arlene asked.

"Got any sweet tea in the refrigerator?"

"Sure do."

"I'll get you a glass, Grandpa." Martha went to get the beverage. When she returned, she placed it in front of him. "I put in some extra ice to help you cool off."

"Danki, that was thoughtful of you." Dad's face sobered, and the wrinkles around his brown eyes deepened. "Saw our bishop at the auction today. He thinks I oughta look for another *fraa*. Even said a few of the widows in the area might be interested in me."

"How do you feel about that?" Arlene asked, already sure of the answer.

He grunted and shook his head. "Don't need another wife. I told the bishop so, too. I'm gettin' along adequately on my own. Besides, no other woman could ever fill your mamm's shoes. My Effie was one in a million. She will always remain my fraa." As if the matter was entirely settled, Dad picked up the newspaper lying on his end of the table and snapped it open.

Arlene looked at her daughter and smiled. The whole family knew he had a stubborn streak. If Dad didn't want another wife, it didn't matter how many widows in their community were interested in him. Unless someone really special came along to change his mind, he'd no doubt remain single for the rest of his life.

⤬

Akron

Holding a glass of orange juice, Joel sank onto his couch with a groan. Lemonade would have tasted better, but orange juice was all he had in the refrigerator right now. At least it was cold. Joel had done a small job today on his own, knowing he couldn't pay anyone to help him right now. For that matter, he'd been trying to dodge several of his subcontractors all day. One he'd seen at the parts store. Another had called, asking for his money. A third man, who did the electrical work for most of Joel's jobs, had shown up at the house he'd been working on this morning, demanding his money. Joel told each of them the same thing: "I'm a little short on funds right now, but I'll get you paid as soon as I can."

Joel would keep his feelers out. He'd need a lot of jobs to get through the mess he'd gotten himself into. Usually he was asleep before his head hit the pillow, but Joel had a hard time getting to sleep last night due to his circumstances.

He rubbed his sweaty forehead. Right now, he felt like a defenseless cat being chased by an angry dog. It was his own fault for spending money he should have used to pay the people he owed. But the mistake had been made, and he wasn't about to give up the car—if he could even find a buyer with that kind of money.

Sweat rolled down Joel's temples as he glanced at the air conditioner he'd placed in the living room window to help beat the heat. One lousy little unit wasn't enough to cool his single-wide, even if his home was small. If the weather cooled later, maybe he would sleep outside tonight.

I can't wait till I have enough money to build a new house. Sure can't marry Kristi and expect her to live in these cramped quarters either. She deserves better than this.

Joel's cell phone rang. He pulled it out of his pocket to check the caller ID. "Wish I could hide myself or become invisible until I have the money I need to right my debts," he muttered. Seeing the caller's name, he realized it was Rick, the plumber who usually worked for him. He probably wanted his money, too. Ignoring the call, Joel let his voice mail kick in. He couldn't deal with this right now. If he didn't get another big job quickly, he may have to do something drastic.

CHAPTER 5

Walnut Creek

On Monday of the following week, Joel had finished a small job at a residence in Zoar and was now approaching Walnut Creek to take a look at another possible job. Unfortunately, neither would bring in a lot of money.

Think I'll stop at Rebecca's Bistro and get something to eat, he decided. After the thirty-minute drive, Joel was even hungrier than before and ready to relax for a spell. He'd eaten at Rebecca's before, and the food had always been good, so he looked forward to it.

As Joel drew close to the small restaurant, he saw the parking lot was completely full. The long line of people standing at the entrance meant only one thing: it would be awhile until he got seated.

Oh, great! Joel's stomach rumbled in protest. Since he didn't have time to wait and was getting hungrier by the minute, he pulled his truck into Der Dutchman's parking lot. It was a bigger restaurant, and he could probably get in and out in half the time.

When Joel entered the building he was taken to a seat near the windows. "Your waitress will be with you soon." As the hostess handed Joel a menu, his stomach growled once again. Embarrassed, he mumbled, "Sorry. Guess my belly is screaming to be fed."

She grinned at him. "It's okay. You're in the right place to take care of that."

Joel nodded and picked up his cell phone,

figuring he may as well check his messages while he waited. The only one he found was from Kristi, asking if he'd like to go for a run with her after work this afternoon. Some exercise might help relieve some of the stress Joel felt, but it would do nothing to earn the money he needed. Even gazing at the beautiful car parked in his shop did little to ease his troubled mind.

Joel slipped his cell phone back into his pocket. *If Kristi knew what I was planning to do when I get back to Akron, she wouldn't want to go anywhere with me. Sure wish I didn't have to do this, but I don't see any other way.*

"Joel?"

He jerked his head, surprised to see his youngest sister standing beside his table. "Doris, what are you doing here?"

"I'm a waitress at this restaurant."

"Oh, I see. I. . .uh. . .didn't realize you worked here." Joel glanced down at his menu. *Wish now I'd waited in line at Rebecca's Bistro.* Doris was two years older than Joel, and they'd been close when they were kids. But once they'd become teenagers, she'd disapproved of everything he did. Doris had lectured him more often than either of his other sisters. Joel hoped Doris wouldn't start in on him now. If she did, he'd get up and walk out.

"How have you been, Joel?" she asked.

"Doin' okay." No way would he admit the financial mess he was in. It would only open the door for Doris to berate him about going English. "How 'bout you? Everything goin' okay in your life?"

She nodded, although not a hint of a smile showed on her face. Was she angry at him for leaving home, or perhaps still grieving Mom's death? Maybe something else was going on in her life.

"Aren't you going to ask how Dad and the rest of the family are doing?" she questioned.

Joel's face heated. "Umm. . .you haven't given me much of a chance to ask. So how is everyone getting along these days?"

"As well as can be expected. We all miss you. Are you too busy to drop by once in a while, or are you deliberately staying away?"

Joel grimaced. *Here we go with the lecture.* "This is not the time or place to be talking about this. Now if you don't mind, I'd like something to eat. My stomach's about to jump out of my throat."

"Certainly. I see your appetite hasn't changed, at least. What would you like to have?"

Ignoring her sarcasm, Joel pointed to the menu. "I'll have a roast turkey sandwich with fries. Oh, and a glass of chocolate milk would be nice."

"I'll get your order turned in right away." Doris paused, moving closer to the table. "Why don't you come by for supper one night next week? I can make your favorite, hamburger and fries. In fact, we can do it picnic-style and get out the grill. I'll invite the rest of the family. I'm sure they'd all like to see you."

Joel folded his arms. "Yeah, I'll bet—especially Dad." It was hard to turn down a grilled burger, but he wasn't ready to face his entire family and be the focus of a thousand questions or the looks of irritation Dad often gave whenever Joel came around.

She frowned. "Don't be sarcastic, Joel. Dad may not say it, but he misses you, and so do the rest of us."

"The last time I visited, Dad didn't say more than a few words to me. Does snubbing me sound like someone who misses his only son?"

"I shouldn't need to remind you that our daed is a man of few words."

Joel shrugged. "If you say so."

"Will you come to supper or not?"

He shook his head. "I have a lot of work-related things going on right now. Maybe some other time."

Doris sighed. "I'll be back when your order is ready."

Joel blew out his breath, wishing once again he had picked another restaurant.

❧

Joel had no more than finished his meal when he caught sight of a horse and buggy pulling into the section of the parking lot reserved for the Amish. That in itself was no surprise, since many Amish people patronized Der Dutchman. What surprised Joel was seeing who got out of the buggy. He grimaced as he watched his older sisters, Arlene and Elsie, accompanied by Dad, heading for the restaurant.

Quickly, Joel grabbed his bill and rushed over to the cash register. While it might not be right to avoid them, he wasn't in the mood for his sisters' questions or Dad's cold shoulder. After he'd paid for his meal, Joel realized if he went out the door right now he'd probably run head-on into his family. Rather than risk an encounter, he ducked into the restroom. He'd wait there until he was sure they'd been seated.

As Joel stood at the sink, combing his hair, he

thought about the last time he and Dad talked. It had been awkward, and there really hadn't been much to say. Joel asked how Dad was doing, and Dad mumbled, "About the same." Joel asked if Dad could spare five hundred dollars, and Dad had given it to him, but not without a lecture. Of course, Joel was used to that. He'd had plenty of lectures from Dad during his teenaged years. "Don't stay out too late." "You don't need an expensive car." "You're full of *hochmut*, and pride goes before a fall." Joel had heard it all.

If Dad saw me driving the Corvette, he'd really believe I was full of pride. Well, it doesn't matter. I deserve that car. I've waited a long time to get one like it.

Thinking he'd given his family enough time to get seated, Joel opened the restroom door and peered out. No Amish in sight. He glanced toward the dining room and saw them seated at a table near the window, not far from where he'd been a short time ago. Relieved, he made a hasty exit. It was bad enough he'd seen Doris; Joel didn't need to deal with Dad, too.

⁓

As soon as Elsie entered the restaurant in Walnut Creek with Arlene and their father, she spotted their younger sister, Doris. "Let's ask the hostess to seat us in Doris's section," she whispered to Arlene.

"Okay, but we'd better not take up too much of her time visiting. We wouldn't want to jeopardize her job."

"Doris is too schmaert for that," Dad spoke up. "She knows better than to carry on a symposium all day with the customers when she oughta be tendin' to business."

Elsie looked at Arlene and rolled her eyes. Their father had always been right to the point and never minced any words—even the big ones, which had become his trait.

Soon after they were seated at a table, Doris showed up to take their order. "This is a pleasant surprise." She gave them each a glass of water. "Seeing my *schweschdere*, daed, and *bruder* all in the same day—what more could I ask for?"

Dad's eyebrows shot up. "Joel was here?"

Doris nodded. "You missed him by five minutes or so."

"Did he come in to see you?" Arlene asked.

"No, he didn't even realize I was working here until I came up to his table to wait on him."

"Humph! Bet you surprised him," Dad muttered.

"What did our bruder have to say?" Elsie questioned.

"Not much." Doris frowned. "I asked Joel if he'd like to come to our place for supper next week, but he used being too busy as an excuse. I even offered to make his favorite meal, but it didn't seem to matter."

Deep wrinkles formed across Dad's forehead as he pulled his fingers through the ends of his beard. "Sounds like he's using the same old excuse, but the truth is, he never comes around unless he wants something." He tapped his thumb on the menu. "Let's place our orders and forget about your wayward bruder. I'm *hungerich*, and Doris needs to put in our orders."

Saying anything more about Joel would get

them nowhere, so Elsie kept quiet. The mention of their brother was a touchy subject where Dad was concerned. It had been this way ever since Joel left the Amish church and walked away from his family in search of what he thought was a better life. Quickly scanning her menu, she looked up at Doris and suggested, "Why don't you start with Dad? He probably knows what he wants already."

"Not really." Dad shook his head. "I can't decide between a hot dog and french fries, or the grilled cheese sandwich, also with fries."

"A hot dog's not very healthy, Dad." Doris pointed to the menu. "Why don't you have a roast turkey sandwich and a cup of soup?"

He scrunched up his nose. "No one can make a turkey sandwich the way your mamm does. I'll stick with a hot dog."

Elsie glanced at Arlene, sitting beside her. *Is she thinking what I'm thinking? Why does Dad sometimes talk about Mama as if she's still alive? Does he forget occasionally, or is it simply his way of coping with her death?*

Arlene merely looked at Doris and said, "I'd like the strawberry crunch salad and a cup of vegetable soup."

"What about you, Elsie?" Doris held her pencil above the ordering pad.

Elsie scanned the menu one more time. "I'll have the soup and salad bar. I like a nice variety of veggies to choose from."

Dad let out an undignified snort. "You girls and your salads. You need a little meat to put on your emaciated bones."

Elsie's forehead wrinkled. She wished her father

didn't use big words so often. "Our what?"

"Emaciated bones. The word means, 'skinny.'" He pointed at Arlene. "Especially you, Daughter. You've gotten way too thin since the boppli was born."

Elsie held her breath, waiting to see how her sister would respond, but Arlene merely picked up her glass of water and took a drink.

Some things are better left unspoken, Elsie thought. *Especially when it comes to knowing when or how to give a reply to something Dad has said.*

"Do any of you want anything other than water to drink?" Doris asked.

Arlene and Elsie both shook their heads, but Dad was quick to say he wanted a glass of buttermilk. While some might find it strange to drink buttermilk with a hot dog, it was not uncommon for Dad. In fact, he had buttermilk with at least one of his meals every day. He'd been drinking it ever since Elsie could remember. Their mother had drunk it, too, but not as much as Dad. In fact, Mama made buttermilk biscuits and pancakes, which tasted so good. Elsie's mouth watered, thinking about it. She missed those days when her mother and father were together. Mama had always kept Dad in good spirits with her heartfelt humor and gentle ways. She had known how to soften his temper and keep him moving in a positive direction. Now it was up to Doris, Arlene, and Elsie to look after Dad. Joel sure wasn't going to help with that.

"I'll put in your orders and be back soon with your buttermilk." Doris smiled at Dad and hurried from the table.

"She looks thin, too," Dad commented. "Bet she

eats like a bird. Your mamm was a well-built woman. She was perfect for me." He stared off into space and grunted. "My girls are just as pretty though. They also attend church regularly and do well by their family, as well as others, which is more than I can say for that wayward son of mine." Dad's closed fist thumped the table. "Joel is spoiled by his wants and neglects those who should matter the most to him. He's pushed his family aside and forgotten his Amish upbringing." He sat back in his chair and slid his feet noisily forward under the table, the way he often did at home when he was upset.

Elsie's shoulders slumped as she let out a soft breath. She didn't remember her father being so critical when Mama was alive. Could he be this way because he missed her so much and felt depressed? She couldn't really blame him. But life moved on, and she hoped he would find some happiness.

Wanting to talk about something else, Elsie looked out the window and pointed to the vivid blue sky. "Sure is a beautiful day. Not nearly as much humidity as last week."

"I know. The weather was miserable, but it's good we got the canning done when we did." Arlene smiled at Dad. "I'll bring you some pickled beets soon. Would you like some?"

He smacked his lips. "Sounds *wunderbaar!*"

Elsie relaxed in her chair. At least the mention of beets had put Dad on a positive note. Now to keep things upbeat throughout the rest of their meal.

CHAPTER 6

Akron

Kristi turned on the coffeemaker and fixed herself a piece of toast. She'd forgotten to set her alarm last night, but fortunately, the early morning light had awakened her. She still had several minutes to spare.

The aroma of freshly brewed coffee drew Kristi to her kitchen for that first cup. Coffee wasn't on her ideal drink list, but she made an exception for her morning brew to get a kick-start to her Friday morning.

As Kristi sat at the table eating her low-calorie breakfast, she thought about Joel, and how, when they'd gone jogging last night, he'd acted strange—almost as if he was hiding something.

But what could it be? She reached for the jar of sugar-free strawberry jelly to put on her toast. *It was probably my imagination. He may have been tired.* Kristi's gaze fixated on her cup, watching the delicate swirl of steam rise from the surface of the coffee. She had a habit of over-analyzing things, especially where Joel was concerned. He had a business to run, which had to be stressful at times. Joel had a right to act sullen or moody when his day wasn't going as planned. Kristi hoped once they were married, Joel wouldn't let his business affect their relationship. *If we ever get married. Joel still hasn't bought me an engagement ring or suggested setting a wedding date. I don't want to push him, but I wish he'd at least introduce me to his family.*

It wasn't fair. Joel had met Kristi's family, but she hadn't met his. Every time the topic came up,

Joel either changed the subject or said she wouldn't fit in with his family, and for that matter, neither did he. Kristi figured he must have had a falling out with someone to be so dead set against her meeting them. She would have to be patient where his family was concerned. Maybe by the time she and Joel set a wedding date, he'd be ready to introduce her to them.

Kristi glanced at her watch, then gulped down the rest of her coffee. She needed to make a sandwich for lunch and get out the door soon or she'd be late for work.

❦

Charm, Ohio

Eustace Byler stood on his porch, gazing at the trees lining the back of his property. The smell of pine filled the morning air, and it seemed to melt his tensions away. Listening to the birds singing brought his thoughts to a sweeter time when his wife, Effie, used to say he ought to build a tree house so they could see things from the birds' perspective. Eustace kept promising to construct the little house in the trees, but had never gotten around to it. The plans had been drawn up, but getting started seemed to be the hard part. Other things seemed more urgent.

During the summer months, Effie spent time nearly every day relaxing in her favorite chair on the front porch with a cup of tea. She'd loved watching the birds and kept several feeders filled with a variety of seeds to lure them in. She would often comment on the birds' activity, listening to the steady chatter in undeniable disagreements as they competed for the best spot to perch. Effie used to say the birds were free entertainment at all times of the year.

Eustace groaned. "Why'd your heart have to give out on you, Effie? Don't ya know how much I still need you here by my side?" Someday he would build the tree house in memory of Effie. Then every time he went up there, he'd be reminded of his dear, loving wife.

Eustace's stomach growled, reminding him that he hadn't had breakfast yet. Turning toward the house, he went inside and made his way to the kitchen. When his gaze came to rest on the gas stove, he was reminded once again how much he missed his wife. When she was alive, Eustace would come inside after doing his chores and could always count on Effie having breakfast waiting for him. The wonderful aromas of whatever she prepared would reach his nostrils before he got to the door. Now he had to fend for himself. Since he wasn't the best cook in Holmes County, he usually ended up eating cold cereal or a piece of bread with peanut butter for breakfast. This morning, however, Eustace had a craving for steak and eggs. *I'll cook the steak on the grill.*

Eustace set the frying pan on the stove; took a carton of eggs, some ketchup, and the steak from the refrigerator; and went back outside. After he poured several briquettes into the bottom of the grill, he squirted lighter fluid over them and lit a match. Nothing happened. He added more fluid, lit a second match, and tossed it in.

Whoosh! The flames shot up. Eustace jumped back, but not soon enough. The sulfur-like smell could only mean one thing: he'd singed his beard.

To make sure the fire was out, he picked up the pot-holder he kept on the porch table and smacked at his beard several times. Then, placing the steak on the grill, he went back inside to check on the damage he'd done.

One look in the bathroom mirror and Eustace realized his beard was more than half the length it had once been. To make matters worse, the singed ends were dark. He opened the medicine chest and took out a pair of scissors. He had no choice but to trim off the scorched part, which made his beard even shorter.

"I'll probably be bombarded with all sorts of questions about this," Eustace grumbled, heading back outside to tend the meat. "Shoulda fixed a bowl of cereal instead of tryin' to satisfy my craving for steak and eggs."

❧

Akron

Even though the cool morning air was invigorating, Joel's jumbled thoughts made it hard to concentrate as he drove his work truck to town. He had been so preoccupied that he'd forgotten to fill his rig with gas last evening before heading home. Now the fuel gage sat on empty. He didn't need this headache on top of everything else.

Sweat beaded on Joel's forehead, but not from the outside temperatures. He hoped there was enough gas in his truck to get to town. He'd ridden on fumes a few times before, so maybe this time would be no different.

In an effort not to be consumed by his anxiety about the gas, Joel concentrated on what he was about to do. He'd convinced himself that taking money from his and Kristi's bank account was the right thing, but his conscience told him otherwise, constantly reminding him that the position he'd put himself in was his own fault. He'd never been one to admit his mistakes however. Even when he was a young boy, it had been easier to wangle his way out of things rather than face the truth and admit he was wrong. He had come up with an idea to fix the mess he was in, and right or wrong, he'd carry out the plan.

Joel had gotten back too late yesterday to make it to the bank, which had given him more time to think things through. But it hadn't helped much, because after looking at his last bank statement, he realized the money in their joint account would only pay a few of his subcontractors. He didn't dare draw it all out either. Thank goodness the monthly statements came to his place and not Kristi's. The last thing he needed was for her to find out he'd taken the money without her knowledge.

Joel swiped at the sweat on his forehead as he approached the bank. The gas station, which wasn't too far away, would be his next stop. With the exception of not telling Kristi about his family, he'd never done anything this deceitful to her. But he couldn't come right out and ask if she minded if he borrowed their money to pay his debts; he'd then have to tell her about the Corvette.

I can't worry about it right now, he thought, stepping into the bank. *I need to solve this problem.*

❧

When Joel left the bank, he squinted against the

glare of the sun. In his hurry to leave this morning, he'd forgotten his sunglasses.

Climbing back into the truck, Joel felt a headache coming on. Was it from the glare on his windshield, or the stress of what he'd just done?

"I'm really in a pickle right now," he muttered. The sun's brightness and his near-empty fuel tank were just a small part of the bigger frustrations plaguing him. All Joel could really hope for was that another big job would come along so he could pay the rest of his men, plus have enough to put back in the bank what he'd withdrawn. If things didn't go his way soon, he may have no other option but to make a trip to see his dad. But that was the last thing he wanted to do.

CHAPTER 7

After a week with only small job prospects, Joel had no choice but to visit his father and ask for a loan. He was almost out the door when his cell phone rang. As soon as he realized it was Kristi, he answered. "Hey, Kristi, what's up?"

"I was wondering if you'd like to go for another run with me this evening."

"Uh. . .I can't do it today."

"How come?"

"I have to go out of town on business, and I'm not sure what time I'll get home. It'll probably be late."

"Oh, I see. Maybe tomorrow then? Since it's Saturday, I'll have the day off."

"Sure, that'll be fine." Joel shifted the phone to his other ear. "Listen, I'd better go. I'll see you tomorrow, Kristi."

"Okay. I hope you have a good day."

"You, too." Joel hesitated a minute, then quickly added, "Love you." Before Kristi could respond, he clicked off his phone, grabbed his truck keys and sunglasses, and headed out the door.

Joel made a face when he glanced at his truck. The outside was a mess and needed a good washing. At least he'd taken the time to clean the windshield. Joel wished he could drive the Corvette to Charm, if for no other reason than to see how it performed once again on the open road. But he couldn't show up with an expensive car and then ask for money to help him out of a jam. Joel hoped his dad would be glad to see him and have no problem opening his wallet.

As Joel stepped into his truck, he reflected on the lie he'd told Kristi about where he was going today. It really wasn't a lie. He technically would be out of town doing business—with his dad. It was either tell a fib or tell Kristi the truth, which he definitely did not want to do. *I may never be ready to tell her about my Amish family,* he thought. *Then I'd have to explain the reasons I left and admit I used to be engaged to someone else.*

Over and over, Joel contemplated how he could tell Kristi about his past, but he found no easy way to announce that he used to be Amish. One thing was certain: Joel would avoid it for as long as possible—maybe indefinitely. If only Dad would give him the money. What a relief it would be to replace what he took out of the bank and be able to pay off his debts. Hopefully by tomorrow, things would be as they should.

⸎

Charm

As Eustace headed to the barn to let the horses into the pasture, he heard the soft cooing of doves, which made him think once again about Effie. Everything around here brought some sort of memory about his wife—the flowers blooming in late August, the birds singing overhead.

Unbidden tears sprang to Eustace's eyes, remembering how, whenever he used to bring the horses in for the night, he'd see Effie waiting on the porch, waving at him. He would remove his straw hat and wave in response. Eustace always drew comfort in knowing Effie would be there to greet him after his chores were done.

It had been a week since he'd singed his beard, and of course, he'd received some comments from family members, as well as friends at church on Sunday, which was embarrassing. Especially the part about how it happened. Now he had to be patient while it grew back.

I wonder if I combed or brushed my beard a lot more if it might help it grow faster, he mused. *Or maybe there's some kind of lotion I could look for at the drugstore that would quicken the process.* Eustace shook his head. *Guess it's probably best to leave it alone and let time take care of things.* Eustace's friend Henry hadn't seen his beard yet, but he was due here anytime, so Eustace was prepared for some ribbing.

Entering the barn, Eustace thought about Joel and how, as a boy, he'd helped bring in and let out the horses every day. Never in all of Joel's years of growing up had Eustace suspected his son would become dissatisfied with the only life he'd ever known. He'd seemed content when he was a boy. Eustace had foolishly convinced himself Joel would someday follow in his footsteps and raise horses, the way he had before he'd agreed to let oil wells be placed on his property. Now that money was no object, Eustace only raised a few horses for his own enjoyment.

"I was sure wrong about my boy. Guess I didn't know him as well as I thought." Eustace yanked off his old straw hat and swatted one of the horses to get her moving. In his exuberance, he missed the critter's rump and hit the side of the barn instead.

"Oh, great. Not what I needed this morning."

Eustace squinted at the brim of his hat where a chunk had broken off. "Guess I deserve it for not payin' attention to what I was doing."

Once the horses were out, Eustace went back into the house. Grunting, he plunked down in his favorite chair with wheels, rolled over to his desk, and pulled the junk drawer open. After removing the roll of duct tape, he proceeded to tape the brim back on his hat.

Effie had bought the hat for him two years before she died, so he wasn't about to throw it out. The only sensible thing to do was mend it the best way he could. If it looked ridiculous, then, oh well! He'd only be wearing it for everyday, so it didn't matter what others might say.

Rolling his chair back across the room, Eustace pulled up to the table and grabbed a banana to tide him over until lunchtime. Rising from his seat, he ambled over to the refrigerator. *Think I'll have a glass of buttermilk to go with the banana. Then I need to go over the plans one more time before I start working on the tree house.*

While getting out the milk, Eustace heard the familiar rumble of a tractor coming up the drive. He knew without looking it was his New Order Amish friend, Henry Raber. Old Henry rode around in that tractor more than his horse and buggy.

Eustace went out the door, leaving his glass of buttermilk on the counter. As soon as he stepped onto the porch he heard Henry's dog, Peaches, howling like a baby from her metal carrier fastened to the back of the tractor. Peaches, so named for the color of her hair, was always with Henry when-ever he came to visit. The cocker spaniel was kind of cute, but she was a fat little thing with a hearty set of lungs.

"Morning, Henry," Eustace called. "Glad ya came by. How's everything with you these days?"

"Can't complain I—" Henry tipped his head. "Say, what happened to your beard?"

Eustace groaned, reaching up to touch his shorter chin hairs. "Got a little too close to the barbecue grill when the flames shot up." He went on to tell his friend the rest of the story.

With a snicker, Henry thumped Eustace's back. "You're lucky ya didn't lose your whole beard."

Eustace nodded. "Indubitably."

"Indu-what?" Henry's brows squeezed together.

"Indubitably. It means 'definitely.'"

"Sounds like you've had your nose in the dictionary again."

"Yep. It's a great pastime, and I learn a lot." Eustace clasped his friend's shoulder. "So what have you been up to so far today?"

"Saw the widow-woman Ida at the post office this morning. She asked how you were doing." Chuckling, Henry yanked on his full gray beard and nodded. "Jah, she was anxious to know that, alright."

"So what'd ya tell her?" Eustace leaned on the porch railing.

"Said as far I knew you were good and I was heading out to see you." Henry walked up to the carrier to let his faithful companion out. The dog looked at Henry and tipped her head. *Yip! Yip!*

"Alright, already." Henry leaned down and, as if in slow-motion, lifted Peaches into his arms. One thing about old Henry—he did things slowly, never in much of a hurry.

"Well, that widow-woman may be interested in me," Eustace commented, "but my heart will never belong to anyone but dear Effie. Now enough talk about Ida. Let's go inside, and I'll get some coffee brewing. Oh, and I've got some blueberry fry pies to go with it that my daughter Doris picked up at Der Dutchman Bakery yesterday. She works next door in the restaurant, ya know."

Henry bobbed his graying head. "She's waited on me a time or two. You have a thoughtful dochder, Eustace."

"Jah. Doris sometimes brings me a sandwich or soup for supper." Eustace smiled. "All three of my daughters go out of their way to help out. They always want to clean around here or just drop by to check up on me, no matter how much resisting I do."

Henry thumped Eustace's back. "I, myself, would be in favor of all that fussin'. But then, you aren't like me."

"That's true. We're different, alright, but still good friends."

Henry took a seat at the table, still holding Peaches like she was his baby. "With most of my *kinner* in Indiana, I get far less attention than you do." He scratched Peaches behind her left ear. "But I'm content with what I've got."

Taking a sip from his glass of buttermilk, Eustace nodded. "I like to do things my own way. If I wanna climb a tree and cut off branches, I do it. No one likes to be told to wait on someone else to help when they can do it themselves." He puffed out his chest. "I may be sixty-five, but I'm more than capable of doing most chores around here myself. In fact, I'm quite proficient. Besides, I enjoy the work. Keeps me from missin' Effie so much. I can't stand to be idle." Eustace moved across the room. "Guess I'd better get the coffee goin'."

⁓

Berlin

"I'm going out to check for phone messages," Elsie called to her fifteen-year-old daughter, Mary. "Will you keep an eye on the breakfast casserole I have in the oven?"

Mary's blue eyes twinkled as she bobbed her head. "Sure, Mom. Hope and I will also set the table."

Elsie smiled. "Danki." She appreciated her two girls and their willingness to help, even without being asked. "The casserole should be done by the time I come back to the kitchen, and then as soon as your daed and brothers finish up with their chores, we can eat."

"Good, 'cause I'm hungerich." Hope, who had recently turned eleven, spoke up.

Mary giggled and poked her sister's arm. "You're always hungry. You could probably eat more than both of our brothers put together."

Hope made no comment as she opened the cupboard door and took out six plates, placing them on the table. Elsie was pleased her youngest daughter could take a little joshing without getting upset. Some children, like her nephew Scott, became defensive when teased. He also had a bit of a temper, but Elsie's sister Arlene and her husband, Larry, had been working with Scott on the issue.

Elsie went out the back door. Stopping at her

garden, she bent to pull a few weeds. If she didn't keep at them, they would soon choke out the plants. Things had been growing well this year. Vegetables were abundant, with plenty of tomatoes, green beans, corn, zucchini, and potatoes. After breakfast she would enlist the girls' help to pick and snap beans so they could have some for supper. She smiled, glancing at the carrots. They were sure getting bigger. This had been a great year for her garden.

Moving on down the driveway, Elsie opened the door to the phone shack to check for messages. She had no more than stepped inside when a spider web hit her in the face. "Eww. . ."

She cleaned the sticky web off her face and then checked her fingers, relieved there was no spider. From the time Elsie was a little girl, she'd had a spider phobia. Whenever she'd seen one, she had nearly freaked and usually asked someone to get rid of it for her. Since Elsie was now an adult, she took care of things like disposing of unwanted bugs, unless her husband was around of course.

Elsie took a seat in the folding chair, and was about to check the answering machine, when an ugly brown spider, hovering on a single web strand, lowered itself in front of her face. She screamed, ducked under the spider, and bolted out the door. Trembling, Elsie drew in a few shaky breaths. She had to go back in and check for messages, but not until the spider was out.

She spotted a twig lying in the yard and bent to pick it up. *I wish John or one of the kinner was here to do this for me right now,* she thought. *Since they're not, it won't get done unless I do it myself. I sure hope that spider is still there and not hiding in some corner waiting to creep me out again.*

Cautiously, Elsie stepped back into the phone shack. Sure enough, the spider was still there, dangling over the answering machine. Despite her trepidation, Elsie held out her hand, wrapping both spider and web around the twig. Then she carefully took the creature outside, placing it on a bush farther away. Once the job was done, she re-entered the phone shack and quickly checked for messages. The first was from her driver, saying she would be available Monday afternoon to take Elsie to her dental appointment. The second message surprised Elsie the most. It was from her brother, Joel, saying he'd be coming for a visit later this afternoon. It had been several months since they'd seen or heard from Joel. Elsie hoped this visit would go better than the last. Did she dare anticipate Joel may have decided to return to his Amish faith? Or was it wishful thinking? The fact of the matter hadn't changed—Dad was still hurt and angry because Joel turned his back on his family, as well as his faith. Deep down, however, Elsie felt sure Dad loved his son as much as his daughters.

Think I'll plan a big supper this evening and invite everyone over to Dad's place. I won't tell Dad though. I want it to be a surprise.

CHAPTER 8

Charm

Joel pulled his truck off to the side of the road and got out. As he leaned against the door and closed his eyes, familiar sounds came to his ears. The dog days of summer had definitely arrived, and it was anything but silent in late August. Instead of hearing the birds' constant melodies, he picked up the sound of certain bugs singing their own tunes. Crickets chirped, cicadas buzzed, and locust sounds were at their peak. *Trrrrrr. . .c-c-c-c. . .*

Memories from Joel's childhood flooded his mind as he stood on the hill above his father's house and looked down. He remembered many afternoons on this very rise, lying on his back, watching the clouds while enjoying the noises surrounding him.

A small grin reached Joel's lips as he wondered how, after all these years, a chorus of bugs could remind him of school days starting soon.

Joel could see the old swing hanging from the big maple tree, still looking as it had when he was a boy. He and Doris, being the youngest siblings and closest in age, had taken turns pushing each other on the swing a good many times. They'd run through the barn, chasing the cats, and climb into the hayloft to daydream and talk about the future. Little had Joel known that he'd someday have his own business, let alone become part of the English world. It surprised him how content he was living a different way of life than his family assumed he would. At least Joel thought he was content. If he were completely honest, part of him still missed some aspects of being Amish, but he'd been English for seven years now. For the most part, it felt right. He was not about to give up the dream he was living, nor break up with Kristi. The Amish way had many good aspects, but it wasn't for Joel anymore.

Turning his back on the farm and surveying the land around it, Joel saw nothing much had changed. He walked over to an area still familiar to him. Except for the weeds encompassing the spot, the seat he had made by arranging two rocks remained in place since the day he'd put them there. This rock-seat, situated in front of a large oak up on the knoll, had always been a happy place—Joel's private spot.

He watched as several dragonflies hovered over the grasses and colorful butterflies flitted from one plant to another, trying to find the last of the late-summer blooms. Joel took a deep breath and ran his fingers through his hair. *If only life could be as simple.*

About to lower himself to the old familiar seat, Joel's head jerked at the sound of a horse and buggy. Turning, he saw it approach and then stop. A few seconds later, his sister Doris got out. "Elsie said you were coming, but I didn't believe her." She moved closer to Joel. "Dad's gonna be surprised you're here." She gave him an awkward hug; Joel felt the strain between them.

"Why would he be surprised?" He glanced down the hill at their father's place. "When I called Elsie, I asked her to let Dad know I was coming."

"Guess she figured it was best not to say anything." Doris looked toward the open buggy, where her husband, Brian, sat holding the reins; then she turned her gaze back to Joel. "Elsie invited all of us to Dad's for supper this evening. She thought he would enjoy having his whole family together again." She folded her arms. "It's been awhile, you know."

"I've been busy with my business."

She glared at him. "Nobody should be too busy for family, Joel. But then you've never gotten that or you wouldn't have left us in the first place. Not to mention how bad you hurt your *aldi*."

Joel held up his hand, defiance welling in his soul as he looked at her. "Let's not even go there, okay? The past is in the past, and there's no going back. I'm sure Anna Detweiler has moved on with her life by now."

"She's still teaching school and keeps busy with other things, but Anna has remained single and hasn't had a serious boyfriend since you broke up with her."

Joel grimaced. The reminder of what he'd done to Anna made his stomach tighten. He still wondered if he and Anna might be married by now if she had been willing to leave with him. *But then I would never have met Kristi,* he thought. *Anna and I had some problems, and I'm sure Kristi's the perfect girl for me.*

Joel's thoughts came to a halt when Doris touched his arm. "Are you ready to head down the hill to Dad's now? I see two buggies near his barn, so I'm sure the others are there already."

Joel gave a nod. What else could he do? He was here and needed to ask Dad for money. He wished his sisters hadn't come though. It would be harder to speak to Dad with the others around.

Glancing at the farm once again, Joel felt like an outsider. Even with all the good memories flooding back, he didn't feel as comfortable as he should be with family.

❦

Akron

When Kristi wheeled Mildred Parker, one of her patients, into the social room at the nursing home where she worked, her attention was drawn to an elderly man sitting in an easy chair near the window. It wasn't his flowing white hair and long Santa Claus beard that caught her attention; however—it was the beautiful music coming from the harmonica he held between his lips.

Joel had a harmonica similar to this man's, but Kristi hadn't heard him play it for several weeks. He'd seemed so preoccupied lately. Whenever she talked to him, he didn't appear to be really listening. What Joel needed was to relax more and have some fun for a change. Having work on his mind all the time wasn't a good thing for Joel—or for their relationship.

I'll bet a trip to Amish country would help Joel relax. It sure did for me, Kristi mused. *I wish he was willing to go there with me. When I catch Joel in the right mood, I'll ask again.*

Smiling, Kristi parked Mildred's wheelchair near the man with the flowing beard and took a seat beside her patient to listen to the melodic sounds of "Amazing Grace." Several of the patients, as well as family members who had come to visit, joined in by singing the familiar hymn. The man playing the harmonica seemed not to notice, as he closed his eyes and lifted his gaze toward the ceiling. Perhaps it was his way of worshipping God. Hearing his song had certainly warmed Kristi's heart and put her in a worshipful frame of mind. It made her look forward to this coming Sunday, when she and Joel could attend church. It might be fun to plan a bicycle ride later in the afternoon. They could either take a picnic lunch along or stop at one of the local restaurants for a bite to eat. It would be fun to be together. Maybe she could talk Joel into bringing his harmonica.

As Kristi let the music envelope her thoughts, her gaze drifted to the window. When she'd first started working at the nursing home, she'd been told this room wasn't always so popular. Now it was a favorite with patients and visitors alike, in part because the view from the window had changed from plain old grass to a landscaped nature garden. Flowering shrubs and unusual rocks surrounded a fish pond. At the far end, facing the window, a small waterfall cascaded into the tranquil pool. Pink-and-white water lilies floated on top, with several koi fish peacefully swimming through the clear water. Their orange-and-white bodies created a sharp contrast to the brown river pebbles on the floor of the pond.

The social room, with the large picture window, was a nice place for the residents to relax and feel comfortable. It was peaceful, and the employees at the nursing home often visited the room during their breaks.

Kristi glanced at her watch. She needed to check on another patient before her shift ended for the day, so reluctantly, she turned from the window. Then, leaning over to tell Mildred she would be back for her soon, Kristi quietly left the room.

❧

Charm

Joel parked his truck near the barn and got out. Looking around, it didn't take him long to realize that, with the exception of a few more old wagon wheels and several antique milk cans scattered around, the place hadn't changed much. Dad was a junk collector and always had been. But then, Joel had to admit, he had a few of his own things he couldn't part with. If he had the chance, he'd have a collection of classic cars—not sitting around the yard of course. Some, he'd fix up and sell for a profit, but others he would keep for the pure pleasure of having them.

"Hey, Joel, it's good to see you. How have ya been?" Arlene's husband, Larry, asked as he headed for the barn with his horse.

"Okay, I guess." As Joel entered the barn behind his blond-haired brother-in-law, he winced at the putrid odor of horse urine and scowled at the cobwebs hanging from the rafters.

Larry stopped and looked back at him. "I'd say this barn could use a good cleaning."

"I agree. When I was a boy, Dad used to keep it much cleaner. Of course," Joel added, "I usually helped him with that. When was the last time Dad cleaned the barn anyway?"

Larry shrugged. "Brian, John, and I have offered to do it for him many times, but he always refuses our help."

Joel frowned. "Figures. He's as stubborn as ever." The place was thick with flies. He swatted at a few as he watched Larry lead his horse into one of the empty stalls. When Joel's mother was alive, Dad always made sure either he or Joel kept the barn and other outbuildings clean and fresh, with plenty of fly strips hanging from the rafters to keep the pesky bugs at bay. Mom had even kept a lid on some of Dad's eccentricities, but no one was there to do that anymore.

Joel shook his head. *Dad shouldn't be living alone. I sure don't have the time or patience to take care of him though. Besides, he wouldn't want to live in my fancy world. You'd think he'd move in with one of my sisters or, at the very least, hire someone to help out around here. With the oil fracking being done on Dad's property, it's not like he can't afford it. I'll bet he has more money than he knows what to do with.*

"So where's my dad?" Joel asked, leaning on the door of the horse's stall.

Larry shrugged. "Don't know. I'm guessin' he must be in the house. I'll bet he'll be glad to see you."

Joel opened his mouth, but as he was about to speak, he inhaled a fly and swallowed the filthy insect before it even registered what had happened. He coughed and sputtered, trying to get it back up, but it seemed to be lodged in his throat.

Dashing out of the barn, Joel flung his truck door open, grabbed a bottle of water, and took a big swig. "Life on the farm," he muttered. "Guess all the memories weren't so good."

"Uncle Joel!" Joel's nephew Scott bounded up to him with a huge smile on his freckled face. "Are ya movin' in with Grandpa, or did ya come to ask him for somethin'?"

Joel's face heated. Apparently there'd been some

talk among family members about him only coming around when he wanted something. *I don't care if they do talk behind my back.* Drawing in a quick breath, Joel collected himself to face his family. Then he gave Scott's shoulder a squeeze and pointed to the house. "I'm sure whatever my sisters have made for the meal will be good." He stepped onto the porch and took another deep breath. "Shall we go inside and see what's for supper?"

CHAPTER 9

When Joel entered the house with Scott at his side, he expected to see his father sitting in the living room in his favorite chair. What he saw instead was his sister Arlene sitting in Mom's rocking chair, holding a baby. Except for a few gray hairs mingled with strands of brown sticking out from under her white head covering, she looked the same as the last time he'd seen her.

Arlene looked up and smiled. "It's nice you came, Joel. Elsie and Doris are in the kitchen, and the menfolk and most of the kinner are in the basement looking at something Dad recently bought."

He gave a brief nod. Then giving the living room a quick scan, he noticed it hadn't changed at all. Every stick of furniture remained in its place. The braided throw rug Mom had made many years ago was missing though. It had probably worn all the way through from Dad wheeling about the house in his favorite chair. The marks on the wooden floor told the story.

Glancing toward the kitchen, Joel heard his other two sisters speaking their traditional German-Dutch language. Even though he didn't use it anymore, Joel understood it all perfectly.

"I'd like you to meet your newest nephew, Samuel. He's four months old." When Joel looked back at Arlene, she motioned to the infant.

Joel looked at Scott, still standing beside him with a cheesy grin, then back at the baby, realizing the brothers were eight years apart. "I—I wasn't aware you'd had another child."

"If you came around once in a while, you'd realize what's going on in our family."

Joel jerked his head at the sound of his father's voice. Dad stood in the doorway between the living room and kitchen with his arms crossed over his chest. "What are you doing here, anyway?"

"I—I came to see you," Joel stammered, feeling like a kid again as his dad scrutinized him. "Figured Elsie would tell you I was coming."

"No, she didn't." When Dad pulled his fingers through his beard, Joel noticed it was much shorter than it had been before. He wondered what happened, but before he could ask, Arlene spoke up.

"We wanted your coming to be a surprise."

Dad tapped his foot, never taking his eyes off Joel. "It's a surprise, alright. Wasn't sure we'd ever see your wayward bruder again."

Joel clenched his fists. He didn't like the way his dad was staring right at him while talking to Arlene like he wasn't even in the room.

Joel's brothers-in-law, John, Larry, and Brian, entered the room, along with Joel's nephews, Doug, Glen, and Blaine. They each took turns shaking Joel's hand. Their cordial welcome made Joel feel a little more relaxed. He was glad Scott had left to use the bathroom and hadn't heard Dad's caustic remarks.

A few seconds later, Doris and Elsie came in from the kitchen, along with Joel's nieces, Martha, Lillian, Mary, and Hope.

"Well, Joel is here now, Dad, so I think we should all eat and enjoy our time together." Arlene stood, and when Doris held her arms out, she handed the baby to her. Joel couldn't help but notice the look of longing on his youngest sister's face. No doubt she wanted a baby of her own.

Soon after, when Scott joined them in the dining room, the hot food was brought out and placed on the table. The aromas caused Joel's mouth to water. Elsie, her brown eyes appearing darker than usual, immediately stepped over to Joel and gave him a hug. "I'm glad we could all gather this way to catch up, like a real family."

When Joel stepped away from her embrace, he nodded.

"The food is ready." Elsie looked at Dad.

"Humph!" He shuffled across the room and took a seat at the head of the table.

Everyone gathered and found seats as well. Joel was relieved he hadn't been asked to sit at a separate table, the way he had when he'd first left the Amish faith and returned home for a meal. But Dad was as cool and unfriendly as ever. Scott, however, was all smiles when he took a seat to the left of Joel.

All heads bowed for silent prayer, which felt strange to Joel, since Kristi always prayed out loud. Joel didn't pray much anymore. He only went along with it for Kristi's sake. If he didn't go to church with her and appear to be interested in spiritual things, she'd probably break up with him. He would do whatever it took to hold on to Kristi and make sure she'd never leave him. They had a good relationship, and he wasn't about to let her go. Meeting Kristi was the best thing that had ever happened to Joel. *If she heard I was sitting here right now with my Amish family, she wouldn't believe it for a minute,* he mused.

Eustace sat across the table from Joel, longing for his son to sit at his table like the guest of honor tonight. Instead, tension filled the room, like it always did when Joel came around.

Brian, Doris's husband, who sat on Joel's other side, leaned closer and asked, "How's the construction business going?"

Joel shifted in his chair; then clearing his throat, he drank some water. "Uh. . .well, my business has been doing fairly well. I have several jobs lined up right now." His cheeks reddened a bit. "How about you, Brian? How's the carpentry business?"

"Doin' good. I like my job." Brian bobbed his brown head. "My corn's growing well this year, too. Looks to be a great crop. It should yield us quite a bit this fall. Doris and I are hoping to save up enough money to take a trip together sometime next year." He leaned back in his chair and grinned at his wife. "We'd like to go to Florida—maybe in January or February—when the weather gets cold here."

Joel nodded briefly. He seemed preoccupied and a bit edgy. *I wonder if he's hiding something,* Eustace thought. *I can sense it in his tone and the way he avoids making eye contact with everyone.*

A muscle on the side of Eustace's neck quivered. Having Joel here was like a two-edged knife. While it was good to have the whole family together, it grieved Eustace to see his son sitting here in English clothes, barely saying a word to anyone unless he was asked a question. Others in their community had children who'd left the faith, but none acted as haughty and distant as Eustace's son. What had happened to make Joel become so dissatisfied? Had Eustace done something to turn his son away? If Effie were still alive, would she be able to talk their son into moving back home and joining the Amish church again? Maybe not. Effie wasn't able to make Joel see reason before she died. Eustace gripped the edge of the table. It had nearly broken poor Effie's heart when their youngest child left to go English.

I need to quit thinking about this, because, short of a miracle, my son will never return to our faith, Eustace told himself. *Joel only comes around when he wants something, and I'm sure it's no different this time. But I'm not going to let his being here spoil my supper.*

"Please pass me the mashed *grummbiere*." Eustace reached out, looking at Elsie.

She smiled and handed him the bowl. "I fixed them the way Mama used to. Plenty of milk to make the potatoes creamy, and of course, salt and pepper."

Eustace plopped some on his plate, squeezed a bit of ketchup out of the bottle, and took a bite. "Not quite as favorable as your mamm's, but not so bad either." He glanced at Joel. "What do ya think of this fine meal set before you? Bet ya don't get food this exquisite anywhere in the English world."

Joel smiled, but the expression didn't quite reach his eyes. "Everything tastes great." He reached for a piece of chicken. "My sisters are the best cooks in all of Holmes County."

"Danki," Arlene and Elsie replied in unison, but Doris remained quiet. She hadn't said more than a few words since they sat down at the table.

It shouldn't be like this. Eustace slid his feet back and forth under the table. *There should be good feelings among everyone here at my table.* He wondered if Doris might still be angry at Joel for breaking up with her best friend, Anna, when he made the decision to go English and move to Akron in pursuit of worldly pleasures. Anna had been devastated by Joel's rejection, and like a good friend, Doris had been there to help her get through it.

Eustace felt bad about what Joel had put Anna through, but the main reason he wasn't happy to see Joel this evening had nothing to do with Joel's ex-girlfriend. Simply put, Eustace was almost sure Joel's only reason for coming here was to ask for money, like he had the last time he'd visited. Well, if that turned out to be the case, he'd be sorely disappointed.

⁓

As Doris ate her meal, she kept watching Joel. He hadn't contributed much to the conversation. The only time he ever smiled was when young Scott said something to him. Why did he bother to come here this evening if he wasn't going to blend into the family and have a good time? Had her brother shown up with an ulterior motive?

Thinking back to her childhood, Doris remembered how close she and Joel had once been. Back then she'd gotten along better with him than either Elsie or Arlene. Of course, she was closer to Joel's age, and they'd had a few things in common. Not anymore though. There was nothing about Joel that reminded Doris of the closeness they'd once had. Going English had changed him, and in her opinion, not for the better.

She sighed, remembering how when they were children she'd seen Joel many times sneak up the hill to sit on the large rocks by the big oak tree. Since Joel had left, she sometimes walked up to his rock-seat when she was visiting Dad and sat awhile. It was quiet there, with a lot of activity from birds and animals. Doris felt drawn to its calming effect. She also felt closer to Joel when she sat on his rocks. Sometimes, she would close her eyes and pray that her brother would see the light and admit the error of his ways.

But it may never happen, she reminded herself. *Joel might always remain self-centered and disinterested in his family.*

"Uncle Joel, did you bring your harmonica with you tonight?" The question from Arlene's twelve-year-old son, Doug, cut into Doris's thoughts.

Startled, Joel blinked a couple of times. "Uh, no. . .I didn't think to bring it." He forked a piece of chicken and plopped it on his plate.

Doug's dark eyebrows furrowed. "That's too bad. It woulda been nice to hear you and Grandpa play together again."

Elsie smiled. "You should bring it the next time you come."

Scott tugged on Joel's sleeve. "Will ya teach me how to play the harmonica, Uncle Joel?"

"Maybe sometime," Joel replied. "But you should really ask your grandpa. You see him all the time; I don't come here that often."

"And whose fault is that?" Doris spoke up. She couldn't hold her tongue any longer. "You don't really live that far from us, Joel. There's no reason you can't take the time to visit at least once a month."

All heads turned to look at Doris. She'd probably said too much, and worst of all, in front of the children. "I—I'm sorry," she murmured. "I spoke out of turn."

Arlene reached over and patted Doris's arm. "It's okay. We've all said things we wish we hadn't."

"What we need is a change of subject," Brian put in. "Eustace, why don't you tell how you singed your beard?"

Doris appreciated her husband's attempt to lighten the mood, but Dad had previously told most of them about the mishap with his beard. If he explained how it happened now, it would only be for her brother's sake. And so far, Joel didn't seem interested in much of anything being said this evening.

"Maybe Dad would rather not discuss it." Doris glanced in her father's direction. "Should we talk about something else instead?"

He shook his head. "No, that's okay. I don't mind tellin' the story again. It's good for a laugh."

While Dad recounted the details of his grilling mishap, Doris concentrated on finishing her meal.

⁓

"If it's alright with everyone, I think we'll wait awhile to have dessert," Elsie suggested when supper was over. "I ate too much and need time for my food to settle."

"That's fine by me." John thumped his stomach. "I'll enjoy my dessert a lot more if I eat it later."

All heads nodded in agreement, even the children's.

Joel glanced at his dad, wondering if he would settle into his easy chair in the living room or head outside for some fresh air. It would be a lot easier to talk to him if he went outdoors. Joel worried about what he would do if he couldn't get Dad alone tonight. He sure couldn't blurt out in front of everyone that he was in a jam and wanted to borrow some money. On the other hand, he didn't want to leave here without asking Dad.

Joel felt a surge of hope when Dad pushed away from the dining room table and said he was going out to the barn to check on the mare that had given birth this morning.

"Mind if I tag along?" Joel asked.

Dad hesitated a moment, but finally shrugged. "Suit yourself."

Relieved that none of the other men or any of the boys had offered to join them, Joel followed his dad out the door. When they entered the barn, he decided to make some idle conversation first, to break the ice. It would be best if he eased into the topic of money, rather than blurting it out.

They talked about Dad's horses awhile and moved on to discussing the warm weather they'd been having.

"I, for one, will be glad when summer's over and the cooler weather swoops in." Joel leaned against the mare's stall, watching her foal nurse.

Dad merely grunted in response as he chewed on a piece of straw.

"Sorry to hear you lost part of your beard, but it'll grow back, right?"

Dad nodded.

Joel stood quietly, watching him check the mare and her colt over good.

Guess it's now or never. I need to ask for the money while I have the chance.

Joel was on the verge of telling Dad his predicament

when Arlene showed up. "I came out to tell you the desserts have been set on the table. Everyone's waiting for you. Seems they all have room now." She smiled at Dad. "Elsie made your favorite peach pie, so you'd better hurry before it's all gone."

Dad didn't have to be asked twice. Without so much as a word to Joel, he hurried from the barn.

"Great," Joel mumbled. At this rate he might never get to talk to Dad alone.

CHAPTER 10

"Why don't we start a bonfire out back?" Larry suggested as they all sat around the table, eating their pie. "I'm sure the kinner would enjoy roasting some marshmallows."

"Good idea. It'll give us more time to visit with Joel," Elsie said.

Joel shook his head. "I should probably get going, but I do need to talk to Dad before I go."

"Why don't you spend the night here?" Arlene suggested. "You don't have to rush off, and it'll give you more time to spend with Dad."

Joel glanced at his father to get his reaction. If he stayed the night, he could get up before the Saturday morning traffic became heavy. With it being the final weekend in August and children soon starting a new school year, travelers would be crowding the highways for those last-minute family vacations. Joel figured if he left at sunup, he'd make it back to Akron in plenty of time to go to his bank, which was open until noon—that is, if he had a check to deposit. Everything hinged on Dad's willingness to loan him the money.

Dad looked at Joel and shrugged his shoulders. "If you wanna stay, it's fine by me."

"Really? I—I mean, I'm fine with it, too." Joel looked at Doris and noticed her scowl. Did she disapprove of him spending the night? Didn't he have the right to spend time with Dad? It didn't matter what Doris thought. Joel was an adult and could make his own decisions. Besides, if he stayed overnight, he'd have Dad all to himself and would be able to talk privately with him.

He looked at his watch, wondering whether he should give Kristi a call. In the message he had left earlier, he'd told her he would be home sometime this evening. He hoped she wouldn't call while he was here with all the family, because he'd have a hard time explaining all the background noise.

"I need to step outside and make a quick phone call," Joel stated after he finished his coffee.

"While you're making your call, I'll get the fire going." Larry jumped up and followed Joel out the door. Several others did as well.

Stepping into the night air felt nice after being inside where it was stuffy. No one else seemed to have minded the heat, so maybe only Joel felt as if he couldn't breathe. It made sense, with him being the center of attention, even among his own family, and feeling like the outsider he was.

The stars, Joel noticed, were far more intense out here at Dad's place then back home in the city where Kristi lived. Joel's own piece of land would also be a great place for stargazing if not for all the lights he had around the place to discourage trespassing or a burglary.

Joel paused on the porch a few minutes, watching the fireflies rising from the lawn. Since July was normally the best month to see lightning bugs, he was surprised to still see a few around. Maybe it was because the nights hadn't turned cooler yet.

He breathed in the refreshing night air and for several seconds watched his family mingle. Joel waited until everyone had headed around to the back of the house where Dad's fire pit was located.

Then, feeling the need for some privacy, he slipped away to make his call to Kristi.

Joel hopped into his truck and closed the door. When he took out his cell, he grimaced. The phone had no bars. "Should have known I would be off the grid way out here," he grumbled. "Guess I'd better make my way to Dad's phone shack and call Kristi from there."

Joel stepped out of his truck and was halfway down the driveway, when his nephew, Scott, called, "Where ya goin' Uncle Joel?"

Joel turned around, cupping his hands around his mouth. "I need to make a phone call. Save me a seat by the fire, okay?"

Scott bobbed his head, then darted off to join the other children playing near the barn.

When Joel entered the phone shack, a sense of nostalgia swept over him, the way it had when he'd been in the barn earlier this evening. When he and Doris were children, playing hide-and-seek, he'd sometimes hidden in the phone shack. Of course, once she'd caught on to his secret hiding place, that was the end of it.

Pulling his thoughts back to the task at hand, Joel punched in Kristi's number. She answered on the second ring.

"Hi Joel. Are you back in town?" Kristi asked cheerfully.

"No, not yet. In fact, I won't be back till sometime tomorrow morning."

"Really? But you told me you'd be back this evening."

"I know, but my business here took longer than I figured. So rather than coming home tonight, I decided it would be best to wait till morning. I'd feel better being fresh and alert when I drive home."

"That makes sense if you're too far away. Where are you anyway?" she asked.

Joel bit his lip. "Umm. . .a little south of Berlin."

"You're in Amish country?"

"Uh, yeah, that's right."

"Lucky you. Wish I had gone with you. I had so much fun the day Mom and I visited there. I'd really like to go back again."

Tap. Tap. Tap.

Joel opened the door and poked his head out. There stood Scott, looking up at him with inquisitive blue eyes. The boy opened his mouth, as if to say something, but Joel spoke first. "I'll be there soon," he whispered, then quickly shut the door.

"Who are you talking to, Joel?" Kristi questioned.

"Uh, no one. I mean, I was talking to you. Just said I'd see you soon."

Joel heard Kristi's intake of air, then waited as she paused before continuing. Kristi's voice was above a whisper when she asked, "Is everything alright, Joel? Your voice sounds strained."

"I'm fine. My job has me preoccupied, is all."

"Okay. I'll let you go. See you sometime tomorrow, Joel."

"Sounds good. I'll drop by your place tomorrow evening." Hoping to reassure her, he added, "Maybe we can go for a run before supper."

"That'd be nice, and I'd be happy to fix whatever you want to eat."

"Okay. We'll talk about it then. See you tomorrow, Kristi." Joel pressed his fingers on the receiver as he pinched his lips together. He missed Kristi and wished he were with her right now.

When Joel headed toward the bonfire, another childhood memory came to mind. Teasing Doris, he'd roasted a marshmallow for her and deliberately made sure it was well-done, to the point of turning black. He'd realized quickly she hadn't been riled one little bit, as she had let it be known how she much liked her marshmallows overly toasted. Joel could still see Doris's smug expression as she ate the ash-covered marshmallow and smacked her lips, with gooey stuff still stuck to her fingers.

I wonder how she'd respond if I made her a burned marshmallow tonight. Bet she wouldn't smile and say she liked it. Pushing his memories aside, Joel took a seat beside Scott to enjoy the rest of the evening.

❧

Akron

Kristi settled into a wicker chair on her deck to watch the sun set in the Ohio skies. Toying with the braid she'd plaited into her hair, an uneasy feeling enveloped her. Why was it she felt Joel had been keeping something from her? Or was it only her imagination running wild and making her feel uneasy?

Kristi picked up the book of crossword puzzles she'd bought a few days ago. Maybe this would keep her mind occupied. In the past, exercising her brain while working the puzzles had helped her relax. Tonight, though, she wasn't so sure.

Kristi got the first couple of words right away, but it wasn't long before her concentration faltered. She chewed on the end of her pencil and stared out across the yard. She noticed the trees had a worn-out look during their last stages of summer growth. Kristi couldn't wait for autumn. She enjoyed watching the leaves turn brilliant with color. But now, as she looked at their dull appearance, she couldn't help comparing them to her relationship with Joel. Lately it seemed their connection with each other was dull and lacked the luster they'd shared when they first started dating. Like the last autumn leaves letting go, was their relationship fading and drawing to a close? Or was it only the stress Joel felt from his job putting distance between them?

Kristi put the crossword puzzle aside. The sun had already dripped below the horizon, and the first stars were coming to light. Closing her eyes and bowing her head, she sent up a silent prayer: *Lord, please be with Joel tonight. And if our relationship is failing, and it's somehow my fault, show me how to make things better.*

⌘

Charm

The house seemed quiet after everyone went home. Eustace wondered if he should go to bed or visit with Joel awhile. He didn't have to wonder long, for Joel quickly engaged him in conversation.

"I need to ask you something, Dad." Joel took a seat on the couch.

"Oh, what about?" Eustace seated himself in his easy chair and reclined it. He was tired from the excitement of the evening and needed to relax.

Joel leaned forward, elbows on his knees. "I'm in a bit of a financial jam right now."

"What else is new? I thought you said at the

dinner table that you were doing substantially well in your business." It was all Eustace could do not to point a finger at his son and exclaim what he'd been wondering all along. But he realized it would be best to keep to himself what he suspected about Joel coming home for more reasons than to visit. Eustace could almost count on the next words out of Joel's mouth, when he'd worked up his nerve to ask for something.

"I was doing well, but something messed me up, and now I'm overextended. So I was wondering if I could borrow some money."

"How much?"

"Twenty-five thousand dollars."

Eustace pulled the lever on his chair so hard it nearly propelled him out. "Are you kidding, Joel? Why do you need so much money?"

"I owe some of my subcontractors." Joel rose to his feet and moved to stand in front of Eustace. "I'll pay it back as soon as my next big job comes in."

Eustace shook his head determinedly. "Absolutely not! It upsets me that the only time you feel the need to come around is when you want something."

Joel's cheeks reddened as he ran a shaky hand through his hair. "It may seem that way, but—"

"Do I need to remind you that the last time you came here you borrowed money but never paid it back? Now you have the nerve to ask my help again." Eustace lifted both hands. "You're profligate."

"Huh?"

"You're reckless. When are you gonna grow up and take responsibility for yourself?"

Joel's eyes narrowed. "I'll bet if it was one of my

sisters asking for money you'd give it to her with no hesitation."

"I may, but none of your sisters are as irresponsible as you. For the most part, they're magnanimous."

"Magnanimous? What's that supposed to mean?"

"Worthy and upright. If they owed me money, you can be sure they'd pay it back."

"I'll pay my debt to you—for the last loan, as well as this one. Please give me another chance." Joel's tone was pleading.

Eustace held his ground. If he gave in, his son would never learn to stand on his own two feet. "You're spoiled, and it's time you grew up and took responsibility for your mistakes without expecting me to come to your rescue. It's not like you care about your family anyway." His tone was flat.

"I do care. I made a mistake and need some money to tide me over till another big job comes along."

"I suspected during supper, actually, that you were up to something." Eustace crossed his arms. "You can't fool me, Joel. A father knows his child's heart. You have truly strayed and need to change the path you're on before you lose any more of your precious money. A man like you will never be affluent, because he loses what he has as soon as he acquires it."

"But—but Dad. . ."

Eustace held up his hand. "Sorry, Son, but you won't be leaving here with a check from me. I will give you no more money. And don't come back here again unless it's strictly to visit. You're not being fair to the rest of the family."

"Fine then! If that's the way you feel, I won't come back at all!" Joel stomped toward the door then turned back around with his index finger in the air. "By the way, those big words you've been using don't make you any smarter than me!" He went to the door again and swung it open, letting it slam behind him.

Eustace sank back into his chair. It hadn't been easy telling Joel no, seeing such a look of desperation on his face. Like most parents, it was in Eustace's nature to want to help his children and see them succeed. But Joel would never learn the value of a dollar or the importance of family if he had everything handed to him. What Joel needed was to follow the example of his brothers-in-law and quit blowing money on things he didn't need. Eustace felt sure that's exactly what had happened. No doubt his son had bought something he couldn't afford, and probably with someone else's money. *Will my son ever stop being so selfish? How far down will he travel before he hits rock bottom? What Joel needs to do is a sincere, selfless act.*

❦

Joel ground his teeth as he headed straight for his truck, never bothering to look back. Struggling with his emotions, he drove out and stopped up at the top of the hill, where he parked and turned off the engine. His dad's harsh voice still rang in his ears, drowning out the relentless chorus of the katydids' rhythmic song, as he stared out the front window into the blackness of night.

He pounded the steering wheel until his hands ached. As Joel calmed down, he rested his arms and head on the wheel and berated himself. *What did I think would happen tonight? I knew Dad would react like he did, but I had to try.* He felt alone and defeated. Without help from Dad, how was he going to pay his subcontractors?

Joel peered down at the now-dark farmhouse. No doubt Dad was sleeping soundly, unconcerned about how he'd refused to help. "He's probably snoring in 'la-la' land and not thinking anymore about me right now." He pounded the steering wheel again, this time accidently honking the horn. "So what if I woke Dad up?" He winced. "I'm his only son. How can he do this to me?"

Joel agonized over his dilemma for a while, but realizing he needed to get home, he started up his truck. *I do care about my family*, he told himself. *They—especially Dad—don't really care about me.*

As Joel headed down the road toward home, his thoughts ran wild, increasing his anger. *Who does Dad think he is, treating me like that? If I had a son who came to me with a need, I'd give him whatever he wanted, no questions asked.*

Joel turned on the radio, trying to drown out his thoughts, but it was no use. He could still hear Dad accusing him of being selfish.

As Joel approached the entrance to the freeway outside of Dover, a car coming from the opposite direction swerved into his lane. Before Joel could react, the vehicle slammed into his truck. The last thing Joel felt was searing pain. Then his world faded into blackness.

The
STUBBORN
FATHER

CHAPTER 1

Charm

"That son of mine can sure get under my skin," Eustace grumbled, pacing the living room floor. Never once had Joel apologized for the hurt he'd caused his family by leaving the Amish church. Even worse, he only came around whenever he wanted something and didn't act interested in being part of their family. With the exception of Eustace's eight-year-old grandson, Scott, Joel had hardly spoken to anyone during his visit here tonight. It would have been nice if Joel had actually stayed the night and the two of them could have visited like any normal father and son. But no, Joel let his temper get the best of him and stormed out the door.

Guess I can't blame him though. Joel was upset because I wouldn't loan him twenty-five thousand dollars. Eustace frowned. *It was a lot of money to ask for—an amount Joel would probably never pay back.*

It wasn't because Eustace didn't have adequate funds in the bank—he had more than enough to loan Joel. *But if I'd given it to him, what would it teach my selfish son? He has to learn responsibility sometime in his life. After all, he's twenty-six years old.*

Eustace stopped pacing and stared at his wife's old rocking chair, empty and void without her. "This is your fault, Effie." He pointed at the chair as if she were sitting there. "Our son has become ungrateful for everything we've done for him. You spoiled him rotten from the time he was born."

Eustace stood by Effie's chair, using his foot to get it rocking in motion. As the chair creaked back and forth, he could almost see his wife looking defiantly back at him. The more he thought about what Effie would have said if she were there, the more he had to admit she'd probably be right. After having three daughters, Eustace had been so excited to have a boy when Joel came along that he'd been a bit too permissive as well. He'd often looked the other way when Joel had done something he shouldn't, and he'd given him things he probably didn't need.

In some ways Joel reminded Eustace of himself. As a youngster he'd been full of energy, anxious to explore the world, and always looking to try new things.

But I was grounded in my faith. Eustace sat down in Effie's rocker, grasping the arms of the chair. *Well, at least in most things. I stayed true to my church and family. That's more than Joel can say.*

Eustace's gaze came to rest on the Bible lying on the small table beside him. Effie's Bible. When the children were all living at home, their mother would gather them around the rocking chair every evening while she read a passage of scripture out loud. Then after the children were grown and out on their own, she'd read to Eustace. Afterward, they would discuss the verses and how they applied to their life. Eustace missed those days. He missed everything about his dear wife and all they'd done together. He and Effie had been deeply in love, and he'd never grown tired of learning more about her.

Because Effie is gone doesn't mean I should neglect Bible reading. Eustace picked up her Bible and opened it to a section in the book of Luke she'd marked with a white ribbon. Holding the book made him feel closer to Effie. He noticed the page had several verses underlined—in fact, a whole passage about the prodigal son that started at verse 11 of chapter 15.

A lump formed in Eustace's throat as he read the story. Joel was like the prodigal, only he had never come back repentant. His vision blurred, and his heart ached for his son. *He needs to repent, Lord,* Eustace prayed. *Even if Joel never comes back to live as an Amish man, I hope he will find his way back to You. If there is anything I can do to help my son see the error of his ways, please show me how.*

Wiping tears with his shirtsleeve, he murmured, "My job as Joel's father is to help him get on the right path. Effie would agree with me wholeheartedly on that. My kinner are too important for me to look the other way. As long as there is breath in my body, I need to keep looking for a way."

He sat staring at the Bible then closed his eyes for a while. Finally, an idea popped into his head. It might not be the right thing to do, and perhaps Joel would never change, but at least Eustace could find solace in making an attempt to bring Joel to the Lord. Rising from Effie's chair, he turned off the gas lamp and made his way down the hall to get ready for bed.

～

Dover, Ohio

"Wh–where am I?" Joel moaned when someone's cold fingers touched his forehead. "Kristi, is that you?" He was surprised when he opened his eyes long enough to see a middle-aged woman with short brown hair looking down at him. *What's going on here?*

"You're in the hospital. Please lie still. I'm Karen,

your nurse, and I need to take your vitals now. Dr. Blake, your attending physician, doesn't want you to try and get up yet."

This couldn't be true, even though Joel's body hurt in places he didn't know he had. A small attempt to shift his weight made every muscle scream out in pain. "Wh–what happened? How'd I get here?"

"You were in an accident and brought here to Union Hospital by ambulance." Her touch was gentle as she lifted Joel's arm and took his blood pressure.

"Oh yeah, now I remember." Joel squeezed his eyes shut as he attempted to block out the pain. "A crazy driver swerved into my lane and came straight at me. I'll bet he was drunk." Joel moaned, a little deeper this time. "How bad am I hurt? Was there much damage to my truck?"

"Your condition isn't serious, but you do have a mild concussion, so we are keeping you overnight for observation. If you're having a lot of pain, we can give you something to help. I'll get in touch with the doctor and see what he will allow for the discomfort." The nurse gently patted his arm. "Try to rest now. The doctor will be in to see you soon."

"But what about my truck?"

"I'm not sure, sir. I imagine a tow truck was called, so your vehicle was probably taken to the impound yard."

"Great." Joel grunted in frustration, turning his head to the side. "Where's my cell phone? I need to make a call."

Speaking softly, the nurse replied, "When you were brought to this room, only your clothes and wallet were with you."

"I have to call Kristi so I can let her know what's happened. Maybe she can find my car, and my cell phone, too."

"Is Kristi a relative?"

"No, she's my girlfriend. I don't have any family. At least none who care about me." Joel couldn't keep the bitterness from his tone. After the way he'd been treated at Dad's tonight, he didn't care if he ever saw any of his family again.

"There's a telephone right here you can use to call your girlfriend." She gestured to the phone near his bed.

A searing pain shot through Joel's head as he shook it vigorously. "Her number is programmed into my cell phone, and I don't have it memorized."

"If she has a landline, we can look it up in the phone directory."

Joel clenched his teeth, which also made his head hurt. "It's a good idea, but Kristi only has a cell phone." A sense of panic rose in his soul. He felt trapped here in the hospital with no cell phone, unable to get ahold of Kristi. Joel needed her now, more than ever.

❦

Akron

"I appreciate you coming over to help me today." Kristi Palmer's mother smiled and leaned on her hoe. "These weeds are getting the best of my garden, and since your dad's back is hurting, he's not up to helping right now."

Kristi dug her shovel into the ground. "I'm glad I could do it, Mom. Since Joel spent the night out of town somewhere, I won't be seeing him until later today."

"I figured he must be doing something else, or you would have been with him, like you are most Saturdays." Mom's tone wasn't sharp, but Kristi sensed an underlying message. Her mother had made her views on Joel quite clear. She didn't approve of Kristi's boyfriend and thought she spent too much time with him.

Kristi's throat felt dry as she swallowed. "I'm going in for a drink; my throat's parched. Want me to bring you something when I come back out?"

"I wouldn't mind a glass of lemonade. Help yourself to some. I made it fresh this morning."

"Thanks, Mom. I'll check on Dad while I'm in there."

When Kristi entered the house, she picked up her cell phone, which she'd left on the kitchen counter, and glanced at the message icon to see if Joel may have called or sent a text. No messages showed, so apparently he hadn't tried to get in touch with her.

He's probably not back yet. Or he might have gotten busy with something and forgotten to call. Maybe I should call him.

After checking on her father, Kristi went back outside with the lemonade and her cell phone. "Here you go, Mom."

Mom smiled and reached for the glass.

Kristi took a gulp of the cold liquid. "This sure tastes good. Do you want to take a break while we cool off?"

"You go ahead if you want to. I'm going to keep working." Mom tucked a wayward strand of hair behind her ear. "I'll join you after I pull a couple of these more stubborn weeds. Some of them feel like their roots go all the way to China."

Kristi smiled as Mom set her glass down to play tug-of-war with a weed. Mom could also be stubborn, so those weeds didn't have a chance.

Taking a seat on the grass, Kristi punched in Joel's number. When it went to his voice mail, she left a message. "Hi, Joel, it's me. Just wondered if you're still out of town or back home by now. I'm at my mom's, helping in the garden, but I'll be home sometime this afternoon. So give me a call when you can and we'll make plans for later."

For the next few hours, Kristi kept busy pulling weeds and then picking green beans and cucumbers. Mom's garden had done quite well this year, even with the weeds threatening to take over. Kristi wished she could have a garden of her own, but living in a condo with only a deck didn't allow for growing much of anything. Kristi had managed to squeeze in a few pots of flowers on the deck, but a barbecue grill, small table, and two chairs took up the rest of the space.

Someday when she and Joel got married, she would have plenty of space for gardening. Joel had two acres of land. Even with his single-wide mobile home, garage, and shop, his yard had plenty of room for a garden as well as fruit trees. She was glad he'd chosen to live outside of town and not in the city like she did.

Of course, being in the city had some advantages. In addition to being closer to stores for shopping, Kristi worked at a nursing home not far from her condo. She'd have to commute once she and

Joel were married, but it was a small trade-off. Having grown up in the suburbs of Akron, where Mom and Dad still lived, she had always longed to live in the country.

Kristi reflected on the trip she and Mom had taken nearly a month ago to Holmes County. The best part of the weekend had been seeing all the Amish buggies, homes, and farms in the area. She'd heard that Holmes County had the largest population of Amish in America, and tourism was on the rise every year. If Kristi had her way, she would live among the Amish, but moving there would be too far from her job. Besides, Joel had shown no interest in even visiting Amish country, so she was sure he'd never agree to move there.

Kristi brushed the dirt from her gloves and stood. "It's almost noon, Mom. Should we stop and have lunch? I'd like to try calling Joel again, too."

Mom wiped her forehead with the back of her hand. "Stopping's a good idea. We've done enough work for one day." She rose to her feet. "I'll go in and start lunch while you make your call."

After Mom went inside, Kristi called Joel again. Still no answer, so she left another message. She tried not to worry, but couldn't shake the feeling that something was wrong. *Please, Lord,* she prayed, *keep Joel safe, wherever he is. And let me hear something from him soon.*

CHAPTER 2

Charm

Eustace sat at the kitchen table, staring at the un-touched bowl of soup he'd heated for lunch. It was hard to eat alone. *Maybe I should have gone into town and had my meal at the newly opened restaurant owned by an Amish family,* he thought, rocking the ketchup bottle back and forth with his hands. *I may have run into someone from the community who could have sat at my table. It would sure beat sittin' here alone. If I'd been thinking, I would have called my New Order friend, Henry, and asked him to meet me there.*

Eustace got up and poured the soup from his bowl back into the pot. Once it cooled off, he'd refrigerate the soup to have another day. Soup season was fast approaching. Over the winter months, any kind of soup was good, as long as it was hot.

He walked out to the porch and breathed deeply of the September air. Where had the time gone? Resting against the porch post, Eustace viewed the swaying trees along the back of his property as soft winds blew past the area. The leaves from the branches fell delicately, like feathers, to the smooth lawn. A smile crossed Eustace's face. *Maybe I can work up a better appetite if I take a walk.*

Eustace headed straight for the tree line. *No better time than the present to pick out the tree where I'll build Effie's tree house.*

Many large trees, especially maple and oak, silhouetted the azure sky. As Eustace walked from tree to tree, he came upon one of the largest: a huge maple standing quite high, with branches jutting out in every direction. This tree had been there since the children were little, and even then it had seemed tall. Many times Effie packed a picnic basket, and the family enjoyed lunch under the shade of its branches.

Eustace stood at the base and looked up. *The view from those branches must be beautiful,* he thought.

Luckily, the tree had enough low-lying branches he could easily latch on to. As he pondered what to do next, the urge to climb won out. Reaching toward the first limb, Eustace was surprised at how effortless it was to get up on it.

Climbing from one branch to the next highest was easier than he expected. Each time he stopped to get a good foothold, he surveyed the landscape. *Maybe the next branch will give an ever better view.*

Midway up, he came to a spot where many branches on the sides and back part of the tree cradled toward the middle, giving him a wider area to stand on. The front had an ample opening. Eustace knew immediately that this was the perfect tree. He leaned back against the main part of the trunk, which at this height was still quite wide.

No wonder Effie wanted to be up here with the birds, he mused, looking out over their property. From here, Eustace could see the entire farm, the rolling fields where his horses lazily fed, and the hill his son used to venture to when he wanted to be by himself. Joel had never been aware anyone else knew of his special place on the hill. Eustace never let on, respecting his son's need to be alone at times.

Without a doubt, Effie's tree house would be built here. He looked toward the sky at a big puffy cloud and imagined his wife sitting upon it. "This is it, Effie. I found a perfect maple for your tree house."

Eustace's goal would be to have it finished before winter set in, so he could enjoy going up there without fear of snow. His excitement grew. Now he'd have a project to do, keeping him busy for the next several weeks.

Guess I better get back to the house. Maybe I'll put the soup away and head into town to try out the new restaurant. I'm gettin' kinda hungry.

Eustace pushed himself away from the tree, but didn't get far. Something felt wrong. Why couldn't he move from the spot where he stood? Something was keeping him in place. Moving this way and that, but to no avail, Eustace suddenly realized his suspenders had gotten hooked on something behind him. He tried reaching back to undo whatever he was caught on, but unfortunately it was out of reach. *Now what in tarnation am I gonna do?*

Eustace's thoughts halted when he heard a whinny off in the distance, followed by the faint *clip-clop* of a horse's hooves coming up the driveway. From his vantage point, he saw his eldest daughter, Elsie, climb down from her buggy.

Cupping his hands around his mouth, Eustace yelled, to get his daughter's attention. He saw her stop and look in all directions, but she hadn't spied him yet. Next, he gave out a shrill whistle. After a few more tries, she finally heard him. He watched as Elsie quickly tied the horse and sprinted up to the tree, now holding him prisoner. "What are you doing, Dad? You're up there pretty high, aren't you?"

"I'll explain later. Right now, I need your help. I'm stuck on something." Eustace pointed toward his back. "Do you think you can climb up and help me? As I recall, you used to love climbing trees when you were little, and I made it up here pretty easily myself."

"You're talkin' years ago, Dad, but I'll give it a try."

Eustace watched his daughter start climbing, as if she were a little girl again. Soon, she made her way up, smiling when she stood next to him. The spot had enough room for them to stand side-by-side.

"See here." Eustace leaned forward. "It seems my suspenders are caught on something. I couldn't reach around to get them unhooked."

"Somehow you got one suspender strap caught on a notch in the tree where a branch snapped off, possibly years ago."

"Thought I felt something digging into my back, but the view up here was so wonderful, I ignored it."

Eustace was glad Elsie had no trouble undoing his suspender. "Danki, Daughter. You came in the nick of time."

"You can tell me why you are up here later. What I want to know now is why didn't you simply unhook your suspenders from the front of your trousers?" Elise looked at him quizzically. "You would have been freed immediately."

"I didn't think of it." Eustace snickered. "Now that you mention it, I feel kinda silly."

"Let's get you out of this tree and back to the house."

As they walked arm-in-arm toward the farm, Eustace looked at his daughter. "Danki again for coming to my aid." He gave Elsie's hand a squeeze. "Now how about some lunch? I have potato soup to reheat."

"Soup sounds good, but I brought us some sandwiches." They paused by her buggy, and while Eustace petted her horse, Elsie drew out a wicker basket.

"We can have both." Eustace smiled as they approached the house. Now he wouldn't have to eat alone. All three of his daughters were good to him and, for some reason, usually sensed when it was time to drop by. He was sure whatever kind of sandwiches she'd made would be good, because, like her mom, Elsie was an excellent cook.

"I brought a jug of tea along, too." Elsie went to the kitchen sink to wash her hands.

"Is it sweetened?"

She shook her head. "But feel free to add sugar if you like."

"Think I will." Eustace opened the cupboard and took out the sugar, while Elsie got the glasses and went to the freezer for some ice. Gasping, she jumped backward. "Dad, what is this huge thing wrapped in a clear bag? Is—is it a dead bird?"

"Now don't start fussing. It's a pheasant I found dead this morning. I'll be taking it to my friend who does taxidermy later, but wanted to make sure it stayed fresh."

Elsie groaned. "Do you really need a stuffed pheasant? I mean, where are you planning to put it?"

"Don't rightly know, but I'm sure I'll find a place for the bird."

Elsie opened her mouth as if to say something more, but then she grabbed the ice cube tray, shut the freezer door, and came back to the table. Eustace sensed she thought his decision to keep the pheasant was weird. Well, she could keep her opinion to herself. This was his house, and he could do whatever he wanted.

~

Elsie frowned as she sat across the table from her father. The wrinkles across his forehead seemed more pronounced than usual, and his shoulders were slumped.

"Guess you're wondering what I was doing up in the tree." Dad looked tired as she smiled at him. "I found the perfect place to build your mamm's tree house."

"Do you think it's still a good idea, since Mama isn't here to enjoy it?"

"You probably see it as pointless, but it's something I feel the need to do. Besides, it'll keep me busy during the lonely times."

"But Dad, the cold seasons are coming soon, and what about snow?"

"I'll take advantage of the nice days we're having now." He heaved a sigh. "It'll keep my mind off other things."

Elsie saw no point in arguing with her father. He had his mind made up.

"Is anything else wrong, Dad?" She took a bite of her soup. "You look kind of *umgerennt* this afternoon—like something might be bothering you."

He nodded. "You're right; there is. I'm upset with Joel."

"Didn't things go well when he spent the night?"

"No, they did not, and he didn't stay." Dad grabbed the bottle of ketchup and squeezed some into his soup, which was nothing unusual for him. With the exception of desserts and fruit, he liked ketchup on nearly everything he ate.

"What happened? Why didn't Joel stay overnight like he'd planned?"

"He left because I wouldn't give him what he wanted." Dad's eyes narrowed and his nostrils flared like a charging bull. "I should have realized he only came here to ask for money. Joel's exasperating and selfish. He doesn't give a hoot about his family."

"Exasperating? Is that another word you found in your dictionary?"

Dad's eyes widened; then he lowered his voice. "How did you know about my dictionary?"

"I've walked past you a couple of times while you were reading it. I'm surprised you never noticed."

"Oh, I see. Well as I was saying, Joel had no intention of trying to amend things with us. I can't remember the last time he didn't come over to ask me for money."

Elsie fidgeted with her hands underneath the table. "If you don't mind me asking, what does Joel need money for?"

"He didn't go into detail, but it was something about owing his subcontractors." Dad's thick brows furrowed. "Guess he must not be runnin' a good business if he's gettin' himself in over his head."

Elsie felt concern for her brother. "Maybe we should all chip in and help him out."

Dad's hand came down hard on the table, causing some soup to spill out of his bowl. "Absolutely not! I've bailed your brother out before, and look where it got me. It didn't teach Joel a thing about responsibility, and he never even bothered to pay back the loan." Dad rolled his chair across the floor and grabbed a roll of paper towels; then he rolled back to the table and wiped up his mess.

After they finished eating their lunch, Dad sat looking out the window. Elsie wondered if he was still thinking about Joel. When she slid out of her chair and rose to start clearing their plates, Dad reached over and grabbed both of their bowls. Then he rolled across the room and placed them in the kitchen sink. Without a word, he rolled back to the table and grabbed his drink.

Elsie poured liquid dish soap into the sink and turned on the water, trying to hide her smile. Watching Dad roll his chair across the floor always made her giggle. It was something he'd done since she was a child.

A few seconds later, she heard the back screen door open and close. When she heard a familiar squeak, she knew Dad had made himself comfortable on the porch swing. While the sink filled with sudsy water, Elsie unwrapped the new sponge she'd brought along today. She wasn't surprised to discover Dad's old sponge lying near the back of the sink. For some reason, he couldn't part with the old thing. Of course, it was one of many things Dad couldn't let go of.

When the dishes were washed, dried, and put away, Elsie poured herself more tea and went outside to join Dad. Taking a seat beside him on the swing, she sat quietly, mulling things over. She felt bad Joel had gotten himself in a bind, but was also concerned for her father. She was sure Dad loved his son as much as he did his daughters. Saying no to Joel's request must have been hard, even if Dad felt he was doing the right thing. It wasn't likely Joel would ever return to the Amish faith, but if he'd come by once in a while to be with his family, things would go better between him and Dad. Joel also needed to be true to his word and pay back any money he'd previously borrowed.

❧

Dover

"I'm not hungry," Joel grunted, pushing aside the lunch tray a young woman had brought into his hospital room.

She smiled. "It's okay; I'll leave it here in case you change your mind."

"I won't, so you may as well take it away."

With a slight shrug, she picked up the tray and started out of the room.

"Say, wait. Would you see if you can find me a phone book for Summit County? I need to make a call, and I don't know the number."

"I'll see what I can do." She smiled and hurried from the room.

Trying not to let his agitation get the best of him, Joel glanced out the window to his left. The sun shone brightly in a blue sky accented by a couple of puffy white clouds. It was too nice a day to be cooped up in a stuffy hospital room. When the doctor had come in that morning to check on Joel, he said that Joel could probably go home before the day was out, but they were still waiting for a few more of his test results.

Don't think my accident would have happened if I'd spent the night at Dad's. Joel gripped the rails on his bed with such force that the veins on his hands stuck out. *I should have stayed there and tried to play on his sympathy instead of losing my temper and storming off. If I'd pled my case long and hard enough, Dad may have relented and loaned me the money I so desperately need. Now what am I supposed to do?*

Joel reached for the remote and turned on the TV. Even though he was now living the English way and owned his own TV, he'd never enjoyed watching most of the shows. Many of them made no sense and seemed like a waste of time. Still, maybe listening to something was better than nothing.

Joel scanned all the stations. Earlier, the aide had explained the hospital rooms were hooked up to cable, and he had many more channels to choose from, along with the local ones. Joel finally found a station, but the show was in black and white instead of color. It looked like an old movie, depicting a time back in the '50s. Joel didn't know about growing up in the '50s, but he'd heard plenty about it from his parents.

Even these days his family lived in their simple ways. The Amish had always lived plain, but the English world had changed. Back then, people didn't have cell phones, computers, video games, or tablets, and they talked rather than texted with each other. In today's world, it seemed Englishers always had some sort of gizmo or gadget in their hands. They were either texting someone or had a cell phone to their ear, even when they were driving. *Times were simpler for the English back then,* Joel thought as he watched the TV family sitting at the dinner table, talking. Although not easier by today's standards, he was sure they had to feel a sense of accomplishment when they worked hard like the Amish folks still did today.

Joel was getting more into the show when the aide bounded into the room. "Here you go, Mr.

Byler—the phone book you requested."

Joel thanked her for responding to his request. He waited until she left the room, then proceeded to look up the number for Kristi's parents.

"Ah, here it is." He held one finger on the listing for Paul Palmer in Akron. "Sure hope someone's home so I don't have to leave a message."

Joel scooted the phone closer to his bed and punched in the number. He felt relief when Kristi's dad picked up.

"Palmer residence. This is Paul."

"Oh, hey, this is Joel. I'm in the hospital in Dover, and I need to talk to Kristi. Could you give me her cell number?"

"Sorry to hear you're in the hospital. Are you ill? Have you been hurt?"

"I was in a car accident last night, but my injuries aren't serious. Now about Kristi's number. . ."

"Kristi is here right now, Joel. She and JoAnn are in the kitchen fixing lunch. I'll go get her."

Joel compressed his lips while he waited several minutes, until he heard Kristi's voice on the phone. "Joel, are you all right? Dad said you were in an accident."

"Yeah, I was, and for the most part, I'm okay." Joel paused and drew in a quick breath. "I have no idea where my truck is, and my cell phone is missing. Kristi, I need you here with me. Can you come?"

"Of course, Joel. I'll leave right now, and if traffic isn't heavy, I should be there in less than an hour."

Joel breathed a sigh of relief. Once Kristi got here, everything would be okay. He wouldn't tell her where he'd gone last evening, though, or why he'd been heading home in the middle of the night.

Chapter 3

Akron

Joel tossed his classic car magazine aside. He had been home from the hospital a week, recuperating. Most of his time was spent lying on the couch, either staring at the TV or reading. While none of Joel's injuries had been serious, his muscles were stiff and sore, making him feel like he'd been trampled by a herd of horses. The headache brought on by the concussion still lingered, and Joel's ribs hurt whenever he took a deep breath or moved the wrong way.

Despite the pain, he couldn't stay around here indefinitely. He needed to round up more jobs and get some money coming in. Since Dad refused to give him a loan, Joel needed cash more than ever. Besides owing some of his men, Joel had a hospital bill and the repair of his truck to worry about. Even though the man who'd hit him had insurance, it could be awhile before Joel received a settlement, and he wasn't sure how much of his medical expenses would be covered. His own insurance would pay 80 percent of the hospital bill, but hopefully neither that nor his deductible would be needed when the other driver's insurance paid up.

Then there was the matter of his truck, which was in the shop getting repaired. Joel was relieved the truck hadn't been totaled. He needed it in order to keep working. Once he got it back from the shop, he hoped he'd be healed enough to begin working again. He had been told when he left the hospital to take it easy for a few weeks, which he wasn't thrilled about. No money coming in meant he'd be further in debt.

Joel tossed the magazine aside. *If only my dad weren't so stubborn and selfish. It's his fault I'm under so much stress. He could make my life easy if he'd give me the money, instead of being so stingy. I wonder if he'd treat my sisters the same way if they were in need. I thought Christians were supposed to be kind and giving.*

It did no good to get himself all worked up, so Joel closed his eyes and thought about the beautiful Corvette out in his shop. He imagined himself gripping the steering wheel at 70 mph on the freeway and hearing the engine roar as it accelerated. Joel would give almost anything to take his new beauty for a drive right now to forget all his troubles. At least nobody could steal his joy when he was behind the wheel.

Kristi would be coming by soon to fix his supper, as she'd been doing since he was released from the hospital. Joel glanced at his cell phone, thankful it had been found on the floor of his truck. *Maybe I should call and tell her not to come by. I'll say I have leftovers and don't need her to cook me anything this evening. It would give me the opportunity to take the Vette out.* Joel really wasn't up to it and shouldn't be thinking about the new car right now. What he needed was something to take his mind off things. He continued to worry about the money he'd taken from his and Kristi's joint savings account. If Kristi knew what he'd done, she'd never trust him again.

The unmistakable sound of Kristi's car interrupted his thoughts. Groaning from the pain in his ribs, Joel pulled himself off the couch and walked stiffly across the room toward the front door, reaching it just as Kristi entered carrying a white sack.

"I hope you're in the mood for supreme burritos tonight, because I stopped at the Mexican restaurant near my condo and got take-out." She smiled up at him and lifted the bag. "I told you I'd cook something special, but since this is Saturday and I didn't have to work, the major part of my day was spent cleaning the house. By the time the chores were done, I was too tired to even think about cooking."

"Burritos are fine, Kristi." Joel motioned to the kitchen. "We can either eat them in there or sit out here in the living room." Joel didn't have a formal dining room in his small single-wide, so when he was alone, he often ate his meals in front of the TV.

Kristi shook her head. "I don't want to compete with the television. It makes it too hard for us to visit."

Joel shrugged his shoulders. "Okay, whatever. If you prefer, we can eat in the kitchen."

"You sound grumpy, Joel. If you'd rather eat out here, it's fine with me. I don't want to cause you more irritation. Let's not turn on the TV, though, okay?"

"It doesn't matter where we eat. I'm irritable because I'm tired of sittin' around here when I should be working. I need money, and none will come in unless I get out there and beat the bushes." He stepped into the kitchen and got out some napkins and paper plates.

Kristi placed the burritos on the table and poured them both a glass of lemonade, which she'd taken from the refrigerator. "Why don't you take some money out of our joint account? After all, you've put money in there, too."

"Umm. . .I'd rather not." Joel felt like a bug trapped in a spider's web. No way could he admit he'd already taken money from their account to pay some of his debts. Truth was, only a small amount of money remained.

"It's okay," she insisted. "If you're not feeling up to going out on Monday, I can stop by the bank on my way home from work and make a withdrawal. How much do you think you'll need?"

Joel's heart hammered in his chest. "No, Kristi, I am not touching our joint account. I'll be going back to work on Monday. I should have some money coming in soon." Joel's conscience pricked him. He should have been honest with Kristi in the beginning, but it seemed too late to explain. He had no choice now but to get back to work and try to put a little in the bank whenever he could. Since the monthly bank statements came to his house, hopefully, Kristi would never be aware of what had transpired.

❧

Charm

Arlene clucked to her horse to get him moving faster. At the rate the gelding had been plodding along it would be way past suppertime before she got to Dad's with the casserole she'd made. She hoped to find him in a good mood. Her sister Elsie had mentioned that when she'd dropped by to see Dad last week he'd been irritated with Joel. She'd said she needed to talk to her about something else, but wanted their sister, Doris, in on the conversation. Of course, their father's irritation with Joel was nothing new. Every time Joel's name was mentioned, Dad became uptight. If Joel came around asking for money, Dad's mood would sometimes be affected for weeks.

It was a shame he and Joel couldn't put their differences aside and enjoy each other's company. But Dad's stubbornness and unwillingness to forgive got in the way. Joel's disinterest in being part of the family didn't help either. While Joel had a right to choose whether he wanted to be Amish or English, he should have made his choice before joining the church. Up until then, everyone thought Joel would marry Anna Detweiler and settle into married life.

Poor Anna. I wonder if she's ever gotten over Joel. Arlene couldn't imagine going through such rejection—especially when it happened only a few days before the wedding. Not only did Anna have to live through the embarrassment of having to call off the wedding at the last minute, but it must have hurt to know Joel didn't love her enough to remain Amish.

"It hurt us, too," Arlene mumbled, tapping the reins until her horse picked up speed again. *When Joel left, it grieved Mom and Dad most of all.*

Forcing her negative thoughts aside, Arlene snapped the reins once more. "Giddyup, Buddy. Time's a-wastin'. We need to get to my daed's sometime today."

When Arlene finally guided her horse and buggy up Dad's driveway, smoke was pouring through the slightly open kitchen window.

She leaped from the buggy, secured Buddy to

the hitching rail, and ran toward the house. Heart pounding, she raced inside, where more smoke billowed from the kitchen. Since it seemed to be isolated to that room, she figured something might be burning on the stove.

Removing her apron and waving it in front of her face, Arlene held her breath as she made her way across the room. Quickly opening the oven door, she realized whatever was baking had been reduced to nothing more than a blackened lump. Grabbing a potholder, she picked up the glass baking dish and carried it outside to the porch. Then she rushed back inside, turned off the oven, and opened the other two kitchen windows. The situation under control, Arlene cupped her hands around her mouth and shouted for Dad.

No response.

She ran through the house, checking in every room, but saw no sign of him. Since she hadn't seen him outside when she pulled in, Arlene figured he might be in the barn.

Sure enough, she found him there kneeling in front of an old milk can, holding a paint brush. "What did you have in the oven, Dad?" she panted. "Do you realize it's burned to a crisp?"

He whirled around, nearly dropping the brush. "Daughter, don't sneak up on me like that!"

"I wasn't sneaking. I'm surprised you didn't hear my horse and buggy pull in."

"Guess I was too deep in concentration to notice." He stood. "Now, what's this about my meatloaf burning?"

She squinted. "So it was meatloaf? It looks like a brick of charcoal now, and the kitchen's all *schmokich.* I could hardly breathe."

"I got so busy out here, I forgot to check on it." Grunting, Dad frowned. "So much for supper. Guess I'll have to fix a sandwich now."

"No, you won't. I brought you a chicken-and-rice casserole. It's in my buggy."

He smiled. "Danki. It was thoughtful of you. And it'll be a heap better than burned meatloaf."

Arlene pressed her hand to her mouth and puffed out her cheeks. "You'd never be able to eat it, Dad. What started out as a meatloaf is burned beyond recognition. And you know what else?"

He tipped his head. "What?"

"You could have burned down the whole house." She sighed deeply. "If you're determined to live here alone, then you need to stay in the house while your supper is cooking. Better yet, Doris, Elsie, and I can take turns either bringing your evening meal or having you to one of our homes to eat."

Dad shook his head. "There's no need for all the fuss, Arlene. You and your sisters do enough for me already. From now on, I'll stay inside whenever I'm cooking."

She pursed her lips. "You promise?"

"Jah, and to put your mind at ease, you'll be happy to know your aunt Verna is comin' next week for a visit. While she's here, she'll probably want to do all the cooking. Besides, if I had a tree house, like your mamm wanted us to build, I could always move into it. At least there'd be no oven to burn down the place." He chuckled, as if to lighten the mood.

"Ha! Not funny, Dad."

He winked at her, then pointed to a birdfeeder

on a shelf overhead. "I picked that up at the farmers' market the other day. Looks like a log cabin, don't you think?"

"You're right; it does. And speaking of feeders, it looks like some of those you have out in the yard need to be filled. Would you like me to do it?"

"No, I'll take care of it after we eat." He pushed his dilapidated straw hat a little farther back on his head. "I have lots to get done before my sister gets here."

Avoiding eye contact, Arlene managed a brief nod. Not only was Aunt Verna hard of hearing, but she easily became preoccupied as well. Arlene hoped between Dad and his sister, they wouldn't burn down the house.

CHAPTER 4

Eustace whistled as he listened to the birds in the trees overhead. Since he'd spent most of the morning pounding nails as he began work on his tree house, he was surprised the birds were singing at all. The blue jays must have been curious as to who was making all the noise, for they squawked in the branches higher up in the tree. After a while, they flew off, seemingly satisfied with their observations. Eustace had been keeping all the feeders full of food, so most of the birds seemed more interested in eating than being bothered by his noise.

He stopped hammering and sipped on the coffee he'd brought out with him. *What a nice morning. Sure wish I had some help with this.*

Eustace had started this project a week ago, two days after Arlene had brought him a casserole for supper. So far he'd managed to nail a ladder to the tree and get started on the base of the tree house. He hoped to finish the floor before his sister got here, sometime this afternoon. He looked forward to seeing Verna again. It had been some time since her last visit. Since she and her husband, Lester, lived in Geauga County, which was nearly a two-hour drive by car, he didn't see her very often. With the exception of going to some of the local auctions, Eustace didn't travel much either. He preferred to stick close to home, where he could putter around and create new things. He felt close to Effie here.

In the spring he'd made several bird feeders out of plastic soda pop bottles. During the summer he had constructed a few wind chimes using old pipe, fishing line, and some CDs he'd received in the mail from an Internet provider trying to drum up business. Like he really needed that! Even Eustace's New Order Amish friend didn't have a computer; although Henry was allowed to have a phone in his house. But after painting the CDs in various shades, the wind chimes had turned out quite colorful.

Eustace was content having a phone in a shack he shared with his closest neighbor. With the exception of a few special things, he'd never had a desire for modern conveniences. But the desires he'd once had were set aside when he joined the church and married Effie forty-seven years ago. He'd had a good life here on this farm, and Eustace appreciated every bit of it—from the large two-story house to the rambling barn where he kept many of his treasures—including his fine-looking horses.

He looked toward the fields. The edges were ablaze with goldenrod, orange jewel weed, and ragweed—the onset of early autumn colors. Even from where Eustace stood, he could see many butterflies flitting from flower to flower on the unappreciated weeds. Most people he knew didn't care for these intrusive plants, but all three had healing benefits. Even Effie didn't mind seeing them when they bloomed in August and September. She loved everything about nature. Many times she'd picked the goldenrod and would mix them in with late-blooming wildflowers for a centerpiece on the kitchen table.

Eustace shook his head. Everything he saw these days, even the colorful weeds, made him think about Effie.

Halting his thoughts and stepping back to view the mature maple tree he'd chosen to build his tree house in, Eustace mentally checked off the things he'd done so far, in addition to what still needed to be done.

The first phase had been to draw a design of the tree house. Then he'd laid out the wood and all the tools he would need to accomplish his task. Next, Eustace had nailed a ladder to the tree trunk, making it easy to trim the extra branches that could get in the way during construction. He was now in the process of nailing some well-polished wooden boards together across two strong branches, close to each other. This would become the floor of his tree house. Following that, he would add wooden boards on three sides of the tree house until a railing was formed. The door and windows would then be installed for cross-ventilation. A wooden roof would follow, and then it would be time for the finishing touches.

A terrace would be nice, so I can sit out there and feel one with the birds, Eustace mused. *Effie would like it.* He gave a decisive nod. "Jah, that's what I'm gonna do all right."

"Are you talkin' to yourself, Grandpa?"

Eustace turned so abruptly, he nearly fell over backward. "Whoa there, Doug. You shouldn't sneak up on me!"

Eustace's twelve-year-old grandson motioned to his bike. "I wasn't sneakin'. I rode right in. Figured you'd hear me comin'."

Eustace shook his head. "Nope. Never heard a thing. Guess it's because I was concentrating on this." He gestured to the pieces of wood lying on the ground beneath the tree.

Doug's mouth formed an *O*. "Are ya finally gonna make the tree house you've been talkin' about?"

"Jah. I'd say it's about time, too, wouldn't you?"

The boy nodded enthusiastically. "Can I help ya with it?"

"It's more than all right with me, if your mamm doesn't mind. You're an assiduous kid, aren't ya, boy?"

Doug's head titled slightly to the left. "Assiduous?"

"Sorry, never mind." Eustace's brows furrowed. "Say, shouldn't you be in school right now?"

"School's out for the day, Grandpa. I told Mama this morning I was comin' by here afterward. I wanted to spend some time alone with you, without my sisters and little brother taggin' along."

Eustace gave his earlobe a tug. "Guess I've been out here longer than I thought. I didn't even take time to eat anything at noon."

"Want my banana, Grandpa? I've got one in my lunch pail I didn't eat for lunch."

Eustace ruffled the boy's thick brown hair. "No, that's okay. Your mamm gave it to you, so you'd better eat it."

"She won't mind. Long as I don't come home with it." Doug wrinkled his nose. "Mama gets upset if any of her kinner waste food."

"We wouldn't want your mamm gettin' upset, now would we?" Eustace reached into Doug's lunch pail and withdrew the banana. He was about to peel it when a gray minivan pulled into the yard and parked. Verna stepped out and grabbed her suitcase.

Eustace cupped his hands around his mouth and gave a yell. "We're back here!"

Grinning like a child who'd been given a balloon, Verna set her suitcase down and began walking toward Eustace, sneezing as she came.

He smiled back at her. *So, let the fun begin.*

They waved as her driver turned the van around and pulled out of the driveway. "I'll give a call to my driver a few days before I decide to return home," Verna said. "She'll be staying in Sugarcreek with some friends while she's here, so I don't think she's in a hurry to get home."

When she approached, Verna gave Eustace a sisterly hug. "It's sure good to see you again. It's been awhile, hasn't it?"

Eustace bobbed his head.

Glancing at Doug, Verna asked, "Now who is this handsome young man with you today?"

"This is Doug—Arlene's son."

She looked at him strangely. "Did you say 'Bug'?"

"No, I said the boy's name is Doug." Eustace spoke a little louder, remembering Verna was hard of hearing.

"Well, goodness me. You've sure grown since I last saw you." She held out her arms. "Now, Doug, how about a hug for your great-aunt Verna?" Her eyes twinkled with merriment.

Doug snickered, and a bit awkwardly, he complied.

"Just to let you both know, my hearing's not the best these days." Verna's voice rose with each word.

"So you may have to repeat what you've said sometimes." Clucking her tongue, she shook her head. "It sure isn't easy gettin' older."

"Let's take you inside and put your things away." Eustace walked to the driveway, where she had left her suitcase and picked it up. "The sheets are clean on the guest bed, and a little tidying's been done. Arlene took care of it when she was here the other day."

"It's nice to be with you, Brother, and to be able to spend time with your family." Verna spoke excitedly. Stepping onto the porch, she stopped and pointed to his boots. "For goodness' sakes, Eustace, those boots of yours are in need of repair. If you're not careful, they'll fall right off your feet." She elbowed him and chuckled. "Maybe you ought to put some duct tape on them. Then they'll match the old hat on your head."

Eustace reached up and touched the spot on the brim of his hat, where duct tape held it together. "You may have a point, Sister. If I repaired the boots I could keep wearin' them longer. Maybe I'll do that while you're getting settled in."

❧

Eustace had no more than finished taping up his boots when Verna came out to the kitchen. "How's this look?" He leaned back in his chair and stuck out his feet.

Covering her mouth with her hand, she giggled like she had when she was a girl. "It might hold them together for a while, but they sure look *schpassich*."

"They may look funny, but they'll serve the

purpose." Eustace rolled his chair across the floor and picked up a flyer off his old desk. "Say, Verna, I have an idea of something fun we could do while you're here." He held the paper out to her.

Pushing her glasses a little higher on her nose, she studied the flyer. "So there's going to be an auction up in Mt. Hope tomorrow morning, huh?"

He gave a quick nod. "Would you like to go, or will you be too tired?"

"I'm not tired at all. In fact, it sounds like fun."

Eustace grinned. "Oh, good. Who knows what interesting things we might find to bid on?"

"Guess we'll have to hire a driver since it's not close by."

"Not a problem. I'll go out to the phone shack and make the call right now." Eustace rose from his chair, but paused at the door. "Would ya mind if I invite my friend Henry to come along?"

She shook her head. "Not a'tall."

"Okay, good. I'll make the phone calls now, and then I need to get back to work on my tree house." He put on his straw hat. "Don't want to keep my grandson waitin' for me all day."

"You go right ahead." Verna gave Eustace's arm a tender squeeze. "I'll stay here in the kitchen and see what I can fix for supper."

Eustace smiled and headed out the door. He found Doug sitting on the top porch step with his chin in his hands. "I'm ready to go to work, Grandpa."

"I'll be with you shortly." Eustace tapped the boy's shoulder. "Just need to make a few phone calls, then we can work till it's time for you to go home for supper."

Akron

Today had been Joel's first day back on the job, and even though all he'd done was drive around in his truck to bid on a few jobs, he was beat. The driving hadn't worn him out though; it was his anxiety over the money he still owed, coupled with the fact he didn't know if any of his bids would even be accepted. Money. . .money. . .money. It seemed the almighty dollar was constantly on his mind. He needed work, and he needed it bad. If something didn't open up soon, he may have to sell one of his vehicles.

"It won't be the Corvette," Joel mumbled after he entered his home and headed for the shower. "If I sell anything, it would be my everyday car, but I need it in case my truck gives out."

Joel stepped into the bathroom and looked in the mirror. He clearly needed a shave, and his eyes were puffy and bloodshot from lack of sleep. *After I get cleaned up maybe I'll take the Vette out for a spin. That should perk me right up.* Since Kristi had said she'd be working the evening shift and wouldn't be coming by like she'd been doing since Joel's accident, he had the perfect opportunity to do whatever he wanted.

Joel ran his fingers through the back of his hair. *Maybe I'll call my buddy Tom and see what he's up to this evening. I'll bet he'll jump at the chance to take another ride in my Corvette.*

When Kristi got off work at ten o'clock that evening, she was tempted to drive by Joel's and check on him. But since today was his first day back on the job, he was probably exhausted and had gone to bed by now. She'd been fixing his supper every night since he got out of the hospital and felt bad she'd been unable to do it for him this evening. Some of the casserole was left over from what she'd fixed him last night. Hopefully Joel had warmed it up for his supper.

Kristi turned on the radio and tried to relax. It seemed like she was always worried about Joel these days. His haggard appearance told her he wasn't sleeping well, and his lack of enthusiasm when they talked most likely meant he was depressed. Either that or he'd become bored with her.

Kristi's confidence in her relationship with Joel often wavered. Things were different from when they'd first started dating.

She gripped the steering wheel as another thought popped into her head. *Could Joel be attracted to someone else? Maybe that's why he isn't opening up to me.*

She turned the radio up, trying to drown out her thoughts, but it was no use. Her concern for Joel was uppermost in her mind—especially when their favorite song began to play. Last night when she'd made supper for him, he'd been moody and had even snapped at her a couple of times. She had tried to ignore it, realizing he was under a lot of stress and probably still sore from his accident, but his sharp tone hurt nonetheless. Even in her worst mood, Kristi had never talked harshly to Joel.

"Lord, please help me with this." She turned off the radio and prayed out loud. "If things are okay between Joel and me, then erase my doubts. If there's a problem and Joel decides we should break up, please help me accept it as Your will and be able to move on with my life."

Tears stung Kristi's eyes. She'd had other boyfriends, but never loved any of them the way she did Joel. She couldn't imagine her life without him. But if they did at some point end up going their separate ways, she would have to deal with it, no matter how much it hurt.

Up ahead, Kristi noticed a nice-looking car parked along the side of the road. When she drew closer, she realized it was Joel and his friend Tom walking from the front of the car as they put the hood back down. *I wonder what's going on. Joel should be home in bed. At least I thought he would be.*

❧

Joel couldn't believe it when Kristi pulled up alongside of them. He and Tom had been out tooling around for a good many hours until something started sputtering in the engine. They had discovered a disconnected hose and been able to fix it. Fortunately, the engine was running smoothly again.

Joel jammed his hands into his pockets. "Hey, what are you doing here? I thought you'd be in bed by now."

"I'm on my way home from work. I worked the evening shift, remember? I thought you'd be in bed by now, too." Kristi bit her bottom lip. "Do you need some help?"

He smacked his forehead. "I knew you planned to work late. Guess I momentarily forgot." He hesitated then quickly explained, "Tom wanted me to go for a ride and take his new car out for a spin. Guess we didn't realize it was this late."

"Nice car, Tom." Kristi smiled. "It looks expensive."

"Uh. . .yeah, it is." Tom looked at Joel, while responding to Kristi.

Relieved that Tom didn't contradict him, Joel explained about the disconnected hose. He'd sure never expected her to come along.

"I can give you a lift home if you like," Kristi offered.

"Thanks but my truck is back at Tom's. I'll give you a call tomorrow."

Joel watched as Kristi waved and pulled away. He also felt Tom's eyes boring into the back of his head.

"I can't believe you would drag me into your lie." Tom pointed a finger at Joel.

"I plan on telling her about this car. I'm just not sure when."

Joel couldn't blame Tom for being upset with him. One of these days, he'd have a lot of explaining to do, and he hoped Kristi would understand.

CHAPTER 5

Walnut Creek

"Hey, Sister, wait up!" Elsie called when she spotted Doris in front of Der Dutchman's Bakery.

Doris halted and turned around. "It's good to see you. Did you come for breakfast?"

Elsie shook her head. "I'm heading to Charm to see Dad this morning and thought I'd stop by the bakery first to pick up some of his favorite lemon fry pies. I also want to see if Aunt Verna is here yet. She was supposed to arrive at Dad's sometime yesterday, and this evening I want to have everyone for supper at my house. Can you come?"

Doris nodded. "Jah, I heard she was coming, and so far, we're free for supper tonight. How long will Aunt Verna be visiting?"

"Probably a week or two. I'm sure Dad's going to enjoy her company. Even though he insists he's getting along fine on his own, Dad's bound to get lonely living there all alone."

"You're right, but I doubt any of us will ever convince him to move into one of our homes." Doris frowned. "You know Dad. He can be so stubborn sometimes."

"I can't argue with that." Elsie touched her sister's arm. "How are you and Brian these days? Are you both working hard at your jobs?"

"Jah. In fact, I need to get going right now, or I'll be late for work. I'm doing the breakfast and lunch shifts today."

"Then I guess you'll be busy with all the fall tourists."

Doris moved her head slowly up and down. "Sometimes I wish I could quit waitressing and stay home." She lifted her shoulders in a brief shrug. "But then what would I do all day with no kinner to take care of?"

Elsie gave Doris a hug. "Maybe you and Brian should consider adopting a boppli."

Tears pooled in Doris's eyes. "I'd like to, but Brian says if God wants us to have a baby, it will happen in His time. He won't even talk about adoption."

Elsie wanted to say more, but she didn't want to upset Doris further or cause her to be late for work. "Always remember, I've been praying for you and will continue to do so."

"Danki. That means a lot." Doris took a tissue from her purse and dried her eyes. "I'd better get going. Unless you hear differently, Brian and I will join you for supper. Oh, and before I forget, can I bring anything to add to the meal?"

"All you need to bring are your hearty appetites." Elsie grinned.

As Doris walked away, Elsie paused. *Heavenly Father, if Doris is never going to have any children of her own, please soften Brian's heart on the subject of adoption.*

Sighing, she headed for the bakery. As soon as she stepped inside, her senses were greeted by the sweet aroma of cookies and pastries. The place was already busy with tourists looking around and trying some samples. Elsie walked by the bakery cases to check out what might interest her. The lemon fry pies looked good. But so did the frosted lemon cookies. Most anything lemon Dad would like. *Maybe I'll get some of each,* she decided. *Dad can take home whatever we don't eat for supper tonight. That way he and Aunt Verna can snack on them later this week.*

As she stood in line, waiting to pay for her things, Elsie noticed an English woman and a young girl ahead of her. The girl had turned to face Elsie and kept staring at her, even though the child's mother told her several times to turn around. When the woman finished paying, she turned to Elsie and cleared her throat. "I apologize for my daughter's behavior. This is our first trip to Amish country, and she's curious about the clothes you're wearing."

"It's okay. I understand." This was not the first time Elsie had caught someone staring at her. What she didn't appreciate was when they took photos without her permission. While some Amish might not care too much, the district she belonged to frowned on having their pictures taken.

After Elsie paid for the cookies and fry pies, she went outside to her buggy and put her things up front. She'd also picked up an éclair to nibble on during her journey. After she untied her horse and climbed in the buggy, she grabbed the bakery bag and took out the tasty treat. Now she was ready to stop by Dad's for a quick visit and to invite him and Aunt Verna for supper tonight.

❧

Charm

"How'd ya sleep last night?" Eustace asked his sister as they sat at his kitchen table eating breakfast.

"Other than my sneezing spell, I slept just fine. Can't think of any reason I wouldn't have though. It's nice and *friedlich* here."

"I can't argue with you; it is peaceful." Eustace reached for the ketchup and squirted some on his scrambled eggs, as well as the hash browns Verna had made. "What got ya to sneezing all of a sudden?"

"I must be allergic to the goldenrod. It's blooming at home as well." Verna wiped her nose with a tissue, then went to the sink to wash her hands. "I'd planned on going to the doctor to see if he could give me something, but haven't gotten there yet." She sat down again.

"It's most likely the ragweed making you sneeze," Eustace explained. "Although goldenrod is often blamed during allergy season, it doesn't have airborne pollen and doesn't cause allergic reactions like ragweed does."

"You learn something new every day." Verna smiled, looking at Eustace over her glasses.

"I read recently that goldenrod's pollen is stickier, and instead of it blowing in the wind, it's spread by the butterflies, ants, and bees."

"That's interesting. Sure hope I'm not sneezing the whole time I'm here." Verna spread some jelly on her piece of toast. "It seems to come in spurts."

"Are you ready to go to the auction today? Maybe you'll feel better there—at least for a while."

She tipped her head. "What did you say?"

Speaking a little louder this time, Eustace repeated his question.

"Jah. I'm looking forward to it." She drank some orange juice. "Will you be looking for anything in particular?"

"Nothing special. Sometimes I don't know what I want till I see it."

Verna chuckled. "I'm the same way whenever I go shopping. Makes Lester a nervous wreck, which is why he doesn't go with me too often."

Eustace sighed. "Effie used to go to auctions with me. It was her time to socialize while I bid on whatever things caught my fancy. I'll never forget the look on her face when I carried a box of old cowboy boots out to the buggy one day."

"What were you planning to do with them?"

"Didn't really know at the time, but I ended up planting some flowers in them." Eustace grinned. "Afterward, Effie kind of liked them."

Verna smiled. "I'll bet you still miss her a lot."

"Jah. There isn't a day that goes by I don't think about my fraa." Eustace glanced out the window at the line of trees behind his house. "The tree house I'm building is in memory of Effie."

Verna's eyes widened. "How nice! I did notice you were working on something when I arrived yesterday afternoon, but I was so excited to be here, I didn't pay much attention to what you'd been doing. How far have you gotten on it?"

"Not much—just built the platform so far. My grandson Doug wants to come help again, and his little bruder Scott will probably do whatever he can as well. Course, he's only eight years old, so he'll mostly be handing us whatever tools we need. He can be our little gofer."

"If my seventy-five-year-old body could still move like it once did, I'd be right in there, helping you build the tree house."

Eustace grunted. "My sixty-five-year-old body

doesn't move as it once did, either, but I figure as long as I keep using my limbs, they're less apt to stop workin' for me." He winked at her. "You've heard the old saying 'Use it or lose it.'"

"You're absolutely right. It's best to keep moving." Verna pushed away from the table. "As soon as I get the *gscharr* done, I'd like to see where you're building the tree house."

"Sounds good to me. Only, let's leave the dishes and go look at it now."

Verna didn't have to be asked twice. Like Eustace, she'd always been eager to try new things and was a spur-of-the-moment kind of person. Eventually, the dishes would get done, but they could soak in the sink until they got back to the house.

Slipping into her black sweater and putting a tissue inside her sleeve, Verna headed out the door with Eustace right behind.

❧

When Elsie pulled her horse up to Dad's hitching rail, she heard voices in the distance. Apparently Dad and Aunt Verna were somewhere outside.

After securing the horse, Elsie stood and listened a few seconds. Then, realizing the voices came from the trees out back, she headed in that direction. *I'll bet Dad's showing Aunt Verna where he plans to build his tree house.*

As Elsie approached the spot, her mouth dropped open. In the week since she'd been here, Dad had built a platform in the tree that once held his suspenders captive. But the work he'd accomplished in such a short time wasn't what surprised her the most. The real shock was seeing both Dad and his sister sitting on the platform.

"Wie geht's?" Aunt Verna called down to Elsie. "It's good to see you again."

"I'm doing fine, and apparently so are you." She tipped her head back, shielding her eyes from the glare of the sun peeking through the tree branches. "I never expected to see you and Dad up there."

"What was it you said?" Aunt Verna leaned her head forward.

"I never expected to see you and Dad up there." Elsie repeated, a little louder this time.

"You never know what we old retired people will do." Aunt Verna grinned. "Or maybe I should've said, 'What we tired old people will do.'"

"I brought her out to see what I've accomplished so far," Dad explained. "And she got the bright idea to climb up the ladder to admire the view."

"That's right." Aunt Verna bobbed her head. "Your daed was trying to describe to me what he wants for this tree house. Maybe a little porch on the front or back and some windows with good views. I can't wait to see the finished project." She stood and rubbed her back. "And what a view it is from here. Why, I can see clear back on your daed's property where the oil wells are located."

Elsie frowned. She'd never mentioned anything to Dad, but she was none too happy about those oil well monstrosities. They'd given Dad more money than he knew what to do with, but money didn't bring true happiness. Truth was, Dad hadn't been happy since Joel left home. Mama dying a few years ago had only added to his despair.

"Why don't you come on up?" Aunt Verna called. "There's room for three of us up here."

"No thanks." Elsie shook her head. "I just stopped by to drop off some cookies and lemon fry pies and see if you two would like to join the rest of the family for supper at my house tonight. Maybe Dad could bring his harmonica along and play some music for us after we eat."

"Sounds good to me," Verna shouted.

"We'll be leaving for the auction soon, but should be back in plenty of time," Dad added.

"I hope I get to see Joel while I'm here. Is your bruder coming tonight?"

"No, he will not be joining the family," Dad answered before Elsie could respond. "Joel doesn't want anything to do with us. But I will bring my harmonica tonight."

Aunt Verna stared down at Elsie, who couldn't help wondering what Dad's sister was thinking. Did she realize how bitter Dad felt about Joel? *If I did invite Joel to supper, would he come?*

CHAPTER 6

Akron

Not more than two minutes after Joel left a job in Canton, his cell phone rang. Since he hadn't started the truck yet, he answered the call.

"Hi, Joel. It's Elsie. Are you busy right now?"

"Uh, no. I'm done working for the day and am getting ready to head home." He rolled down his window to get some air flowing.

"I won't keep you, but I wanted to tell you Aunt Verna came down from Burton to spend some time with Dad. We're all having supper at our house this evening, and I was wondering if you'd like to join us." Elsie paused. "I'm sure Aunt Verna would love to see you."

Yeah, well, she'd probably be the only one. Joel drew in a sharp breath. He had fond memories of his aunt, but Dad would be there. After their last confrontation, Joel wasn't about to put himself in a similar situation. Most likely, Dad would give him the cold shoulder all evening, or they could end up having angry words again.

"Sorry, Elsie, but I can't make it tonight," Joel responded. "Would you tell Aunt Verna hello for me?"

"Of course I will, but I'm sorry you won't be able to join us."

"Yeah, me too."

"Guess I'd better let you go."

"Okay. Thanks for calling. Bye, Elsie." Joel grabbed his bottle of water from the cooler on the floor and took a drink. It was good to get in some work today. Tomorrow looked promising as well. Putting his water in the cup holder, he realized his cell phone was still in his grasp. After he put it away, he sat in his truck for a while, staring out the front window. He was glad his sister hadn't pressed him further when he'd declined her invitation. Sometimes Joel felt like a buggy without a horse, no longer being close to his family. But it was a choice he'd made. He only wished he felt free to visit without harsh words between him and Dad. Deep down, Joel figured there might come a day when he'd regret all this. He wouldn't have the memories his sisters had of family events, get-togethers around the holidays, and other fun times. If only his family would be more accepting of the choice he'd made for his life. Didn't he deserve to be happy, too? If they had accepted his choices—especially Dad—maybe he'd feel more comfortable around them.

Of course, Joel reasoned, *it's partly my fault because I asked him for money.* He tapped his knuckles against the steering wheel, wishing once more his father wasn't so stingy.

"Dad didn't even give me a chance. I would have paid it back," he muttered. "Just like I'll return the money to Kristi's and my bank account. It's going to take a little time, that's all."

~

Walnut Creek

"So what did you and Grandpa do today?" Elsie's oldest son, Glen, asked, smiling at Verna from across the dining room table.

She leaned slightly forward, cupping her hand around her ear. "Sorry, I didn't hear what you said."

Glen repeated his question, while Eustace waited to see if his sister would respond. If she still didn't get what Glen said, Eustace was prepared to answer for her.

"We spent some time looking at his tree house. Then we went to an auction with his friend Henry." Verna smiled as her gaze touched each person gathered around Elsie's table.

"It's so nice to be here with all of you this evening. The whole family is here tonight—everyone except Joel."

Eustace curled his toes. He was tempted to blurt out about Joel never coming around unless he wanted something but thought better of it. This wasn't a topic to be discussed in front of the children.

Why couldn't my son be a part of this family? Eustace asked himself. *Doesn't he realize how much he's missing? Of course, he probably wasn't told about our family gathering in honor of Verna being here. Even if he had known, I'm sure he wouldn't have come.*

Quickly redirecting his thoughts, lest he give in to negativity, Eustace announced he'd brought his harmonica along and would accompany Verna on her autoharp after the meal.

Elsie's daughters, Mary and Hope, clapped their hands, which brought a round of applause from everyone else.

"We can listen to the music and sing all night," enthused Lillian, Arlene's eleven-year-old daughter.

Lillian's father, Larry, tweaked her nose. "We can stay for a little while after supper, but it won't be late. You have school tomorrow, remember?"

"Jah, I know." Lillian looked over at Verna.

"Would ya teach me how to play the autoharp?"

Verna grinned, after wiping her nose on a tissue. "I don't see why not. I was about your age when I learned, so I bet you'll catch on mighty fast."

Lillian's eyes brightened even more. "Oh, good. I can hardly wait!"

"Do ya have a cold?" Eighteen-year-old Blaine looked intently at Verna.

"No, it's only my allergies kicking up from the ragweed pollen in the air right now."

Eustace nodded his head as Verna glanced over at him and winked. She'd been paying attention earlier when he'd explained the difference between ragweed and goldenrod.

Scott turned to Eustace and clasped his arm. "Think I could learn how to play the mouth harp, Grandpa?"

"I believe so." Eustace remembered back to the days when his father had taught him to play the harmonica. "It's easy, my boy. Like my daed taught me, all you have to do is suck and blow."

A knot formed in Eustace's stomach as he thought about the day he'd told Joel those same words. Joel had caught on right away and was soon able to play nearly as well as Eustace. What a joy it had been whenever the two of them played duets, with Effie and Joel's three sisters singing along. Those days were gone for him and Joel, but at least Eustace could enjoy the camaraderie of his grandchildren. He felt grateful for the new memories being made.

He reached for his glass of buttermilk and took a drink. *I wonder if Joel will ever have any children of his own.*

Akron

Joel didn't feel much like eating, so he grabbed a cup of coffee, along with his harmonica, and went outside. Fall-like breezes piggybacked on what was still left of summer—a perfect evening to enjoy the outdoors. Autumn was only one week away, and Joel couldn't help anticipating what it would bring. He was definitely ready for it, especially with his type of job. Working in the construction business brought in good money when he had work to do and the jobs were big enough. It had its downside though—especially during the sweltering summers and bitter cold winter months. Some days were so hot, he and his subcontractors had to start work before the sun came up and stop before the hottest part of the day. In the winter, it could get so cold at times that he couldn't feel his fingers, even with work gloves on. With those extreme temperatures, Joel felt he really earned his pay. He just wished spring and autumn, with their more moderate temperatures, would last longer.

A niggle of guilt hit him, knowing he still owed money to the guys who worked hard for him. Plus, he needed to get the money back into the joint savings account.

Taking a seat at the picnic table, Joel lifted the harmonica to his lips and began to play a familiar tune—one his dad had taught him when he was a boy.

The longer Joel played, the more he thought about the past—days when everything seemed so much simpler. Soon, the calmness he'd first felt when he came outside was replaced with anxiety.

He and Dad used to do many things together when Joel was a boy, but they'd drifted apart during Joel's teenage years. From there, things went downhill quickly, and when Joel left the Amish faith, his close relationship with Dad ended.

"I've got to stop thinking about the past." Joel put the harmonica in his pocket and headed for his shop to look at the Corvette. "I'm not going to get all sentimental about this. It is what it is." If he sat in the comfortable car seat for a while, he might feel better. Maybe he'd take the Vette out for a spin. Driving around on the open road had helped the last time he'd done it—that is until Kristi showed up. He'd felt so humiliated dragging his friend Tom into a lie and had endured even more shame by being dishonest with Kristi. Yet he still didn't have the nerve to tell her the truth.

When Joel entered his shop, he paused and looked around. The building was huge—more than enough room to house all his tools, plus several classic cars. Of course, at the rate things were going, it didn't look like Joel would own any more than the one he had now. Classics—especially the kind he was after—cost a lot of money.

"Guess it's just wishful thinking," Joel mumbled. He was about to take a seat inside the car when he heard what sounded like Kristi's car pull into his yard. Joel jumped out of the car, covered it with a tarp, and left the shop, closing and locking the door behind him. He was surprised to see her because she hadn't mentioned anything about coming over.

Smiling, Kristi walked over to Joel. "You look surprised. Aren't you happy to see me?"

"Of course I am." Joel pulled her close and gave

her a hug. "I didn't realize you were coming. Didn't you say something about going to the gym to work out tonight?"

"That was my original plan, but I jogged after I got off work so I didn't think I needed any more exercise." Kristi reached for his hand. "What's in your shirt pocket, Joel? Is it your harmonica?"

"Yep, it's my harmonica. I played it awhile before you got here." He stifled a yawn.

"Would you play something for me?" Her eyes lit up. "I haven't heard you play in a long while."

"Okay." Joel placed the harmonica between his lips.

Kristi seemed to enjoy his song. Soon, she started clapping and singing along.

"How about we take a break now?" Joel paused after several songs. "I've had a long, busy day, and I'm tired."

"No problem. Maybe someday you'll teach our child to play." She looked at him sincerely.

"Yeah, if we ever have any kids. To tell you the truth, I'm not sure I'm cut out to be a father."

Kristi's forehead wrinkled. "You've never mentioned not wanting children before. I've always thought. . ." She dropped her gaze as her voice trailed off.

"Didn't say I don't want any." Joel shrugged his shoulders. "I'm not sure I have what it takes to be a good dad."

Looking up at him again, Kristi squeezed his hand. "Of course you do. You're kind, smart, talented, and a hard worker." She ruffled his hair. "You'll make a great father."

Joel thought about his own father and how he

used to think the world of him. Since Joel was no longer a child, he saw Dad for what he was—eccentric, stingy, and unfeeling. *A good father who loves his children would not look the other way when his son has a need.*

"Oh Joel, there's something else I wanted to talk to you about." Kristi's voice halted Joel's thoughts.

Joel led the way to the picnic table and gestured for her to take a seat on the bench. "What's up?"

"As I'm sure you've heard, our church is sponsoring a marriage retreat next week."

"Guess I did read something about it in last Sunday's bulletin."

Nodding, she smiled. "How would you like to go?"

"To the seminar?" His jaw clenched. Seminars or spiritual retreats were not for him.

"Yes."

"Why would we need that? We're not married yet, Kristi."

"It's not only for married couples. It's also for people who are planning to be married."

"Oh, I see."

Kristi's forehead wrinkled. "We are still planning to be married, aren't we? Or have you changed your mind about us?"

Joel shook his head. "Where did you get such an idea? Of course I haven't changed my mind. Now's not a good time to be making any plans."

"I realize that, but if we go to the marriage seminar it might help strengthen our relationship."

He crossed his arms. "What's wrong with our relationship?"

"I...I can't put my finger on it, Joel," She paused

and swallowed. "Things have been strained between us for a good many weeks. Even before your accident, I felt it."

Joel's chest tightened when he saw tears forming in her eyes. He slid over on the bench and pulled her into his arms. "Sorry, Kristi. I've had a lot on my mind." Kristi felt so warm in his arms; he never wanted to let her go. Joel closed his eyes and held her even tighter. *I'd never be happy if something happened between us.*

"I. . .I know you've been busy."

He gently patted her back, then slowly pulled away, gazing deeply into her ocean-blue eyes. Joel's body flooded with warmth. He could almost feel himself drowning in the depths of her eyes as he gently caressed her cheek. "If it'll make you feel better, I'll go to the marriage conference."

"Thank you, Joel." Kristi sniffed and dabbed at the tears on her cheeks. "I'm confident this will be a good thing for both of us."

He nodded, softly brushing a strand of hair away from her face. Joel wasn't so sure about going to the event, although he wouldn't admit it to her. He didn't need some so-called expert on marriage telling him how to be a good husband. Maybe between now and then he'd get a few more jobs lined up and would be too busy to go.

CHAPTER 7

Kristi pulled up to her parents' house, turned off the engine, and checked her watch. She thought about how she and Joel sat under the stars together last week. It had been wonderful to hear him play the harmonica. It was so nice to see Joel having a good time and looking so relaxed.

Tonight, Kristi and Joel would attend the marriage seminar, and she didn't want to be late. But Mom had called and asked her to stop by. Even though it was Kristi's day off, her Saturday schedule was filling up.

Entering the house, she found her father in the living room, watching TV. "Hey, Dad. How's your back doing?" Kristi bent down and gave him a hug.

"It's better, but the doctor reminded me about taking it easy so I don't reinjure it."

"You should listen to his advice. In the end, you'll be happy you did. It's important to take good care of yourself, because—"

He gestured toward the kitchen and grinned. "Your mother's in there, doing one of her domestic things."

"Okay, Dad, I can take a hint." Kristi smiled. "Guess I'll go join her."

Placing her purse on a chair, Kristi entered the kitchen and spotted her mother lifting a quart jar from the canner. "Looks like you've been busy."

Mom placed the jar on the counter, then gave Kristi a hug. "I've been making applesauce all morning and thought you might like to take some home."

She pointed. "I did all those at the far end earlier, so you can take from them if you like, because those have already cooled."

Kristi studied the jars lined up in a row. The lids on the more recent ones started popping as they cooled.

"I always like to hear that sound." Mom wiped her hands on her apron. "Then I know the lids have sealed."

"They look good, Mom. I'd be happy to take a few jars home." Kristi hoped to do things like this when she and Joel got married. She looked forward to canning and freezing produce from a garden and having fruit trees someday, but recently, some things she'd been wishing for seemed to be getting further out of reach. Kristi almost hated to wish for things, for fear they'd never happen. More than anything, she wanted to become Joel's wife. Lately, though, something felt different between them. Kristi hoped she was wrong about the inner voice, warning her to be on guard. She wanted to trust Joel; after all, along with love, trust was the basis of any relationship.

"I got the applesauce recipe from the Amish cookbook I picked up when you and I visited Holmes County last month." Mom glanced over at Kristi and snapped her fingers. "Hey, are you daydreaming? Didn't you hear what I said?"

"Sorry, Mom. Guess I was zoning out for a bit. I did hear you though."

Kristi traced the rim of one jar with her finger. "Our trip to Holmes County was a fun weekend. I only wish I'd had enough money to buy a quilt."

Mom gave a nod. "We did see a lot of beautiful quilts. It's too bad they're so expensive."

"It's understandable though. A lot of work goes into making one."

"It certainly does." Mom opened the refrigerator and removed a jug of apple cider. "Boy, I'm glad it's autumn now. The cooler temperatures make doing this canning a whole lot easier."

"I'm with you, Mom. I love running when the air is cool and crisp and there aren't a lot of bugs swarming around my head."

"Would you like something cold to drink?"

Kristi smiled. "Maybe half a glass, and then I need to get going."

"What's the rush?"

"Joel and I are going to the marriage seminar our church is hosting this evening. Besides, I have a few things I need to get done at home before it's time to go."

Mom handed Kristi a glass of cider. "Your dad and I thought about going to the seminar, too. Events like this are beneficial, even for people who have been married a long time. All couples need a reminder of the things they need to do to keep their marriage healthy."

"I suppose that's true." Kristi took a drink, allowing the tangy cider to roll around on her tongue before swallowing. One of the best things about fall was enjoying the mouthwatering apples coming into season. "I'm certainly looking forward to going tonight. I hope the things we learn will strengthen Joel's and my relationship." She sighed. "Things have been a bit strained between us lately."

Kristi waited for Mom's response, expecting a reminder of what the Bible says about being unequally yoked. To her surprise, Mom merely patted Kristi's arm and said, "I'm sorry, Kristi. I hope things will go better for you soon."

Nodding, Kristi finished her cider and set the glass in the sink, filling it with warm water to soak. "I'd better get going or I won't get any of the things done on my list today." She gave Mom a hug and started for the back door.

"Don't forget your jars of applesauce." Mom put six jars in a cardboard box and handed it to Kristi. "If your dad and I decide to go, we'll see you at the seminar this evening."

"Sounds good." Kristi headed out the door. She'd barely gotten into her car when her cell phone rang. The caller ID spelled out it was Joel.

"Hey, Joel, I was just thinking of you. I'm looking forward to our evening together."

"Umm. . .about that. . .I'm sorry to have to tell you this, but the job I started yesterday isn't done. I'm here right now at the jobsite, working on it again."

"What time will you get done?"

"I'm not sure—probably not till quite late."

"Can't you finish it on Monday?"

"Nope. It's a rush job and needs to be finished today. So I won't be able to attend the marriage seminar with you tonight after all."

"Oh, I see." Kristi couldn't hide her disappointment. But Joel needed the work, so she would try to be understanding. "Guess I'll go without you then. Maybe I'll get some helpful hints about being a good wife."

"Sorry, Kristi. I feel bad about letting you down."

"No, it's okay. Sometimes work needs to come

first. If you're free after church tomorrow, maybe we can have lunch and I'll share with you what I learned."

"Okay, sounds good. See you tomorrow, Kristi."

Kristi hung up, leaned her head back, and closed her eyes. *I hope Joel really does have to work tonight and isn't using it as an excuse to get out of going to the seminar.* She opened her eyes and started the car. *I'm sure he wouldn't lie to me.*

$\diamond$

Charm

When Doris arrived at her dad's place later in the afternoon, she was surprised to find him outside working on the tree house, along with her nephews Scott and Doug, as well as Eustace's friend Henry.

"I see you have quite a crew working here today." Doris walked around some of the boards as she stepped up to the maple Dad had chosen for his tree house.

Dad removed his hat and fanned his face. "Jah, and they're all good helpers." He smiled at Doris. "Did you come to help, too?"

She shook her head. "I heard Aunt Verna will be heading back to Burton this evening, so I came to say goodbye."

"That's right. She's inside doing a little cleaning she insisted needed to be done before she leaves." Dad's forehead wrinkled. "I told her not to bother, but she was adamant."

"Yoo-hoo!" Aunt Verna opened the door and waved. "I saw you pull in, Doris. I've got something I need to show you from the auction the other day." She ambled toward them with a bird cage swaying by her side. It looked old and ornate. A blur of red flapped inside it, too.

Doris couldn't believe her eyes when she recognized the blur as a beautiful red cardinal. The poor thing looked confused. No matter how pretty the cage was, the wild bird would be miserable enduring its sentence. Besides, it wasn't a pet.

"How do you like my new bird cage and its occupant?" Aunt Verna spoke rapidly, her eyes dancing with joy.

Dad cleared his throat. "She's a little proud of her purchase, I'd say." He took over the conversation. "Did you notice my homemade table over there? The base is a wooden wire spool I picked up at the auction. When we got it home, I put a top on it. Not too shabby of a picnic table either. Henry's coffee cup is setting on it already."

Henry nodded enthusiastically. "It was fun going to the auction with you and Verna. And with all the walking we did, we sure got our exercise, didn't we?" He leaned down and rubbed the calf of his leg. "But it was worth it, because I left there with a few things myself." Using a hanky he took from his pocket, he wiped his brow.

Doris turned to Aunt Verna. "What I'm wondering is how you ended up with our state bird in your birdcage?"

Aunt Verna cupped her hand over her ear. "What was that?"

Doris repeated her question.

"Oh, well, it was stuck inside one of your daed's bird feeders, so I rescued it. Of course, I cleaned out the bird cage first, then added food and water before I saved the critter from its cramped quarters and heat exhaustion. It was a hot day when I discovered it there."

"But Aunt Verna, the cardinal looks okay now. Wouldn't he be happier if you released him instead?"

Scott and Doug stepped over right then. "The poor bird looks sad." Doug scrunched up his nose. "It ain't fair. You oughta let him go."

"You're probably right. Guess it would be better to let him fly free like the other birds here in the yard." She unlatched the cage door. "Okay everyone, I'm letting the cardinal go."

All eyes watched in anticipation to see what would happen next. Aunt Verna opened the cage door. The cardinal sat for a moment; then it hopped out and flew away. Dad, Henry, and Aunt Verna smiled. The boys clapped. Doris felt relief. She couldn't believe anyone would try to make a pet out of a wild bird. But then, like Dad, Aunt Verna had a good many eccentricities.

"How's your mare doing with the new foal?" Doris asked, turning to Dad.

"They're both doing well."

"Wanna go out to the barn and take a look?" Scott tugged on Doris's arm.

She smiled and took his hand. "I'd like that. Lead the way."

"I'll walk with you. I need a break from housecleaning." Aunt Verna set the empty bird cage on the ground.

"After we see the horse, I'll be happy to help you finish cleaning Dad's house," Doris offered.

Aunt Verna slipped her arm around Doris's waist and chatted as the three of them made their way to the barn.

When they returned from the barn, Doris noticed Henry crouched near a metal bucket with nails scattered on the ground. She knelt beside him and offered to help pick them up.

"That's nice of you." He grimaced. "Guess I'd better pay closer attention to what I'm doing. I'm gettin' clumsy in my old age."

"Everyone drops things from time to time, Henry." Doris patted his arm. "It's good of you to help Dad with his new project."

"That's why Grandpa's tree house is goin' up so fast." Scott pointed overhead. "He's got plenty of help to get the job done."

Doris smiled. "I'm sure he appreciates each of you being here today."

Aunt Verna nodded. "I bet, too."

Scott grinned up at Doris. "I can't wait till the tree house is done and we can all go up in it."

Doris squeezed his shoulder. "You can count me out. I've never liked heights."

"What about Uncle Joel? Does he like bein' up high?"

"He used to," Dad answered before Doris could respond. "Joel was like a monkey when it came to climbing trees."

Scott's eyes lit up. "Wish I'd known him when he was a *bu*."

"You'd have gotten along well, I'm sure."

"You're probably right." Doug nodded. "My little bruder gets along with everyone. Course, he can be kinda stubborn sometimes, and he—"

"I wish Uncle Joel was here workin' on the tree house with us," Scott interrupted.

"We have plenty of help." Dad motioned to

Henry. "My good friend came to work on the tree house."

"Yep." Henry's eyes twinkled. "Even my dog, Peaches, wanted to come along." He winked at Scott. "She's not afraid of heights either."

"You mean she'll climb the ladder up to the tree house?" Doug questioned.

"That's right." Henry chuckled. "When it comes to climbing, my *hund's* like a mountain goat."

The boys laughed, along with Aunt Verna. Doris rolled her eyes. "Henry you're such a tease."

He wiggled his silver-gray brows. "Wasn't teasing. If I climbed a ladder, or even a tree, Peaches would come right up after me. Wanna see?"

"I do! I do!" Scott bounced up and down on his toes. "I've never seen a dog climb a ladder before."

"And you're not gonna see one today either." Dad gestured to the pile of wood on the ground. "We're supposed to be working, not foolin' around."

"I'll tell ya what, son." Henry bent over to stroke Peaches on the head. "When the tree house is finished, I'll let Peaches climb up to the top."

"Okay." Scott looked toward the house. "Is it all right if I go get a drink?"

"Course you can. While you're in there, would ya bring the rest of us some bottles of water?"

"Sure, Grandpa." Scott headed for the house. Doris and Aunt Verna followed.

When they stepped inside, Scott paused and turned to her. "Have ya seen Uncle Joel lately, Aunt Doris?"

"No. Why would I?" she asked, a bit too sharply.

"Thought maybe he's come in to eat at the restaurant where you work."

Doris shook her head. "If he has, it's been on the days I haven't worked."

"I liked being with Uncle Joel the last time he visited. Sure wish he'd come around more often."

Doris nodded. "We'd all like that, Scott, but it's probably not going to happen."

"How come?"

"My bruder is a busy contractor. He doesn't have much free time." Doris could have told him a lot more, but thought better of it. Scott was too young to understand everything concerning Joel. She would not be guilty of talking badly about him.

CHAPTER 8

Yipe! Yipe! Yipe!

Eustace turned to Scott and shook his finger. "You'd better be prudent with what you're doin' now, 'cause ya stepped on the dog's tail."

The boy jumped back. "Oops! Sorry about that. Didn't realize she was sittin' behind me."

"It's okay." Henry bent down and picked up his dog. "Peaches has a way of getting underfoot." He stroked her tail. "She'll be fine. Probably scared her more than anything."

"Would it be all right if I hold her?" Doug questioned.

"Don't see why not." Henry handed the pooch to Doug and stood watching as Peaches licked the boy's nose. In no time, Peaches grew limp in Doug's arms. Her big brown eyes drifted lazily closed as the boy twirled his fingers around her cottony curls.

It was time to get back to work, so Eustace climbed the ladder to the floor of his tree house. He picked up his hammer to begin working on the next phase of the project—the railing and deck, when he heard Doug mention Anna Detweiler's name.

"Ya know what, Henry? My teacher let the scholars bring their pets to school last Friday."

"Is that so?" Henry leaned against the ladder, as if he was in no mood to work.

"Jah, but the only pet I have is my pony, Flicker, and my folks wouldn't let me take her to school." Doug's voice lowered a bit, and Eustace had to strain to hear what he said next. "Sure wish I had a hund like Peaches. She's real nice."

"You and me think alike," Henry agreed. "If she wasn't around, things wouldn't be the same."

"Teacher Anna has a cocker spaniel, too, only hers is all black. When she brought the dog on pet day, everyone in the class got to pet it."

"Anna sounds like a nice teacher."

She would have been a nice daughter-in-law, too, Eustace thought. *But wishing for what could have been won't change the facts. Joel left a girl everyone believed he would marry, and now he probably doesn't even give her a thought.*

"Say, Henry. Are you gonna stand there all day watchin' the dog, or did you plan on helping me build the tree house?" Eustace called down to his friend.

Henry tipped his head back and looked up. "I'm old. Leave me alone."

"And I'm not?" Eustace laughed so hard, tears ran down his cheeks. He figured he and Henry could probably outwork his two grandsons put together.

"I'll help ya, Grandpa." Scott scampered up the ladder. "Tell me what you want done, and I'll do it."

"You can start by handing me a few of those." Eustace pointed to a can of nails. "We can only work another hour, and then it'll be time for you boys to go home for supper."

"Sure, Grandpa, whatever you say."

Eustace was pleased at the young boy's eagerness to help. Joel had been the same way when he was Scott's age—always helpful and eager to please. Why couldn't things have stayed the way they were back then?

Holding a board in place, Eustace clenched the hammer and drove a nail in so hard, his hand ached. *I need to stop thinking about Joel and concentrate on the joy of building this special tree house in memory of Effie.* Looking down at Henry and Doug, Eustace cupped his hands around his mouth and hollered, "We could sure use more help up here! Could one of you bring me another batch of boards?"

"I'll do it! Can't let my little bruder do all the work." Doug handed Peaches back to Henry, grabbed some boards, and climbed up the ladder.

Eustace smiled. He hoped these two boys would grow into strong men who followed the Lord's leading in all they said and did. If they put God first, He would lead and guide them through all of their days.

Eustace closed his eyes briefly and sent up a prayer. *It's what I want for my son, too, Lord. I pray the decision I made awhile back about Joel and the rest of my kinner was the right thing to do.*

❧

"It's been nice visiting with you, but now it's time for me to head home. Brian will be there soon, and I need to get supper started." Doris gave her aunt a hug, then turned toward the door. "I hope we will get to see you again soon."

"What was it you just said?" Aunt Verna asked.

Doris turned back around. "I'm sorry, Aunt Verna. I said, 'I hope we get to see you again soon.'"

"No harm done. The ole' hearing isn't what it used to be." Aunt Verna smiled. "Maybe the next time I come, my husband will join me."

"That would be nice. I haven't seen Uncle Lester in some time."

"He doesn't travel as much as he used to, with his arthritis and all."

"I understand." Doris gave Aunt Verna another hug. "What time will your driver be here to pick you up?"

"She's supposed to come around seven. It will give your daed and me time to have supper and say our goodbyes." Aunt Verna walked with Doris out to the porch. "Maybe next time I come, Joel will be here. It would have been nice to have seen him this time."

A lump formed in Doris's throat. She swallowed hard and gave a brief nod. At this point, the chance of Uncle Lester leaving Burton to travel anywhere was greater than Joel coming here—unless he wanted something.

Doris went out and told everyone goodbye, then headed for the barn to get her horse. As she walked the mare out to hook her up, Doris couldn't wait to share with Brian about her day. She would make homemade pizza and a tossed salad. Then she and Brian could sit down to a quiet meal and visit. She thought it strange how the English liked to watch TV. Even some restaurants would have it on. Doris was thankful TVs held no place in an Amish home. It would only be a distraction. And from what she'd heard, some things shown on the television could lead a person astray.

A yawn escaped her lips as she climbed into the buggy and gathered up the reins. It had been busy at Dad's today, but she and Aunt Verna had gotten a lot done. Doris would miss her father's sister. It felt nice to have a mother-figure around.

After guiding her horse onto the main road, Doris relaxed in her seat, pleased there wasn't much traffic. The fall scenery was beautiful, too—so many leaves already turning color. It was enough to melt away her cares.

With the sun beginning to set over the hills, it was almost time to send the boys home. Eustace didn't want them riding their bikes home in the dark. "Okay, fellas, let's put your tools away, and then you two need to get going. My guess is your mamm has a meal cookin' for you by now, and you don't want to be late for supper."

Before leaving, Doug and Scott gave their grandpa a hug.

"You two ride your bikes home safely, and danki for your help today. Oh, and don't forget to stop up at the house and let your great-aunt know you're leaving." Eustace peered at Doug and Scott over the top of his glasses.

The boys dashed off to the house, but before they could open the door, Verna stepped out and greeted them on the porch. "You boys be good while I'm away, and always listen to your folks. Hopefully, I'll bring your great-uncle Lester with me on my next visit here." She gave them both hugs.

"Have a nice trip home, Aunt Verna," Doug called as he and his brother mounted their bikes.

"Bye, Aunt Verna." Scott waved at her before the boys peddled down the driveway and onto the road.

Eustace watched his grandsons leave the yard in a matter of seconds. Soon after, Verna popped over to where he and Henry stood, all smiles. "Those are two good boys. I will miss them while I'm away." She sniffed. "Their folks are doing a fine job raising their kinner."

"I can't complain about that. Larry and Arlene have a good group of children, and so do John and Elsie. Except for Joel, my wayward son, I haven't had any problems with my kinner." Eustace glanced down at his worn-out, taped-together boots, before looking back at Verna.

Her eyes filled with tears as she rested her hand on his shoulder. "Keep praying for Joel. Perhaps in time, he will turn his life around."

Eustace could only manage a nod. His throat suddenly felt swollen.

"Well, my friend, shall we call it a day?" Henry stepped up to Eustace and set his hammer on the picnic table.

"Might as well. Let's get the stuff put away." Eustace swatted at a fly buzzing him.

"There's still some coffee left over. Would either of you like a cup?" Verna stood with one hand on her hip.

"No thanks." Eustace shook his head.

"How about you, Henry?" Verna asked.

"Sure, I'll take some to go. Here's my coffee mug." He picked it up from the picnic table and handed it to her.

After Henry helped Eustace put everything away, he grabbed Peaches, carried her over to his tractor, and put the dog inside the pet carrier. When he'd closed it up tight, he checked the bungie straps. "Yep. Everything looks good and secured to travel for my hund. Sure hope she doesn't yelp like a baby all the way home. It can get on a fellow's nerves after a while."

Eustace chuckled. Henry liked to complain about his dog. Truth was, he'd be lost without Peaches.

"Here comes Verna with your coffee." Eustace pointed at his sister.

"Here you go, Henry. I'm not sure when I'll see you again." She handed him the coffee mug.

"Danki. This will be good for the trip home. It's been nice to visit with you, Verna. Eustace, you have a good sister." He took a sip of his coffee.

"I can't complain, Henry. Verna likes to take care of me. No matter how old I get, she still acts like a mother hen whenever she comes around." He chuckled and winked at her. "Guess it's what big sisters do."

She smiled at him.

"Have a safe trip home, Verna. And you'll see me again soon, my friend, Mr. Byler." Henry tugged on Eustace's straw hat. Then he climbed onto his tractor and started it up. Soon, Henry and Peaches were heading down the road toward home.

"I've made turkey sandwiches, and there's some leftover beef vegetable soup I can heat." Verna bumped Eustace's arm with her elbow.

"Sounds tasty. I could handle both of 'em for supper." He stretched and yawned. "What a busy day we've had, jah?"

"It's been busy, all right, but my day isn't over yet. I still need to travel home this evening. I miss Lester and can't wait to see him. Now let's go eat and visit before it's time for me to go." She pushed back a strand of gray hair from her face as they walked together toward the house.

Eustace hated to see his sister go. It would seem lonely without her. But he would do as he'd done since Effie died: keep busy.

⌒

Canton, Ohio

When Joel left the jobsite that evening, he pulled out his cell phone to check the time. Eight o'clock.

The marriage seminar must be halfway over by now. *I wonder if Kristi's upset with me for not going. She needs to realize my job comes before anything else right now.*

Joel's reasons for not going jabbed his conscience. If he hadn't gotten himself into debt by bidding on the Corvette, he wouldn't be in the position of needing money so badly right now. He'd maxed out his credit cards, too, and didn't dare apply for another one, or he'd really be in over his head.

Joel yawned as he leaned against his truck, watching the sky turn from blue to orange hues. It had been a long day, and the sun was already low in the western sky. He was dog tired, and his body ached from being on his feet all day. His toes cramped inside the confines of his work boots. He couldn't wait to get home to kick them off, take a shower, and relax.

Kristi would have gotten paid yesterday, he thought. *I wonder if she put any money in our bank account. If so, I might be able to take out a bit more.*

Joel admitted he had put himself at risk taking money from their account the first time. Sooner or later, Kristi was bound to find out what their balance was. Because the statements came to Joel's house didn't mean she wouldn't ask at the bank the next time she made a deposit.

"I'm playing with fire," Joel muttered as he climbed into his truck. "I need a way out, and I need it soon."

❧

Akron

When Kristi got ready to leave the church that evening, she had mixed emotions. While she'd enjoyed the seminar and learned a lot, it wasn't the same without Joel. He needed to hear what the guest speaker said about marriage and the importance of good communication. He'd stressed the need for honesty between a couple and talked about spending quality time together. While Kristi and Joel got together fairly regularly, lately she felt as if his mind was always on other things. The fact that Joel couldn't take a few hours off tonight really bothered her—maybe too much. But couldn't Joel have gone to work earlier this morning so he could attend the seminar?

Kristi was almost to the door when she bumped into her mother. "Oh, sorry. I didn't see you and Dad standing there."

"No harm done." Mom touched Kristi's arm. "Where's Joel? I thought he was coming with you tonight."

"He was, but he had to work late." Kristi dropped her gaze. She didn't want to let on how disappointed she felt or mention that she thought Joel might have used work as an excuse not to come.

"I'm sorry he couldn't be here," Dad interjected. "He sure missed out on some good stuff."

Kristi held up the packet of information they'd been given, along with the notes she'd taken. "I'll be sharing all the information when I see Joel tomorrow."

"Good to hear." Dad gave Kristi a hug. "If Joel's gonna be my son-in-law someday, then he needs to know how to take care of my daughter."

Avoiding her mother's gaze, Kristi smiled at Dad. "I'm sure he will, Daddy. Joel's a good man."

CHAPTER 9

Charm

Monday morning, Eustace was up at the crack of dawn. He ate a quick breakfast and got all his outside chores done so he could work on the roof. Several shingles were missing, and with rain in the forecast, he needed to get some patching done or he could be in for a few leaks.

It was a good thing Eustace wasn't afraid of heights, because his two-story house had a steep roof. He might have asked one of his sons-in-law to help, or even some of the boys, but Eustace enjoyed working and liked to keep busy, so he didn't view it as a chore. He couldn't see asking any of his family for help. They had their own responsibilities to keep up with. This way, he could work at his own pace. Any work he did on this home that he loved so much gave him a sense of satisfaction. At Eustace's age, completing tasks, such as fixing the roof, meant by tonight, every bone in his body would ache. Even so, it was fulfilling to see the results of the work he could still do.

If Effie were here now, she'd be standing beneath my ladder shaking her finger at me and saying I ought to come down and let someone younger take care of this chore, Eustace thought after he'd climbed the ladder and gotten settled on the roof. Of course, Effie had always worried about him, often saying he took too many chances.

Eustace remembered one time he'd made a huge kite, and Effie was sure it would lift him into the air and carry him away. It hadn't, of course, but it probably could have if the wind had been strong enough. *Now, wouldn't that have been something— me sailing through the air like a bird?*

Soon after Eustace became rich, he'd bought a trampoline for his grandchildren to enjoy when they came to visit. Effie was certain it wasn't safe and worried one of the kids might get hurt jumping on it. To put her mind at ease, Eustace had climbed onto the trampoline and jumped as high as he could. When no great tragedy occurred, he even did a few flips. Of course, he'd been a few years younger then. He'd also added a safety net around the perimeter of the trampoline to ensure his grandchildren's protection.

Eustace chuckled as he began patching the roof. As his father used to say, "We only live once, so we may as well have a little fun and take a few chances, or life will become boring."

After he'd worked a while, Eustace began to sweat. *Should have brought some* wasser *up here with me.* He smacked his forehead with the palm of his hand. *Sometimes I can be so forgetful. Guess it comes with age.*

He was about to climb down, when he spotted Elsie's rig coming up the driveway. *Oh, good. I can ask her to get me the water.*

"Hey, Elsie," Eustace called after she'd gotten out of the buggy and secured her horse to the hitching rail. "Would you mind goin' in the house and bringing me a glass of water?"

Elsie looked up, and her mouth opened wide. "What are you doing up there, Dad?"

"Some of the shingles are missing, and I'm

replacing them before I end up with a leak in my roof. Since fall is here, we're bound to see more rain."

"John could have replaced shingles for you, Dad. All you needed to do was ask."

"It's okay. I'd rather do it myself. Besides, John's a bricklayer, not a roofer." Eustace chuckled. "That's why so many folks around here call him 'Bricklayer John.'"

"You're not a roofer, either, and you're up so high. What if you fell and no one was here to help?"

Eustace flapped his glove at her. "Stop pestering me. I'm not afraid of heights, and being on the roof is no big deal. I'm perfectly capable of taking care of the job, and I have everything under control. I've done things like this for years. Today is no different."

"But Dad, don't you realize—"

"Are you gonna bring me a glass of *wasser* or not?"

"Will you come down here to drink it?"

"Why? Are you afraid to climb the *leeder*?"

"No, I am not afraid to climb the ladder." Elsie huffed. "But there's no place to set a glass of water on the roof, now is there?"

"I wasn't gonna set it down. I was planning to drink it."

"Okay," Elsie finally conceded. "I will bring it up the ladder, and then I'll wait there till you drink it."

Smiling, Eustace nodded. "You're a good daughter. Now hurry inside."

A few minutes later, Elsie returned with a plastic bottle. She made her way up the ladder and handed it to him. "I put water in this bottle instead of a glass. If it gets dropped, it won't break."

Eustace took the bottle, opened the lid, and

drank. "Danki. Sure hits the spot." He started to hand it back to her but changed his mind. "Guess I'd better keep the bottle with me in case I get thirsty again."

She remained on the ladder, with lips pursed as she looked up. He figured she was about to plead with him to come down and let John finish the job. So before she could say anything, Eustace spoke. "There's a pile of sullied clothes in my bedroom needing to be washed. Would you mind doing 'em for me?"

Elsie hesitated at first, but finally nodded. "Sure, Dad. I'd be happy to take care of the laundry." She started down the ladder, then suddenly yelled out.

Eustace crawled to the edge of the roof to make sure his daughter was all right. "What happened, Elsie?"

"I missed one of the rungs and almost fell."

"Are you okay?"

"Jah. My legs are kind of wobbly on the ladder right now."

Wiping his brow, Eustace felt relief. Thank goodness she was all right. "I'm holding my end of the ladder till you get down. Now take it slow, one rung at a time." He watched as Elsie went the rest of the way down. What was wrong with him? He should have known better than to ask his daughter to bring him water. Elsie was only forty-two, but it was a risk for anyone climbing a ladder this high. The last thing he wanted was to put any of his loved ones in danger.

Guess I should have been thinking about that the day I asked Elsie to climb the tree and rescue me. But then, Verna went up in the tree house, and so did the boys.

When Elsie's feet touched the ground, she turned and looked up again. "I'll check on you as soon as I get the clothes washed and ready to hang. Please be careful, okay?"

"I'm always prudent."

Elsie shook her finger, reminding him of Effie. "No big words, now, Dad. I want you to take it easy."

Eustace promised. When the screen door shut, he smiled. *Now maybe I can finish my task without interruptions. My daughter means well, but like her mamm, she worries too much. But then, how can I blame Elsie for being concerned? Look what almost happened to her.*

❧

Eustace was nearly finished with his chore when Elsie came out to hang the wet clothes. "How's it going?" she called before heading over to the line.

"Almost done. I'm gonna sit here a spell and enjoy the sights. You can see forever from up here."

He heard Elsie sigh. Then she headed out to the line and began hanging some towels, as well as his clothes.

Eustace looked out across the pasture, watching his beautiful buggy horse running about in the field. He chuckled as the horse kicked up his heels like a frisky colt and some of the other horses followed, doing the same.

His gaze went to the oil wells, going at a steady speed. *I'm a fortunate man to have all of this.* He drank the last of his water. *Someday, when I'm gone, I hope each of my kinner appreciates what they will eventually receive.*

By the time Eustace climbed down from the

roof, Elsie had gone back inside. After putting the ladder and his tools away, he entered the house. When Eustace stepped into the living room, he was surprised to find Elsie going through a stack of mail piled up on an end table near the couch.

"What are you doing?" he inquired.

"I was sorting, to make sure there was no important mail before tossing all the ads and catalogs."

Eustace vigorously shook his head. "No, don't do that! I'm keeping all of those."

She quirked an eyebrow. "Whatever for?"

"I may want to order something. I've been so busy building the tree house I haven't had time to go through all my catalogs."

Elsie sighed. "Okay, Dad, whatever you want."

Eustace was glad he'd caught her in time. If he'd come in a few minutes later, she may have thrown all the mail in the trash. Then he wouldn't have been able to order anything.

"Say, Dad, it's getting close to noon. Why don't I fix you something to eat?"

"Only if you'll agree to eat with me. It would be nice to have some one-on-one time for a change, and eating by myself is not much fun." Eustace chuckled. "I kinda got used to your aunt's constant chatter."

"Of course I'll stay." Elsie smiled. "What would you like to eat?"

"I'll tell you what. Why don't you make a salad, and I'll grill some steaks? It would be nice to have someone to share the meal with, because I've never gotten used to eating alone."

She gave him a hug. "I understand, which is

why I don't understand your insistence on living here by yourself."

"I feel close to your mamm in this home, Elsie. Sometimes, when I look at her rocking chair or some of the clothes she used to wear, I feel like she's still here, watching over me."

"But you know she's in heaven with God, right? And no matter where you are, whether it's at home or someplace else, she'll always be here."

He nodded as Elsie pointed to her heart. "I look forward to joining her in heaven someday."

Elsie slipped her hand through the crook of Eustace's arm as they walked toward the kitchen. "We don't want it to be anytime soon, which is why you need to be careful."

He patted her hand, thankful for his daughter's love. *Too bad Joel doesn't care much for me. I hope he regrets his actions someday.*

CHAPTER 10

The following morning, after Eustace had enjoyed his first cup of coffee, he opened the back door and stepped onto the porch. The humidity was high, with the smell of rain accompanying a light breeze. Wrinkling his nose, the air actually smelled like earthworms. He glanced at the rocks, where years ago, Effie had meticulously positioned them to border the flowerbed. Her "Suzies" were still in bloom but would soon be dropping their seeds. She always loved those black-eyed Susans, and now they were Eustace's favorite flower, too. He could see the slimy trails from slugs where they'd crawled across the bordering rocks and into the landscaping. *Guess I better look for something soon to get rid of those slugs before they eat Effie's flowers.*

Eustace leaned forward, holding onto the porch post, and stuck out his hand. For now, only a slight mist fell. He hoped any heavier precipitation would hold off until he got his outside chores done. He also wanted to put finishing touches on his tree house.

Eustace made his way out to the barn to let the horses out to the pasture. As soon as he did, they took off running, kicking, and bucking to the far end of the field. Instead of stopping to graze, they seemed to be a little fidgety as they pranced along the fence row. *Maybe they're feeling their oats, needing to stretch their legs.*

After he made sure the horses' water trough was full, Eustace returned to the barn to clean the stalls.

With so much of his time spent building the tree house, he'd neglected some other things.

As Eustace began to muck out the first stall, his thoughts went to Joel. While cleaning had never been Joel's favorite thing to do, he'd always enjoyed spending time with the horses. When Joel turned sixteen, Eustace had given him his first buggy horse. For a year or so afterward, all Joel talked about was Speedy, and how fast he could run. He'd also bragged on his horse, saying the gelding looked finer than any of his friends' buggy horses. Effie used to warn Joel about boasting, and Eustace had as well. But the older their son got, the more he bragged about things. When Joel turned eighteen, he'd bought a car, and everything began to change. He rarely took the horse and buggy out after that, and Speedy didn't seem so special anymore. Joel's convertible became his passion. At first, Eustace figured it was a passing fancy, and when Joel was ready to settle down and join the church, he'd sell the car and that would be the end of it. And it was for a while—until Joel broke poor Anna's heart and took off to seek his fortune in the English world. What a heartbreak it had been for all the family.

By the time Eustace finished cleaning all the stalls, he was sick of reminiscing and more than ready for something to eat. Back in the house, he fixed himself another cup of coffee and set out the cinnamon rolls Doris had brought by last evening on her way home from work. The mere sight and smell of those sweet rolls made his mouth water. He couldn't wait to take his first bite and sip the fresh, hot coffee.

Walnut Creek

As Doris approached the table she would be waiting on, she noticed two little blond-haired girls sitting in high chairs—one on each side of their mother. Dressed alike, and with the same facial features, they were obviously identical twins. The girls looked to be one or two years old, but Doris couldn't be sure. She'd never been good at guessing children's ages.

She was about to ask the young woman if she was ready to order, when one of the little girls started to howl and kick her feet. Patting the child's back, the mother whispered soothing words, but to no avail. The blond-haired cutie continued to cry. Soon, her twin sister followed suit. The poor woman looked fit to be tied. "I'm so sorry," she apologized, looking up at Doris, then quickly glancing around the restaurant. "They're both hungry. We've been out shopping and waited too long to eat."

"Is it all right if I bring them some crackers?" Doris asked. She had done the same thing with fussy children before, and it helped tide them over until their meal was brought out.

The mother smiled. "Oh, would you? If we can get them to stop crying, I can finally order something to eat."

Doris hurried off and returned with several crackers, which she handed to the children's mother. As soon as the girls were each given one, they stopped fussing and seemed content.

The mother offered Doris a grateful smile. "Thank you. I didn't want them bothering the other patrons."

"You're welcome." As Doris watched the little girls eat, she struggled with feelings of envy. *Why did God bless this woman with two babies when I have none?* She wished she could trade places with the twins' mother. *I need to stop feeling sorry for myself and learn to count my blessings,* she reminded herself. *I have a wonderful husband, five nephews, four nieces, two sisters who are also my best friends, and a father who loves me. There are many people who have no families at all. So with God's help, I will try to remember this and be grateful.*

Smiling, Doris gestured toward the woman's menu. "Are you ready to order now?"

$\sim$

Akron

Kristi scurried about the kitchen, setting the table and stopping to check the crockpot to see if the roast, potatoes, and carrots were done. The aroma coming from the beef caused her stomach to growl. She'd invited Joel to her place for supper this evening and wanted everything to be ready when he got there. She was eager to talk with him about the seminar she'd attended Saturday night.

When Kristi saw Joel on Sunday and gave him a copy of the seminar handouts, along with her notes, he'd promised to look them over once he was settled in for the evening. She was eager to find out what he thought.

Originally, Kristi planned to have Joel over for supper on Monday. But one of the other nurses at the nursing home called in sick, so Kristi worked in her place that evening. It wasn't fun to work two shifts, but others had done it for her when she'd gotten sick, so she felt the least she could do was return the favor. Kristi remembered her grandmother saying that when a person does you a favor, you should pass it on to someone else who has a need.

As she stood there looking at the table, Kristi heard thunder in the distance. "I hope we don't lose electricity." At least the meal she had prepared was already good and hot, so even if the power went out, they'd still be able to eat. "Maybe I better get a few candles out, too. A candlelight dinner might be a nice touch."

Kristi had begun filling the water glasses when the doorbell rang. *Good. Joel's here.* She lit the candles, and after blowing out the match, quickly checked her appearance in the hall mirror and opened the door.

Charm

Eustace had planned to go up in the tree house earlier, but there had been too many interruptions. First, the mail came, followed by paying several bills. Then his friend Henry dropped by and invited him to have lunch at Carpenter's Café, which was upstairs in Keim Lumber. Eustace always enjoyed eating there, so he couldn't say no. Since Henry had driven his tractor over and didn't have Peaches with him, they'd taken Eustace's horse and buggy into town. After their meal, they had stopped by the Shoe and Boot in Charm so Eustace could look for some boots. The ones he'd taped together weren't holding up well, so he figured it was time to get a new pair. By the time they'd come back, Eustace was tired, so as soon as Henry left, he'd laid down on the couch and taken a nap. When he awoke a few minutes ago, he looked out the window, saw the darkening sky, and realized it had started to rain.

He yawned, stretching his arms overhead. "I'm not about to let a little rain keep me from putting a couple of Effie's birdhouses on the railing of my tree house."

Eustace put on his new boots, grabbed his dilapidated straw hat, and headed outside. It was as good a time as any to break in the boots, which right now felt a little stiff. Hopefully, he'd get used to them soon.

The rain came down a bit harder, and clouds blocked out the sun. In the distance he saw a bright flash of lightning and heard the booming clap of thunder, but it was too far away to worry about.

Determined to complete his task, Eustace carried the first birdhouse up the permanently-fixed ladder to the tree house. After nailing it in position on the railing, he stopped and looked toward the west where the storm was slowly approaching. Being up this high, Eustace had a panoramic view, and what he saw made him a little nervous. He noticed a wall of rain like a huge white veil set against the blackened sky, but to him it still looked miles away. Hastily, he went down and got another birdhouse, then came back up. As he anchored the second one in place, the sky opened up in a torrential rain. The wind came in strong and blew Eustace's hat right off his head. Thunder boomed, while a bolt of lightning flashed across the sky.

When Eustace's hair stood straight up, he grabbed his tools. *I'd better get back in the house before lightning comes any closer.* Eustace had heard and read about how when lightning produced electrical charges in the atmosphere before a strike, it could lift a person's hair into the air, providing nature's last warning of a bolt coming out of the blue.

Quickly, he started for the ladder, but not soon enough. Another jolt of lightning came, this one hitting the tree and engulfing it in the brightest light Eustace had ever seen. Suddenly, it seemed as if everything had slowed down. Then came a sensation of weightlessness, followed by a deafening explosion. His hearing went silent, and as all grew quiet, the last thing Eustace saw was a vision of dear Effie's face.

The
BETRAYED
FIANCÉE

CHAPTER 1

Akron

Thunder and lightning streaked across the sky as Joel waited for Kristi to let him in. If not for the jacket he'd thought to put on before leaving home, he'd be drenched from this deluge of rain.

"Quick, come inside befre you get any wetter," Kristi said as she opened the door. "Let me get a towel so you can dry off."

Joel handed her his jacket and waited until she returned. "Thanks." He dried his face, blotted his hair, and ran the towel over the front of his legs. Before they walked into the living room, he kicked off his wet shoes.

"You look tired. Did you have a busy day?"

He reached up to rub the back of his neck and groaned. "Busy, but unproductive."

She tipped her auburn head to one side, looking at him with curious blue eyes. "What do you mean?"

"Let me get off my feet, and I'll tell you about it."

"No problem. Supper is ready, but it can wait a few minutes." Kristi gestured to the couch. "Let's sit so we can talk."

Joel took a couple of shuffled steps toward the couch but turned back to her when his stomach growled. "Are you sure? I don't want to spoil the meal you cooked."

She shook her head. "It's fine, Joel. The Crock-Pot's on low so the food will stay warm."

Joel grabbed the arm of the sofa and took a seat, reaching over his shoulders to place a throw pillow behind his head. When Kristi sat beside him, he took her hand, wrapping his fingers around hers. After a day like he'd had, it felt good to sit beside the woman he loved and relax for a bit.

"So tell me about your busy day," she prompted. "Why was it unproductive?"

Joel sighed as he closed his eyes and leaned against the pillow. Should he tell her what all had gone on today? What would be the point? It was his mess, not hers. "Never mind, Kristi. On second thought, I'd rather not to talk about my day right now. I'd like to enjoy the evening with you." He turned his head and gave her a gentle kiss. "Truthfully, I am kind of hungry, so why don't we eat?"

Hands dropping to her sides, she rose from the couch. "The table's been set, and it'll only take me a couple of minutes to bring out the food."

"Is there anything I can do to help?" Joel offered.

"No, stay where you are and relax. I'll call you when the food's on the table."

Joel didn't argue. He was beat and felt hollow. He'd bid on four different jobs today, with no guarantee he'd get any of them. He'd also finished up a small job, but the people asked him to bill them, saying they didn't have the money right now. He clenched his fists. *They should have told me they couldn't pay right away before I started the job. I was countin' on the money.* At least he'd finished working before the storms broke loose. One nasty front after another had gone through the state, but on the way here, the station on his car radio announced the storms would be ending soon.

Joel rubbed his finger across the top of the end table next to the couch, noticing there wasn't a speck of dust. Kristi was an immaculate housekeeper. Her condo was always clean and orderly. His fiancée was warm and caring, and when she looked deeply into his eyes, he could feel her love. To Joel, Kristi was perfect in every way and would be the ideal wife—if the day ever came they could be married. If things didn't shape up with his finances soon, they may never be able to set a wedding date. No matter how many times Joel tried to think positive, his financial situation always jumped in the way. The only thing right in his life was Kristi, but their relationship could end if she learned every truth about him.

Joel's eyes grew heavy while he waited for Kristi. He released a warm yawn and stretched out on the sofa. If she didn't call him to eat soon, he might fall asleep.

"Everything's ready now."

Joel's eyes snapped open. "Okay." He stood slowly and followed Kristi into the dining room, taking a seat beside her.

She clasped his hand tenderly and smiled. "Would you like to pray this time, Joel?"

"Uh. . ." His throat constricted as Kristi watched him intently. "Why don't you do it? I like hearing you pray."

Kristi's lips pressed tightly together. "You never pray, Joel. Is there a reason?"

Joel felt trapped—like a mouse getting caught in a trap with nowhere to run—as he struggled to get his breath. He moistened his lips. "I pray silently. It's the way I've always prayed." It was halfway true. Joel's family prayed silently, as most Amish did, but Joel hadn't lifted many prayers—silent or otherwise—since he left home.

I don't have time to waste on prayer, he thought. *Even if I did, what good has it done in the past?* Joel had talked to God plenty of times while he was growing up, but he'd mostly prayed because everyone else in his family expected him to. He remembered when his mother had gathered him and his siblings together and taught them the purpose of prayer. She used to say God answered and rewarded prayers offered in persistent faith—meaning prayer should be continued until something happened. But none of his prayers were answered, even when he was persistent.

He wasn't about to share his thoughts with Kristi however. Kristi's religion was important to her, like it had been to Joel's mother. Joel was sure Kristi would break things off with him if she knew where he stood spiritually. Oh, he would keep going to church with her on Sundays, but Joel didn't think he needed religion to get what he wanted in life.

"Okay, if you'd rather, I'll pray." Kristi bowed her head, and Joel did the same. He felt a twinge of guilt when she prayed for him, asking God to bless his life and thanking Him for this time they had together. *The love of my life prays for me; yet my life is only getting worse, it seems.*

When Kristi finished praying, she released Joel's hand and passed him the platter of meat. "It should be nice and tender, since it's been slow-cooking all day while I was at work. Even if the storm had knocked out the power, dinner would still have been good and hot."

"It's raining a little yet, but at least the worst of the storm has passed." Joel looked toward the window before pointing to the center of the table. "Are the candles because you thought the lights might go out?"

"Partly. I also like eating by candlelight. Don't you?"

"It is sort of relaxing," he agreed.

"To me, it's romantic." Kristi offered him a playful smile.

Joel noticed how Kristi's blue eyes sparkled as he cut a piece of beef and took a bite. "It's good, Kristi. My compliments to the chef."

She handed him the bowl of carrots and potatoes. "Why, thank you, sir. Now try some of these."

Joel spooned some onto his plate and passed it back to her. Kristi was a good cook, and he was glad she'd invited him for supper this evening.

"What did you think of the information I gave you on Sunday?" Kristi asked.

"What information?" Joel reached for his glass of water and took a drink.

"The brochures I got at the marriage seminar on Saturday." Kristi forked a piece of carrot. "Remember, you were going to look them over so we could talk about it tonight."

"Oh yeah." Joel stared at his plate. "Sorry, Kristi, but I was too tired Sunday evening, and Monday I worked late and fell into bed a few minutes after I got home."

"So you haven't looked at any of the information?"

"No."

Her shoulders drooped. "I was hoping we could talk about it now."

"We can. You can tell me whatever you learned."

Kristi blotted her lips with a napkin. "Oh, we learned a lot. Let's see. . . . Where do I begin?"

"Guess you can start at the beginning. What was one thing you learned?"

"The speaker pointed out how necessary it is for married couples to have good communication."

"Makes sense to me."

"He also stressed the importance of honesty and trust."

Joel nearly choked on the piece of potato he'd put in his mouth. He and Kristi weren't married yet, but he'd already been dishonest with her. First in not telling her about his family. Second, he'd bought a classic car and kept it hidden in his shop. And last, he'd taken money from their joint savings account without her knowledge. Joel felt like a heel, but if Kristi knew what he'd done, she'd probably break up with him. The best thing he could do was get the money back in the savings account as soon as possible.

His jaw tightened. *I could have taken care of the problem if my dad would've loaned me some money.*

"Joel, have you been listening to me?" Kristi nudged his arm.

"Uh, sorry. Guess I was zoning out. What was it you were saying?"

"I was telling you how the speaker explained about the importance of a couple spending quality time together."

"You mean like we're doing now?"

"Yes, but I'm not sure you're with me. You seem preoccupied tonight."

Joel blew out his breath. "I have a lot on my mind. But you're right. I should be paying attention to what you're saying. Go ahead, Kristi."

As they continued to eat, she shared with Joel more of what she'd learned at the marriage seminar. When they were done, Joel helped Kristi clear the table and do the dishes, thinking he might redeem himself.

When the dishes were done, they returned to the living room to visit and watch TV until they felt ready for dessert.

They had no more than gotten comfortable on the couch when Joel's cell phone rang. Pulling it from his pocket and looking at the caller ID, he realized it was his sister Elsie. Joel had no desire to be interrupted, and he certainly didn't want Kristi knowing who the call was from, so he let it go to voice mail.

Later, when Kristi went to the kitchen to get their dessert, Joel hurriedly accessed his voice mail, to listen to his sister's message.

"Joel, it's Elsie." Her voice sounded shaky. "There's no easy way to tell you this, but. . ." Elsie's silence made the hairs on the back of Joel's neck rise. "Dad is dead."

He's dead. No, that can't be. I must've misheard her message.

Joel shuddered when he heard a sharp intake of breath before his sister continued. "Dad was up in his tree house, and he. . ." Elsie's voice broke. "He got hit by lightning. Please call as soon as you can. We need to talk about the funeral."

Joel's arms went limp as he lowered the phone to the couch. Seconds seemed like hours while he slowly shook his head, trying to grasp his sister's words and let them sink in. He felt as if he'd been the one hit by a bolt of lightning. It didn't seem possible. Dad couldn't be dead. Joel's body felt numb. *What was Dad doing in a tree house?*

༄

Kristi returned to the living room with two pieces of apple pie but stopped suddenly when she saw Joel sitting still, a vacant look in his eyes. Her stomach quivered as she rushed over to him. "What's wrong, Joel?" She set the serving tray on the coffee table and took a seat beside him. "You look upset."

He gave no response.

"Joel, you're scaring me." She touched his arm. "What is it?"

"Huh?" Joel blinked, as though coming out of a daze.

"Are you upset about something?"

Joel squeezed his eyes shut then opened them again. "My dad's gone," he mumbled. "He—he passed away after being struck by lightning." He picked up his cell phone. "My sister left a message."

Kristi covered her mouth to stifle a gasp. "Oh, Joel, I am so sorry."

"I'll have to go to the funeral."

"Of course. I'll go with you."

Joel shook his head. "No, you don't need to go. You didn't even know my dad, and—"

"It's because you never wanted me to. I've asked many times to meet your family, but you've always said no."

Joel shrugged his shoulders. "I didn't see any reason for you to meet them. Like I told you before, they're different. I don't think you'd be comfortable around them."

Before Kristi could respond, Joel stood. "I have to go now. I'm tired, and I need to call my sister back and let her know I'll be there for Dad's funeral. In fact, I should go the day before, for the viewing."

"Okay, but I'm going with you to the funeral, Joel."

He shook his head more vigorously. "I told you, it's not necessary."

She stood, looking up at him with determination. "It is to me. If I'm going to become your wife someday, then it's time for me to meet your family and pay my respects."

He continued to shake his head.

"I don't understand why you're pushing me away and why you would object to me going to your father's funeral. Are you ashamed of me?" She crossed her arms.

"No, of course not."

"Maybe we shouldn't get married, if you don't want your family to meet me."

Joel pulled her into his arms. "I'm sorry, Kristi. If it means that much, you can go." He stroked the top of her head.

Joel's hugs were always so affectionate. Although they'd had their share of disagreements, every time he held her in his arms, Kristi knew he cared.

∾

Millersburg

When Elsie left the phone shack after making several calls, her legs trembled so badly she could hardly walk. While she hadn't spoken with anyone in their district directly, she'd left messages about Dad's untimely death. That had been difficult enough. She could hardly believe he was gone.

After walking through puddles she barely noticed, then trudging slowly up the stairs to her porch, Elsie entered the house and closed the door. Leaning against it for support, she heard the rain continuing to fall, even though the worst of the storm had finally passed.

"Did you call everyone on the list?" her husband

asked when she joined him in the living room.

Elsie nodded slowly as she took a seat beside him on the couch.

"How about Joel? Did you get ahold of him?"

"He didn't answer his phone, but I left a message." Elsie leaned her head on John's shoulder for support. She felt drained and woeful as she slouched on the sofa. "Oh John, I can't believe Dad is gone. I can only imagine how horrible it was when Arlene and Larry stopped by his place earlier this evening and found Dad's body." She choked on the sob rising in her throat.

John pulled Elsie into his arms, gently rubbing her back. "I can't understand what he was doing up in his tree house during such a storm."

"Maybe it wasn't storming when he climbed up. It rained awhile before the *dunner* and *wedderleech* came upon us."

"Could be. I don't think your *daed* would have taken any chances if he'd known he was in danger of being struck by lightning."

Elsie sniffed. "I need to go upstairs and tell the *kinner*, but it won't be easy. All of our children loved their *grossdaadi* so much."

"I know," John agreed. "It won't be easy, but we can take comfort with the assurance of knowing he's at peace and in heaven with your *mamm*." He stood and held out his hand. "If you'd like, I'll go up with you."

Elsie nodded. Some folks who didn't know the Lord personally did not have such hope. She couldn't imagine how horrible it must be. If not for her faith and trust in God, she wouldn't be able to deal with any of life's tragedies.

CHAPTER 2

L
isten, Kristi. There's something I need to tell you." Joel hesitated as they headed south on I-77 early Friday morning.

"What is it?" Kristi wondered why Joel was being so evasive. He hadn't told her exactly what town his dad lived in, only that he lived south of Akron.

"Umm... It's about my family. Remember when I told you they were different?"

"I remember, but you never explained in what way they are different from me."

"The thing is..." Joel glanced over at her and then quickly looked back to the road. "They're Amish."

Kristi's eyes opened wide. "Your family is Amish?"

"Yes."

"So what you're saying is all this time I've been dating an Amish man without being aware of it?" She blinked rapidly as a rush of adrenaline tingled through her body.

"I used to be Amish, but not anymore." Joel gripped the steering wheel so tightly his knuckles turned white. "I left the Amish faith seven years ago."

"So you speak Pennsylvania Dutch and everything?"

"Jah. It means yes."

Kristi's thoughts were all over the place, wondering why Joel had kept this from her and what made him leave the Amish faith. She glanced at him, then looked at the dashboard, unable to form a response.

"Kristi, did you hear me?" Joel's voice sounded strained.

"Yes, I heard." Kristi swallowed hard, struggling not to cry. Apparently, this man she'd come to care for so deeply wasn't the person she knew. No wonder Joel hadn't wanted her to meet his family and kept saying they were different. Did he think she was so shallow she couldn't have accepted his heritage?

"Don't you have anything to say?" Joel placed his hand over Kristi's and tenderly held her fingers.

Feeling a painful tightness in her throat, Kristi pulled away from his grasp, bringing her arms close to her chest. "Joel, would you please pull over?"

Up ahead, he found a safe place to pull off the road and then turned off the ignition.

She rubbed her temples, trying to comprehend his startling confession. "Look at me, Joel." Kristi waited until she had his full attention. "I can't believe you would lie about something so important."

"I—I didn't lie. I just didn't volunteer the information."

"Why was it necessary to keep this from me?" Her forehead wrinkled.

He shrugged, looking toward the highway. "I—I don't know. Guess I assumed you might be uncomfortable around my family and wouldn't understand why I gave up the Amish way of life."

Kristi reached out and touched his chin, turning him to face her. "Why did you?"

Joel raked shaky fingers through the side of his hair and groaned. "I wanted something more than the Plain life could offer."

"Like what?"

He tapped the steering wheel a couple of times. "A car, for one thing. I had one when I went through my *rumschpringe*, and it was hard to give it up."

"Rumschpringe? What's that?"

"It means 'running around.' It's a time when young people who have grown up in an Amish home have the chance to explore the world outside their faith." Joel cleared his throat. "Then they have the right to choose between joining the Amish church or going English."

"So you went English."

He nodded. "But not till after I'd joined the Amish church, which, of course, made it worse when I left."

Kristi massaged the bridge of her nose and sighed. After her shopping trip to Holmes County with her mother, she'd done a little reading about the Amish culture and remembered one article stating how hard it was on a family when one of them left the faith. No wonder Joel prayed silently and not out loud. This also explained why he was able to find Bible passages easily whenever they went to church and followed the pastor's message. *I should have questioned him more about it.*

"Did you ever plan to tell me your family is Amish, or did you only blurt it out now because we're on our way to your father's funeral?" Kristi tried not to let her irritation show, but this was unnerving.

Joel remained silent for several seconds. "I—I would have told you eventually, but I was worried about how you'd respond."

"I would have dealt with it better if you'd told me right away." Kristi's muscles tightened.

"I'm sorry, Kristi. I didn't think you'd understand, and I was wrong to assume how you'd react."

"All I know is you weren't honest with me,

and that bothers me a lot."

His ears reddened. "Look, can we talk about this later? It's gonna take all my strength to get through the funeral today."

Kristi felt bad about being pushy, but she wanted to know everything Joel kept hidden from her. *I have to be considerate of his feelings right now. If one of my parents passed away unexpectedly, I'd want him to do the same.*

She sighed, slipping down a bit in her seat. *But it's difficult to be supportive when he's kept his family hidden from me for so long—especially since I've told him everything about my family, and even shared some things from my childhood. I wish I'd have met Joel's father and known what kind of person he was.*

Kristi pushed herself back up with her elbows to get repositioned in her seat. In sympathy, she placed her hand on Joel's arm. "Today will be difficult, but God will help you endure the pain."

Joel made no comment as he started the car and pulled back onto the road.

"Is your mother still alive?" Kristi spoke quietly, hoping Joel wouldn't be upset with all her questions.

He shook his head. "She had a heart attack and died two years ago."

"I'm sorry, Joel." Kristi couldn't imagine losing both of her parents, especially in such a short span of time. "You had said it was your sister who called with the news of your father's death. Do you have other siblings?"

"I have three sisters—Elsie, Arlene, and Doris. They're all older than me." Joel changed lanes to pass a slow-moving vehicle.

"Where do they live?"

"Arlene and her family live in Farmerstown. Doris lives in Berlin with her husband, Brian. Elsie, the oldest, lives in Millersburg. Oh, and my dad lived in Charm." Joel rubbed the back of his neck. "That's where I went for the viewing yesterday. The funeral will be held there today as well."

"I see." Kristi had wanted to attend the viewing with Joel, but didn't want to ask for two days off in a row. They were shorthanded at the nursing home right now, and one of the other nurses who normally worked Saturdays had traded with Kristi so she could attend the funeral.

"In case you don't know, Amish church services, weddings, and funerals are held in church members' homes or in one of their outside buildings. Sometimes they rent a large tent if there isn't room to accommodate everyone indoors. So no church or funeral home is used at any Amish funeral," Joel explained.

Kristi gripped her armrest as he increased the speed. Now he'd begun passing everyone on the highway, probably to make sure they got to the funeral on time. Trying to keep her mind off how fast Joel was driving, Kristi thought more about the Amish. She had read something concerning their funerals, as well, but experiencing an Amish funeral service firsthand would enlighten her further. But she couldn't help wondering if Joel's sisters knew about her and how they would accept an outsider.

❧

Charm

The only thing in their favor today was the weather. Although the sky was gray, at least it wasn't raining. As they drew closer to his father's house, Joel's palms became sweaty, and his heart pounded. In addition to concern over how Kristi would respond to his family, he worried that she might say or do the wrong thing at any moment simply because she was unfamiliar with Amish ways.

On second thought, it might be me who says or does the wrong thing. Joel's jaw tightened. It seemed to be the norm whenever he visited his family.

He glanced to his right and observed Kristi, noticing her head turned toward the side window, with both hands resting on her lap. Was she looking at the scenery or thinking about all the things he'd told her so far?

I shouldn't have waited so long to admit I used to be Amish, he berated himself. *It didn't do a thing to strengthen our relationship. If anything, it probably made it worse.*

Sweat beaded on Joel's forehead as he continued to mull things over. *If she knew about my other deceptions, she'd probably never talk to me again. Sure wish she hadn't gotten so quiet all of a sudden.*

Releasing one sweaty hand from the steering wheel, he rubbed it dry on his pants. Joel tried to relax, but as they approached his father's driveway, he was hit with a wave of nausea. It was hard to believe Dad was actually gone, but all the buggies parked in the field gave truth to the fact of how many people had come here today to pay their last respects and uphold Joel's family. It was the Amish way.

Joel pulled his car up beside Dad's barn and turned off the engine. Reaching across the seat, he took Kristi's hand. "Are you sure you're ready for this?"

Squeezing his fingers, she nodded.

❦

Doris peered out the living room window, watching as her brother got out of his car. He strode around to the other side and opened the door for another passenger. Then the two started walking toward the house. "There's a young woman with Joel. I wonder who she is." Doris turned to her sister Arlene who stood beside her, holding baby Samuel.

Arlene stepped closer to the window. "I have no idea, but her auburn hair is sure pretty. When Joel was here yesterday, he didn't say anything about bringing anyone to the funeral with him."

"Maybe she's his girlfriend. Look, he has his arm around her waist."

"Or maybe she's his fraa. Could Joel have gotten married without telling any of us?"

Arlene shrugged her slender shoulders. "I wouldn't put anything past our brother."

"Me neither." Doris sniffed and dabbed at her tears. "Whoever the woman is, I'm afraid she's going to see us with red-rimmed, swollen eyes. These past three days it's been hard for me not to cry every time I think of Dad."

"Same here. It's so difficult to accept his death."

Their sister, Elsie, joined them at the window. "I see our bruder made it. Who's the young woman walking up the stairs with him? Do either of you recognize her?"

Arlene shook her head.

Doris turned her hands palm up. "I don't know. Let's open the door and find out."

CHAPTER 3

As Kristi stood beside Joel at his father's grave-side service, she observed those around them. Everyone wore somber expressions, and the four girls, whom she'd learned were Elsie and Arlene's daughters, wept openly. Kristi had a difficult time, herself, as she swallowed around the lump in her throat. She thought about how Joel and his family must feel right now. Since she hadn't met any of them until today, Kristi could only try to put herself in their shoes.

She'd always been emotional when it came to these types of situations. Even when it was a joyous occasion, she could cry at the drop of a hat. When-ever Kristi heard "Taps" or a sentimental song on the radio, her eyes would well up with tears. As soon as she heard the "Wedding March" in a marriage scene in a movie, her tears flowed. But right now, Kristi wanted to be strong for Joel.

Taking a deep breath, she fought for control and reached for Joel's hand—not only to give herself comfort, but to offer him reassurance as well. She glanced at him, unable to read his stoic expression. Throughout the funeral service held in his father's home, Joel hadn't shed a single tear. Nor had he cried when the family filed up to the coffin to view the deceased's body. Even on the night Joel learned of his father's death, he had shown little emotion—at least not in Kristi's presence. Perhaps he had done his crying privately or yesterday at the viewing. She hoped it was the case, because holding one's feelings in was not a good thing.

While Kristi never had the opportunity to meet Eustace Byler, her heart went out to his family as they huddled together. Joel had been right when he'd told her what to expect today. This was not the typical funeral she'd attended in the past.

A slight wind blew, scattering golden leaves across the cemetery and filling the air with a damp, musty aroma. Dismal gray clouds covered the sky, but at least it wasn't raining. In the distance, Kristi noticed a tree giving off hints of an autumn blush. It stood vivid against the drab, colorless sky.

Turning her head to the left, Kristi noticed a young woman with golden-brown hair glance in her direction, then look quickly away. Was she part of Joel's family—someone she hadn't met? Or perhaps she was a member of Joel's father's church. The woman appeared to be around Joel's age. She was pretty, even though her blue eyes were puffy from crying. It appeared the young woman had come alone, for she stood off to one side by herself.

Since Joel and Kristi were the only people dressed in English clothes, others were probably curious about them. Of course, many of them knew Joel personally. But since he'd left the Amish faith so many years ago, some might not realize who he was.

Before long, the four pallbearers, each bearing a shovel, began taking dirt from the pile near the grave and covering up the coffin. While the grave was being filled in, a men's group sang a hymn. Without the aid of any instruments, their voices filled the air with the sobering music. Once again, Kristi had to blink rapidly in an attempt to keep her eyes dry. At the conclusion of the graveside service, the bishop asked the people to pray the Lord's Prayer silently.

"I'm expected to go back to the house now for a meal and to visit awhile," Joel whispered to Kristi. "Are you okay with it?"

She gave an affirmative nod. In addition to doing the right thing, she was eager to become more familiar with Joel's family. Those Kristi had been introduced to so far seemed kind. How could Joel keep from mentioning such a wonderful family to her all this time?

⚬⚭⚬

After the simple funeral dinner, many people lingered. While Joel was outside visiting, Kristi went into the house to talk to his sisters.

"What a beautiful piece. Did someone in your family make it?" Kristi asked Doris, when she noticed a lovely blue-and-pink quilted wall hanging with a star pattern draped across the back of the couch.

Doris's eyes mirrored an inner glow as she trailed her fingers over the material. "My mother made it. She was always making full-sized quilts, wall hangings, table runners, and even potholders. Mama gave quilts to each of her daughters, as well as to many of her friends in the area."

"I'm impressed. She did beautiful work."

"I agree. My sister Elsie's hobby is needlepoint." Doris motioned to the wall across the room. "See the wall hanging there with the two hummingbirds and flowers? She made it for Mama as a Christmas gift one year."

"Your sister does nice work." Kristi moved closer to take a better look. "I'm sure it takes a lot of patience to finish such a project."

"Actually, Elsie says she finds it quite relaxing to sit and needlepoint. She's spent many hours making special items for family members and friends." Doris smiled. "We all enjoy doing things meaningful with our hands during the long hours of winter." She moved over to the couch and lifted the quilted wall hanging into her arms. "I'm surprised Dad kept all the quilts she didn't give away, but then he had a hard time parting with anything. Some have called him a hoarder, and I guess it's true."

Kristi reached out to touch the wall hanging, gently tracing her fingers on the stitches. "It was thoughtful of your mother to make something so lovely, especially for her children." She sighed. "Someday, after Joel and I are married, I hope to own a quilt. Even a small one like this would be nice."

"Are you and my brother engaged?" Doris questioned.

Kristi nodded. "Well, not officially. I don't have a ring yet, but he did propose, and my answer was yes."

"Then you'll soon be part of our family." Doris handed Kristi the quilt. "Since you will become Joel's wife, I'd like you to have one of Mama's wall hangings. I'm sure my sisters would agree."

"I saw some Amish-made quilts in a shop in Berlin, and they were expensive. How much would you charge?" Simply holding the quilted piece gave Kristi a warm feeling.

"Oh my, not a penny. It's a gift from our family." Doris clasped Kristi's arm. "You can either take this or choose one from some others in a box under my folks' bed."

"I'd like this one." Kristi fingered the edge of

the quilt. She couldn't believe she'd been presented with such a special gift. "I'll take good care of it. Thank you so much." She laid it down and gave Doris a hug.

"You're more than welcome. Before you go home, I'll put it in a plastic bag so it doesn't get dirty." Doris placed her hands on the back of the couch. "Now I have a favor to ask."

"Anything. Anything at all."

"I was wondering, if you have any influence over Joel, could you ask him to come visit more often?"

"Doesn't he do it now?"

"He rarely comes around, and when he does. . ." Doris's voice trailed off.

"Joel works long hours because of his business. There are times when we've had plans to do something together, and he ends up working instead." Kristi didn't know why she felt the need to defend Joel. Working long hours was hardly an excuse for neglecting his family. "I'm sorry. I'll have a talk with Joel about coming to visit more often." Kristi took out a pen and tablet from her purse. Then she wrote down her phone number and handed it to Doris. "If there's ever a time you can't reach Joel, please give me a call."

"I appreciate it. I'll give you my number, too." After Doris wrote her phone number down for Kristi, she gestured to the kitchen. "Why don't we go find Elsie and Arlene? I'd like them to get to know you better, too."

⚮

As Joel wandered around the yard, trying to avoid certain people, he glanced toward the back of Dad's property. The tree house had been destroyed, but the heavily damaged section of the tree showed Joel where it had been. All that was left of the tree house were a few pieces of burned wood in a heap at the bottom of the tree. Even the steps, still nailed to the trunk, had been charred and blackened by the force of the lightning.

Joel stopped and stared at the giant maple. From the blown-away bark at the top of the tree, the lightning had made a visible path all the way down its trunk. Some long pieces of splintered maple lay scattered on the ground a few feet from the tree. Other fragments of wood clung to the trunk, curled back like a banana peel.

Stubborn man. Joel grunted. *Can't figure out why he'd want to build a tree house. Going up there with a storm approaching was a dumb idea.*

He leaned against a fence post, reflecting on his childhood. He and Doris had spent many hours playing hide-and-seek in Dad's barn. They'd also climbed trees, taken turns on the swing, and chased after the cats. *Wish Dad would have built a tree house when I was a boy. I could have had a lot of fun playing in it and maybe even camped out during the hot summer months.*

Joel glanced to the top of the hill that overlooked his parents' farm. It wasn't as exciting as a tree house, but at least he'd had a special place up there. It was too late for any of that though. Joel's childhood was over, and Dad was gone.

Joel watched as his aunt Verna visited on the porch with Arlene's two girls, Martha and Lillian. She was showing them how to master some techniques with a yo-yo. It was typical of Aunt Verna.

She'd always had a way with children, even though she'd never had any of her own. Her yearning for children may have drawn her to them. Joel remembered one time when Aunt Verna came to his tenth birthday party and brought him a big jar of marbles. Joel had never expressed a desire to have a marble collection, but watching Aunt Verna get down on her knees to compete with him in a game of marbles got his attention. Surprisingly enough, she was good at it. Joel wondered if Aunt Verna and Dad had played with those same marbles when they were children. Although Joel's aunt wasn't a hoarder, like Dad, she did enjoy a few collections. Joel had to admit he liked to hang on to some things, himself. He'd even kept those marbles from long ago and had packed them away in one of his closets.

Glancing at his watch, Joel started for the house to find Kristi. He figured she was visiting with his sisters and could only imagine what they might be talking about.

Wouldn't be surprised if I'm the topic of their conversation. Sure hope no one has said anything negative about me.

Joel had only made it halfway there when he spotted his ex-girlfriend, Anna Detweiler, heading in his direction. His heart raced as she came closer. *Oh, great. I wonder what she wants. If Kristi sees me talking to her, how will I explain? Anna is the last person I want to speak to right now.*

CHAPTER 4

Joel was almost to the porch when Anna stepped up to him. "Hello, Joel."

He paused and turned to look at her, sweat trailing down his forehead. "Oh hey, Anna."

"I—I wanted to say I'm sorry for your loss." Anna's smile quivered. "I also wanted to let you know I'll be praying for your family."

Joel noticed Anna was fidgeting with her hands and realized that the situation was as awkward for her as it was him, but he couldn't be rude. "Thanks, Anna. I appreciate your concern." He shuffled his feet a few times. It felt strange speaking to her after all these years. Anna had matured and was as pretty as ever. With golden-brown hair peeking out from her head covering and clear blue eyes, she was stunning. He noticed the pill-sized mole on her neck. "Uh, so how are you these days?" he stammered.

With her gaze fixed on him, Anna answered, "I'm doing all right. How about you?"

Joel wasn't about to admit his life was a train wreck, so he forced a smile and lifted his shoulders in a brief shrug. "I'm doin' great. I have my own business, and it keeps me plenty busy. What about you? Are you still teaching at the school in Farmerstown?"

She nodded. "Unless I get married someday, I'll probably keep on teaching."

"I'll bet my nieces and nephews enjoy having you as their teacher."

"I enjoy them, too." Anna's face turned pink. "Did you hear that my folks moved to Indiana?"

He shook his head. "Why'd they move?"

"They wanted to be close to my sister Nancy. She recently had a baby."

"I'm surprised you didn't go with them."

Her cheek color deepened. "I like my job and the area here."

"Oh, I see." Joel shoved his hands into his jacket pockets. He was tempted to ask if Anna had a suitor but thought better of it. It wasn't his business, and she might think he had regrets about breaking up with her.

"Who's the auburn-haired woman who came with you today? Is she your wife?"

Anna's question caused Joel to stumble back a step. "What? Uh, no, but Kristi and I are planning to be married. We haven't picked a date yet."

Anna lowered her gaze. "Well, she's beautiful."

"Yes. Yes, she is. However, Kristi's beauty is more than skin-deep." Joel slid his hands out of his pockets and fiddled with his shirt collar. "She's the most amazing woman I've ever met."

Anna lifted her gaze to meet his again and blinked several times. "You once told me the same thing."

A surge of heat shot up the back of Joel's neck and spread quickly to his face. His body felt like it was encased in concrete. Anna was right of course. When they had been courting, he'd often told her how special she was. Back then, she was everything to him. But things changed once Joel made the decision to leave the Amish faith.

Unsure of how to respond to Anna's statement

or whether he should say anything at all, Joel awkwardly touched the side of her elbow. "It's been nice seeing you again, but I'd better go check on Kristi." Without waiting for Anna's response, he hurried up the stairs onto the porch. He was about to open the door when a hand rested on his shoulder. He twisted his head to see who had touched him.

"Well, for goodness' sake. If it isn't my favorite nephew." Aunt Verna held out her arms and gave him a hug.

He patted her back tenderly. "Nice to see you, too." As Joel hugged his aunt, he couldn't help noticing how abruptly Anna turned and headed toward the backyard.

"I missed seeing you the last time I was here, but Elsie explained you were busy with work and couldn't come for a visit." Aunt Verna motioned for them to take a seat in two empty chairs on the porch.

When Joel sat down to face her, he noticed her sorrowful expression. He felt bad seeing his aunt like this, but he couldn't tell her that he'd missed seeing her during her last visit because his dad wouldn't appreciate his presence. After the last encounter they'd had, Joel was sure his dad never wanted to see him again. *I needed money from Dad.* Joel pinned his arms against his stomach. *Sure wish things had played out differently. Maybe I shouldn't have gotten so irritated with him. But he was the one who got mad first, and for no good reason.*

"I'm sorry I couldn't be here then, but it's good to see you now, Aunt Verna." He reached over and patted her hand.

"I know. I only wish it could be under more

pleasant circumstances." She sniffed and dabbed at the tears on her wrinkled cheeks. "I'm gonna miss your daed so much. He was the best bruder. We always had such fun together."

Joel listened while his aunt reminisced about some of the things she and Dad had done while growing up. Then she told him about her last visit and how excited Dad had been when he was building the tree house. "He did it in memory of your mamm." Tears trickled down her cheeks as she spoke. "Eustace told me Effie had always wanted a tree house."

"Really? I didn't realize that." He raised his eyebrows. "I don't recall it ever being mentioned when I was a boy."

Aunt Verna shook her head. "I don't think Effie brought it up till you were grown and had left the Amish faith."

"Oh, I see. After all these years, guess there's a lot I don't know." Joel glanced at the house, wondering why Kristi hadn't come out. She'd been in there quite awhile.

⁓

Kristi stood at the kitchen window, watching Joel visit with an elderly woman. But that wasn't what had initially drawn her attention to the window. She'd seen him talking to the young Amish woman she'd noticed during the graveside service. Kristi wondered, yet again, about the woman and was tempted to ask one of Joel's sisters who she was, but she didn't want to appear nosey. Kristi felt vulnerable being around so many people she didn't know and who spoke a different language when they conversed with one another. Thankfully, Joel's sisters were warm and friendly and had made her feel welcome. She felt drawn to their quiet demeanor and plain lifestyle. Kristi wondered what it would be like to live a simpler life without the distractions of TV, computers, and cell phones. Not that those things were bad. But most people seemed to focus on electronic gadgets instead of concentrating on developing good relationships with others. Kristi wasn't sure she could give up all her modern conveniences, but she longed for an unpretentious way of life.

"We believe in putting God first, and our family second," Doris had told Kristi a few minutes ago, when she'd commented on the caring attitude she'd sensed in the people who had come to the funeral.

Earlier, Kristi had noticed an older man who had his dog with him. When she and Joel ended up sitting on the same bench in the yard after their meal, he'd introduced himself as Eustace's good friend Henry. He was a real gentleman and even introduced his dog. It seemed strange that someone would bring a dog to this somber occasion, but Henry had kept Peaches in her cage until they'd eaten. Kristi thought the dog was cute, and the cocker spaniel seemed to like her. While Kristi had listened to Henry talk, Peaches had curled up beside her feet. Kristi could tell Henry hurt from losing his best friend, and he'd recalled nothing but good things about Eustace. Henry even had Kristi laughing at times, which felt good on this sobering day. No wonder he'd been Eustace's good friend.

After talking with Henry, and hearing Arlene

mention how many people helped set things up for the service, as well as the meal, was it any wonder these people were so closely knit? Helping out during times of need seemed to be a normal occurrence among the Amish. *We English could learn a lesson from them* Kristi thought.

A light tap on her arm caused Kristi to turn away from the window. She'd been so caught up in her thoughts she hadn't realized Elsie stood beside her.

"You look tired." Elsie slipped her arm around Kristi's waist.

Kristi nodded, stifling a yawn. "I am a bit. It's been a long day. Joel and I got up early so we could be here on time."

"Would you like to lie down in the guest room awhile?" Arlene offered.

"No. Thank you though. Joel will probably want to go soon anyway."

"How about another cup of coffee or a piece of zucchini bread?" Doris motioned to the desserts sitting out on the table. "Feel free to help yourself to anything you like. It looks like there will be lots of leftover chocolate-chip cookies. I'll get some for you to take home so you and Joel can share." Doris opened the container on the counter.

Kristi watched her put a paper plate into the bag before placing the treats inside. She'd already sampled one of the soft, chewy cookies and found them to be quite tasty. She was on the verge of pouring a cup of coffee when Joel stepped into the room. "Kristi and I should go, but first I need to ask you a question, Elsie."

"What is it, Joel?" She looked at him curiously.

"Where's Dad's will? We need to find out how much he left us."

Kristi couldn't believe Joel would bring up this topic on the day of his father's funeral when the pain of losing him was so raw. She felt embarrassed. The last thing Joel should be concerned with right now was his father's will. And why had he been avoiding his family? What was wrong with him, anyway?

"Listen, Joel." Elsie's chin quivered as she looked at him with watery eyes. "This is not the time to be discussing Dad's will. We can talk about it in a week or so, once things have settled down for all of us."

"That's right," Arlene agreed.

Joel's eyes narrowed into tiny slits. "We don't have to discuss the will right now. I just want to know where it is."

"We don't want to discuss this today." Doris spoke up.

"Well, I do!" Joel shouted.

"I couldn't help overhearing you talking from the other room, and there's no need for knowing right now," Elsie's husband, John, intervened as he entered the kitchen.

Kristi held her breath, watching Joel's ears turn pink and waiting to hear his response.

Joel strode across the room until he was mere inches from John. The men were about the same height, so they were eye to eye and practically nose to nose. Kristi feared Joel might be about to punch Elsie's husband. "Listen to me, John, this is between me and my sisters, so I'd appreciate it if you'd just stay out of it and mind your own business."

John's face colored, too, and his brown eyes narrowed through his glasses. "Whatever involves my fraa is my business, plain and simple. Furthermore, if you were truly interested in a relationship with your family, you'd come around more often, and without always asking for money. It seems now you are concerned about money again, or you wouldn't be worried about Eustace's will."

"I'm not worried. I'd just like to know—"

John held up his hand. "We don't want any trouble here today. Our family is under enough sorrow and strain."

The room got deathly quiet. Kristi was sure if a feather floated from the sky, she would hear it drop. These last few minutes, watching her fiancé's expression and listening to the anger in his voice, gave a pretty clear picture of why he hadn't previously told her about his Amish family. He obviously did not get along with them, and for good reason. From what she'd heard here in this kitchen, the man she loved and hoped to marry cared more about money than he did his own family. Didn't Joel feel remorse that his father had been killed less than a week ago? Wasn't he grieving like his siblings were? She clenched her teeth. *Maybe I don't know Joel as well as I thought.*

Joel whirled around, his dark brown eyes blazing as he looked at Kristi. "You'd better gather up your things. We're leaving!" He turned and pointed his finger at Elsie. "I'll call you in a few days to talk about Dad's will."

CHAPTER 5

The first thirty minutes on the road, Joel remained quiet. Kristi did, too. She needed time to process everything—especially the scene when Joel had asked about his father's will. *More like demanded,* she thought, glancing at Joel and noting his smooth, expressionless features. Kristi still couldn't believe the scene she had witnessed. Everyone in the room had looked like codfish, the way their jaws dropped open. *How could Joel be so insensitive? Or had he spoken in frustration from grief over losing his father? If so, how can I help Joel or support him when he needs it? He seems to keep things bottled up most of the time.*

Earlier, Kristi had wondered how she would be accepted by Joel's family. She'd hoped they would all like her and had felt comfortable with his sisters, but things had been awkward after Joel's confrontation with his brother-in-law.

Unable to bear the silence any longer, Kristi reached across the seat and touched Joel's arm. "Mind if I ask you a question?"

"Sure, ask me anything you want." His gaze remained fixed on the road.

"Who was the Amish woman you were talking to in the yard before you came in the house to get me?"

"Which Amish woman? I talked to a lot of people today."

"The younger one with golden-brown hair. You talked to her for a while, before you stepped onto the porch and began a conversation with an older woman."

"The older woman is my aunt Verna. She's Dad's only sibling."

Kristi sighed as she nudged Joel's arm. "Okay, but she's not the woman I was asking about, Joel. It's the younger one."

"Uh. . . Her name is Anna Detweiler."

"Is she a relative?"

"No, she's not."

"Then a friend, perhaps?"

"Yeah, I guess." A muscle on the side of Joel's neck quivered.

"Is there something you're not telling me? Is Anna more than a friend?"

He turned his head and frowned. "What's with the twenty questions?"

"I haven't asked you twenty questions. I simply want to know about Anna Detweiler."

"She was my girlfriend. We were engaged to be married." Joel glanced out his side window, then back to the road again, avoiding her stare. "Satisfied?"

Kristi flinched, as if he'd thrown a glass of cold water in her face. She wasn't about to let this matter drop. "No, I am not satisfied, and I don't appreciate the tone of voice you're using."

He let go of the steering wheel and clasped her hand. "Sorry, Kristi. I'm not myself today."

Although it was a considerate gesture, his touch felt unsympathetic. Usually, Kristi would wrap her fingers around Joel's, but her hand rested lifeless in his grasp. "I can't argue with you there. I'm not even sure who the real Joel is anymore."

"Can't you understand, Kristi? I'm stressed out.

I've got a lot on my plate, trying to run a business. Now with my dad dying and my sisters refusing to talk about his will, I'm very upset."

"I do understand, but as your brother-in-law mentioned, today was not the best time to discuss the will."

Joel let go of Kristi's hand. "Didn't you hear what I told Elsie before we left? I ended the matter by telling her I'd call her in a few days to talk about it."

"Yes, I heard, but what I'm wondering is why it's so important to you. Are you expecting a big inheritance?"

Joel bobbed his head. "My dad was a millionaire, Kristi. There are oil wells on the back of his property."

"Really? Guess I didn't notice."

"That's because you never saw what's out back. I'm sure he has more money in the bank than most Amish people see in a lifetime."

She tugged on the end of her jacket while shaking her head. "Money isn't everything, Joel."

"It is to me."

Kristi rubbed her forehead to ward off the headache she felt coming on. Were Joel's business struggles making him desperate for money? Even if they were, he needed to take time to grieve the loss of his father, not worry about the will. She'd heard her pastor say on more than one occasion how sad it was when someone died and the family fought over who would get what. It was not the Christian thing to do and did nothing to cement a family's relationship. People needed to bind together during difficult times, not worry about their selfish ambitions.

"Let's talk about something else, shall we?" Joel maneuvered his car into the right-hand lane. "I don't want to discuss this the whole way home."

Figuring it would be best to comply, Kristi pointed to the plastic bags by her feet. "Before I tell you what's in the bigger bag, Arlene gave us some chocolate-chip cookies in the smaller bag."

"That's nice. I'm sure they'll be good."

"And best of all. . ." Kristi pointed to the larger bag. "Doris gave me one of your mother's beautiful quilted wall hangings."

"Did she?"

Kristi opened the bag and pulled out one edge of the quilt so he could see the pattern and pretty colors. She didn't want to risk getting it dirty if it touched the floor. "Yes. When I admired this and she found out I was your fiancée—"

"You told her?" Joel's mouth twitched as he glanced her way.

"I figured she already knew." Kristi's spine stiffened. "Why didn't you tell your family about me, Joel?" She folded the edge of the wall hanging so it was safely tucked inside the bag.

"I would have—eventually." He looked back at the road.

"When? Would you have waited till we were married? After we had kids?" Her voice choked with tears, Kristi tugged at her jacket collar. "Would you have ever told them?"

His shoulders slumped. "Of course I was gonna tell them. I was simply waiting for the right time."

"Why did there have to be a right time?" Kristi was beyond frustrated. "Your sisters were so kind and welcoming. I would have liked to have become acquainted with them from the time we started dating." Her tone softened.

"Sorry, I thought. . ." He lifted one hand. "Oh, what does it matter? I can't change the past. We need to focus on our future."

Do we have a future? Kristi wondered, but she didn't voice her question. Now wasn't the time for them to get into a heated debate about this—especially since she wasn't composed enough to reason with him.

Kristi observed Joel as he kept driving. She couldn't begin to imagine what was going through his head. Yes, she was upset that he'd kept his heritage from her, but he had just lost his father. Kristi poked her tongue on the inside of her cheek. Was it fair to be irritated with him when he had so much on his shoulders right now? Joel needed a few days to work through the initial shock and grief over losing his father.

❧

Charm

"I can't believe the nerve of our bruder." Arlene looked at Elsie and shook her head. "His insensitivity must have been embarrassing for Kristi. She seems like a sweet woman. I can only imagine what she thinks of our family."

"Hopefully Kristi only thinks good thoughts. When she brought up the fact that she and Joel were planning to get married, I gave her one of Mama's quilted wall hangings. It's the one that was on the back of the couch." Doris rested her hands on the back of a chair. "Kristi was admiring it, and she seemed quite happy when I gave it to her."

"I'm glad you did. She got along well with every-one today," Arlene commented. "I doubt she has any ill feelings toward us, but it makes me wonder why she got involved with Joel. He can be such a *schtinker* sometimes."

"You took the words right out of my mouth." Elsie motioned to the leftover desserts on the counter. "Joel and Kristi left in such a hurry I'm sur-prised you were able to get her to take the cookies before they went out the door."

Frowning, Doris leaned against the kitchen sink with her arms folded. She probably knew Joel better than any of them, and yet she couldn't fig-ure him out. Just when, and why, had he become so desperate for money? Joel had his own business and should have been doing well with it by now. If he'd remained Amish and kept working with Dad, things would be better for everyone. Joel would be married to Anna, and maybe they'd have one or two children already. Instead, he was engaged to an English woman they knew little or nothing about. Even if Joel came around more often after they were married, Kristi would probably never fully under-stand the Amish way of life and might never fit in. But it would be best not to overthink things right now. It was better to take one day at a time. Perhaps everything would work out in the end.

"I wonder if Dad even made a will." Arlene's statement pushed Doris's thoughts aside.

"I'm sure he did," Elsie responded. "Once things have settled down a bit, we'll look for it." She walked over to the cups and saucers still left in the sink. "At the moment, we have more dishes to do."

"While you two work on those, I'll take the

paper trash out to burn." Doris scooped up two bags and headed behind the barn, where the burn barrel was located.

∽

After Doris lit a match to light the paper in the barrel, she made sure the flames took hold. She'd stay here until the fire turned to embers, to make sure it was safely out.

Doris turned her attention to the maple, where the remains of the tree house still clung. She could hardly look in the direction of the tree and tried to rethink the event, to tone down the harshness of Dad's death. *At least he died here at home and in a place he was happy.*

Not everyone agreed with Dad building the tree house, but how could one deny his happiness? Dad's face had lit up each time he announced he was doing it for their mother.

Gazing heavenward, Doris imagined her parents walking hand in hand. *Mama and Dad had a special bond, and now they're together.*

As she looked closer at the wood scattered around the maple, Doris saw the sun reflect on something. It looked like a piece of metal lying among the splintered wood. She glanced in the barrel and stirred up the contents. Since the flames were at a low burn, Doris thought it was safe to go see what was there.

She picked up a board, then another, and discovered birdhouses attached to each one. While the wood they were nailed to was blackened from the force of the lightning, somehow the two birdhouses remained untouched.

I'll bet, for Mama's sake, Dad nailed these to the railing of the tree house. Doris remembered fondly how much her mother loved the birds. She looked at the small-framed houses, so meticulously made by her father. The tiny perch at the opening, the imitation windows with cute little shutters on both sides, and the tin roof to keep the baby birds dry showed the love Dad had for his wife and for the birds she'd cared so much about.

Doris walked through the debris, making sure nothing else was hidden under the pieces of wood. Then she spied her dad's tool box. Incredibly, beside the open box, Doris found a third little house. It was as cute and undamaged as the first two, only shaped a bit differently. How it happened, she would never understand, since the toolbox and birdhouse were only a few feet from the tree.

Doris gathered the birdhouses and put them in the small wagon Dad had often used to carry supplies. In some ways, maybe these birdhouses would bring a bit of peace to her, as well as to Arlene and Elsie.

Doris stopped at the burn barrel to check it again. She was glad the paper products burned quickly, as she was anxious to take what she'd found back to her sisters. She stirred the ashes to make sure the fire was out and was satisfied when no more smoke wisped up.

Putting the lid back on the barrel, Doris pulled the wagon around the barn. When she came to the front, she heard a noise coming from inside and halted. She noticed the barn door slightly ajar. Was it the colt's whinny, a cat's meow, or something else she'd heard? Tilting her head to one side, Doris leaned forward and listened. It sounded like someone crying.

She dropped the handle of the wagon and slowly entered the barn. Doris let her eyes adjust to the dimness, with only the light coming through the windows. Slowly, she followed the soul-wrenching sobs. Hearing it made tears come to her eyes. *Who is in so much pain?*

As she rounded a stack of hay, Doris's hands flew to her mouth. Lying on a bed of straw in an empty horse stall was Anna.

She ran quickly to her friend's side, crouched down, and held Anna in her arms. "Are you okay? I thought you'd already left."

Sniffling and choking on sobs, Anna sat up. "I shouldn't be blubbering like a boppli, but seeing Joel today with his fiancée upset me. I thought I'd gotten over him, but my feelings for Joel are still here." Anna placed one hand against her heart. "I've kept them buried."

Using the corner of her apron, Doris dried Anna's tear-stained cheeks. Anna was a good person, and she hated to see her suffer this way.

~

Akron

After Joel dropped Kristi off at her condo that evening, he went straight home and got out the Corvette. Today had been stressful, and he needed some time alone. A few hours on the open road in his shiny black Vette might be what Joel needed to ease some of his tension.

He headed down the driveway and turned onto the highway with his high beams on, always on the lookout for deer. The last thing he needed was to hit one of them tonight and total his priceless classic, not to mention hurt a deer.

Today didn't go well with Kristi, Joel thought. *She thinks it was terrible I brought up Dad's will. If she realized how badly I need money, maybe she'd understand. But if I tell her I'm in debt up to my neck because I spent big bucks on a fancy car, she'll be even more upset.* He gripped the steering wheel and bit his lower lip. *Not to mention how angry she'd be if she found out I took money from our joint account without her knowledge.*

Joel felt like he was walking a tightrope with no net under him. One wrong move and he could lose his balance, falling straight to his death.

I've got to find out soon if Dad has a will, and if so, how much of his money I'm entitled to. I'll wait till the middle of next week, and then I'm calling Elsie. If Dad left each of us a fourth of his assets, my sisters and I will have all the money we need. And I, for one, need it bad.

CHAPTER 6

"Y ou look tired, honey. Did you and Joel get back from his father's funeral late last night?" Kristi's mother asked when Kristi stopped by the following morning on her way to work. She was working Saturday to complete the trade she'd made with a coworker so she could go to the funeral.

"Not too late. I'm tired because I didn't get much sleep." Kristi went over to the coffee pot and poured herself a cup, making sure it didn't overflow. After refilling the water reservoir on her parents' coffeemaker, she picked up her mug and took a seat at the kitchen table. "I stopped by to give you a treat and fill you in on a few things." She placed a bag of chocolate-chip cookies on the table. "One of Joel's sisters sent these home with us yesterday, and I wanted to share some with you."

Mom sat across from Kristi. "That was thoughtful. So why didn't you get much sleep last night?"

Kristi sighed. "Because I was, and still am, deeply troubled." When she'd learned about the death of Joel's father, Kristi had called her parents to let them know she would be traveling to the funeral with Joel.

"About Joel?" Mom took a cookie and also a napkin.

"Yes." Kristi's stomach tensed as she explained about Joel's Amish background.

"How long have you known this, Kristi?"

"I didn't know anything until yesterday. As we were driving to his dad's place in Charm, where the funeral was held, Joel blurted out his family was

Amish. And get this—Joel left the faith seven years ago."

"Oh my!" Mom touched her parted lips. She seemed at a loss for words.

"I don't have anything against his Amish heritage, but I was hurt by his deception."

"And well you should be. Given all this time you've been dating Joel, he should have told you about his family long before now." Mom's gaze flicked upward. "I've always thought it a bit strange that he'd never introduced you to his family. It's not normal, Kristi. Not in a healthy, loving relationship."

Staring into her coffee cup, Kristi could only nod.

"Did you feel out of place at the funeral?"

"A little." Kristi brought her mug to her lips, but the coffee seemed to lack any taste when the warm liquid touched her tongue.

"Was Joel's family accepting of you?"

"They seemed to be. His sister Doris gave me one of her mother's quilted wall hangings." Kristi smiled. "It's so beautiful, Mom. I can't wait for you to see it."

"Oh, how nice. Was Mrs. Byler okay with her daughter giving away one of her quilts?"

"Joel's mother is also deceased."

"How sad. Does Joel have any other brothers or sisters?" Mom asked.

"Besides Doris, he has two other sisters. Joel's the youngest. Doris, Elsie, and Arlene all seemed so nice. I'm looking forward to knowing them better." Kristi wiped her mouth on a napkin and rested her elbows on the table. "I felt a sense of peace when I was with them—at least, I did until Joel caused some tension."

Mom's eyes blinked rapidly. "What happened?"

Kristi recounted the details of what had transpired when Joel asked about his father's will. "It was so embarrassing. I couldn't believe he would be insensitive enough to bring it up on the day of his dad's funeral, when everyone was grieving."

Mom's mouth opened, as though about to respond, but she allowed Kristi to keep talking.

"What's more puzzling is he didn't shed a single tear during the funeral or graveside service."

Mom placed her hand gently on Kristi's arm. "It sounds like Joel has some serious issues he needs to deal with, Kristi. Do you see now why I've been concerned about your relationship?"

"I understand, but—"

"He's been keeping things from you, and that's never good. It's a shame Joel didn't attend the marriage seminar with you. If he'd heard what our speaker taught us, he might realize the importance of honesty between a couple." Mom leaned slightly forward. "For that matter, we should be honest with everyone. It's the Christian way. But since I'm not sure Joel is a Christian. . ."

"I'm sorry to interrupt, but I need to go." Kristi glanced at the clock on the wall. "I don't want to be late for work." A tingly sensation shot up Kristi's spine as she pushed her chair aside and stood. She said a quick goodbye to Mom and hurried out the door.

As she stood on the porch, rubbing her temples, Kristi wished she hadn't told her mother Joel had asked about his father's will—although she couldn't keep the truth about his Amish heritage from her folks. *If I hadn't told Mom about Joel's family being*

Amish, she would have fainted in shock when she saw them at our wedding. Dad may have been surprised, too. No, she'd done the right thing sharing with Mom about Joel's family being Amish. But she wished she had kept quiet about what went on after the funeral dinner.

I'll give Joel a little more time to work through things, Kristi told herself as she got in the car and headed to work. *But I'm not giving up on him, no matter what Mom thinks.*

❧

Charm

Doris's boss had given her a week off to deal with the funeral and other issues, so despite exhaustion and queasiness, Doris had gotten up early to help her sisters clean their dad's place. She'd just walked her horse into the corral and closed the latch when she heard Aunt Verna and Uncle Lester in the barn.

"Now, Lester, don't overdo. You could hurt yourself bending too far and end up straining your back."

"Aw, Verna, you worry too much. The horses' stalls need to be cleaned, and someone has to do it."

"Speak up, Lester. You're mumbling."

Uncle Lester repeated himself.

"It can wait till one of the younger men or boys comes over," she retorted.

"Are you sayin' I'm old?"

"I didn't say anything about you being cold."

"*Old,* not *cold.*" His voice rose. "You should quit being so stubborn and get a hearing aide."

"*Guder mariye,* Aunt Verna and Uncle Lester." Doris entered the barn.

"Morning, Doris," they answered in unison. Aunt

Verna gave her a hug.

"I'll help you clean the stalls, as well as feed and water the horses, Uncle Lester." Doris rubbed the mane of Dad's buggy horse. It saddened her to think he would never drive this horse again.

"It's nice of you to offer." Uncle Lester leaned on his pitchfork. "I still need to let the mare and her colt out to run."

"I'll take care of it before I begin cleaning," Doris offered. "We'll get this work done in no time at all."

"Would you like a cup of coffee, Doris?" Aunt Verna plucked a piece of hay off her dress.

Doris nodded. "Jah, please."

"What did you say, dear?"

"She said 'jah.' And would you bring me a cup, too?" Uncle Lester spoke loudly.

"Okay, will do." Aunt Verna shuffled out of the barn.

Doris wondered if her aunt's hearing was steadily getting worse. She could see Uncle Lester working as hard as he could, but he moved a bit slow, no doubt due to the pain and stiffness caused by his arthritis. Doris hoped Elsie and Arlene would arrive soon to help with things in the house.

A short time later, a rig pulled into the yard. Doris ran out and waved at Elsie.

Uncle Lester stuck his head out to check what was happening. "I see your sister's here." His brows furrowed. "I wonder where our coffee is."

"I bet Aunt Verna got sidetracked." Doris watched Elsie unhitch her horse and take him to the corral. When she finished, they walked together to the barn.

"How's it going?" Elsie asked.

"We're cleaning the horses' stalls, but we could sure use some coffee." Uncle Lester grunted. "Don't know what your aunt's up to. Would you go in and remind her that we're still waiting?"

Elsie nodded. "I'll get your coffees. Maybe Aunt Verna is busy with something."

When Elsie returned a few minutes later holding cups of steaming coffee, she smiled and said, "Aunt Verna was sitting in the living room, reading. I didn't mean to, but I made her jump, because she hadn't heard me come in. I gave her a hug and then mentioned the coffee."

"What'd she say?" Uncle Lester cocked his head.

"She forgot, so I told her to relax and enjoy her book, and I'd bring out the coffee."

Doris wasn't surprised when Elsie handed them their cups and picked up a broom. She never had been one to stand around when work needed to be done. This gave Uncle Lester a chance to sit on an old stool and drink his coffee.

Doris sipped her own coffee and set the cup on a wooden box so she could help Elsie. Soon, they had the horses taken care of and each of the stalls cleaned. When they were done and the tools had been put away, they headed for the house. "Look!" Doris pointed toward the driveway. "Here comes Arlene now."

Uncle Lester went on ahead, but Doris and Elsie waited for Arlene. Once her horse had been put away, they walked into Dad's house together. They'd gotten a lot done yesterday, cleaning up after the funeral, but it had been an exhausting day for everyone. All were in agreement to go home and get a good night's rest and return in the morning to do more. Aunt Verna and Uncle Lester would be staying at Dad's for the next few weeks to help out, but Doris and her sisters didn't expect their aunt and uncle to do everything on their own. It was their place to clean Dad's house and sort through all his things.

"Did you sleep well last night?" Arlene asked Doris while she swept the kitchen floor. "You left in such a hurry yesterday."

"No, not really. I had a troubling night. All I did was toss and turn. I'm sorry Brian and I left so quickly." Doris sighed, setting a container on the table before plopping down on a chair. "I brought some apples, oranges, grapes, and celery filled with peanut butter. What we don't eat today, we can put in the fridge, since we'll be coming back on Monday to finish cleaning and begin the sorting process."

"Seems like now's a good time to have a snack and talk a spell." Elsie found a box of crackers in the cupboard and called their aunt and uncle to join them.

Opening the refrigerator, Arlene took out a block of cheese left over from the funeral and then grabbed a knife from the counter. "Elsie, why don't you slice the apples and cheese, while I make us some hot tea?" she suggested.

Soon everyone was seated at the table.

"This sure hits the spot." Aunt Verna reached for a slice of cheese. "I think we all needed a break."

Arlene blew on her steaming cup of tea and glanced at Doris. "I was concerned when Brian rushed in and told us you were leaving yesterday. I figured the day's events might have hit you all of a sudden."

"You're right, it did, but it wasn't just the exhaustion from the funeral. I was upset by something else." Doris closed her eyes and drew a deep breath. "Even now, thinking about it, makes me feel nauseous."

"Did something happen?" Uncle Lester asked.

Doris nodded, then quickly explained how she'd discovered Anna when she was heading back from burning the trash. "I never heard such a gut-wrenching cry."

"Come to think of it, I don't remember saying goodbye to Anna yesterday." Arlene handed Doris a napkin. "Why was she crying so hard? Was it because of Joel?"

"Jah." Doris went on to say how, once Anna had calmed down, she'd confessed her love for Joel had never died. "I thought after all these years she'd gotten over him. Apparently, Anna did, too, until she came face-to-face with our bruder yesterday."

"Oh dear." Elsie sighed, and Aunt Verna slowly shook her head.

"Anna said when she looked into Joel's eyes, she realized she'd buried her feelings. Then when Anna found out who Kristi was and how much Joel's girlfriend meant to him, she was devastated." Doris wiped the tears on her cheeks. "All this time Anna's been hoping Joel would return home to the Amish faith and their relationship could be rekindled. Now she feels all is lost, realizing her dreams were for nothing."

"Our brother!" Elsie grumbled. "I don't understand him at all. Joel is a different person than he was growing up. He had a good thing with Anna."

Arlene nodded. "I hardly know him anymore."

"After Anna and I finished talking, I drove her home in her buggy while Brian followed me in ours," Doris continued. "That's why we left in a hurry with no explanation."

"Poor Anna." Aunt Verna patted Doris's arm. "It's good she confided in you."

Doris nodded. "Now that I know, I want to offer her my support."

Everyone ate in silence until Doris jumped up. "I almost forgot something I want you to see. I'll be right back." She rushed out the door.

Shortly after, as Doris pulled the little wagon toward the porch, Arlene and Elsie came out.

"What do you have there?" Arlene asked.

"It's something I found yesterday up by the maple tree that was hit by lightning. Something for each of us in memory of Mama and Dad."

As Doris handed her sisters each a birdhouse, she explained how she had come upon them.

"Looks like I may need a tissue." Teary-eyed, Elsie stared at the birdhouse she'd been given. "This is so special."

"When I took the trash out to be burned and found the birdhouses unscorched by the lightning's heat, I believed it was meant to be," Doris said. "I think I was meant to find Anna as well."

~

Akron

When Kristi got home from work late in the afternoon, the first thing she did was call Joel. She drew a deep breath when he answered.

"Hi, Joel. How was your day?"

"Okay, I guess."

"How are you doing? Were you able to get a good night's sleep?"

"Not really, but I'm fine." Joel's tone lacked emotion.

"Why don't we work out at the gym for a while?" she suggested, hoping it might perk him up. "Afterward, we can go somewhere for a bite to eat."

"I'm too tired from work, and I don't feel like getting cleaned up to go out."

"Would you rather come here for supper? It's a bit chilly outside but not too cold to put burgers on the grill."

"Not tonight, Kristi."

Kristi winced. "Please don't shut me out, Joel. Whether you realize it or not, you need support right now."

"I'm fine, really. I just need to be alone."

"Okay, I'll let you go, but don't hesitate to call if you want to talk."

"Thanks for understanding. Maybe we can do something tomorrow."

"That'd be nice. If the weather cooperates, why don't we go on a picnic at the park after church?"

"Whatever you want to do is fine." Joel's words were positive, but the tone of his voice was not. Was he telling her what he thought she wanted to hear, or was he looking forward to being with her? She hoped it was the latter.

"Okay, I'll see you tomorrow. Have a good evening."

"You too, Kristi. Bye."

Kristi set her cell phone aside and went to the

bedroom to change into her sweatpants. It wouldn't be dark for another hour or so, and she thought about going for a run. While getting dressed, however, Kristi saw her laptop lying on the bed. She stared at it a few seconds, wondering if she should go online or head out for a run. *Maybe I won't feel like an outsider if I do more Amish research.*

She picked up her laptop and carried it to the living room. *If I'm going to be part of Joel's family someday, I need to learn all I can about their way of life.*

Chapter 7

Millersburg

Monday morning, as soon as the children were off to school and John had left for work, Elsie slipped into her shoes and went out to the phone shack to check for messages.

Cautiously peering in to make sure no spiders lurked about, Elsie stepped inside the small wooden building. She took a seat on the folding chair and started replaying the first message.

"Hey, Elsie. It's Joel. I'm calling to see if you've located Dad's will."

Elsie's fingers curled into her palms. *I can't believe him! When does he think we would have had time to look for Dad's will? And why does he need money so bad? I have half a mind not to even call him back.*

She took in a couple of deep breaths, trying to calm herself. Joel could be so insensitive. Didn't he realize how badly they were all grieving? Wasn't he grieving the loss of their dad, too?

"Maybe not," Elsie grumbled aloud. "Our brother might only be thinking of himself. I'll bet Joel doesn't realize how unfeeling he sounds."

Struggling with whether to call Joel or not, Elsie finally picked up the phone. She felt a release of tension when she heard Joel's voice mail play. It would be easier to leave him a message. Less chance of getting into an argument, which neither of them needed right now.

"Hello, Joel, it's Elsie returning your call. We

haven't had time yet to look for Dad's will. Aunt Verna and Uncle Lester are still here. They'll be staying at Dad's house for a few weeks to help us sort through things. We'll call you if his will turns up in the process. Please try not to worry about it for now. When things settle down a bit, we'd like to have you and Kristi over for supper. Doris, Arlene, and I enjoyed meeting her. She seems nice, and we're happy she has one of Mama's quilted wall hangings. I'll get back to you in a few weeks."

Elsie placed the phone back on the receiver, letting a soft breath escape her lips. She was trying her best to be confident throughout this whole process, but she felt frail, struggling against the urge to break down and scream.

She closed her eyes. *I'm the oldest child. I have to stay strong, not only for myself but also for my sisters. Imagine how they'd feel if they saw their oldest sister acting like a scared, overly emotional child. Please help me, Lord. I can't do it without Your help.* Elsie quoted Philippians 4:13, "'I can do all things through Christ which strengtheneth me.'"

A crawling sensation tickled her arm. Elsie opened her eyes, raised her arm, and shrieked. Feeling rather foolish, she brought her hand close to her face, eyeing a strand of long hair dangling from her fingers. Elsie chuckled slightly. She was glad it wasn't a spider.

She was about to leave the phone shack when the phone rang. Hoping it wasn't Joel, Elsie was tempted to let the answering machine pick up. But it could be someone else. "Hello," she said hesitantly.

"Hi, Elsie. It's Doris. I'm sorry I won't be able to meet you and Arlene at Dad's house today.

Unfortunately, I've come down with the flu." Doris spoke softly, her voice trembling.

Elsie's forehead wrinkled. "I'm sorry to hear you're feeling poorly, but don't worry about it. We'll manage without your help today. Aunt Verna is itching to help us, since she got some much needed rest on Sunday."

"Danki. I appreciate it. I'm glad I have the day off and can stay home and take it easy."

"That's what you need to do, all right. Have you taken your temperature to see if you have a fever?"

"I did, and it's normal. I don't ache anywhere, either, but I'm quite nauseous. I couldn't keep my breakfast down."

"Please get some rest and let me know if you need anything. I'll be over at Dad's helping Aunt Verna and Arlene most of the day, but I'll make sure to check Dad's answering machine in case you need us to bring you anything."

"Thanks so much. I'll talk to you later, Elsie."

As she started back to the house, Elsie felt torn. Part of her wanted to help out at Dad's, but she also wished she could go to Doris's place to check up on her. Since Brian was no doubt at work, Doris would be alone. *Of course,* Elsie reasoned, *she has no little ones to look after, and I did tell her to call if she needs anything. She'll probably be fine. I need to stop acting like a mother hen.*

When Elsie entered her house, she went to the kitchen to put a casserole together for lunch. After placing it in the oven and setting the timer, she wandered around the house, looking for something else to do. She would be heading over to Charm soon, but the thought of sorting through Dad's things nearly broke her heart.

She paused in the living room to look out the window. Her gaze came to rest on the old wagon wheel leaning against a tree in the yard. Elsie remembered the day she'd acquired the wheel. She and Dad had gone to the local farmers' market. When she'd spotted the wheel, he'd bought it for her. Then Dad found another one and bought it for Mama. *I'll find a place to put it when I get home,* Elsie remembered him saying.

Swiping at the tears rolling down her cheeks, she headed back to the kitchen to check on the casserole. *Maybe I'll bake the peanut butter cookie dough resting in the refrigerator for snacks this afternoon.* Elsie closed her eyes. *Lord, please help me and my family through this difficult time.*

⤬

Charm

When Elsie arrived at Dad's, she noticed Arlene's rig wasn't there yet. She tied her horse to the hitching rail and carried the box with the casserole and cookies up to the house.

Uncle Lester let her in. "Guder mariye, Elsie. You're the first to arrive."

"Good morning. Arlene should be here soon, but Doris won't be coming. She has the flu and stayed home to rest."

"Sorry to hear it. I hope she feels better soon." He closed the door and headed to the living room.

Elsie carried the food to the kitchen, where she found Aunt Verna going through a drawer in Dad's old desk. "I'm glad you're here." Aunt Verna looked up and gestured to the drawer full of pens. "We certainly have our work cut out for us today."

"We sure do, but it doesn't have to all be done in a day. In fact, it's going to take a good many weeks to sort through all my daed's collections."

Her aunt nodded. "Will your sisters be coming today?"

"Arlene will be here as soon as she drops off baby Samuel at a friend's, but Doris is sick with the flu."

Aunt Verna's brows puckered. "Did you say, 'Doris is sick and doesn't have a clue?'"

Elsie bit back a chuckle. "I said she has the flu."

"Oh, what a shame. Then she needs to rest and drink plenty of fluids."

"Jah." Elsie pointed to the casserole dish she'd set on the table. "This needs to be refrigerated, but I'll take care of it as soon as I tend to my horse."

"You go ahead. I'll deal with the casserole."

"Danki." Elsie went out to her buggy and was about to unhitch her horse when her sister pulled in. "Guder mariye," she called as Arlene guided her horse up to the hitching rail. "Doris won't be joining us today."

Arlene hopped out of the rig. "Is she okay?"

"She thinks she has the flu."

"Oh, no. Is the flu bug going around?"

Elsie shrugged. "A lot of people were at the funeral on Friday, so someone may have been coming down with it."

Arlene secured her horse then reached inside the buggy and took out a box. "I brought some pickled eggs and dilled green beans." She smacked her lips. "Both are recipes from Mama, so you know they'll be tasty."

"I brought a chicken-rice casserole and some cookies. Lunch will be good, but the reason we're here today isn't." Elsie swallowed hard.

Arlene slipped her arm around Elsie's waist. "We'll get through this. We need to trust God and pray for strength."

"You're right. Now let's put our horses in the corral so we can go inside and get started." Elsie fought the lump in her throat. "There's a lot to do."

⁊

Akron

Because Kristi's shift didn't start until ten, she planned to stop at the bank on the way to work. Friday was payday, but since she'd been at the funeral that day, she had to do the banking today. She planned to put half the money she'd earned in her and Joel's joint savings account. The rest would go in her checking to pay bills and for incidentals.

As Kristi got in her car and pulled onto the street, she thought about Joel and wondered how he was doing this morning. Yesterday, he'd called to let her know he was too tired to get out of bed and go to church with her. He sounded depressed, but Kristi wasn't sure if his fatigue and mood was from working too hard or if he was emotionally drained because of his father's death. She'd been tempted to go over to Joel's place Sunday evening to check on him but thought he might need more time alone. If Kristi had lost either of her parents, she would need all the support she could get. Joel, however, tended to withdraw when faced with an unpleasant situation. Kristi had witnessed this after Joel's accident, when he'd been unable to work for a few weeks. Every evening, she'd gone over to fix his meal, but sometimes Joel hardly seemed to notice she was there.

Maybe I'll give him a few days before I try calling again, she decided. *I don't want to appear pushy or make Joel think I'm too controlling by forcing him to talk about things when he's not ready.*

By the time she pulled up to the bank, Kristi felt a little better. She was sure Joel would call when he was ready, so stressing about it would do her no good. When he decided to open up, she would be ready to listen and offer support.

Kristi got out of her car and hurried into the bank. Fortunately, no one was in line ahead of her, so she stepped up to the teller and handed her the check. "I've filled out two deposit slips," she told the middle-age woman. "The rest, I'd like in cash."

"Would you like a balance on both your accounts?"

Kristi nodded. It had been awhile since she'd asked for a balance on her and Joel's account. She was curious to see how well they were doing. If they had enough money, maybe they could set a wedding date soon.

Kristi waited until she got back in her car to look at the deposit slips. When she did, she had to do a double take. What was written there sent a chill up her back. The account she and Joel shared had less than half the money in it since the last time she'd checked. *Wait a minute. What's going on here?* She crimped the slip between her thumb and index finger. *Did Joel withdraw money from our account without telling me?*

Kristi shook her head in disbelief as she leaned

heavily against the seat. She could hardly believe Joel would do such a thing. But then, lately nothing surprised her. Too bad she didn't know where he was working today, or she'd go there right now and confront him.

Looking at her watch, she saw it was impossible. Kristi barely had time to make it to the nursing home before her shift started. She would talk to Joel when she got off work. One way or another, before the day was out, Kristi would get to the bottom of this.

CHAPTER 8

Charm

I hardly know where to start," Arlene commented as she and Elsie entered their father's bedroom.

Elsie opened the closet door and peered in. "Maybe we should begin by going through his clothes. We can see if there's anyone in our community who might have a need or give them to the Share and Care thrift shop in Berlin."

Tears welled in Elsie's eyes. "I realize we can't keep everything, but it's going to be so hard to part with any of Dad's things."

Arlene gave a quick nod. "A lot of Mama's things are still here, too, and we'll need to decide what to do with those."

"I'm so glad Doris found those birdhouses." Elsie paused. "I can't believe no one saw them in all the rubble before."

"I suppose they would have eventually been discovered, but it was perfect timing all the way around." Arlene stared at Dad's Sunday shoes, sitting by his dresser. "I believe Doris was right. Finding the birdhouses was meant to be."

"I may keep mine inside for a while," Elsie said. "I'd like to put it in a special place as a reminder of Mama and Dad."

"I may do the same thing," Arlene agreed.

Elsie sat on the end of the bed, viewing the clothes peeking out of the closet. "Maybe it would be best not to dispose of anything but the clothes until the will has been found. That way, if Dad specified anything in particular should go to certain people, we can respect his wishes."

"If there is a will." Arlene sighed. "Maybe Dad didn't make one."

"Jah, he did." Aunt Verna stepped into the room. "He told me the last time I came here for a visit."

"Did he say where he put it?" Elsie questioned.

Aunt Verna tipped her head. "What was that?"

Elsie repeated her question. It was amazing how sometimes Aunt Verna heard whatever had been said, while at other times people had to repeat themselves. *Perhaps I spoke too quietly. I need to make sure I speak loud enough and look in her direction when I'm talking to her.*

Aunt Verna moved closer. "My bruder said he'd made out a will, he even showed it to me. But. . ." her voice trailed off. "I can't remember now where he put it. Didn't he tell one of you about the will?"

Elsie and Arlene both shook their heads. "I'm sure he didn't tell Doris either," Elsie said.

"And I'm even more certain he didn't tell our brother, because if he had, Joel would not have asked about the will," Arlene interjected.

"Maybe we need to box things up and wait until the will is found before deciding what to do with them." Elsie rose from the bed. "In the meantime, I'm hungerich. Should we stop and heat the casserole for lunch?"

"No need for that. The reason I came in here was to tell you I put the dish in the oven forty-five minutes ago. It's nice and warm and on the table." Aunt Verna smiled. "Lester's waiting for us, so why don't we join him?"

"Sounds good." Elsie and Arlene followed Aunt

Verna out of Dad's room.

"Oh, before I forget, I wanted to ask you something." Aunt Verna paused in the hall, peering at them over the top of her glasses.

"What is it?" Elsie and Arlene asked in unison, stopping beside their aunt.

"I hate to ask, but if you happen to come across Eustace's worn-out boots, would you mind if I have them?" She pursed her lips. "It would be the ones held together by duct tape."

"Certainly." Elsie put her arm around her aunt's shoulder.

"Danki." Aunt Verna wiped her eyes with the corner of her apron. "When I arrived last month to visit Eustace, I had to chuckle when I saw his old boots. I suggested he use duct tape to hold them together."

"They're probably in the barn somewhere. Even though he bought a new pair, I can't imagine he'd get rid of the old ones." Arlene paused, blinking against tears about to spill over. "He was wearing those new boots the day Larry and I found him."

"Well, your daed mentioned how he'd bought a pair of old cowboy boots at an auction one time and your mamm couldn't imagine why."

"I remember those," Elsie exclaimed. "Dad planted flowers in them."

"Jah, and he told me your mamm ended up liking the idea." Aunt Verna grinned. "So if you find those old duct-taped boots, I'd like to plant flowers in them. They hold a good memory for me of my bruder."

"We'd be pleased if you turned Dad's old boots into your own special memory." Arlene hugged

Aunt Verna, and Elsie did the same.

When they entered the kitchen, Elsie stopped in mid-stride as soon as she saw Uncle Lester sitting in Dad's roll-about chair at the head of the table. Her chin trembled as she pressed her hand to her chest. The tears didn't seem to want to stop today. The sight of Uncle Lester sitting in Dad's spot was a vivid reminder that he was gone and would never occupy his special chair again. She would miss seeing Dad roll around as he often did, going from room to room. It had become his trademark of sorts. Elsie blinked rapidly. *Oh Dad, if only you hadn't gone up in the tree house.*

❧

After lunch, Elsie helped put stuff away. "I'm going to walk to the phone shack and check for messages. I doubt Doris has called, but there may be a chance. I shouldn't be long." She headed out the door.

"Hey, wait up!" Arlene called. "I'll walk with you."

Elsie waited for her sister to catch up. "Oh, good, you can hunt for *schpinne* for me." She laughed.

Arlene snickered. "Well, it wouldn't be anything new. You could never handle it when a spider was in the bedroom we shared growing up. You'd say, 'Arlene, would you please take care of it for me? Schpinne are creepy.'"

"I can't deny it. I called on you a lot to do the nasty deed—only because Doris was too small, and the spiders were nearly as big as her." Elsie elbowed her sister, chuckling. It felt good to find something to smile about.

When they got to the phone shack, Arlene

stepped in and brushed away a web. "No messages," she announced.

"Our sister must be doing okay. Guess we'd better get back to the house and box up some more stuff. I brought peanut butter cookies for us to snack on. I'll set them on the table soon." Elsie pushed a wayward strand of hair back under her head covering before linking arms with Arlene.

As they headed to the house, Elsie hummed a silly tune their father used to play on his harmonica. There were so many memories of Dad she would always treasure. Someday, she would see him again in heaven.

&

Akron

When Kristi got off work that afternoon, she didn't bother going home to change out of her nursing uniform; she headed straight for Joel's place, hoping he'd be there. She had to find out why he'd taken money from their account and thought it would be better if they talked face-to-face. She didn't know how she'd gotten through the day without leaving early to confront Joel.

A light rain trickled down the windshield, so Kristi turned on her wipers. Listening to the steady *swish-swish* of the wiper blades, she thought about her perplexing relationship with Joel. *Could Mom be right about Joel? Maybe he's not a Christian. He could only be pretending to be one by going to church with me on Sundays. But it doesn't make sense. Joel grew up in the Amish church. He should be spiritually grounded.*

Kristi reflected on the information she'd found on the Internet. One site talked specifically about baptism and confession of faith. She'd learned those wishing to be baptized and join the Amish church must first take a series of instructional classes. On the Saturday before baptism took place, the candidates would be given the opportunity to change their mind.

I wonder why Joel didn't do that. Why'd he wait to leave until after he joined the church? There were so many unanswered questions.

Kristi had also learned from the website that during the baptismal service, each of the young men and women were asked three questions: (1) if they were willing to renounce the world and be obedient only to God and the church, (2) if they were willing to walk with Christ and His church and remain faithful throughout their life, and (3) if they could confess Jesus Christ as the Son of God. They had to answer affirmatively to each question. Then the deacon poured water into the bishop's cupped hands, which he dripped over the candidate's head. The ritual of baptism signified the individual had formally become a member of the church.

"If Joel complied with all three things, how could he not be a Christian?" Kristi murmured. She pressed her lips tightly together. *But if Joel is a Christian, why is he ignoring his family and being deceitful with me? But then, we're only human, and everyone makes mistakes. I have my own faults to deal with.*

❧

The first thing Joel did when he got home from work was to take a shower and change his clothes. Following that, he went to the kitchen to make a sandwich, since he didn't feel like cooking.

Joel was about to sit down when he heard a car pull into the yard. Going to the window and looking out, he was surprised to see Kristi get out of her car, wearing her nurse's uniform.

He hurried to the door, hoping everything was okay. Normally Kristi called before coming over.

The minute she stepped onto the porch, Joel sensed something was wrong. No cute dimpled smile or friendly greeting. Kristi's lips were pressed into a white slash as she held tightly onto her purse.

"Come in before the wind blows rain under the porch eaves." Joel opened the door wider, and Kristi stepped inside.

He leaned down and pressed his lips against her cold cheek. "I'm surprised to see you. I didn't think we were getting together this evening. Is everything all right?"

"I—I'm not sure." Kristi opened her purse and pulled out a slip of paper. "I went to the bank on my way to work this morning. When I made a deposit to our savings account, I was given this." Kristi's hand shook as she handed it to him.

Joel didn't have to look at the deposit slip to know what was on it. The teller had printed the new balance on the back.

"Did you take money from our account without telling me?" Kristi's sharp tone hit Joel like a dagger.

He shuffled his feet a few times, while clearing his throat. "I. . .I admit, I did make a withdrawal, but you told me awhile back if I needed money I could borrow some from our account."

She looked up at him defiantly. "You assured me you would never take any of the money without telling me about it."

Joel gave his shirt collar a tug before rubbing the back of his neck. "Guess I must have forgotten to mention it. Sorry. I'll make sure it never happens again."

"What I would like to know is what kind of problems are you faced with that you would need to take over half the money we'd saved?" She continued to stare at him through squinted eyes.

Joel squirmed uncomfortably. He wasn't about to tell her that because he'd bought an expensive car he couldn't pay his subcontractors. She'd think he was a louse—not to mention a risky choice as a husband.

Joel clasped his fingers around her hand. He felt relief when she didn't pull away. "As you may recall, I lost out on a big job a few months ago, and it set me back."

She gave a slow nod. "You've been busy with work since then. I figured you were making enough to get caught up."

Heat rushed to his cheeks, and he let go of her hand. "I'm not. Most of the jobs I've taken on have been small and didn't pay a lot. To save money, I've done many of them myself."

Kristi's face softened some. "I wish you would have talked to me about this, Joel. Remember how I told you the speaker at the marriage seminar stressed the importance of communication?"

"Yeah, I know. I didn't want to worry you though."

"I'm more worried about you pushing me out of your life." Her voice trembled.

Joel felt a sudden coldness deep inside. "I'm

not pushing you out of my life, Kristi. I didn't want you to worry about something that was out of your control."

"We could have talked about it and prayed together. I love you, Joel. I want honesty and trust between us."

Joel pulled Kristi into his arms, holding her close. "I love you, too, sweetheart. Am I forgiven?"

"Yes," she murmured against his chest. "But from now on, no more secrets please."

Joel stroked her silky hair, then bent to kiss her lips. He hated keeping information from Kristi, but some things were best left unsaid.

CHAPTER 9

Wednesday evening, Kristi had finished eating supper when she heard the doorbell ring. Thinking it might be Joel, she hurried to answer it.

"Oh, hi," Kristi said, when she opened the door and saw her mother on the porch, holding a paper sack. "What are you doing out and about?" Kristi held the door open while her mother entered.

Mom stepped into the hall then turned to face Kristi. "Your dad had a deacon's meeting at the church this evening, so I seized the opportunity to come by and see your new wall hanging."

"It's draped over the back of the sofa in the living room." Kristi gave her mother a wide grin. "Come on in. I'm anxious to see what you think of it."

Mom handed Kristi the bag she held. "First, I have something for you."

"What's in here?" Kristi asked, peeking inside.

"I stopped at the market on my way over and got a few things I thought you might like—apples, a butternut squash, and some spareribs they had on special."

"Thanks Mom. I'll take these things to the kitchen and put the meat in the fridge. If you'd like to come along, I'll pour us a glass of cider."

Mom smacked her lips. "Sounds good. I love cider this time of the year."

"Same here."

When they finished up in the kitchen and

started for the living room, Mom paused and tipped her head. "Kristi, you look like you've lost some weight."

"You think so?" Kristi wasn't about to admit she had lost a few pounds from all the stress of worrying over Joel and their relationship. Needing to change the topic, she hurried into the other room and pointed toward the couch. "There's the quilted wall hanging Joel's sister gave me. What do you think?"

"It's lovely." Mom slid her fingers across the material. "How could she part with such a beautiful family heirloom?"

"Each of Joel's sisters has her own. Doris said their mother made even more, so it's not like I was given the only one."

Mom removed her jacket and took a seat on the sofa. "How come you haven't hung the quilt on the wall?"

"I'm waiting until after Joel and I are married. Then we can decide where we want to hang it in our house." Kristi sat beside her mother.

"How are things between you and Joel these days?" Mom inquired.

"We're going on a picnic after church this Sunday." Kristi's stomach tightened. No way was she going to tell her mother about Joel taking money from their joint account. It would give her one more reason to question his ability to be a good husband. She would probably say Joel was deceitful and couldn't be trusted. Lately, Kristi had to admit, she felt the same way, but her love for him always won out. He'd apologized for taking the money, and Kristi was confident he wouldn't do it again.

"I hoped you hadn't made any plans for Sunday afternoon." Mom touched Kristi's arm. "I planned to ask if you and Joel could come over to our house to eat after church. Your dad mentioned it's been some time since we've visited with both of you."

"Can we do it next Sunday instead? Joel called last night and said he has something special to give me, and he'd probably prefer being alone." Kristi had a suspicion Joel might be planning to give her an engagement ring, but wondered how he could afford it, given his financial circumstances. *If it is a ring, I hope he didn't charge it, or we'll be stuck with making payments for a long time.*

As eager as Kristi was to make their engagement official and set a wedding date, she didn't want to start their marriage deeply in debt. She'd been praying Joel would land a big job soon and be able to replace what he'd taken from their account. Surely, with all the building going on in the area, something would open up.

"Next Sunday will be fine." Mom rested her arm on the sofa pillow. "We can confirm it when the time gets closer and you've had a chance to speak with Joel. He might not be interested in having lunch with us."

Kristi couldn't imagine why he wouldn't. After all, Mom and Dad would be his in-laws once she and Joel were married.

❧

Berlin

"Are you feeling all right, Doris?" Brian motioned to her half-eaten supper plate. "You've barely touched your food."

Doris exhaled as she pushed her beef stew around with a fork. "My stomach is queasy and has been all day. This flu bug I came down with on Monday is determined to stick around. I may have picked something up the day of the funeral with so many people around."

"Maybe it's not the flu. Have you called the doctor and told him your symptoms?"

"No, but if I had called, he'd probably tell me all the usual things to do for the flu—drink lots of fluids and get plenty of rest—which is what I've been doing."

Brian touched her forehead. "You don't have a fever. Do you feel achy?"

"No, only my stomach's upset."

His eyes darkened, and a sly grin appeared on his lips. "You don't suppose. . . ."

"Suppose what?" Doris reached for her glass of water and took a sip.

"Is it possible? After all this time, could you be having morning sickness because you're expecting a boppli?"

"I don't think so, Brian. Besides, the nausea I've felt isn't just in the mornings. Sometimes it lasts all day."

"Have you talked to your sisters to get their opinion? They've both experienced what it's like to be pregnant. I'm sure they'd know if what some folks call 'morning sickness' could occur at other times of the day."

"I suppose I could ask them." Doris fiddled with the napkin beside her plate. "But I'm sure it's a lingering flu bug." She forced herself to take another bite of stew and closed her eyes. *Wouldn't it be something if I was actually pregnant? I won't get my hopes up, but it would truly be a miracle and an answer to prayer.*

⸻

Akron

Joel leaned back in the recliner and checked his phone messages. There were two from people asking for bids on small jobs, and a message from Elsie saying the will had not been found.

He leaped from the chair and started to pace. *This is ridiculous! How long can it take for my sisters to find Dad's will? There are three of them, after all, plus Aunt Verna and Uncle Lester, if they decided to stick around awhile.*

Joel had half a mind to get in the car and go over to his dad's house and search for the will himself. But he didn't feel like making the hour's drive, since Charm was more than sixty miles away. It would take too much time to drive there, search the house for the will, and drive back home. If at all possible, he wanted to hit the hay early tonight. Right now, he had a few jobs lined up, which he needed to get started on early tomorrow and Friday. Fortunately, he'd given a few of his subcontractors part of the money he still owed them, so they'd agreed to do the jobs Joel couldn't do, such as the wiring and plumbing.

He stopped pacing long enough to grab his cup of coffee and take a drink. *If I don't hear anything from Elsie by the time those two jobs are finished, I may drive over to Millersburg and talk to her in person.*

This Sunday, Joel would be taking Kristi on a picnic, and he'd like to tell her the will had been found. With the exception of his relationship with Kristi, it was hard to find much good in his life these days. " 'Course, there's also my beautiful Corvette," he mumbled. "Think I'll get it out right now and take a short spin." Looking at his watch, Joel realized he still had enough time to go out and be back in plenty of time for bed. One thing Joel had discovered since he'd gotten the classic car: driving around in it helped him to relax and forget his troubles—if only for a little while.

∽

Millersburg

Elsie had been thinking about Doris and was considering going to Berlin to see how she was, but the day had gotten away from her. She'd rushed about cleaning; had stripped all their beds; and washed sheets, towels, and clothes. Now it was time to get supper on the table.

Her thoughts jumped to Joel, another family member to be concerned about. *Dad was right. Joel acts spoiled and only thinks of himself.*

Elsie paused in the hall and took a couple of deep breaths to calm herself before going to the kitchen. She still had some laundry to take down from the clothesline, so she asked Mary to get it.

"Sure, Mom, I'll do it right now."

On entering the kitchen, Elsie was pleased to see Hope peeling potatoes and putting them into a kettle for boiling. The roast was in the oven, and Elsie had sliced some tomatoes she'd picked from the garden this morning. So far, they'd had no frost, and if the weather held out, they could get tomatoes for a few more weeks. John was home from work and was out in the barn with the boys, so they would eat soon after they came in from doing their chores.

Hope dropped a potato into the kettle and turned to face Elsie. "I miss Grandpa so much." Tears welled in her eyes.

"I do, too." Elsie gave her youngest daughter's shoulder a tender squeeze. "Let's try to remember all the good times we had with him."

"I will, but it's hard knowing both he and Grandma Byler are gone."

Elsie's eyes filled with tears as she gave her daughter a hug.

"Hey, are you two all right?" John asked when he stepped in from outside.

Elsie patted her damp eyes. "We miss my daed."

"We all do." John moved closer and rubbed Elsie's back.

She sniffed. "Did you get all the chores done? Where are the boys?"

"They're feeding the cats. I told 'em to hurry. Oh, and I checked phone messages. There was one from Doris."

"What did she say?"

"Said she's felt nauseated off and on all day." His forehead wrinkled. "She's been *grank* for a few days now. Has she seen the doctor?"

"I'm not sure. I'll give her a call after supper."

"Might be a good idea." John sniffed the air. "Dinner smells good. How long till we eat?"

"Fifteen minutes, maybe," Hope spoke up. "As soon as the potatoes have cooked."

"I'll go out and hurry the boys. Then we'll all wash up."

Elsie watched out the window as her husband returned to the barn. *I wonder what's going on with Doris.* She thought back to when she was expecting. *Could my little sister be pregnant?*

"I got the clean laundry off the line and brought in." Mary bounded into the kitchen.

"Danki." Elsie placed a serving fork on the table for the meat. "After you wash your hands, would you please help your sister set the table?"

"Sure, Mom." Mary headed down the hall toward the bathroom.

Elsie was sure her oldest daughter missed her grandfather, too, but she seemed to be holding it inside, going about her business as though everything was normal.

Elsie leaned against the counter and closed her eyes. *We all need to grieve—even Joel. I hope he feels some remorse for the way he talked to Dad when he was alive.*

Chapter 10

Akron

"What a beautiful day for a picnic." Kristi sighed as she set her wicker basket on the blanket Joel had spread on the grass. "Fall is my favorite time of the year. Look how pretty the leaves are getting." Kristi pointed to a grove of sugar maples with leaves of red, orange, and yellow.

Joel stared blankly at them as he took a seat on the blanket beside her. He didn't seem interested in the beautiful trees. He had been quiet and pensive ever since church let out. Kristi wished she could read his mind.

"Before we start eating, I have something for you." Joel reached into the pocket of his denim jeans and pulled out a small velveteen box.

Kristi's heart quickened as he placed it in her hand.

"Go ahead. Open it." Joel's sudden smile caused her heart to beat a little faster.

Kristi's fingers trembled as she untied the ribbon. When she opened the lid, an attractive pair of pink earrings, sparkling in the sun, peeked out at her. She lowered her head, staring intently at them. Although disappointed he hadn't given her a ring, in one sense Kristi felt relief. She was certain Joel hadn't spent nearly as much on the earrings as he would on a diamond ring, which meant he hadn't put himself in financial jeopardy.

"They're beautiful, Joel. Thank you," Kristi murmured. "But you didn't have to get me a gift. It's not my birthday or anything."

He smiled. "It's a token of my affection, and a reminder of how much I love you."

"I love you, too." She closed the box and put it inside the picnic basket.

"Aren't you going to wear them?"

"Not right now. I'll save them for a special occasion." She reached for his hand.

He leaned over and gave her a kiss. "Should we eat? I'm hungry."

"Of course. Should we pray the Amish way before I take out the food?"

"Sure, that's fine." Joel bowed his head, and Kristi did the same.

When they finished silent praying, Kristi handed Joel a paper plate and got out the bucket of chicken they'd picked up on the way. They also had bottles of sparkling lemon water, as well as some sliced veggies she had fixed this morning.

As they ate, Kristi noticed how quiet it was. Except for her and Joel, no one was at this end of the park. Sitting there, with no noise except the chatter of a few birds, she almost felt Amish. No cars were in sight, since the parking lot was farther down the path. Everything in their presence was natural and seemed like a gift from God.

Don't be silly. Kristi chided herself for feeling Amish. *You're living in a fantasy world.* She had to admit there was something about the Amish she found enchanting. She didn't want to idealize them though. Like people from all walks of life, the Amish had their share of troubles, and none of them were perfect. Still, Kristi admired their values, love for their family, and dedication to a way of life that had been established hundreds of years ago.

They worked hard, but their lives were simplified, without all the gadgets the English world seemed to need.

"A nickel for your thoughts." Joel tweaked Kristi's nose.

"I was thinking about your Amish heritage and wishing I could incorporate more of their ways into my life."

Joel's brows lowered. "Now don't tell me you've decided to start hanging your laundry out to dry or get rid of your computer and TV."

She swatted his arm playfully. "I may not give them up, but there are other things I'd rather do than watch TV or hang out on the Internet reading posts on social media sites. Truthfully speaking, I believe I could live without either of them."

"What would you like to do?"

Kristi held up her index finger. "For one thing, I'd like to learn some Pennsylvania Dutch words." She leaned in closer to him and lowered her voice. "Would you teach me, Joel?"

His nose wrinkled. "What for? The Amish world is no longer part of my life. It's behind me."

"No, it's not. You still have family who remained Amish. When they're speaking Pennsylvania Dutch, I'd like to understand what they're saying."

Joel grunted. "You don't realize what you're asking. It would take years for you to learn the language well enough to grasp it."

Unwilling to give in, Kristi folded her arms. "Could you at least teach me to say a few words?"

"I suppose, but I don't see much point in it."

"You might be surprised what a quick learner I am." She smiled. "Give me a couple of words and tell me their meaning."

"What? Now?"

"Uh-huh. There's no time like the present."

"Okay, here's an easy one. Jah. It means yes."

"That's easy to remember. What else?"

"*Gut* is for good, and danki for thanks."

"Jah, gut, danki," Kristi repeated the words. "Now give me a sentence to learn."

Joel rolled his eyes. "Okay, but then let's talk about something else."

"That's fine."

Speaking slowly, Joel pronounced each word clearly. "*Geld zwingt die welt.*"

"What does it mean?"

"Money rules the world." He bobbed his head. "And I have to say it's true."

"It doesn't have to be," Kristi argued. "There are many things we should focus on rather than money—important things like our relationships with people."

Joel folded his arms. "*Humph!* Some people I can't have a relationship with."

"Are you thinking of anyone in particular?"

"My brother-in-law, for one." Joel frowned. "John should have stayed out of Elsie's and my discussion the day of Dad's funeral. The subject of Dad's will was between her and me."

"If you were married and someone talked to your wife the way you did Elsie, wouldn't you step in and say something?"

Joel shrugged his shoulders. "It all depends on what was being said. If it was something that didn't pertain to me, I'd keep quiet." Joel grabbed his bottle of sparkling water and took a drink. "Okay, that's enough for now. Let's talk about something else."

"Have you spoken to any of your family since the funeral?" Kristi asked.

He shook his head. "Got a message from Elsie though. Said she'd let me know when they found Dad's will. It's been over a week since his funeral, and I haven't heard a thing."

"They may not have found it yet, and they're most likely busy with other things." Kristi repositioned herself on the blanket. "I wish you weren't putting so much emphasis on getting some of your father's money. Have you even grieved your loss? Don't you feel sad that he's gone?"

Joel set his bottle down and looked right at Kristi. "I'm sorry he died, but there was no love lost between me and my dad. He didn't give a hoot about me."

Kristi's heart went out to Joel. She could see by his pained expression that he was miserable. Harboring ill feelings toward anyone, let alone a parent, could do nothing but tear a person down. If Joel didn't rise above his anger and forgive his father, he would never be at peace.

She touched his arm. "Have you prayed about this? Have you asked God to help you with your feelings of bitterness?"

Joel's face flamed like a bonfire being lit. "I don't need any lectures, Kristi. And I sure don't need you preaching at me."

"I wasn't. I'm only trying to offer my support."

"Support is fine. I don't appreciate being preached at though." He rubbed his hand against his cheek. "I got enough lectures from my dad to last a lifetime." Grabbing the empty tub the chicken had been in, Joel tossed it into the wicker basket. "You know what, Kristi? We need to go. I have some things to do at home before I go to work tomorrow."

All Kristi could do was nod. How could such a pleasant day have turned sour so quickly? Maybe she ought to give Joel some time to mull over the things they'd discussed. Surely after he'd had a chance to analyze his behavior he would realize he was wrong.

Later in the day after Joel dropped Kristi off at her condo, he'd gone home and taken the Corvette out of his shop. Since he'd washed the car the day before, Joel wanted to get a fresh coat of wax on so it would shine even more.

As Joel began working on the hood, he thought about the things Kristi said to him at the park. She'd meant well when she suggested he pray about his bitterness, but Joel didn't put much stock in prayer. *I shouldn't have gotten so upset with her. She probably thinks I'm mad. I'll give her a call as soon as I'm done with the car and try to smooth things over.*

Joel moved to the back of the car and was almost finished waxing when he heard a car coming up his driveway. As soon as he realized it was Kristi, he panicked. *I can't let her see the Vette. If she sees the car, I'll have some explaining to do.*

Joel reached in his pocket and fumbled with his keys. But he couldn't get them out quickly enough, let alone get in the car and start it up. Kristi had already seen him.

"What are you doing with Tom's car?" she asked after she'd parked her car and gotten out. "Is he here? Did you two have something planned for today? Is that why you wanted to leave the park in such a hurry?" Kristi glanced around.

Tom's car? Why would she think it's his Corvette? Then Joel remembered Kristi had seen him and Tom together with the car one night several weeks ago. He couldn't say Tom was here. She might want to talk to him. Then what? Joel needed to come up with some excuse as to why he was waxing the car Kristi thought belonged to Tom, without him being present. Or he could come right out and tell her the truth. Kristi had made it clear she didn't appreciate being lied to, so maybe it would be best to admit the Corvette was his. First, though, he needed to find out why she was here.

"I'm surprised to see you. Why'd you come by?" he asked, avoiding her question.

"I left my cell phone in your car."

"Oh, I'll get it for you right now." Joel left the chamois on the Corvette's hood and raced into the garage. When he returned with Kristi's cell phone, he found her staring at the Vette. "This looks like an expensive car. Tom must be making good money."

Joel's face heated. "Actually, the car's not Tom's."

"Oh? Who owns it then?"

"I do."

Kristi's posture stiffened. "This is your car?"

"Yeah."

"But I thought. . ." Her eyes blinked rapidly. "How come you let me believe it was Tom's?"

Sweat beaded on Joel's forehead and dripped onto his cheeks. "The thing is. . .I got the car at an auction back in August, and I paid a hefty price for it."

"Is that why you took money from our account—to pay for this?" Kristi's voice quivered as she pointed at the car.

Joel shook his head forcefully. "I used money I'd gotten from a big job for the car—money I'd planned to use to pay my subcontractors."

Her mouth twisted. "How could you do something like that, Joel?"

"Figured I could make up the money when I got paid for another job I'd bid on." Joel grimaced. "Unfortunately, I didn't get the second job, which left me in a bind. So in order to pay some of the men who'd worked for me, I borrowed money from our savings account."

Kristi's hand shook as she motioned to the Corvette. "So all this time, you've had the car and never said a word to me about it?"

Joel's face tightened as he lowered his head. "Sorry, Kristi. Guess I haven't been thinking straight lately."

"You're right, you haven't! I can't believe you would be so deceitful." She choked on her words. "Don't you care about anyone but yourself?"

Joel moved toward Kristi and grasped her wrist. "I care about you."

"Let go of me!" She pulled her arm toward herself, but Joel gripped it tighter.

"No, Kristi, I need you to listen to me."

"Do you really care, Joel? If you did, you wouldn't sneak around behind my back and do whatever you pleased." Kristi's chin quivered as tears pooled in her eyes. "I looked past you taking money from our account and not telling me about your Amish heritage until your father died, but another deception is too much."

"What are you saying?"

Kristi turned her head away from him, remaining silent for a few minutes. She sniffled before speaking again. "It. . .it's time for us to go our separate ways."

"You can't mean it, Kristi." Desperation welled in Joel's chest. "You're angry right now. Please give me another chance and let me explain a little more."

"You've already explained. There's nothing more to be said. You've kept too many things hidden from me." Using her free hand, she pried Joel's fingers loose. "Without honesty, our relationship will never work. I'm sorry, Joel, but we're done."

A sense of panic welled in his soul as he watched Kristi get into her car. "Kristi, please wait!"

After she slammed her door shut, Joel could do nothing but watch Kristi back out of his driveway. He fell to his knees, his body hunched over, as he tried to choke down a sob. *Why? Why?* His nails bit into his palms. Heat flushed through his body, and he pounded his fists against the gravel. *Haven't I had enough to deal with?* He glared up at the sky. "Well, haven't I?"

Once Joel calmed down a bit, he headed up to his trailer house. His hand trembled as he reached for the doorknob. *It can't end like this. I need to get her back. There has to be a way.*

The
MISSING
WILL

CHAPTER 1

Akron

Blinking against tears threatening to spill over, Kristi struggled to keep her focus on the road. Breaking up with Joel had been one of the hardest things she'd ever done. But it was the right decision. Her fingers turned white as she gripped the steering wheel. *I can't believe all the lies he's told me.*

Nothing about Joel made sense anymore. She'd been blinded by his good looks and charm. *I should have listened to Mom.* Kristi still didn't understand the reason he'd kept his Amish heritage from her for so long or why he'd taken money from their joint account without telling her. If he hadn't foolishly used money he'd earned on a job to buy a classic car he didn't need, Joel wouldn't be in a financial bind.

Kristi reflected on how desperate he'd seemed when he asked his sister Elsie about the will on the day of his father's funeral. Joel had acted selfishly and unfeelingly. She couldn't picture herself asking about her parents' will so soon after one of them had passed away. Was Joel really that desperate for money?

Her throat constricted as she changed lanes. "'For the love of money is the root of all evil,'" she murmured, quoting 1 Timothy 6:10. She reflected on 1 Timothy 6:7, as well: "For we brought nothing into this world, and it is certain we can carry nothing out." Kristi had committed those two verses to memory when she'd attended a Bible study on money management a few years ago. *Too bad I didn't think to quote those scriptures to Joel when he told me how desperate he was for money. If he needed funds for a good cause, that would be one thing, but to waste it on a car he could certainly live without was foolish.*

The longer Kristi thought about things, the more she wanted to pull to the side of the road and break down in tears. It would probably do her good to go for a run to release some tension, but right now she needed a listening ear. Turning at the next road, Kristi headed for her parents' house. She hoped they were home.

❦

Farmerstown

"Are you okay?" Arlene's husband, Larry, looked at her with concern. "You were quiet on the buggy ride home from church, and since we've gotten here, all you've done is sit and stare out the kitchen window."

Arlene sighed as she clutched her damp handkerchief. "I miss my daed, Larry. Remember how almost every Sunday when his district didn't have church, he would attend service with us? Looking at the men's side this morning and not seeing him there didn't seem right." Tears pooled in her eyes. "Then the three of us always came here for a meal, and afterward we'd visit, sing, or play games."

Larry sat beside Arlene and placed his hand on her shoulder. "I'm here for you, no matter what. We all miss your daed, but it's been the hardest for you, Elsie, and Doris."

She sniffed, raising her handkerchief to wipe tears from her eyes. "The kinner miss him, too. Dad loved our children, and they looked forward to spending time with him after church." She pointed to the birdhouse on a post outside the kitchen window. "Every time I look at that, I'll think of Dad and be glad Doris found it."

"When the lightning struck your daed's tree house, it's amazing everything in and around the tree didn't burn to a crisp."

She lowered her arm and turned toward him. "It's a shame Doris didn't find four birdhouses on the ground beneath the tree—then Joel could have had one, too."

"Do you think he would have wanted a birdhouse?" Larry's brows furrowed. "From what I can tell, the only thing your bruder wants is your daed's money."

Arlene swallowed hard, remembering how Joel had acted after the funeral dinner. When he'd asked about Dad's will, everyone in the room became upset. "We do need to find the document. It's the only way we'll know how he wanted things divided among us. I only hope when Joel comes around here again he won't create another scene."

"If he does, one of us will set him straight."

With shoulders slumped and head down, their youngest son, Scott, shuffled into the room.

"What's wrong, Son? You look umgerennt." When Scott looked up, Larry motioned for him to come over to them.

Scott stepped up to the table. "I ain't upset. I'm *bedauerlich*."

Arlene slipped her arm around him. "Why are you sad? Do you miss your grossdaadi?"

"Jah. Not only that, but I won't get to watch Peaches climb the ladder to Grandpa's tree house."

Arlene tipped her head. "Peaches?"

"You know—she's Henry Raber's hund. Henry

said Peaches likes to climb. Since the tree house is gone now, me and Doug won't get to see her do it." Scott kicked the floor with the toe of his shoe and lowered his gaze. "Won't get to go up there and enjoy the view with Grandpa neither."

"I'm sorry, Son." Larry pulled the boy into a hug. "Your mamm and I know you miss your grossdaadi, as we all do, but we have lots of fond memories of him."

Larry was right, but Arlene couldn't stop thinking about their children having lost their grandfather, whom they all loved and respected. She had hoped he would see them grow up, get married, and have kids of their own. It was hard to accept the changes in life that she couldn't control and were not what she'd planned.

"Why don't we gather the rest of the family together in the living room? We can sing some of our favorite songs for a while," she suggested.

"It won't be the same without Grandpa here, playin' his harmonica." Scott frowned. "Guess I'll never learn to play the mouth harp now neither."

"Maybe your uncle Joel can teach you." Larry ruffled the top of Scott's thick brown hair. "As I recall, he's pretty good at playing the harmonica."

I doubt that's ever going to happen. Joel doesn't seem to care about anyone but himself. Arlene made sure not to voice her thoughts. Even though she was upset with her brother, the last thing she wanted to do was turn any of her children against him.

"Say, I have an idea." She rose from her chair. "After we sing awhile, I'll fix some snacks."

"Can we make popcorn?" Scott's eyes brightened a bit.

She nodded. "Jah, we'll do that."

"How about hot chocolate and marshmallows to go with it?" Larry smacked his lips. "That always tastes good with popcorn."

"We can have some of those peanut butter *kichlin* in the cookie jar, too." Arlene gave her son's arm a tender squeeze. "Now why don't you go let your brother and sisters know what our plans are for the rest of the afternoon?"

"Okay, Mom." Scott grinned at his parents and hurried from the room.

Larry looked over at Arlene and smiled. "It's nice to see our boy smiling again."

"Jah. A little joy is something we all need right now."

᠙

Akron

Kristi felt relieved when she pulled up to her parents' house and saw their car parked in the driveway. She was desperate to talk to someone right now—someone who would understand and offer support.

She'd no more than stepped onto the porch, when the front door swung open. "This is a surprise. I thought you and Joel went on a picnic today." Mom stood in the doorway, drying her hands on a towel.

"We did, but we ended it early, so I. . .I decided to come here."

"Are you all right?" Mom asked as she let Kristi into the house. "Your eyes are red. Have you been crying?"

Kristi looked at her shoes, struggling to keep her emotions in check. "You don't have to worry about fixing lunch for us next Sunday, because Joel and I won't be coming."

"How come?"

"Is Dad here? I'd like him to hear this, too."

"He's in the living room, reading the newspaper." Mom gestured in that direction. "Let's go in, and you can tell us all about it."

After Kristi took a seat on the couch between her parents, she told them everything that had been discussed at the picnic and explained how Joel had taken money from their account without her knowledge.

"You need to pull out the rest of the money and close that account before every penny is gone." Dad's expression was somber.

Kristi cupped her cheeks in her hands. "Oh, you're right. I'll take care of it first thing tomorrow morning." Since Joel had taken over half of the money they'd saved, she was certainly entitled to what was left.

Dad's eyebrows furrowed, and he gave a quick snort. "I can't understand why he'd do something like that. Didn't he realize what it would do to your relationship?" He slapped the folded newspaper on the coffee table. "I'm disappointed in him. Joel is obviously not the man I thought he was."

Kristi dabbed at the tears dribbling down her cheeks. "I think. . .Joel's so caught up with his need for money. . ." Her voice broke on a sob. "He's not thinking of anything but himself."

To her surprise, instead of Mom saying something negative or reminding her of what the Bible said about being unequally yoked with an unbeliever, she pulled Kristi into her arms. "I know you must be hurting right now, but perhaps in time you'll find someone else—someone better for you."

Kristi sniffed against Mom's shoulder, returning the hug. "I. . .I can't even think about that right now."

"And you shouldn't either." Dad reached over and took Kristi's hand. "You need time to work through your pain and heal. Always remember, your mom and I are here for you."

"That's right," Mom agreed. "If you need to talk or want someone to pray with you, come by anytime or give us a call."

"Thanks. I will." As Kristi reached into her purse for a tissue, her cell phone rang. Seeing it was Joel, she let her voice mail answer the call.

∽

Joel held his cell phone up to his ear and grimaced when he heard Kristi's voice mail pick up. It was the fourth time he'd tried to call since she'd left his place, and he was desperate to talk to her. "If she's not going to answer my calls, then I'm going over to her place and talk to her."

Joel had already put the Corvette away in his shop, so he hopped in his everyday car and headed down the road. He hoped Kristi would listen and give him another chance. He was determined to patch things up. As he neared Kristi's place, Joel's palms began to sweat. Could he convince the woman he loved to change her mind about him?

When he pulled in front of Kristi's condo, his stomach clenched. Her car wasn't in the driveway. *I wonder where she could be.*

Joel sat for several minutes, running his hands

through his hair. He tried calling her again, but she didn't answer. When her voice mail finally came on, he left a message: "Listen, Kristi, we can't let it end like this. I love you, and we need to talk things through. Please call me."

As his heartbeat continued to race, he decided to drive over to Kristi's parents' house, thinking she might be there. When he turned onto their street, he saw Kristi's car parked in their driveway. At first, he felt relief, but then he realized why she probably was there. *I'll bet Kristi came here to tell her folks about our breakup.*

Joel had always felt a sense of coolness from Kristi's mother, JoAnn, so it wasn't likely she'd have anything positive to say to him right now. He'd gotten along better with her dad, but Paul might side with his daughter and ask Joel to leave.

"Nope, I wouldn't have a chance or a prayer in there," Joel murmured as he drove on by. "I'll give Kristi a few days to calm down, and then I'll call her again."

CHAPTER 2

When Kristi entered the nursing home Thursday morning, she was greeted with a cheery smile from Dorine Turner, one of the other nurses. "A bouquet of flowers came for you a few minutes ago. I put them in the break room."

Kristi's forehead wrinkled in puzzlement. "Are you sure they're for me?" she asked as she placed her belongings in a cubby. Many of the nursing home residents received flowers, but in all the time Kristi had worked there, no floral delivery had been for her.

Dorine nodded. "I saw your name on the outside of the card."

"Hmm... Guess I'll go take a look before I start my rounds."

When Kristi entered the room and spotted the glass vase filled with six lovely pink roses—her favorite flower—she blushed with pleasure. She walked over to the table and cupped the petals gently in her hands, leaning in to smell their delicate scent. *Whoever sent these must know me well. Maybe they're from Mom and Dad.*

When she opened the card attached to the ribbon, she flinched. *To Kristi. Love, Joel.*

Her warm feeling vanished like a candle flame snuffed out by a gust of air. She bit her lip, then released an irritated huff. *So now Joel thinks he can win me back with flowers?* She shook her head determinedly. *I think not.*

The roses were too pretty to throw out, but there was no way she would take them home. She couldn't believe Joel expected her to take him back and forget everything he'd done to her. *I know what to do. I'll give these flowers to one of the patients.*

After removing the card and tossing it in the trash, Kristi picked up the vase and started down the hall. When she approached Audrey Harrington's room and spotted the elderly woman sitting in a chair by her window, she rapped on the open door.

"Come in." A radiant smile spread across Audrey's wrinkled face when she turned to look at Kristi. "Is it time for my medicine?"

"Not yet." Kristi set the vase on the table beside Audrey's bed. She noticed some gardening magazines stacked neatly next to the lamp. The table looked like it had been cleaned recently with furniture polish, as it glistened in the sunlight shining through the window. Audrey's room was definitely one of the most orderly in the nursing home. While all the rooms received attention from housekeeping, Audrey also made sure her personal items were either lying neatly on the table or tucked away in one of her drawers. "These flowers are for you. I hope you will enjoy them."

"Oh my!" Audrey's arthritic fingers touched her parted lips. "Who are they from? No one has ever sent me flowers before. At least not since my husband passed away."

"There's a first time for everything." Kristi smiled, placing her hand gently on the elderly woman's slender shoulder. "These pretty roses are from me."

Audrey's hazel-colored eyes blinked rapidly as she gazed at the bouquet, then back at Kristi. "Why, thank you, dear. It was so thoughtful of you."

As much as Kristi disliked Joel trying to worm his way back into her life, she was glad he'd sent the flowers to her place of employment and not her home. It did Kristi's heart good to see the look of joy on Audrey's face as she rose from her chair, shuffled over to the flowers, and bent to smell them.

"The pleasant odor equals their beauty. I hope they last several days."

"I'll make sure when I come in to check on you that the roses get plenty of water," Kristi assured her.

Grinning like a child with a new toy, Audrey seated herself again, before picking up the worn-looking Bible lying on the foot of her bed. "God answers prayer." She lifted the book and held it to her chest. "I had prayed earlier that something good would happen in my life today, and it has." She gestured to the roses.

Kristi had not even thought to pray such a prayer when she'd gotten up this morning, but if she had, she, too, could proclaim that her prayer had been answered. The "something good" in her life today was seeing the joy she'd brought to a sweet lady who had never had a single visitor in the year she'd been here.

It grieved Kristi to see lonely patients with relatives who either didn't care or lived too far away to come for a visit. Smiling down at Audrey, Kristi decided to take a few minutes each day to visit this sweet lady and any other patients who appeared to be lonely. It would be good for them, as well as her.

೦ഌ

Charm

When Elsie arrived at her father's place to do more organizing and sorting, she was surprised to find Aunt Verna sitting at the kitchen table, drinking a cup of tea, still dressed in her nightclothes.

"*Ach*, you must think I'm a *faulenzer* this morning." A circle of pink erupted on Aunt Verna's cheeks.

"I don't think you're a lazy person at all." Elsie removed her shawl and outer bonnet, hanging them on a wall peg before taking a seat across from her aunt.

"Compared to Lester, I am lazy. He got up early to take care of the horses. Then, as soon as we had our breakfast, he went back out to the barn to do a few more chores." She opened her mouth and yawned loudly. "I slept longer than usual and don't have much get-up-and-go this morning."

"You've probably been working too hard, which is why I'm here to help out."

Aunt Verna tipped her head. "What was it you said?"

Elsie repeated herself.

"Oh jah, I've been keeping busy."

Elsie stared at the vacant chair positioned at the other end of the table. Tears sprang to her eyes. Oh, how she missed seeing her father in his chair with wheels. It may have seemed quirky to some, but there had always been something fascinating about watching him roll about the room in his special chair. Sometimes he'd even roll into the living room or down the hall to his bedroom. It wasn't that Dad couldn't walk. He simply enjoyed the ride as he pushed himself along with his feet, sometimes singing, whistling, or even playing his harmonica. To Elsie, seeing him do this was a treat.

What a unique character our daed was, she mused. *We never knew what he might say or do.* Growing up with Dad's spontaneity and peculiar habits had kept life interesting, even after Elsie had become an adult.

"Will your sisters be coming to sort through your daed's things today, too?" Aunt Verna's question invaded Elsie's thoughts.

"Uh, no. Doris has a doctor's appointment this morning, and if she feels well enough, she'll work at the restaurant this afternoon." Elsie made sure to speak louder this time.

Aunt Verna's silver-gray brows drew together. "I'm sorry to hear she's still not feeling well. It's good she's finally going to see the doctor."

"I agree."

"What about Arlene? Will she be joining us soon?"

"Not today. Baby Samuel is teething and kind of fussy, so Arlene decided to stay home."

"It's okay. We won't get as much done without their help, but I'm sure the three of us will manage. Although I'm not sure how much Lester will help here in the house. He said during breakfast that there's still plenty of work in the barn to be done."

"We will do the best we can." Elsie left her seat, filled the sink with warm water and detergent, and started washing the dishes.

"You don't have to do that." Aunt Verna got up and put her empty cup in the sink. "These are mine and Lester's breakfast dishes, so I'll take care of them. There are plenty of other things you can do, and you surely didn't come all the way from Millersburg to wash our dirty *gscjaar*."

Elsie knew better than to argue with her aunt. She'd tried it before and hadn't gotten anywhere. Besides, she really did need to get started sorting through more of Dad's things and looking for his will.

"All right then, if you insist." She handed the sponge to her aunt. "Guess I'll head upstairs to the attic and go through some of the items there."

"Good idea. Oh, and don't forget to keep a lookout for your daed's old boots. I still want them, you know."

Elsie nodded, even though she was sure Dad wouldn't have put his boots up there. More than likely he'd tossed them out. Elsie didn't understand Aunt Verna's interest in having Dad's tattered old boots, but if they did turn up, she could certainly have them.

As she made her way upstairs, Elsie thought about how many times she'd climbed these steps when she was a girl. Sometimes, she and her siblings would slide down the stairs on their stomachs, giggling all the way.

Her stomach fluttered at the memory, and she brought her fingers to her lips as a chuckle escaped. *Mama and Dad always told us to stop, otherwise our tummies would get a floor burn, but it was so much fun, we didn't mind. Oh, to be young and carefree again.*

She paused at the door to her old room and peeked inside. Her bed and dresser were no longer there, since her parents had given them to her when she and John got married. Now the bedroom was filled with boxes that hadn't been gone through yet. Elsie thought she would wait on those until one or both of her sisters were here to help. Until it was time to go downstairs and fix lunch, she would concentrate on rummaging through the stuff in the attic.

Turning the knob on the attic door, she decided to leave it open while she worked, so the room could be aired out. Her gaze came to rest on an old wooden chair under a box. It seemed inviting to sit on while she worked, so she moved the container to the floor and brushed off the chair with a rag she'd brought up with her.

Looking intently around the room for spider webs and seeing none close by, Elsie took a seat and gave the rag a few vigorous shakes to chase off the dust. The chair was kind of wiggly and squeaky. She hoped it wouldn't fall apart while she sat on it. But it was easier on her back than squatting beside every box. Elsie snickered, remembering how this old chair used to be downstairs in the kitchen. It didn't match the others at the table, so when Mama said it wasn't worth keeping, Dad hauled it up to the attic, unwilling to throw it out.

Elsie couldn't believe how much her parents had accumulated over the years. Sometimes sorting things out was like stepping back in time. So many memories. . . Some happy. . . Some sad.

꧁

"Look what I found!" Elsie announced when she stepped into Joel's old bedroom, where Aunt Verna was on her knees in front of an old trunk.

"What was that?" Still focused on the open trunk, Aunt Verna tipped her head.

Elsie spoke a little louder. "Look what I found."

Turning to look at her, Aunt Verna let out a whoop. "Ach! You found your daed's old duct-taped boots!" She rose to her feet. "Were they in the *aeddick*?"

"Jah, they were behind a stack of boxes up there." Elsie rubbed the duct tape with her thumb as she set the boots on the floor beside her aunt. "Now when you and Uncle Lester go home, you can take these along."

Aunt Verna grinned. "They'll make such nice planters. I'll probably wait till spring to plant something in them though. Since fall is here and the temperatures are dipping, there would be no point in putting any kind of *blumme* in these old boots now."

Elsie smiled. "It'll give you something to look forward to in the spring."

"So true. We all need something positive to think about."

"We surely do." Elsie gave her stomach a thump. "I don't know about you, but I'm getting hungerich. Should we go downstairs and see if Uncle Lester is ready to eat?"

Aunt Verna nodded and picked up the boots. "You know what though? I have a feeling he's still outside. If he ever came in, I didn't hear him."

Elsie wasn't sure how to respond. With Aunt Verna's loss of hearing, it was more than possible that Uncle Lester had come into the house without his wife being aware of his presence. And with Elsie having been up on the third floor for the last few hours, she wouldn't have heard her uncle come inside either.

"Let's go down and see where he is." She placed her hand in the crook of Aunt Verna's arm, and they left the room.

There was no sign of Uncle Lester downstairs, so Elsie headed to the kitchen to start lunch while Aunt Verna went outside to look for him.

She had finished preparing the sandwiches and was about to step outside to call her aunt and uncle, when the back door flew open and Aunt Verna rushed in. "They're gone!" she shouted, frantically waving both hands in the air. "Your daed's mare and her colt are missing!"

CHAPTER 3

Seeing the look of panic on her aunt's face, Elsie slipped her shoes on, flung the door open, and dashed into the yard.

Uncle Lester stood near the pasture gate, slowly shaking his head. "I thought I closed it when I let 'em into the field this morning, but I either forgot, or it must have blown open." Squinting, he rubbed the back of his neck. "I was in the barn, movin' some bales of hay around, and stepped outside for a breath of fresh air. That's when I discovered the gate was open and the mare and her colt were gone."

"What about my daed's other horses? Did any of them escape?"

"Nope. Just the mare and her foal." He gestured to the pasture. "Can ya see the other horses way out there, grazing?"

Elsie moved closer to the fence. Sure enough, the other horses were where Uncle Lester pointed. She curled her shoulders forward. "Should we walk up the road a ways and see if we can find them, or would it be better to use a buggy?"

"It'll take some time to get a horse and buggy ready, so I'm inclined to walk." He reached under his straw hat and scratched the side of his gray head. "On the other hand, my old arthritic knees won't let me do much walkin' without pain these days. Besides, I have no idea how long the two horses have been missing or how far they've gone from here."

"Why don't you call one of your drivers, Elsie?"

Aunt Verna suggested when she joined them by the fence. "If you can get someone to pick Lester up, they can drive up and down the roads looking for those horses."

Elsie tapped her finger against her chin. "That might be a good idea, but it could take awhile for me to find someone who's free to come. For now, at least, I think I'll walk down the road a ways and see if I can spot either of the horses." She gestured to her aunt and uncle. "Why don't you two go into the house? I've made some sandwiches. You can eat lunch while I look for the mare and her baby."

Wrinkling her brows, Aunt Verna looked at Uncle Lester. "What'd she say?"

"Said we should go inside and eat lunch while she looks for the *geil*," he shouted.

Aunt Verna shook her head forcibly. "That wouldn't be fair; we should all look for the horses."

Elsie didn't want to hurt her aunt's feelings, but truthfully, she could move much faster if she went looking on her own. She was about to comment, when she spotted Dad's neighbor, Abe Mast, coming up the driveway, leading the mare and her colt.

"I found these critters down by my place," Abe announced. "As soon as I saw 'em, I realized they belonged here."

Elsie breathed a sigh of relief. At least one problem had been solved today. "Danki for bringing them back to us."

"That's right," Uncle Lester agreed. "I was worried they might get hit by a car."

"What did you say to that man?" Aunt Verna nudged her husband's arm.

"Said I was worried the horses might get hit by a car!"

"There's no need to shout at me, Lester. I'm not deaf." She straightened her head covering and ambled into the house.

Elsie watched as he followed Aunt Verna, closing the door behind him. Those two sure kept life interesting.

Abe cleared his throat. "I miss your daed, Elsie. There was no one like him. Eustace was not only a good neighbor, but a friend to me as well." He walked up to her with the two horses and passed over their lead ropes.

"Jah. You probably never knew what my daed might say or do sometimes." Holding the ropes, she stood close to the colt and stroked its mane.

"Eustace wasn't afraid to state his opinion on things. He wasn't shy about his faith in the Lord either." Tears shone in Abe's dark eyes. "Your daed gave me encouragement when I was having doubts about my own beliefs. He saw me through some of the worst of times. Eustace knew the Bible and could quote scriptures so well. He told me to read the Word daily—that it would help get my head thinking straight." A big grin shot across Abe's face. "Need any help getting the horses into the barn?"

"Thanks anyway, but I think I can manage. I'll put them in the corral and bring back your spare tack." Without waiting for Abe's response, Elsie headed for the gate, horses in tow. When she returned with Abe's lead ropes, she asked, "Say, would you like to stay for lunch?"

"It's a nice offer, but I already ate. Besides, I've got work to do at my place."

Elsie smiled. "Thanks again, Abe. Have a nice rest of your day."

After Abe headed for home, Elsie turned toward the house. She was glad the horses were safely home and happy to hear Abe's story about her dad. Hopefully, the rest of the day would be uneventful.

⁓

Akron

"I can't believe you're working another double shift," Dorine said when she passed Kristi in the hall. "I'm dead on my feet and more than ready to go home. Figured you would be, too."

Kristi glanced at her watch. It was four o'clock. Normally she'd be getting off work about now. "Working keeps me from thinking too much," she responded. "Besides, I need the extra money right now."

Dorine's gaze flicked upward. "I know what you mean about money. Seems like there's never enough to go around." She gave Kristi's arm a tap. "Just don't spend too much of your time here. Besides burning yourself out, it can get pretty depressing at the nursing home, with so many sick and aging people in our care."

"That doesn't bother me," Kristi replied. "But you're right. If I work too many back-to-back shifts, I will burn out."

"Take the time to do something fun." Dorine moved toward the door. "See you tomorrow, Kristi."

After Kristi waved at her and started down the hall, she decided to check on Audrey. She hadn't seen her in the social room today or even in the patients' lunchroom.

"Are you feeling okay?" Kristi asked when she entered the elderly woman's room and found her sitting in the same chair she had been in that morning.

Audrey turned to look at her and smiled. "I'm fine, but thank you for asking."

"I was worried about you." She moved to stand beside Audrey's chair. "Didn't you eat lunch today?"

"Oh, I ate. Just asked to have my lunch tray brought to my room."

Kristi wondered why Audrey stayed in her room to eat and didn't resist the urge to ask.

"It's not that I didn't want to be with other people," Audrey explained. "I wanted to spend the day in solitude, praying and meditating on God's Word." She lifted the Bible from her lap and nodded at the flowers Kristi had given her. "I've also been enjoying those beauties only God could create."

"Everyone needs to take more time in God's presence and appreciate all the things He's created." Kristi exhaled softly. "Now let me give those roses more water before I forget."

The wrinkles above Audrey's eyes rose as she tipped her head. "So you're a Christian?"

Kristi nodded, adding more water to the vase. "I'll admit, though, sometimes I get caught up in the busyness of life and neglect my devotions and time of prayer." She dropped her gaze as her throat constricted. "I've been going through a rough time in my life lately, and I haven't sought answers from God." She placed the floral arrangement back on the table beside Audrey's bed.

"Thank you for taking care of my flowers."

"You're most welcome."

Audrey clasped her hands under her chin, in a prayer-like gesture. "If you feel inclined to share your need, I'd be happy to pray for you."

Taking a seat on the edge of Audrey's bed, Kristi shared some of her situation with Joel, without giving all the details. Her throat felt tight and began to ache as she continued to speak. "As much as Joel wants me to take him back, I'm convinced it's not the right thing to do."

Audrey's lips pressed tightly together. "It sounds like your ex-fiancé needs the Lord. Have you been praying for him?"

"Praying for him?" Heat tinged Kristi's face. "Guess I've been too consumed with my anger and disappointment." She sniffed deeply, attempting to thwart oncoming tears. "I will pray for him, but it's time to move on. Looking back on it all now, I realize we weren't meant to be together."

~

Joel tried calling Kristi as soon as he finished work that evening. Once again, she didn't answer. "Big surprise," he muttered, directing his truck onto the highway. *Think I'll drop by her house and see if I can catch her there. I'd like to know if she got the flowers I sent.*

The last few days had been hard for Joel, with Kristi not returning his calls, and no word from Elsie about Dad's will. On top of that, he still hadn't landed a job big enough to cover all of his debts.

Disappointed when he pulled up to Kristi's house and saw that her car wasn't there, Joel glanced at his watch. It was five o'clock. *She should've been home from work by now.* He scraped his fingers through his hair, noticing how greasy the roots felt. *Maybe she went to the store. Or she could have gone to the gym to work out.*

Inhaling deeply, Joel made a decision. He'd drop by Kristi's parents' house and see if he could enlist her dad's help. Paul Palmer had always seemed like a reasonable fellow. Whenever he and Kristi got together with her folks in the past, Joel felt as though he and Paul had made a connection. If he could talk to him without JoAnn intervening, he might have a chance.

He turned his truck in the direction of the Palmers' home. When he arrived and saw a dark blue SUV parked in the driveway, he knew at least one of Kristi's parents was there. Hopefully, it was Paul.

Pressing his finger on the doorbell, it only took a few seconds before Paul answered the door.

"Oh, it's you." The man's cool response caused Joel to take a step back. "If you're looking for Kristi, she's not here."

"No, I...uh...was hoping I could talk to you."

Paul's blue eyes narrowed as he peered at Joel over the top of his reading glasses. "About what?"

"About me and Kristi." Joel moistened his lips with his tongue. "She won't respond to any of my calls, and—"

Paul held up his hand, leaning against the doorframe. "Can you blame her, Joel? You've shattered her trust, and she's deeply hurt."

Joel blinked a couple of times to refocus his vision. His eyes felt gritty from lack of sleep. "I realize that, but I need another chance to prove myself." He shifted from one foot to another. "Would you speak to her on my behalf? Tell her how sorry I am and that I'd like to start over?"

Paul's lips pressed together as he shook his head. "I won't play gobetween for you. It would be best if you leave Kristi alone and move on with your life so she can do the same."

Scowling, Joel felt an uncomfortable tightness in his chest as he turned away. "Thanks for nothing." He stomped off the porch, gritting his teeth as he made his way back to his vehicle. *There has to be something I can do to get Kristi back. I need to figure out how to make her see she can't live without me.*

CHAPTER 4

Berlin

Doris turned toward the kitchen window, smiling when she saw it was no longer raining. Some puddles remained in the yard, rippling occasionally from the slight wind blowing leaves about. *Guess I'll go to the phone shack to check for messages.*

She glanced at the clock on the far wall. It was six-thirty. Brian would be in from doing his chores soon. There would barely be time for him to eat breakfast before leaving for work, so he wouldn't have a chance to check messages.

Slipping into a heavy sweater, Doris stepped outside, pausing to breathe the chilly air into her lungs. Things always felt so nice after a heavy rain. They'd had three full days of it, and the ground was saturated.

Doris dodged the puddles scattered on the ground as she made her way out to the phone shack. When she opened the door and stepped inside, she saw the light on the answering machine blinking.

Her hands felt like they were clasping icicles when she lowered herself onto the metal chair. Doris flicked the button and listened. The first message was from Elsie, reminding her that she and Arlene planned to be at Dad's place this morning and hoped if Doris wasn't working and felt up to it that she could join them.

I hope I can go. Doris touched her stomach. She'd been faced with some nausea again this morning but had gotten it under control after drinking a cup of ginger tea.

She turned her attention to the next phone message and listened intently, realizing it was her doctor's nurse. "We have the results of your blood tests, Doris. I'm calling to let you know the pregnancy test was positive."

Doris sat in stunned silence with her hand pressed to her chest. "Oh my."

"Congratulations, Mrs. Schrock. We already have your next appointment scheduled, so please call back to let us know if you're able to come in on that date. We look forward to hearing from you."

This news was almost too good to be true. It was the miracle she and Brian had been praying for.

Without bothering to listen to any of the other messages, Doris left the phone shack and hurried back to the house.

She found Brian in the kitchen, standing in front of the sink with a glass of water. "Are you all right, Doris? Your cheeks are red as a rose, and you're panting for breath."

"It's cold outside, and I've been to the phone shack." She rushed to his side and clasped his arm. "Oh, Brian, I have the best news."

"What is it? Did one of your sisters find your daed's will?"

"No, this is much better news than anything concerning his will. There was a message for me from Dr. Wilson's nurse."

"What'd she say? Is it a lingering kind of flu you've been dealing with?"

"Jah. I have the baby flu."

Brian blinked a couple of times. "Huh?"

"I said, 'I have the baby flu.'" Doris could hardly contain the laughter bubbling up in her throat.

He tipped his head. "What?"

Tears trickled down her cheeks as she placed both hands on her stomach. "She said my blood tests came back and I am *im e familye weg*."

Brian's eyes widened. "You. . .you're in a family way?"

"That's correct." Doris rubbed her stomach and smiled. "I can hardly believe it, Brian. God has answered our prayers."

He set the glass on the counter and pulled her into his arms. "This is the best news. Better than anything I could have imagined."

She leaned her head against his chest as more tears fell. The only thing dampening her joy was the knowledge that her parents would not get to meet their grandchild. But at least Brian's folks were still alive, although Doris wished they lived closer. Geauga County, where her aunt Verna and uncle Lester also lived, was over two hours away.

"I can't wait to share our good news with my sisters," Doris said after she'd dried her eyes. "I'll tell them this morning when I go to Charm to help sort through more of Dad's things."

"Do you think that's a good idea?" Brian gazed into Doris's eyes. "You haven't been feeling well, and now that you're expecting a boppli, I don't want you doing too much. In fact, I think you ought to quit your job."

"The nausea is better when I drink ginger tea." She gave his arm a reassuring pat. "I'll be careful not to do too much. As far as my job goes. . . We could use the extra money, so I'd like to keep working awhile longer—at least till I start to show."

"Okay, but if it gets to be too much, you'll need to quit working sooner than that."

"Agreed."

⁓

Charm

"Do you think Doris is coming? If so, she ought to be here by now." Arlene looked briefly at the clock above Dad's refrigerator. "It's nine o'clock."

"I called and left her a message last night." Elsie shrugged. "But if she's not feeling well or had to work, she may not be able to come."

Arlene sighed deeply. "Our poor *schweschder* has not been feeling up to par for too many days."

"She was supposed to see the doctor last week, but I haven't talked to her since. I'm anxious to find out how the appointment went." Elsie pinched the bridge of her nose. "Guess we should get busy while we're waiting to see if Doris shows up. What room do you want to start in today?"

Arlene tapped her toe against the worn linoleum floor. "I'm not sure. Do you have a preference?"

"Not really. I worked in the attic when I was here last week, but we still have a lot more boxes up there to go through."

"I can only imagine. It seems boxes are in nearly every room of this house, not to mention the barn and buggy shed. Sure will be glad once we get through all of it."

"Too bad Uncle Lester and Aunt Verna went home last Saturday. We could still use some extra help."

Arlene glanced at baby Samuel, lying in his

playpen. "If my little guy wakes up and starts fussing, I won't be much help for a while either."

"We could ask some of the women in our church district to help, but Dad's things are personal, and only we know what we want to keep or throw out."

"True." Arlene moved toward the stove. "The water's hot now. Would you like a cup of tea?"

"That'd be nice. I'll get out the cups and put our teabags in." Elsie placed the cups on the table.

Arlene waited for her sister to add the tea bags before she poured the hot water. Opening the refrigerator to get some cream, her gaze came to rest on the pie Elsie had brought. Her mouth watered, thinking how good it would taste. It was tempting to sample a piece now, but it would be better to wait until later to cut the pie.

"How are things working out with your son staying here since Aunt Verna and Uncle Lester left?" Arlene asked Elsie.

"From what Glen said when I got here this morning, everything's been fine. He's been getting up early to take care of the horses and does some other chores after he gets home from work."

"I bet it's kind of lonely for him being here all alone."

"If it is, he hasn't complained. He's probably glad to be by himself, after spending a good piece of the day at work with his daed and the other fellows John has working for him." Elsie laughed. "I think Blaine misses his big brother, though he'd never admit it."

"That's often how it is with siblings. Sometimes Doug and Scott don't always get along, but when Doug's old enough to move out of the house, I'm sure Scott will miss him."

"You're probably right."

They'd just started drinking their tea when Arlene heard the whinny of a horse from outside. "I'll bet that's Doris."

"Oh, good. It must mean she's feeling better." Elsie jumped up. "Think I'll go help her unhitch the horse and get it put in the corral."

Arlene smiled. "I'll make sure to have a cup of tea ready for Doris when you come in."

"I'm sure she'll appreciate it on this brisk fall morning." Elsie wrapped her shawl around her shoulders and slipped out the back door.

While Arlene waited for her sisters to come in, she fixed another cup of tea. Glancing at the wall peg near the back door, she noticed her father's old hat. He had ducttaped part of the brim, like he'd done with his worn-out boots.

Sniffing, she reached for a tissue to dry her eyes and wipe her nose. The old hat was reminiscent of Dad, but she doubted anyone would want it. And they sure couldn't take it to the thrift store. Nobody would buy a hat in that condition, even if the price was reasonable.

As Arlene continued to gaze at the hat, a memory from her childhood came to mind. When Joel was five years old, he'd found Dad's straw hat somewhere in the barn. He had emerged from the building wearing the hat, which was much too big for him and nearly covered his eyes. Then he'd sauntered over to the swing, where Arlene was pushing Doris, and announced, *"Someday, when I'm big like* Daadi, *I'm gonna be rich. Then I can buy whatever I want."*

Arlene shuddered, gripping the back of Dad's chair. Little did she realize back then that her brother's quest for money would continue into his adult life. All Joel seemed to care about was finding the will so he could get his share of the money.

We all could use money, Arlene thought. *But I'd rather have Dad here than any fortune he may have left us. Nothing on earth is more important than my family.*

The back door opened, and Doris and Elsie stepped in, putting an end to Arlene's musings. "I'm glad you could make it." She gave Doris a hug. "How are you feeling this morning?"

"I was a little nauseous when I first woke up, but a cup of ginger tea took care of it." Doris lifted the plastic sack she held. "I brought more teabags with me, in case I feel sick to my stomach again."

"I heard you went to the doctor's last week. Did you find out what was wrong with you?" Arlene questioned.

"They took blood tests, and I got the results this morning." Doris's face broke into a wide smile. "I'm im e familye weg."

"Ach my!" Elsie, who stood closest to Doris, gave her a hug. "That's such good news."

"Congratulations!" Arlene rushed forward and wrapped her arms around both of her sisters. She quoted Psalm 107:1: " 'O give thanks unto the Lord, for he is good: for his mercy endureth for ever.' "

For the next half hour, the sisters sat at the table, drinking tea and rejoicing over Doris's good news.

"As nice as this is, I think we ought to get busy and do some sorting now." Doris pushed away from the table.

"You're right," Elsie agreed. "Should we all work

in the same room, or would you rather each take a separate room?"

"It might be better if we work separately," Arlene replied. "If we work together, we'll be apt to visit and get less sorting done."

"Maybe I'll continue working in the attic." Elsie smiled at Doris. "Would you mind going through some boxes in your old room, and Arlene can sort boxes in the room she used to sleep in? That way, we'll all be upstairs, and if any of us needs something, we'll be able to hear each other."

Doris nodded, and Arlene did the same. "If you start feeling sick to your stomach or get tired and want to lie down, please don't hesitate to do so." Arlene touched Doris's arm. "There's no way we can get all the sorting done today, so we shouldn't push ourselves too hard."

"I'll rest if I need to."

❧

"Did either of you find Dad's will?" Elsie asked when the sisters stopped working to fix lunch.

"The only thing I found were a lot of old copies of *The Budget*, plus way too many catalogs." Doris groaned. "I don't understand why Dad thought he had to keep all those."

"I don't either," Arlene agreed. "All I can say is Mama was lenient on Dad's behalf. Each time one of us moved out, she'd let him put his things in the empty rooms. Using our old bedrooms to store boxes only gave him more places to keep all that junk."

"To Dad, it wasn't junk. He must have had a purpose for all his collections." Elsie picked up the box of pens she'd found in the attic.

"Maybe we shouldn't throw out any of the magazines or catalogs until we've had a chance to look through every page." Arlene took out a loaf of bread to make sandwiches.

"Why would we want to do that?" Doris questioned.

"It may seem strange, but Dad could have stuck his will inside one of the magazines or even at the bottom of one of the boxes."

Doris went to the refrigerator to get the mustard, mayonnaise, meat, and cheese. "If we take time to thumb through every magazine, catalog, and newspaper, I'll be helping here sorting till my boppli's born—maybe longer."

Elsie was about to comment when she heard a familiar rumble. She went to the window and watched as a tractor entered the yard. "Henry Raber is here, and it looks like he brought his hund."

Arlene gestured to the food Doris placed on the counter. "There's plenty to make several sandwiches. We should invite him to stay for lunch."

"I'll bet he came over because he misses Dad so much," Doris interjected. "Poor Henry has no family living in the area. I'm sure he gets lonely."

"He and Dad were best friends, even though Henry was New Order and Dad was Old Order. Their friendship was special." Elsie opened the back door just as Henry, holding Peaches under one arm and a book in his other hand, stepped onto the porch.

"I won't trouble you." Henry handed Elsie the book. "I borrowed this from your daed some time ago and thought I'd better return it. I heard your son Glen was staying here and hoped I might find him at home."

"Glen's at work," Elsie explained. "I'm here today with Doris and Arlene. We've been going through some of Dad's things." She glanced at the book—a fiction novel set in the Old West. "Why don't you keep this, Henry? I'm sure Dad would want you to have it."

Henry nodded slowly, his eyes misting as Elsie handed the book to him. "I have many good memories about Eustace. It's hard to believe he's gone."

"It is for us as well." She opened the door wider. "We're about to have lunch. Why don't you come in and join us?"

"Oh, I don't want to put you out." Henry turned his head in the dog's direction. "Besides, I have Peaches with me, and if I put her back in the cage, she'll whine and carry on like a squalling baby."

"It's okay, bring her in. She can lie on the throw rug near the door." Elsie felt sure the dog would stay there because she'd witnessed how well-behaved Peaches was before.

After Henry came inside and washed his hands, he told Peaches to lie on the rug. Everyone gathered around the table, and once their silent prayer was said, Elsie circled the table and passed around the platter of sandwiches. As they ate, their conversation covered several topics, including the weather.

"Can't say I'm lookin' forward to snow, but I'm sure it'll be comin'." Henry's bushy eyebrows drew together. "I'm thinkin' about spending the winter in Florida, like so many other Amish and Mennonite folks my age do."

"Maybe you should." Doris handed Henry the

bag of chips she'd brought along to share. "I bet Peaches would love romping on the beach."

"Jah." He looked over at Peaches. "I was hoping Eustace would want to go there with me, but I guess going with my hund would be better than not goin' at all." He motioned to Dad's old hat on the wall peg. "I'll never forget the day I came to visit your daed and he was wearing that old hat held together with duct tape. Seeing it hangin' there now makes me feel as though he might come through the door any time. Course," he quickly added, "I know it's not gonna happen."

In a spontaneous decision, Elsie rose from her chair and took the hat down. "How would you like to have this, Henry?" She held it out to him.

"Ach, no, I can't take that. You already gave me the book. Besides. . ." He lowered his gaze. "It's your daed's special hat."

"It's okay, Henry. I want you to have it. We have plenty of other things here to remember him by." She smiled. "Besides, none of us have a reason to wear a straw hat. As long as you're wearing it, it'll be put to good use."

His eyes filled with tears as he took the hat from her. "Danki. Think I'll hang it in my kitchen. Then every time I look at it, I'll think of your daed."

Seeing how choked up Henry had become, Elsie moved over to the refrigerator and took out the pie she'd brought for dessert. "Who wants a piece of millionaire pie?" she asked.

Doris and Arlene held up their hands, but Henry continued to sit, while staring at the hat.

"Henry, would you like piece of millionaire pie?" Arlene asked.

He looked over at her and blinked. "I've never heard of millionaire pie. Did one of you make up the name on account of your daed?"

Elsie shook her head. "No, it really is the name of the pie." She placed it on the table while Doris got out four plates and forks. She was thankful Henry had stopped by today. Having him here made her feel somehow closer to Dad.

"So what do you hear from your bruder these days?" Henry asked.

A thin line of wrinkles formed above Doris's brows. "We haven't seen Joel since Dad's funeral."

Henry pushed a strand of gray hair aside and scratched behind his ear. "That's too bad. You'd think he'd want to spend time with his sisters."

Elsie clutched the folds in her dress. She wasn't about to tell Henry what she thought of her selfish brother, but she couldn't help wondering why she hadn't heard from Joel in several days. *Has he been too busy to call me, or has my brother decided to be patient and wait for me to let him know once we find the will?*

CHAPTER 5

Berlin

It was the last Saturday of October, and for the first time since her breakup with Joel, Kristi felt a sense of excitement. Moments ago, she and Mom had left the quilt shop where they'd taken their first quilting lesson. Since her Saturdays were free now and she needed something fun to do, learning how to quilt seemed like a good idea. It was also an opportunity for her and Mom to spend time together, doing something they both enjoyed. Kristi had certainly enjoyed today's lesson, although most of the morning had been spent learning the basics of quilting and cutting the pieces of material they would use to make their quilts. Kristi had chosen two shades of purple for the queen-size quilt she planned to put on her bed.

Another reason she liked the class was because their Amish instructor was kind and patient. Kristi's desire to know more about the Amish way of life could be somewhat fulfilled by spending time with Mattie Troyer. It was a shame she'd have no connection with Joel's sisters now that she and Joel had no plans to be married.

"You're awfully quiet over there." Mom removed one hand from the steering wheel and tapped Kristi's arm. "It was beginning to feel like I was alone in the car."

Kristi's lips parted slightly. "Sorry, Mom. I've been deep in thought."

"Mind if I ask what you were thinking about?"

"Oh, nothing exciting—just reflecting on our first quilting class. I enjoyed it so much and appreciated how patient our teacher was with all my questions."

"Yes, she was very kind and helpful. I had fun, too, and look forward to our class next week."

"Same here." Kristi pulled down the visor to check her hair.

"Are you sure you don't mind taking a side trip to Charm so I can get more of that good cheese I bought for your dad the last time we were here?"

"I don't mind at all. I'll probably buy some cheese, too." Looking in the visor mirror, Kristi pulled her hairband off and brushed every strand back in place before securing it in a ponytail.

As they drew closer to Charm, she spotted the road she and Joel took to his dad's place. She was on the verge of asking Mom to turn there so she could see it but changed her mind. One of Joel's sisters, or even Joel, might be there, and it could be awkward. It was best to say nothing and keep going. If she even pointed out the road and said it led to Eustace Byler's home, Mom might say she was better off without Joel. Kristi didn't need the reminder; she still felt she had done the right thing. She would continue to pray for Joel, as Audrey had suggested, but it wouldn't be for them to get back together. She'd ask God to help Joel see the importance of developing a close relationship with his sisters and their families and, most of all, to know God personally.

"Say, I have an idea." Mom broke into Kristi's thoughts a second time. "When we leave the cheese store in Charm, why don't we head up to Walnut

Creek and eat lunch at Der Dutchman? I really enjoyed our meal the last time we went there."

"That's fine with me." Kristi leaned back in her seat. Being in Amish country made her feel nostalgic. *If only things had worked for me and Joel.*

༉

Walnut Creek

Doris was glad her shift would end at two o'clock. She'd arrived at the restaurant early today to serve the breakfast crowd, but a lot more people had come in for lunch. In addition to a few waves of nausea she'd experienced during her shift, her feet hurt from being on them so long. Fortunately, she only had another hour to go; then she'd head for home and take a nap.

Maybe Brian was right when he said I should quit my job. But with a baby coming, we need the extra money, so I'll try to keep working as long as I can.

Glancing toward her section of tables, Doris noticed the hostess seating two women. One she recognized immediately—Joel's girlfriend. She moved over to their table. "It's nice to see you again, Kristi."

Blinking rapidly, Kristi offered Doris a brief smile. "Oh, hi. I'd forgotten you worked here." She motioned to the auburn-haired woman sitting across from her. "This is my mother, JoAnn. Mom, I'd like you to meet Joel's sister Doris."

"It's nice to meet you." Doris lifted the pencil and order pad from her apron pocket.

"Actually, this isn't our first meeting." JoAnn glanced briefly out the window, then back at Doris. "My daughter and I ate lunch here a few months ago. You were our waitress then as well. But that was before Kristi had been formally introduced to you the day of your father's funeral." She paused and moistened her lips. "I'm so sorry for your loss."

Doris fought for control. Nearly every time someone offered their condolences, she teared up. "Thank you," she murmured.

"How's your family?" Kristi asked. "Are you and your sisters getting along okay?"

"Under the circumstances, we're doing the best we can." She paused. "How's Joel? None of us have seen him since the funeral."

Kristi's cheeks flushed as she spun the bracelet around her wrist. "Umm. . .Joel and I aren't together anymore."

Doris drew in a quick breath, nearly dropping her order pad. "I—I'm so sorry. I didn't know."

"It's all right. If you want to hear what happened, feel free to give me a call some evening, and I'll explain everything." Kristi picked up the menu in front of her.

"Oh, okay." Doris had almost forgotten she and Kristi had exchanged phone numbers the day of Dad's funeral. She was curious to know why Kristi and Joel had broken up, so she would definitely give her a call. Based on Joel's past history with Anna, Doris felt sure the breakup was his fault.

Akron

When Joel stopped working at two o'clock to eat lunch, he decided to check his cell phone for messages. He'd been busy remodeling a closet for a newly married couple and had absentmindedly left his phone in the truck. Due to the stress from his breakup with Kristi and her refusal to return any of his calls, he'd forgotten a lot of things lately. Joel was consumed by his desire to be with Kristi. He couldn't believe she wouldn't talk to him or respond to any of his text messages.

Maybe I should send her more flowers. Joel climbed into his truck and picked up his cell phone. *Doesn't she realize how desperate I am to get her back?*

Joel typed in his password, hoping one of the messages he'd received was from Kristi. The first two were prospective customers. The next one was the carpenter to whom he still owed money. The final message was from Elsie, asking Joel to check with Kristi to see if they could come to supper one evening.

"There's no point replying to that message," he mumbled, placing the cell phone on the passenger's seat. "Sorry, Sis, but you're a little too late. And what about Dad's will? You made no mention of that."

Joel's face tightened as he rubbed at the knots in the back of his neck. Elsie promised to get back to him about Dad's will, but so far there had been no word. Did it mean they hadn't found it yet, or was she keeping it from him? "Could Dad have cut me out of his will?" Joel grunted. "He'd better not have done something like that."

He sucked in a couple of deep breaths, trying to calm himself. Elsie had always been a straightforward person. If they'd found the will, she would have said so. He reached over to the passenger seat and grabbed his lunch pail. Looking inside, he decided to start with the bag of chips. While he ate them, he thought about how to deal with his situation. He still had another hour or two before he finished working today.

Clutching the steering wheel, Joel decided he would go home, take a shower, get a bite to eat, and head to Charm. He was going to take the quest for Dad's will into his own hands. Surely it couldn't be that hard to find.

$$\approx$$

Charm

When Joel arrived at his father's house, he wasn't surprised to see all the windows completely dark. He figured by now his aunt and uncle would have returned to their home. Since no one lived here anymore, it was his perfect opportunity to look around.

He pulled his truck up near the barn and turned off the engine. Fortunately, he'd had the good sense to bring a flashlight along, because it would have been nearly impossible to find his way to the front door in the dark.

Stepping onto the porch, Joel turned the knob and was surprised to find the door locked. He kicked it and gritted his teeth. In all the years he'd grown up in this house, Dad had never locked any of the doors. Joel figured his sisters had locked the place to keep anyone from breaking in.

Guess in a way, that's what I'm doing, he thought as he headed around back, hoping to find that door unlocked. Irritation welled when he discovered it, too, was locked.

"Sure wish I had a key," Joel mumbled. "Now I've gotta check every window and hope one is open."

He shined the light on the first window. In so

doing, he caught sight of the basement door. *Maybe that's unlocked.*

Making his way carefully down the stairs, he turned the knob. *Bingo!* The door opened. Joel figured there had to be a gas or kerosene lamp down there somewhere, so he shined his flashlight around until he found one. After lighting it, he began his search—looking through box after box for anything that resembled a will.

This could take forever. He blew out his breath. *If I don't find something soon, I may as well head home and come back another day when I'm not working and have plenty of time to look around.*

Joel had to be desperate to be in Dad's basement, searching through all this junk. "Really, what are the odds the will would be down here anyway?" he muttered.

He decided to check another box, but just as he opened the lid, the kerosene lamp went out. *Oh, great.*

Feeling his way, Joel moved slowly across the room, hoping he was heading in the direction of the door. After he'd turned on the lamp, he'd stupidly laid his flashlight down, and now that he was in the dark, he couldn't find it. If he could make it to the door, he'd have to find his car in the blackness of night.

Joel continued to move around and managed to knock something over. The metallic sound resonated throughout the basement, and he reached out to see if he could tell what it was. From the feel of the object, he was fairly certain it was one of the old milk cans Dad was so fond of. Grunting, Joel moved it aside. Trying to walk through the maze of clutter wasn't working out too well, so he went down on his knees. As he crawled across the floor, he moved his hand around, searching for the flashlight. A chill went up Joel's spine when he heard a noise behind him. *What was that?*

Suddenly, an intense light shone in his face, stinging his eyes. A deep voice shouted, "What are you doing here?"

CHAPTER 6

"Maybe I should be the one asking 'What are you doing here?'" Joel blurted, when he realized the young man holding the flashlight in front of his face was Elsie's son Glen.

"I've been stayin' here since Aunt Verna and Uncle Lester went home."

"Oh, I see." Joel found his own flashlight and clambered to his feet. "How come the house is so dark? It was only seven o'clock when I got here. I doubt you were in bed."

"Just got back from havin' supper at my folks. Sure was surprised to see your truck parked out by the barn." Glen pointed his flashlight at Joel again but avoided his face. "What were you doin' down here in the dark, and how'd ya get in?"

"The basement door was unlocked, and not that it's any of your business, but I've been looking for my dad's will."

"My mamm and her sisters have been doin' that. Do they know you're here?"

"No, they don't, but even if they did, I don't care." Joel tightened his fingers around the flashlight. "This is my dad's house, and I have as much right to be here as anyone else in the family."

"So, did ya find Grandpa's will?" Glen leaned against a stack of folding chairs.

"Not yet, but I'll do more looking tomorrow."

Glen's eyebrows squished together. "You're comin' back on Sunday?"

"I won't have to come back, because I'm already

here." Joel didn't know why he hadn't thought of it before, but since he was at his dad's house and didn't have to work tomorrow, he may as well spend the night. It didn't matter that tomorrow was Sunday, because he had no plans to go to church. In fact, he hadn't attended even once since Kristi broke up with him. What would be the point? He'd only be going to impress her, which probably wouldn't work, since she'd no doubt be there with her folks. Since Kristi's dad didn't want Joel bothering his daughter, Joel figured he'd better stay clear of Kristi's parents.

"What are you saying—that you plan to spend the night here?" Glen stared at Joel as though in disbelief.

"Yeah, that's right. I'll bed down in my old room tonight."

"There are a lot of boxes up there. You'd probably have to move some of 'em to get to the bed."

"It won't bother me. I'll do what needs to be done in order to make the room comfortable. Maybe I'll look through those boxes before I go to bed." Joel pointed toward the stairs that led up to the kitchen. "Let's head on up."

Glen led the way, as he continued to speak. "You can do whatever you want, but it won't do ya no good. I think the boxes in your old room have already been gone through, and no will was found."

Joel's pulse quickened. This twenty-year-old man seemed determined to keep him from spending the night. But Joel wasn't about to be dissuaded. If he didn't find what he was looking for tonight, he'd continue his search in the morning.

The following morning, Joel woke up to the sound of soft winds blowing against his bedroom window. He groaned, slowly pulling the covers over his head. It felt like a herd of horses had trampled his back. The mattress on his old bed was a lot harder than he remembered.

He let out a few breaths, while slowly rising from the bed, then winced when his bare feet touched the cold hardwood floor. He might as well have been standing on a frozen lake. Joel's trailer house had carpeting in the bedroom, so he wasn't used to walking on a frigid floor as soon as he stepped out of bed. Stretching his arms overhead, Joel ambled over to the window and looked out. The sun was hidden behind the clouds, but at least it wasn't raining.

He hurried to get dressed, and shortly after, caught a whiff of coffee brewing. *I could sure use some caffeine to kick-start my day.*

Closing the door to his room, Joel hurried down the stairs, following the enticing scent. He found his nephew in the kitchen, slathering peanut butter on a piece of toast.

"Mornin'. Coffee's ready if ya want some, and there's bread to make toast. Or if you'd rather have cold cereal, there's some of that, too." Glen pointed across the room.

"I'm good with coffee for now." Joel took a mug out of the cupboard and filled it with the steaming brew. "Thanks for making the coffee." He took a sip and smacked his lips. "This hits the spot. Not too bad at all."

"You really oughta eat some breakfast. My mamm always says, 'Everyone needs a hearty breakfast to begin the day.'"

"Your mom's not here, so I'll do as I please." Joel pulled a chair toward him and took a seat at the table, ignoring his nephew's finger tapping on the tabletop. *Glen probably wishes I wasn't invading his space. Well, if he does, it's too bad. I'm here, and I plan to make the day count for something, even if I don't locate the will. If I look long enough, at least I'll know where it isn't.*

"How long will you be sticking around?" Glen's serious brown eyes seemed to bore right into Joel's soul.

He shrugged his shoulders. "Don't know yet. Could be a good part of the day."

"You gonna keep lookin' for Grandpa's will?" Glen got up to warm his coffee.

"It's important for somebody to find it. . .and soon."

"Sure seems odd no one's located it yet. Makes me wonder if there even is a will. What do you think, Joel?" Glen bit into his toast and brushed the fallen crumbs off his black vest.

Joel's internal temperature heated as he gripped his fingers around the handle of his mug. "There has to be a will. My daed was no *dummkopp*. I'm sure he'd want to provide for his kinner." He scratched his cheek, unsure of why he'd spoken several Amish words. When Joel walked away from his heritage, it took awhile to quit speaking Pennsylvania Dutch, but he'd left it behind. Except for the few words he'd shared with Kristi, Joel hadn't spoken it in a long time. *Being here in Dad's house and speaking to Glen must be what caused me to revert.*

"Come to think of it, my mamm said Aunt

Verna told her that Grandpa did make out a will." Glen finished eating his toast and washed it down with a swig of coffee. "The only trouble is Aunt Verna can't remember where he put it."

"That's ridiculous. He should have told some-one else where it is." Joel wondered if his dad had gone to a lawyer to have the will made up, or if he'd done his own and had it notarized. He guessed the latter, because if Dad had a lawyer, surely one of Joel's sisters or Aunt Verna would know who it was and have contacted him by now. *Don't know why Dad had to be so closemouthed about things.*

"Whelp, I need to get outside and hitch my *gaul* to the buggy." Glen pushed away from the table and put his dishes in the sink, rinsing them off. Then he brushed off his dark-colored dress trousers, where a few crumbs had stuck. "Today's a church Sun-day for our district, and I don't want to be late." He turned to face Joel. "Would ya like to go with me? My folks, as well as my brother and sisters, will be there. I'm sure they'd like to see you."

"Yeah, I figured by the way you're dressed that it was a church day. I won't be going with you, but I will walk out to the barn. It'll be nice to see my dad's horses." Joel grabbed his jacket and followed Glen out the door.

After they entered the barn, Joel watched Glen get his horse ready and lead it outside to the buggy. "Do you ever take my dad's buggy horse out for a ride?" he asked.

Glen shook his head. "No way! That crazy gaul is too spirited for me."

"He will only get worse if he isn't taken out sometimes." Joel slid his hand into his jacket pocket and pulled out a piece of gum. A memory from the past popped into his head. Dad used to carry gum in his pockets. Whenever Joel went out to the barn to help clean or take care of the horses, he was usually rewarded with a stick of gum. Of course, he was just a boy then, and any little treat from Dad was appreciated.

Glen broke into Joel's musings. "You're most likely right about Grandpa's horse, but my daed said he'd take care of doing that."

"Bet I could make the horse do what I wanted." With legs spread wide, Joel thrust out his chest. "I grew up with Dad's horses. I could always make them do what I wanted."

Glen tipped his head slightly but made no comment.

"Has anyone in the family talked about selling Dad's horses? It makes no sense to keep them, now that Dad is gone." Joel pulled his fingers through the sides of his hair. "Besides, the money could be split among me and my sisters."

"That's something you'd have to discuss with them." Glen led his horse to the front of the buggy shafts.

"Yeah, I'll do that." Joel caught sight of Glen's straw hat lying on the floor of his open buggy. He wouldn't be wearing it today however. For church, all Amish men wore their black dress hats. He reached in and picked up the hat. Holding it brought back memories from when he was Amish. It was strange how moments like this made him feel a sense of nostalgia and actually helped him relax. Other times, certain thoughts from his past put him on edge or seemed like nothing more than a distant dream.

Farmerstown

"Say, Mom, can me and Scott go over to Grandpa's after church today so we can jump on the trampoline?" Arlene's son Doug asked as they finished eating breakfast.

Arlene pursed her lips. "I don't think so, Son. It's not a good idea for you boys to be hanging around over there alone."

"I wanna go, too," Lillian spoke up.

Her sister, Martha, bobbed her head in agreement. "If we all go, then none of us will be alone."

"Our daughter has a point," Arlene's husband interjected. "Besides, now that Glen is staying at your daed's house, they'll have adult supervision."

Arlene frowned. "Glen is not a self-sufficient adult yet. He's twenty years old, and until he moved into Dad's place, which is only temporary, he lived at home."

"He's old enough to stay by himself. And he has a full-time job, so I think he's capable of supervising our kinner today, don't you?"

Arlene sighed. "I suppose you're right." She looked at Doug. "Just make sure you and your siblings are *achtsam* today. No craziness on the trampoline, okay?"

"We'll be careful," the boy promised.

"Are you going to ride your bikes, or would you like me to take you there with my horse and buggy?" Larry questioned.

"We'll ride our bikes." Doug looked at his siblings. "Is that okay with you?"

Scott, Lillian, and Martha nodded.

Smiling at Arlene, Larry reached over and

patted her arm. "While the kinner are at your daed's place, you should take a nap. You've been working too hard lately, trying to keep up with all your chores here, plus helping your sisters sort through your daed's things. If you're not careful, you're gonna wear yourself down and may even get grank."

"I won't get sick from doing a little work, so please don't worry." She rose from her seat and scooped her dishes into the sink. "Hurry now, everyone. We don't want to be late for church."

◦◦◦

Charm

After searching for the will for two hours, Joel decided he needed some fresh air. *Think I'll take Dad's closed-in buggy and hitch up his spirited horse. I'll bet he's not nearly as hard to handle as Glen thinks.*

Thirty minutes later, Joel plunked Glen's straw hat on his head, climbed into the buggy in an easygoing manner, and took up the reins. It felt strange to be sitting on the right-hand side of the buggy, in readiness to take the horse out on the road. Joel had become used to driving his cars and truck, where he felt more in control. He'd never admit it to his nephew, but Joel felt a bit vulnerable right now.

Don't be such a coward, he chided himself. *If you learn how to ride a bike, you never forget what to do. Same goes for driving a horse and buggy.*

With a renewed sense of confidence, Joel directed the horse up the driveway and onto the road. So far, the animal was behaving, and he began to relax. The sound of the horse's hooves hitting the pavement caused Joel's breaths to slow down. He pictured himself when he was younger, riding in the buggy with his family on their way to church every other Sunday. He would watch his father intently as he guided the horse down the road. There was something about controlling a thousand-pound steed that Joel had found intriguing, and he'd wanted nothing more than to try it himself. He had been given a pony when he was a boy, but training the small animal to pull the pony cart had been too easy.

Joel reflected on the first time Dad had let him drive the horse and buggy. He'd been eleven years old and had begged to try it. His lips curved into a smile. *Dad thought I was too young, but I proved him wrong when he finally handed me the reins.*

A mile or so up the road, something spooked the horse, which caused Joel's thoughts to scatter. The spirited gelding began to act up, flipping his head from side to side, while balking at Joel's every request. Then, as if he'd been stung by a bee, the critter took off like a flash. "Whoa, boy!" he hollered, pulling back on the reins. "There's no need to rush."

Joel heaved a sigh of relief when he finally got the animal under control and going at a slower, even pace. "What's wrong with you?" He spoke to the horse with assurance. "Are you trying to make me look bad?"

Joel was surprised when the gelding responded with a whinny. *Maybe he was purposely testing me, and now he knows who's boss.*

Rounding the next bend, he spotted an open buggy heading in the opposite direction. He recognized the driver immediately—Anna Detweiler. She didn't wave while passing, so Joel figured

Anna hadn't recognized him. Of course, being in the closed buggy, he wouldn't have been as easy to recognize as if he'd been driving an open rig.

Joel's thoughts took him back to the months he'd courted Anna and all the fun things they'd done together. He remembered how they used to play volleyball with some of their friends in the evenings during the summer. The soles of Joel's feet would tickle as he maneuvered on the grass, trying to win a point for his team. Joel wasn't as good at the game as Anna; she was a natural. She'd tried to show him the correct way to serve the ball, by tossing it in the air, striking it with a hand or lower part of her arm. But Joel continued to mess up when it was his turn to serve.

He couldn't help but smile when he thought about her. In addition to being pretty, and a good volleyball player, Anna was easygoing, smart, and had a special connection with children, which was what probably made her want to be a teacher. Joel, on the other hand, had never been patient with children. They usually got on his nerves. Of course, if they were his own kids, he might feel differently.

His brows pulled in as he pinched the bridge of his nose. *What would my life be like now if I'd stayed Amish?* He clutched the reins tighter as he weighed the issue. *Did I make a mistake breaking up with Anna to go English? If we'd gotten married, could I have learned to be content living the Plain life?*

CHAPTER 7

Joel guided the horse and buggy into his dad's yard and was surprised to see five children playing near the house. As he drew closer, he realized four of them were Arlene's—Doug, Scott, Martha, and Lillian. Joel didn't recognize the other boy. He figured it was one of their friends from school or church district.

He climbed down from the buggy and secured the horse. Holding Glen's straw hat in his hand, Joel stood a few minutes, watching the children play. Fortunately, they were preoccupied and hadn't seen him yet. "Great! The last thing I need is five rambunctious kids hanging around, asking a bunch of questions and distracting me from looking for Dad's will," Joel mumbled under his breath. *I'll have to make sure they stay outside or convince them to go home.*

Joel had begun unhitching the horse when Scott ran up to him. "Hey, Uncle Joel! I didn't know you were gonna be here today." His face glowed pink—most likely from playing.

"I didn't expect you either." He squinted at the boy. "What are doing here, anyway?"

Scott grinned up at him. "Me, my brother and sisters, and my friend Alvin came to jump on the trampoline Grandpa bought a few years ago."

"Do your folks know you're here?"

"Jah. My daed and mamm said it was fine 'cause our cousin Glen's stayin' here at the house." Scott tipped his head back and stared up at Joel with a

333

curious expression. "Why did you come, and why were you drivin' Grandpa's horse and buggy?"

Already with the questions. "I came to look through some of my daed's things, and I needed some fresh air, so I took the gaul and buggy out for a ride." Joel's jaw tightened. He'd spoken some Pennsylvania Dutch again.

Scott's eyes blinked rapidly. "Did ya have trouble with the gaul? Grandpa used to say his gaul could be a feisty one."

"At first he tried to act up, but I got him under control." Joel led the horse to the barn and grimaced when he noticed Scott trailing behind him. He wished the kid would go back and play.

Scott followed Joel into the horse's stall. "Did ya bring your harmonica with ya today?"

"No."

The boy's shoulders drooped. "Sure wish ya had."

"I don't take my harmonica everywhere I go."

"I was hopin' you could teach me how to play it. If ya had the mouth harp with ya right now, then—"

"Maybe some other time." Joel focused his gaze on the horse's mane and began brushing it. He was about to suggest that Scott go back to jumping on the trampoline, when Doug darted into the barn. Joel's neck stiffened as he lowered his arm. *Terrific! Now I have two of them to deal with.*

"Sure am surprised to see you here." Doug crossed his arms and stared up at Joel. "Did my folks know you were comin'?"

Joel's knuckles whitened as he continued to brush the horse. "No, and I didn't see a need to tell them." He managed to keep his composure, but his patience was wearing thin.

Doug looked at Scott and his eyebrows lifted slightly, but neither of them commented.

When Joel finished with the horse, he hurried from the barn. The boys were right on his heels.

Joel stopped when he got to the house, then turned to face them. "If you kids and your friend want to jump on the trampoline, that's fine with me, but I've got things I need to do in the house. So unless you have to use the bathroom or get a drink, would you please stay outside? I don't want to be disturbed."

They nodded soberly.

"By the way, where's Glen? I didn't see his horse in the barn."

"Guess he ain't home from church yet," Doug answered. "He has farther to go than we do. Besides, he may have gone to his folks' house after church. Or maybe he went to visit his aldi."

"Didn't know he had a girlfriend."

"A lot of stuff goes on here that you don't know." Doug's tone was so matter of fact, it took Joel by surprise.

He frowned. "I'm sure there is."

Scott tapped Joel's arm. "Ya know, Uncle Joel, if ya smiled once in a while, people might like you better."

Taken aback, Joel forced a hard smile. "Maybe you're right, but I don't have much to smile about these days."

"There's always something to smile about. Our daed says laughter's good medicine." Doug rocked back slightly on his heels as he looked up at Joel. "In case ya didn't know, that's right outa the Bible."

Joel rolled his eyes as he bit the inside of his cheek. If he hung around here much longer, one or both of the boys would probably follow him inside and start preaching or quoting more scriptures at him. He glanced at his truck, still parked by the barn. Since Glen hadn't returned from church yet, Joel thought he should probably stick around. Arlene had allowed her children to come here because she assumed Elsie's oldest son would be available if there was a problem.

Joel mulled things over a few minutes, until his heart hardened. *This isn't my problem. Arlene should have made sure Glen was here before she allowed her kids to play on the trampoline.* He looked at his truck again. *Think I'd better head for home.* Truth was, he needed some time to unwind and didn't want to babysit a bunch of kids. *Maybe I'll go for a run or head over to one of the fitness centers that are open on Sundays.*

"Come back soon," Scott called as Joel climbed into his truck. "And don't forget to bring your harmonica next time."

Joel gave a brief wave, turned the truck around, and headed up the driveway. If he didn't hear something about Dad's will from one of his sisters soon, he'd come back and try searching for it again.

※

Berlin

"It was nice having you and Brian join us for church today," Elsie said as she and Doris sat at the kitchen table, drinking hot apple cider. The men were visiting in the living room, and the girls had gone upstairs to play in Hope's room. Glen and Blaine had gone to see their girlfriends a short time ago.

Doris smiled. "We always enjoy visiting other districts on our off Sundays."

"How are you feeling today? Any nausea?" Elsie

swirled the steaming cider in her mug.

"Just a bit, when I first woke up. Drinking ginger tea seems to help a lot."

"I'm glad." Elsie raised the mug to her lips and sipped her cider, inhaling the spicy aroma. "Oh, I forgot to mention—I called Joel last night and invited him and Kristi to have supper with us one night this week."

"What'd he say?" Doris gave her a curious look.

"I got his voice mail, so I left a message. I hope they can come. It will be nice to get to know Kristi better."

Doris shook her head slowly. "That's probably not going to happen."

"How come?"

"I waited on Kristi and her mother at the restaurant the other day. She informed me that she and Joel broke up."

Feeling a bit dazed by this news, Elsie placed her mug on the table. "How come?"

"Since we were in a public place, and I was working, it didn't seem appropriate to ask for details," Doris replied. "Kristi did say I could call and she would fill me in."

"Have you done that yet?"

"No, but I plan to sometime this week."

Elsie tapped her fingers, pondering the situation. "I wouldn't be at all surprised if the breakup was Joel's fault. He can be so insensitive sometimes."

Doris's mouth twisted grimly. "I know. Just ask Anna how badly he hurt her."

Elsie stared at the table. "I hate to say this, but both Kristi and Anna are better off without him. Unless Joel gets his life straightened around, he will probably never have a happy, meaningful relationship with a woman."

⚬

Akron

Kristi breathed deeply as she jogged down the trail. She felt exhilarated whenever she ran, and today was no exception. Time and keeping busy seemed to help get her through the breakup with Joel. She hadn't forgotten about him of course—that would take awhile. But her emotions were more stable, and she didn't think about him all the time, the way she had at first. *I did the right thing,* she reminded herself once more. *Joel isn't the right man for me.*

Up ahead, Kristi spotted one of her friends from church. "Hey, Sandy," she called. "Wait for me!"

Sandy slowed to a walk until Kristi caught up; then they ran side-by-side. "Looks like I wasn't the only one needing some fresh air and exercise today." She pulled on her hairband and tightened her ponytail.

"Jogging won't be nearly as much fun once the colder winter months set in." Kristi shivered, thinking about it. "I'll probably get most of my exercise at the fitness center."

"Not to change the subject or anything," Sandy said, "but I haven't seen Joel in church with you the last few weeks. Has he been sick?"

Kristi cringed. "Guess you haven't heard..." She drew in a sharp breath before continuing to speak. "Joel and I aren't seeing each other anymore."

"Sorry to hear that." Sandy kept her eyes on the trail in front of her. "Any chance you might get back together?"

"No, our relationship is over." Kristi was glad her friend didn't pursue the topic. Talking about Joel made her feel worse.

Slowing her pace, Sandy glanced at her watch. "Well, it's almost four o'clock. Guess I'd better head home before Ed comes looking for me. He was watching a game on TV when I left, but he's probably getting hungry by now."

"Okay. I'll see you at church next week, if not before."

Sandy turned and headed in the direction of the parking lot, while Kristi continued down the trail. It would be getting dark soon, and she'd have to head back to her car. But for now, it felt good to run.

She'd only gone a short ways, when she came face-to-face with Joel, who'd been running in the opposite direction. "Wh–what are you doing here?" she stammered, trying to push her way past him.

Joel grasped Kristi's arm, halting her footsteps. "Please don't go. We need to talk."

As he stood beside her, she saw the longing in his eyes. *That might have worked at one time, but not anymore.* Kristi wasn't sure if her body felt hot from running or because of unexpectedly seeing Joel. *Probably both.* Shaking her arm free, she looked up at him through squinted eyes. "Did you follow me here?" Her tone was sharp, and she stepped away from him.

He shook his head vigorously. "'Course not. I came here for some exercise and to wind down. How was I to know you'd be here?"

"You've been calling me nonstop, and you even went to see my dad, so I wouldn't put anything past you." Kristi's voice trembled. It was hard to look at Joel and not be reminded of what they'd once had.

So much for keeping my emotions stable.

"I didn't follow you here. I've been in Charm most of the weekend and had no idea where you were right now." Joel slid his fingers through his scraggly beard. "Spent last night at my dad's place, in fact."

Her gaze flicked up. "Don't tell me. I'll bet you went there to look for his will. Or has it already been found?"

"No, it hasn't. That's why I decided to take charge and search for it myself." He paused. "My sisters don't understand how important it is for me to find the will. My situation is far more complicated than theirs, and they don't get how much stress I'm under right now."

"If you need money so bad, then sell your fancy Corvette."

"I can't do that. I've waited a long time to have the car of my dreams." A muscle on the side of Joel's neck quivered as he folded his arms. "I deserve my share of that inheritance."

Kristi didn't comment. What would be the point? Joel's focus was still on money. It seemed to be what drove him to do things that hurt other people. As much as it upset her to see him again, she was glad they'd crossed paths today. It was the reminder she needed that she'd done the right thing by breaking their engagement.

"I can't talk to you anymore, Joel. I need to go." Kristi turned abruptly and sprinted up the trail in the direction of the parking lot. She glanced back briefly and felt relieved that Joel wasn't following her. Maybe he'd finally realized there was no chance of them getting back together. She hoped so, anyhow.

CHAPTER 8

Walnut Creek

On Wednesday afternoon of the following week, Doris had just left the restaurant where she worked, when she saw Anna coming out of the bakery. She hurried her steps, hoping to catch up to her friend.

"It's good to see you, Anna. How have you been?" As Doris came alongside Anna, she gave her friend's arm a gentle squeeze.

Anna shrugged. "I'm doing okay. How about you?"

Doris smiled. "Real well. In fact, I have some *gut noochricht*."

Anna perked up. "I'm anxious to hear it. I always appreciate good news."

"I am im e familye weg."

Anna gave Doris a hug. "Congratulations. I'm happy for you. When is the baby due?"

"Not till this spring. I can hardly wait." Doris's excitement mounted. "Brian and I didn't think we could have any kinner, so this is a *wunner* to me."

"You're right, it is a miracle. I'm sure everyone in your family is happy about it."

"My sisters know, but I haven't told Joel." Doris fidgeted with her purse strap. "In fact, I haven't seen him since our daed's funeral."

Tugging her shawl tighter around her neck, Anna leaned forward. "Speaking of your bruder, I think I may have seen Joel Sunday afternoon—or at least someone who looked like him."

Doris folded her arms over her stomach, tilting her head down, hoping to see a little bump. Her abdomen still appeared flat. Letting out a soft breath, she looked back at Anna. "Where did you see him?"

"On the road between Charm and Farmerstown. I was heading home from church in my open buggy, and the driver of the horse and buggy going in the opposite direction looked like Joel."

Doris gave her head a slight shake. "It couldn't have been him. Why would he be out riding with a horse and carriage?"

"That's what I thought, but then as I said, it may have only been someone who resembled Joel."

"Jah, it's probably how it was, all right." Doris couldn't picture her brother going anywhere with a horse and buggy when he could ride in his car. He had enjoyed driving a horse and buggy when he was young, but he'd lost interest after driving his first car during their running-around years. Besides, if it had been Joel, which wasn't likely, whose rig could he have been driving? Most likely, Anna thought the man she'd seen was Joel because he had been on her mind since the funeral.

❧

Berlin

Doris went to the phone shack as soon as her driver dropped her off at home. After Anna had mentioned Joel this afternoon, she was even more anxious to call Kristi and find out what had caused her and Joel's breakup.

She looked in her purse for Kristi's phone number and dialed it. Doris felt a release of tension when Kristi answered, because she wasn't sure she'd be home from work by now.

"Hi, Kristi, this is Joel's sister Doris Schrock."

"It's good hearing from you. I've been wondering if you would call." Kristi's tone sounded a bit uncertain.

"I'd like to know what happened between you and my brother. Are you free to talk about it now?"

"Yes, I am. I got home from work twenty minutes ago, and except for fixing supper later, I have nothing planned for the evening. So I have plenty of time to talk."

"Okay, good. I just got home from work myself." Doris pulled out the folding chair and took a seat.

"Things were strained between me and Joel for several months," Kristi began. "He did some things he knew I wouldn't approve of and kept them from me."

Doris listened as Kristi explained about Joel's deceit and desperation for money.

"It took me a long time to realize that Joel cares more about his selfish desires than the needs of others." Kristi's voice faltered. "As difficult as it was, I couldn't go on seeing him, so I broke our engagement."

"I understand, and you did the right thing. My brother is not the same person he was when we were growing up. I don't know why he became so self-centered, but I fear he's in for a lot of problems if he doesn't get right with God and change his ways."

"I've been praying for him," Kristi said. "Not so we can get back together, because it's too late for that. I'm asking God to soften Joel's heart and open his eyes so he can see what a wonderful family he has."

"I appreciate your prayers on our and Joel's behalf." Doris sniffed. Using her sleeve, she dabbed at her tears. "I'm praying for my brother, too, and hoping someone, or something, will help him see the error of his ways."

"You might also pray that he will move on with his life and stop pressuring me to take him back." Kristi's words were rushed and sounded shaky. "I was out jogging at the park Sunday afternoon. Joel nearly bumped into me there. He denied it, of course, but I'm almost certain he followed me to the park. You know what he told me?"

"What?"

"Said he'd spent the weekend at his dad's place, looking for his will." Kristi sighed. "It saddens me to think Joel is focused so much on his need for money."

Doris's body tensed as she felt a sudden coldness. *So it could have been Joel Anna saw on Sunday. As strange as it seems, I bet he took Dad's horse and buggy out for a ride.*

She shifted the receiver to her other ear. "I appreciate you telling me all this, Kristi. I'm going to check with my sisters and see if either of them knows what Joel was up to on Sunday. It's not good for him to rummage through things in Dad's house if none of us are there. Joel might throw something out that's important or meaningful to one of us."

$\sim$

Charm

When Elsie arrived at her dad's place the following day, she was surprised to discover her sisters' rigs already there. After putting her horse in the corral, she stopped at her buggy and pulled out a cardboard box. Shivering against the chill in the air, she hurried for the house.

"I'm either late or you two are early," she said when she entered the living room where Arlene and Doris sat on the sofa, going through some paperwork.

Doris looked up at her and smiled. "I think we're early."

"I don't suppose you've found Dad's will." Elsie clicked her tongue. "But then if you had, you'd both have probably been waiting for me on the porch, excited to share the news."

"No will yet, and I'm beginning to think we'll never find it." Arlene held up some of the papers in her lap. "All we've come across so far in the boxes we found in the downstairs spare bedroom are receipts from things Dad ordered a long time ago."

Elsie groaned, shifting the box she held for a better grip. "I don't understand why he kept so many unnecessary things." She set the box on the floor and went to the coat rack to hang her purse, shawl, and outer bonnet. "I can understand why Dad would keep receipts from recent purchases, but to hang on to old paperwork doesn't make sense."

Doris flicked her hand in front of her nose, as if to rid the room of a bad odor. "You know Dad. He thought he had to keep nearly everything."

"We can complain about it all we want, but it won't change the fact that we're stuck going through everything." Arlene grabbed another stack of papers from the box near her feet.

"True, but before I get to work, I'd better take care of the things I brought with me today." Elsie went to the kitchen and placed her box on the counter. First she removed a plastic container filled with pumpkin muffins and set it on the table. Then she checked the refrigerator to see how much food there was for Glen. She'd brought him a jar of homemade soup, which she took from the box and placed in the refrigerator. She'd also included several apples, bananas, a loaf of bread, lunchmeat, and cheese. Since Glen often ate supper at their house when he finished work for the day, he didn't need a fully stocked refrigerator or pantry. Still, Elsie wanted to make sure her son didn't go hungry.

"I'm ready to help," Elsie announced when she returned to the living room, where her sisters sat, going through more paperwork. She grabbed a handful of papers and seated herself in the rocking chair across from them.

Sorting through their father's mound of paperwork while rocking the chair caused Elsie's eyelids to become heavy. It reminded her of when she was in school. Whenever the teacher wrote their assignments or list of spelling words on the chalkboard, the letters sometimes turned into squiggly shapes as Elsie stared at them. The next thing she knew, her body would relax and her vision fade. Then, she'd jolt her head back up, realizing she had dozed off.

"Before we get too busy, there's something I need to tell you both," Doris said. "It's about Joel."

"What's he done now?" Elsie asked, relieved she could take a short break.

"Well, as I mentioned last Sunday, Joel and Kristi broke up. I finally had a chance to call and ask her about the details."

"Now that's a surprise." Arlene frowned. "Although, with our bruder, maybe it's not. Don't forget—he broke up with Anna before he left our Amish way of life."

"True, but this time it was Joel's aldi who broke things off with him." Doris went on to share everything Kristi told her when they spoke on the phone.

"It's a shame." Arlene spoke softly. "I liked Kristi

and looked forward to getting to know her better."

"Me, too," Elsie agreed.

Doris leaned slightly forward, resting her elbows on her knees. "There's more."

"More about Joel?" Arlene questioned.

"Jah. I found out from Kristi that our impulsive bruder spent the weekend at Dad's house. Did Glen say anything about this to you, Elsie?"

"No, he did not." Elsie narrowed her eyes. "But then I've only seen him briefly the last few days, when he's come to the house to meet up with his daed before the two of them went out on a job."

"Maybe Glen said something to John about Joel coming here to Dad's," Doris interjected.

Elsie compressed her lips. "If John knew about it, I'm sure he would have told me."

"We can't have Joel showing up here whenever he feels like it, going through Dad's things without our knowledge." Arlene's nose crinkled. "I wonder what rooms he looked in while he was here."

"Hard to say. Maybe Glen knows." Elsie rocked in her chair. "Next time I see him, I'll ask for details about what his uncle did during his stay."

"If he spent the night here, I wonder if he found anything interesting." Arlene rose from her seat. "Think I'll go check the upstairs bedrooms to see if anything looks disturbed." She headed for the stairs.

Elsie sorted papers quietly for a while, then glanced over at Doris and frowned. "It would be nice to work with our bruder through all of this, instead of dealing with the tension he causes." She remained quiet a few minutes, watching Doris look through more of Dad's papers. Several minutes later, she spotted Arlene coming down the stairs.

"Did you notice anything out of the ordinary?"

"It looks like Joel picked his own room to sleep in, because not one box was on the bed, as it had been before. He didn't bother to make the bed, either, so I did." Arlene sighed. "Like I said before, we can't have Joel showing up here whenever he feels like it, going through Dad's things without our knowledge."

"But isn't that what we're doing?" Doris spoke up. "Joel has no idea we're here now or what rooms and boxes we've gone through so far."

Elsie put her hands on her hips. "That's different. Joel knew we were going to be looking for Dad's will. He's just too impatient to wait for it to be found. I think I'm going to call him this evening and let him know we don't appreciate him spending the weekend here without our knowledge."

Arlene held up her hand. "Why don't you let me call Joel? I was going to anyway to invite him to Scott's birthday party next Friday evening."

Elsie clutched the piece of paper she held with such tightness, it began to crinkle in her palms. "I don't see why Joel has to be included. He's never cared to come around and take part in family functions unless he wanted something."

"Elsie's right," Doris agreed. "Besides, I doubt he would come."

Arlene's hands formed into a steeple. "I'm hoping and praying he does, because for whatever reason, Scott has taken a liking to his uncle Joel."

Elsie leaned back in her chair and tried to relax. She hoped if Joel did come to Scott's party, he wouldn't mention the will or say anything upsetting to anyone there.

CHAPTER 9

Farmerstown

Is Uncle Joel comin' tonight?" Scott asked when he entered the kitchen, where Arlene was mashing potatoes.

"I invited him, Son, but please don't get your hopes up." She sighed deeply, turning toward him as she placed the potato masher down. "My bruder has his own business, and he may be too busy to come." Arlene figured even if Joel wasn't busy, he wouldn't come, but she chose not to say so to Scott.

The boy's lower lip protruded. "I hope he comes, 'cause the party's gonna be fun, and Uncle Joel needs to laugh."

"We all need to laugh more." She tapped his shoulder before adding more butter to the potatoes. "Now go get washed up. We'll be eating as soon as the rest of our family gets here."

As Scott headed down the hall, Arlene went to the dining room, where her daughters were setting the table.

Guests began to arrive for Scott's birthday party a short time later. First Doris and Brian, followed by Elsie, John, and their family. The only one missing was Joel.

After everyone gathered at the table, all heads bowed for silent prayer. Then the food was passed from one person to the next, until everything had made it around.

"Ya know what?" Doug looked over at his mother. "I miss Aunt Verna. Sure wish she and Uncle Lester coulda stayed here longer."

Arlene nodded. "I miss her, too, but she and Uncle Lester needed to get back to their home in Burton."

"Aunt Verna reminds me of Grandpa, with all the funny things she says and does." Doug passed the salad bowl to Martha. "Remember when she put that wild red bird in her cage and was showing it off?"

"But she let it go," Scott reminded his brother.

"Too bad Uncle Lester and Aunt Verna couldn't be here for the party this evening," Hope chimed in.

Arlene had to agree with her daughter, for she wished it, too. When her aunt and uncle visited their family, it was like having her dad there in some ways.

Conversation continued around the table as they began to eat their meal of baked chicken, mashed potatoes, tossed green salad, and creamed corn. It did Arlene's heart good to see their smiles and hear the happy banter. Everyone had been so somber since Dad passed away.

I wish he was with us tonight, she thought. Some of the stories her dad used to share about his childhood had always brought a round of laughter. *Maybe he's peeking down from heaven and celebrating Scott's ninth birthday with us tonight.*

~

Akron

Joel's day had been busy and gone longer than he'd hoped. He had meant to finish working sooner, but here it was, evening already. He dashed into his mobile home, took off his work jacket, and tossed it on the couch. Then he headed down the hall to take a shower. He'd worked on the remodel of a house an hour north of Akron today and gotten caught in traffic on the way home. He didn't want to disappoint Scott by not showing up at his party but was sure he'd already missed the meal.

Better late than never, he told himself. *With any luck I'll get there in time for cake and ice cream.*

He reflected on the invitation he'd received from Arlene when she'd called a few days ago and left a message. In addition to inviting Joel to Scott's party, she'd made it clear she didn't want him looking for Dad's will unless one of the sisters was with him. This didn't set well with Joel, but he wouldn't bring it up this evening. No point spoiling Scott's party.

Joel slapped the side of his head. "Oh, great. I don't even have a gift for the boy." It wouldn't look good for him to show up at the party without a present. He had a certain fondness for the kid, probably because Scott reminded Joel of himself at that age—adventuresome, full of life, and equally full of questions.

He removed his dirty shirt and stared at his reflection in the mirror, rubbing the prickly stubble on his face. He needed a shave but didn't have time for that right now. *Just a quick shower, change, and I'll be out the door. Still, wish I had something to give the boy.*

Joel's stomach growled loudly, which only magnified his hunger. Bananas and a pear were in a bowl in the kitchen. He might have to eat the fruit as he drove to Charm, since he'd be too late for the home-cooked meal he could have had at Arlene's with his family.

An idea popped into Joel's head, and he forgot about his hunger for the moment. He did have something Scott might like for his birthday.

❦

Farmerstown

Arlene had no more than placed Scott's cake on the table when a knock sounded on the door.

"I'll get it." Larry pushed back his chair and hurried from the room. When he returned, Joel was with him, holding a banana peel and a pear core.

"Sorry I'm late. I had to work later than I hoped, and traffic was bad, but I wanted to wish Scott a happy birthday and give him this." Joel fumbled with his garbage, while he tried to reach into his jacket pocket.

Arlene noticed his dilemma and stepped up to him. "I'll throw that away for you." She took the banana peel and what was left of the pear, and handed him a napkin to wipe his hands.

"Sorry about the mess. Since I was running late, the fruit ended up being my dinner, which I ate on the drive down here."

"There's some leftover chicken in the refrigerator. You're welcome to eat some of that," she offered.

"Sounds good." Joel gave her a sheepish grin.

"I'll fix you a plate after I've served the cake."

"No hurry." Joel wiped his hands on the napkin, handed it back to Arlene, then slipped his hands into his pockets and withdrew a harmonica, which he gave to Scott.

The boy's eyes widened, and his lips curved into a huge smile. "Wow! Is this your mouth harp, Uncle Joel?"

Joel nodded. "Well, one of 'em anyway. I have a few, in different keys. The one I'm giving you is in the key of G. I chose it because a lot of songs are played in that key."

Scott's face beamed as he held the harmonica as though it were a piece of gold. "Will ya teach me how to play it, Uncle Joel? Will ya show me what to do right now?"

"Don't you think you oughta blow out your candles and eat some of your birthday cake first?"

"Your uncle is right." Arlene pushed the cake plate closer to Scott. "After we've had cake and ice cream, we'll let you open your gifts, and then Uncle Joel can give you a lesson on the harmonica."

Scott glanced at the others, as if to see what they thought. When everyone nodded, he smiled up at Joel. "Why don't ya take off your coat and pull up a chair? I bet you haven't tasted any cake as good as my mamm makes."

Arlene waited to see what her brother had to say about that, then smiled when he said, "Well, she had a good teacher. Our mother, your sweet grandma, baked cakes so good they made your tongue beg for more." Joel reached up to his ear and gave it a couple of tugs.

Scott snickered. "Sure is good to see ya smilin', Uncle Joel. Don't it feel good to you?"

Giving a quick nod, Joel led the others in singing "Happy Birthday" to Scott.

Arlene's heart warmed. Seeing the sincerity on her brother's face brought back memories of when they were young. It was the first time in a good many years when his defenses seemed to be down. *Maybe... just maybe, things are looking up in this family.*

Akron

Kristi stifled a yawn as she prepared to take several of the patients their prescribed medication before they went to sleep. She'd worked a double shift again today but wondered if it had been a mistake. She would be getting up early tomorrow morning to go with her mother to another quilting class in Berlin, and she looked forward to it. But working the later shift meant she wouldn't get to bed until well past midnight. *If it weren't for me breaking things off with Joel, Mom and I probably wouldn't be taking the quilting class because I'd be spending my Saturdays with him,* Kristi thought. *So I guess at least one good thing came out of it.*

Glancing at her watch, she noticed it was only eight o'clock, so she had a few hours to go. Unintentionally, Kristi thought of Joel again. When they were dating, they often went out on Friday nights, so she rarely volunteered to work the evening shift. Those had been carefree evenings.

How could I have been so blind? she berated herself. *Joel had me fooled for a long time. I'll never allow myself to be taken in by him or any other man.*

With a shake of her head, Kristi pulled her thoughts back to the task at hand. It did no good to think about the past. She needed to focus on the needs of her patients and make sure everyone had what they needed before they went to sleep.

After she'd distributed medication to all the patients but one, Kristi remembered the new magazines she'd brought for Audrey. She hurried back to the nurse's station to grab them.

When she entered Audrey's room, she found

the pleasant woman sitting in her favorite chair near the window. "Good evening. I have a few flower magazines for you." Kristi pulled them out of the plastic bag she carried and handed them to Audrey.

"Oh, how nice of you." She smiled sweetly and began to thumb through the first one. "This has some lovely flower pictures."

"I hope you enjoy them." Kristi watched as Audrey turned the pages. Then she glanced beyond her and looked at the window. Even though it was dark outside, the curtain was open.

"I have your medication for you to take now." Kristi handed Audrey a glass of water and the small paper cup with her pills. "How are you feeling this evening?"

"I'm fine." Audrey placed the magazine in her lap with the others and smiled. "Even if I wasn't, I wouldn't complain. I have much to be thankful about."

Kristi was amazed at this pleasant woman's positive attitude. She always seemed to look on the bright side of things, despite the fact that she was dying of cancer. It was hard for Kristi to understand why Audrey had refused treatment. Perhaps it was because she'd had cancer before, and it had come back. Maybe Audrey was content to live out her life with nothing but pain medication to see her through until the end. It was an individual choice, and Kristi respected that. But it hurt her to know the dear lady had no living relatives or close friends to help her through this rough time in her life. *But she has the Lord,* Kristi reminded herself. *And I will be here for her as much as I can.*

"How are you, dear?" Audrey asked after she'd

taken her pills. "I've been praying for you."

"I'm doing better and appreciate your prayers." Kristi took a seat on the end of Audrey's bed. "I've been praying for Joel, too, but he's still up to his old tricks."

Audrey tipped her head, raising a quizzical brow. "Is it something you'd like to talk about?"

Kristi hesitated at first but then told Audrey how she'd met up with Joel when she'd been jogging at the park and that he'd said he had spent the weekend at his dad's house, looking for the will.

"Joel's concentration seems to be on how he can get his hands on more money, yet when he does have money, he spends it foolishly—like he did when he bought a classic car he didn't need. I think he's obsessed with it." She drew in a quick breath and released it with a huff. "Maybe my prayer for Joel will never be answered."

Audrey stood and moved slowly over to Kristi. Placing her hand on Kristi's arm, she said in a confident tone, "God always answers our prayers. Sometimes it's yes. Sometimes no. And sometimes He wants us to wait. When your faith begins to waver, dear, remember the words of Psalm 46:10: 'Be still, and know that I am God.'" She smiled pleasantly and released a soft sigh. "I am more than ready to meet the Lord."

CHAPTER 10

When Kristi entered her parents' house to share their Thanksgiving meal, a sense of sadness enveloped her. Joel had come here with her last year to celebrate the holiday. She wondered what he was doing right now. Had he been invited to one of his sisters' homes? Or maybe he'd gone to his friend Tom's place to eat. She was sure he wouldn't have spent the day at home alone, because Joel didn't like to cook that much.

Kristi had gone to the bank like her dad suggested, withdrawn what was left of the money, and closed her and Joel's joint account, which the bank teller said she could do. She hoped if Joel tried to take more money out, the closed account would give him another indication that their relationship was definitely over.

Up until a week ago, he had been calling and leaving Kristi messages almost every day. She hadn't heard anything from him since then and wondered if he was too busy to call or had finally figured out she wasn't going to take him back and had given up his pursuit. She hoped it was the latter, because listening to his voice messages or reading his texts was a constant reminder of her loss. It would be a lot easier to move on with her life if she didn't hear from Joel anymore.

The delicious aroma of turkey cooking drove Kristi's thoughts aside, so she hung her coat in the hall closet and made her way to the kitchen.

"Happy Thanksgiving." Kristi gave her mother

a hug. "The turkey smells delicious. Is it done?"

"Yes, but I'm keeping it on low until the potatoes are cooked. Would you like to see how it looks?"

"Sure, Mom."

Her mother grabbed a potholder and opened the oven door.

Kristi stepped up to the stove as Mom slid the bird out far enough to remove the foil and expose the golden brown meat. "Yum! That looks and smells so good. As always, you've roasted a beautiful Thanksgiving turkey."

"Thanks, hon." Mom put the foil back on and slid the pan into the oven again. "I hope it tastes as good as last year's turkey."

"I'm sure it will." Kristi moved over to look at the holiday wall hanging. "Is there anything you'd like me to do?"

"Not at the moment." Mom gestured to the stove. "The veggies are cooking, the dining room table is set, and the salad and pies are in the refrigerator, so there's not much to do until it's time to serve the meal. Would you like to sit here in the kitchen while I keep an eye on things, or visit with your dad in the living room, where he's watching TV?"

TV. Why am I not surprised? Kristi stared out the kitchen window with an unfocused gaze as she thought about Joel's Amish family. *I wonder if his sisters know how fortunate they are that their husbands don't have a television for entertainment.* Kristi didn't have anything against TV per se; she just thought for many people it was a distraction that robbed them of time they should be spending with family.

"Are you all right?" Mom placed her hand

gently on Kristi's shoulder. "You didn't even respond to my question."

She turned to face her mother. "Oh, you mean about whether I want to stay here or sit and watch TV with Dad?"

Mom nodded.

"I'll stay here. You'll need my help when the potatoes are ready to be mashed."

"Okay." Mom went to the cupboard and took out two cups. "While we're waiting for the vegetables to cook, let's have a cup of tea. Would you like regular or decaf?"

"Do you have any peppermint tea?" Kristi asked, licking her lips. She'd had some iced mint tea the day of Joel's father's funeral and enjoyed it.

"Sorry, honey. I only have black tea and a pumpkin spice blend that's decaffeinated."

"I'll try that."

After Mom poured them both a cup of tea, she took a seat at the table beside Kristi. "I'm glad you didn't have to work today, because it would have been a lonely Thanksgiving without you."

"I'm glad to be here, too." Since both sets of Kristi's grandparents lived in another state, they rarely got together for Thanksgiving and sometimes not even Christmas. Since Kristi was their only child, with the exception of some friends from church, she was all Mom and Dad really had.

She enjoyed their company—even more so since she'd broken up with Joel. Her parents had been supportive, which was what she needed, and had refrained from reminding her that Joel had been a poor choice for a husband. The only thing she didn't appreciate was when Mom hinted at Kristi becoming involved with one of the young single men from church. Kristi needed the chance to heal from the pain she felt whenever she thought about Joel's deceptions. It would be some time before she felt ready to begin a new relationship with a man.

∽

Joel sat on the couch, staring at the TV, barely noticing the weather report on the screen. He felt miserable today—not only from the nasty cold he'd come down with, but the loneliness permeating his soul. Last year on Thanksgiving, he'd gone to Kristi's parents' house for dinner. It had been a good day, despite her mother's coolness. Joel had known from their first meeting that JoAnn Palmer didn't care much for him. She probably thought her daughter could do better than a struggling contractor. Or maybe there was something about Joel's personality JoAnn didn't like. If only there was some way he could convince Kristi to give him another chance.

Joel reached for a tissue and blew his nose. He hadn't tried calling Kristi for a week, thinking it might be good to give her a chance to cool down. Hopefully, she'd realize she missed him as much as he did her.

Remembering how Kristi had been there for him during his dad's funeral, Joel's thoughts turned in another direction. The will had still not been found, but he'd decided not to bug his sisters about it until after Thanksgiving. Everyone had been nice to him when he'd gone to Arlene and Larry's place for Scott's birthday. Joel figured if he didn't bring up the will for a while, they might see him in a different light. He wouldn't wait forever, though, because he still needed his share of Dad's money. He also planned to talk with them about selling Dad's horses and sharing the profit. At least that would give them some money until the will was found.

Elsie had invited Joel to her house for Thanksgiving, but he didn't want to expose anyone to his cold, so he'd declined. Besides, he probably wouldn't be the best company when he felt so crummy. Scott would probably want another lesson on the harmonica, and Joel wasn't up for that.

Grunting, he pulled himself off the couch and headed for the kitchen. He felt hungry and was glad he'd bought a few frozen dinners the other day. He opened the freezer and pulled one out with turkey, dressing, and mashed potatoes. "Guess I may as well put the frozen meal in the oven now. At least I'll have a taste of turkey, even if it's not the best."

Joel ambled over to the stove and adjusted the setting. He had time to wait since the oven would take awhile to preheat. In the meantime, he grabbed a tray to eat his dinner on and took it to the living room, placing it on the coffee table. Then he went to his room and got the comforter from his bed to cover up with while he watched TV and ate his meal.

"Might as well take care of myself, since my fiancée isn't around to baby me anymore." He grimaced. "I really don't like the sound of that."

❧

Millersburg

"Sure wish Uncle Joel woulda come for dinner today," Scott mumbled as everyone sat around Elsie's dining room table. "The night of my party he

WANDA & BRUNSTETTER & JEAN BRUNSTETTER

said if I wanted to learn to play the mouth harp, I should blow and suck." He wrinkled his nose. "I've been doin' it for the last week, but still can't make *schee myusick* the way Uncle Joel can do."

"Grandpa made pretty music, too," Martha spoke up. "I liked his playing the best."

Scott frowned at his sister. "Never said I didn't like the way Grandpa played, but he never got around to teachin' me. Besides, Grandpa's not here anymore."

The room got deathly quiet, and Elsie sucked in her breath. She didn't need the reminder that her father wasn't here. This was the first Thanksgiving he hadn't shared the meal with their family. Dad's dry sense of humor and quick comebacks always kept the conversation lively.

Arlene tapped Scott's arm. "Even though your grossdaadi isn't here today, we have many good memories of him, for which we can be thankful."

"That's right," Doris agreed. "In fact, I think it would be nice if we went around the table and everyone said one thing they remembered about our daed that makes them feel thankful."

"That's a good idea," Brian said. "Who wants to go first?"

Doug's hand shot up. "I will."

Larry gave a nod. "Go ahead, Son."

"I'm thankful Grandpa let me and Scott help build the tree house." His head dipped as he mumbled, "But I wish he hadn't died."

Elsie fought to keep her emotions under control. By the time they all said what they were thankful for concerning Dad, she'd have to pass a box of tissues around.

❧

After the meal was over, the women and girls cleared the table, while the men discussed what board games they should get out to play after the dishes were done. Since everyone was full from the meal, they'd decided to wait awhile to eat their dessert of pumpkin and apple pies. Doris had also brought some pumpkin bread from the bakery in Walnut Creek.

Elsie stood in front of the sink, rinsing the dishes, and thought about Joel, while Arlene prepared coffee for anyone who wanted it after dinner. Elsie couldn't help wondering how Joel had spent his Thanksgiving. He'd left her a message, saying he appreciated the invitation, but wouldn't be coming to dinner because he had a cold. She figured he was probably spending Thanksgiving alone.

How sad that he messed things up between him and Kristi, Elsie thought as she ran warm water into the sink, adding some detergent. *It would have been nice if both Joel and Kristi could have joined us today. I wanted to get to know her better.*

Elsie's muscles relaxed as she submerged her hands in the water. She grabbed the sponge on the edge of the sink and scrubbed one of the plates. Most people didn't enjoy hand washing dishes, but it felt pleasant to Elsie. The water surrounding her skin was cozy—like wrapping up in a warm blanket on a cold evening. It was one of the simple things that made her feel content.

Elsie's thoughts returned to Joel. She had hoped her brother would change from his old ways, and maybe the family would grow, with Kristi joining them. But apparently, it wasn't meant to be.

"I should wipe down the table before we have

dessert." Arlene took a clean sponge from the drawer, and reaching around Elsie, she wet it in the soapy water.

Doris picked up the dish towel to dry the dishes Elsie had washed, but suddenly dropped it, wrapping her arms around her torso. "I—I'm not feeling well all of a sudden. I think I may have eaten too much."

"Sorry to hear that. Why don't you go lie down and let the rest of us worry about the dishes." Elsie suggested.

"I probably should." Doris started out of the room but turned back around. "Since we all put our coats on your bed, would it be okay if I went upstairs and rested in one of the kinner's rooms?"

"That's fine. You can lie on one of the girls' beds."

"Danki." Doris's face looked pale as she hurried from the room.

"I think she's been overdoing it lately," Arlene whispered to Elsie. "Even though she's only working part-time at the restaurant, it means having to be on her feet a lot."

"You're right. I hope she's able to quit working there soon." Elsie picked up her sponge and was about to wash another dish when she heard a blood-curdling scream. A few seconds later, Doug dashed into the room. "Aunt Doris fell! She's lying at the bottom of the stairs." His voice quivered. "And—and she's not moving at all."

Elsie threw the sponge and raced from the room. *Please, God, let my sister be okay.*

The
DIVIDED
Family

CHAPTER 1

Dover

Elsie stood trembling at the foot of her sister's hospital bed, listening to the doctor give Doris and her husband distressing news. In addition to a broken leg, plus a nasty bump on the head, the fall Doris took down the stairs earlier this evening had caused her to miscarry. It wasn't fair. The broken leg would heal, but Doris and Brian had waited a long time for her to become pregnant. The joy they'd felt over the pregnancy, which Doris had seen as a miracle, disappeared before their eyes, like a glass of ice melting on a hot summer day.

Elsie glanced at Arlene, standing beside her with tears trickling down her cheeks. She, too, felt their sister's pain.

When Doris had been taken by ambulance to Union Hospital, Brian rode along. Elsie and Arlene had hired a driver to take them, leaving their husbands at home with the children. Right now, and for many days ahead, Doris would need her family's help and support.

It hurt Elsie to hear her sister's anguished cries after the doctor left the room. Brian took the news hard as well, yet seemed unable to offer Doris the comfort she needed. Even if sometime in the future Doris got pregnant again, she might never get over her loss.

Elsie and Arlene moved to the other side of the bed, across from Brian. Elsie reached out to clasp her sister's cold hand. "I'm so sorry. . . ." The words nearly stuck in her throat as she swallowed around the lump that seemed to be lodged there.

"I'm sorry, too." Arlene placed her hand on Doris's trembling shoulder. "Elsie and I will do everything we can to help you get through this."

Doris just closed her eyes and continued to weep.

Brian looked up at Elsie with a distant stare. "Would you mind leaving us alone for a while?"

Elsie slowly nodded. Her body felt heavy as she let go of Doris's hand. As much as she wanted to remain at her sister's bedside, she understood Brian's request to be alone with his wife. This tragedy was something the two of them needed to deal with together. At least for the time being. Hopefully Doris would eventually be more receptive to their sympathy.

"We'll be in the waiting room if you need us." Arlene turned toward the door, and Elsie followed. They took seats in the waiting room down the hall.

Dabbing at her tears, Arlene turned to Elsie with puffy eyes. "What if Doris never recovers emotionally from this? What if she's unable to conceive again?"

"We must pray for her and try to think positive. If it's meant for Doris and Brian to have a boppli, then it will happen in God's time."

"You're right. Larry and I never expected to be blessed with another child after Scott was born. The doctor said due to the damage done to my uterus, it wasn't likely I'd get pregnant again." Arlene smiled, despite her tears. "Then eight years later, along came baby Samuel."

Elsie nodded as she reached for her sister's

hand. "You've been blessed all right."

"Doris is going to need our help when she leaves the hospital in a few days. That means we'll have to put looking for Dad's will on hold for a while."

"It's not a priority right now." Elsie was sure their brother wouldn't be happy about the delay, but it couldn't be helped. Their sister's needs came first. She would give Joel a call later on and tell him what happened.

❦

Akron

Joel had been sneezing and blowing his nose so much it felt raw. He hated being sick—especially while spending Thanksgiving alone with a less-than-exciting frozen dinner. With only the company of his television set during the holiday, he'd given in to self-pity. Kristi was probably at her folks', eating a moist turkey dinner with all the trimmings, while he sat at home on the couch with a box of tissues and a bottle of cough syrup that was six months past its sell-by date. Joel didn't care how old the stuff was; he needed something to relieve his nagging cough.

Pulling himself off the couch, he ambled out to the kitchen to replenish his glass of water. He remembered how his mother used to stress the importance of staying hydrated when a person had a cold or the flu. Joel felt like he had both, because, in addition to coughing and sneezing, his body had begun to ache. "I probably have a fever, too," he mumbled, going to the sink and filling his glass with cold water. He would have taken his temperature, but he'd misplaced the thermometer.

Joel set the glass on the counter and pulled a tissue from his pocket as he felt another sneeze coming on. *Ah-choo! Ah-choo! Ah-choo!* As the final sneeze hit, a muscle in Joel's back spasmed, and he fell to his knees from the pain. *Oh, great! How much worse can it get?*

He gritted his teeth, pulled himself up, and tried to straighten, but the pain was too intense. Walking bent over while holding his back, he shuffled across the room to the refrigerator. He grabbed an ice pack from the freezer compartment and wrapped it in a dishtowel. Since the living room was closer than Joel's bedroom, he headed in that direction, grimacing as he inched his way along. When he reached the couch, he somehow managed to lie down and stuff the ice pack behind his back. This was one time Joel was glad he didn't have any work lined up for a few days. It would give him time to recover from the pain surging up and down his back. But it would be a long weekend, being alone and feeling so miserable.

Joel wished he could lie back on the sofa and relax while someone tended to his every need— making sure he was fed and being there to keep him company. He would have had the help he needed if he hadn't lost the special woman in his life.

Pouting, Joel glanced at his cell phone lying on the coffee table. He thought about calling his friend Tom, but Tom had gone out of town to spend Thanksgiving with his family and wouldn't be back until Sunday evening.

Maybe I should call Kristi. If she knows I'm not feeling well, and that my back's acting up, she might feel sorry for me and come over. It would give me the chance to tell her once again that I'm sorry for messing things up.

Another jolt of pain shot through Joel's back as he reached for the phone. It would be worth the agony if Kristi responded to his call. In desperation, he punched in her number and held his breath. Several rings later, her voice mail picked up. "Kristi, it's Joel," he said, groaning. "I have a bad cold, and during a sneezing attack, my back went out. I'm really miserable and barely able to function. Would you please come over to my place and put your nursing skills to work so I'll feel better?" He paused, searching for the right words. "Please call me or drop by. I really need you, Kristi."

When Joel hung up, he kept the cell phone by his side so he wouldn't have to reach for it if she called.

✺

"Was that your cell phone I heard buzzing?" Kristi's dad asked as they sat at the dining room table eating pumpkin pie and drinking hot chocolate.

"It may have been." She scooped a dollop of Mom's homemade whipped cream off her pie and dropped it into her cup. "I turned the ringer off before I put the phone in my purse so I wouldn't be bothered with any calls while I'm here." Truthfully, Kristi half expected Joel to call, and he was the last person she wanted to talk to today. Even though he hadn't called her for several days, she had a hunch, with this being a holiday they'd previously spent together, he might get nostalgic and decide to call.

"Why don't we play a card game after we finish our dessert?" Kristi's mother suggested. "All the food we ate today has made me sleepy, and a rousing game is what I need to keep awake."

Dad yawned and leaned back in his chair. "I'm with you, JoAnn. There's something about eating turkey. Even if I don't stuff myself, it causes me to feel like I need a nap."

"It's the tryptophan," Kristi said. "Tryptophan is an amino acid found in turkey, and it's known for making people sleepy."

"Our daughter's smart." Mom smiled at Kristi. "I'll bet you learned that in nurses' training."

"I may have, but it's something I read about a long time ago in a magazine article." Kristi stirred her hot chocolate and took a drink. "Yum. I like it when you whip heavy cream. It's much better than the spray kind you buy in a can, and I like the subtle way you sweeten it, without too much sugar or vanilla."

Mom's smile widened. "I enjoy cooking for you and your dad, and I'm glad you appreciate it."

"I appreciate it, too." Dad reached over and helped himself to the fluffy white topping, added some to his mug, and took a drink. "Ah. . . now that's what I call good."

Thinking about all the delicious food she'd just shared with Mom and Dad caused Kristi to reflect on one of the patients at the nursing home where she worked. *I wonder if Audrey felt up to eating any turkey today. Poor thing. She looked so pale when I checked on her yesterday.*

"Is anything wrong?" Mom tapped Kristi's arm. "You look so serious all of a sudden."

Kristi slumped in her chair. "I was thinking about my patient, Audrey, who's dying of cancer. I'm sure I mentioned her before."

"You did. Has she gotten worse?" Mom's gentle tone revealed her concern.

"Yes. Up until recently, she's been able to be out of bed and get around on her own, but now she's pretty much bedridden."

"Cancer's an ugly thing." Dad spoke up. "Seems like there's hardly a family who hasn't been touched by it."

"I know." Kristi sighed. "I've been praying for a miracle on Audrey's behalf, but with her getting worse, I have to think my prayer won't be answered."

"All prayers are answered," Dad reminded. "Just not always the way we would like."

Kristi thought about Joel again and how she'd been praying for him, as Audrey suggested. It had only been a little over a month since they'd broken up, so he was still fresh on her mind. She continued to wonder if anything in his life had changed. Obviously, Joel wouldn't be a different person right away, but maybe he'd receive the help he needed from God sometime soon. Before Joel could change, however, he had to let Jesus come into his heart.

Redirecting her thoughts, she smiled and said, "As much as I'll miss Audrey when she's gone, I'm convinced she's a Christian and will be in a better place. She's told me more than once that she's ready to go home and be with the Lord."

"The sting of death lessens a bit when we know someone we care about has been transported to heaven." Dad reached for the pot of hot chocolate in the middle of the table and poured himself another cup.

Kristi finished eating her pie and pushed away

from the table. "I'll take my dishes to the sink and then get out one of our favorite games." Hopefully once they started playing, she could concentrate on something more uplifting.

After she rinsed her dishes, Kristi decided to check her phone messages, in case someone from the nursing home had called with an update on Audrey's condition. Dorine was working this evening and had promised to let Kristi know if Audrey took a turn for the worst.

Listening to the only message she'd received, Kristi inhaled a long breath when she heard Joel's voice. She took a seat at the kitchen table and pressed the phone closer to her ear. For a split second, hearing him say he wasn't feeling well touched a soft spot in her heart and she felt pity for him. Kristi was aware of how miserable a person felt when they had a bad cold, much less a sore back. But common sense kicked in when she remembered Joel lying to her about why he'd taken money from their joint account. He was probably either making up the situation, or using it as a means to get her there so he could try and talk her into taking him back.

Kristi's lips pressed together as she pushed her shoulders against the back of the chair. *Sorry, Joel, but it's not going to work. I'm staying right here for the rest of the evening.*

CHAPTER 2

Berlin

How are you feeling? Are you comfortable there on the couch, or would you rather lie on your bed?"

Doris clenched her teeth in an effort to keep from shouting. Today was Monday, the last day of November, and she'd only been home from the hospital a few hours. But in those few hours, all her sister Elsie had done was fuss. *How does she think I feel? I'm laid up with a broken leg and sore head. Worse than that, my hopes of giving Brian a baby have been destroyed.* "I'm fine here on the couch for now," she murmured.

Elsie placed a pillow under her cast, with a reminder that the doctor said she should keep her leg elevated as much as possible. "You'll probably have less pain that way, and it will help with the swelling."

"Jah, okay." Doris blinked back tears threatening to spill over. *It won't help the pain in my heart, though, will it?*

"Is there anything you need me to bring you before I wash the breakfast dishes?"

"No, I don't need a thing." *Except my baby.* Since Doris had been pregnant less than twenty-four weeks, there would be no funeral. In some ways, she saw it as a blessing, for she wouldn't have to endure the agony of watching a tiny coffin being lowered into the ground. On the other hand, a funeral service brought closure.

Elsie placed her hand gently on Doris's shoulder. "Arlene should be here soon, and then the two of us can do your laundry and get some cleaning done."

After her sister got busy in the kitchen, Doris sat on the sofa awhile, pondering the loss of her unborn child. With the aid of her crutches, she pulled herself up and made her way down the hall to the room next to her and Brian's. It would have been the baby's nursery.

Inside the doorway, Doris paused and looked around the small room with anguish. Her vision blurred as she gazed at the wall where the crib would have gone. Across from it, Brian had placed a rocking chair—the same one he had been rocked in as a baby. Doris's leg throbbed as she hobbled over to the chair and collapsed into it. Strong sobs shook her body. Her heart felt as if it was broken in two. She thought her tears would never stop flowing. So many feelings hit her all at once; it was hard to feel any hope.

In no time it seemed, both of Doris's sisters were at her side. Arlene, wearing her jacket and outer bonnet, held baby Samuel in her arms and placed him gently on Doris's lap. "Will you hold him for me awhile?"

Doris sniffed. "Jah, of course."

Elsie and Arlene stood quietly beside her, looking down as she rocked the baby. Doris found comfort in the little guy's chubby, warm body. Did Arlene know how fortunate she was?

"What about the sorting we'd all planned to do at Dad's house this week?" she asked, looking up at Elsie. "How's that going to get done if you two are here helping me?"

"It can wait. Right now, your needs take priority over finding Dad's will."

"I bet Joel won't be happy about that."

"I still haven't called him, but I need to do it soon."

Doris figured Elsie had put off making the call because she dreaded Joel's reaction to the news that the search for the will had been suspended. She couldn't blame her. Their brother could be quite difficult when he didn't get his way.

❦

"I'm worried about Doris," Arlene said after she and Elsie had gotten their sister settled on the living room couch and gone to the kitchen.

"She looked tired, so hopefully she'll sleep awhile," Elsie replied.

Arlene had brought the baby to the kitchen with them so Doris could rest. "I hope Samuel doesn't get fussy and wake her. With my older children in school and Larry at work, I didn't have anyone to watch him today."

"I'm sure it'll be fine. We can set his playpen up here in the kitchen, if you brought it."

"Jah, it's in my buggy. I'll go get it." Arlene handed Samuel to Elsie and went out the door.

Elsie looked at the precious infant in her arms. The little guy's eyes closed slowly then opened. He was no doubt ready for a nap. "You're so adorable and sweet," she whispered, reflecting on how soothing it felt when her children were babies.

A short time later, Arlene returned with the playpen. Elsie waited for her to set it up before passing the little one to his mother.

"When I finish the dishes, we can move him to whatever room we decide to clean."

"That's a good idea." Arlene placed the baby in the playpen, then grabbed a dish towel to dry the dishes. "I feel sorry for Doris. She wanted a boppli so badly."

Elsie's chest felt heavy. She stared at the sponge she held. "It's hard to stay positive during times like these, but for our sister's sake, we must encourage her to look for the good in things. As Dad used to say, 'This too will pass, and things are bound to go better soon.'"

~

Akron

Joel blinked against the light streaming through the blinds in his living room. He'd spent another miserable night on the couch, which had probably done his back more harm than good.

Groaning, he forced himself to sit up and winced when he tried to straighten. *How am I going to do any work today when I'm still in pain?* Joel had spent the last four days alternating between using a heating pad and an ice pack on his back. *Probably should see a chiropractor, massage therapist, or doctor—maybe all three. This isn't getting better on its own.*

Joel rubbed the sides and top of his head. His hair felt greasy. He really ought to take a shower, but his back hurt worse when he stood too long. His cold lingered, which didn't help either. He wished he could call on someone to take care of him. He'd tried calling Kristi several times over the weekend, but she hadn't returned even one of his calls. He'd called Tom last night, but his friend couldn't help because he'd gotten stuck at his folks' in bad weather and didn't know when he'd make it home.

Guess I could call one of my sisters, but they'd have to hire a driver to bring them here. He winced. *Bet they wouldn't even care that I'm here alone with a bad back and a horrible cold.*

Joel picked up his cell phone and searched for local chiropractors. He found one a few miles from where he lived and dialed the number. After explaining his predicament, he was given an appointment for three o'clock that afternoon. It would not be easy, but somehow he'd muster the strength to drive there. In the meantime, he would force himself to take a shower and put on some clean clothes. He wrinkled his nose. "Bet I smell as bad as I look."

"How'd your weekend go? Did you have a nice Thanksgiving?" Dorine asked when Kristi arrived at the nursing home.

"It was good. I spent Thanksgiving Day with my parents, went shopping on Friday, attended another quilting class with my mom Saturday, and had dinner at my folks' house after church on Sunday." Kristi smiled. "How was yours?"

Dorine pressed her palm against her chest. "Thanksgiving was kind of rough here at work, and when I had a late meal at my boyfriend's house that evening, I had a hard time feeling thankful."

"What happened?"

"Mr. Riggins had a heart attack and was rushed to the hospital." Pausing to pick up a magazine someone had dropped on the floor, Dorine's shoulders drooped. "It happened in the lunch-room, and the patients who were eating there became quite upset. It took awhile to get them settled down."

"I'm sorry to hear it." Kristi spoke softly. "Have you heard how he's doing?"

"No, but then I was off Friday, Saturday, and Sunday, same as you."

"What about Audrey? How's she doing?" Kristi slipped off her hat and matching gloves, as well as her coat, and put them away.

Dorine gave a slow shake of her head. "She was in a lot of pain on Thanksgiving, and the medica-tion kept her sleeping most of the day. She's get-ting nourishment from her IV, but even when she's awake, she doesn't want to eat anything."

Kristi's arms pressed tightly against her sides. "I wish I had worked Thanksgiving. I could have sat with her awhile and maybe coaxed her to eat a little something."

"It wouldn't have done any good, Kristi. Short of a miracle, Audrey doesn't have much longer to live." Dorine's eyes filled with sadness as she looked down the hall toward Audrey's room.

Tears stung Kristi's eyes, but she tried to sup-press her emotions. She enjoyed tending to the patients who lived here, but at times such as this, she felt like quitting her job and looking for work that didn't involve sickness and death. It was hard not to become depressed while performing her nursing duties—especially when faced with the imminent death of Audrey, who had helped her get through the breakup with Joel. "Think I'll go to Audrey's room right now to check on her."

"Go right ahead, but don't be surprised if you find her sleeping."

As Kristi started down the hall, Dorine called, "Hey, Kristi, before you go, I could use a little help." She pushed the vitals cart along.

Kristi paused. "Sure, what do you need?"

"A new patient came in earlier, and I could use your help turning him. He was transferred here from the hospital and needs a lot of assistance right now."

"Okay, I'll follow you in." Kristi motioned for Dorine to lead the way.

When they finished getting the gentleman situated a short time later, Kristi headed down the hall to see Audrey. She found the dear woman in bed, hooked up to an IV. Her eyes were shut. Her skin was nearly as pale as the bed sheets.

Kristi stood at the foot of Audrey's bed and closed her eyes. *Heavenly Father, as much as I want to keep her here, please don't let Audrey suffer. If it's not Your will to heal her, then please take her home to be with You.*

She kept her eyes closed and reflected on the times Audrey had ministered to her when she'd been trying to deal with the end of her relationship with Joel. "If only there was something I could do for you," she whispered.

"There is. You can sit beside my bed."

Kristi's eyes snapped open. She was surprised to see the elderly woman looking at her, a slight smile on her thin lips. "Oh, you're awake. I'm sorry if I disturbed you."

Audrey lifted a bony finger, beckoning her to come closer.

Kristi took a seat beside the bed and reached out to clasp this special patient's hand.

"Where have you been? It seems like such a long time ago that we talked." Audrey spoke so faintly, Kristi had to lean closer in order to make out her words.

"I spent Thanksgiving with my parents, and then I had Friday, Saturday, and Sunday off. I'll be working for the next five days, so we'll get to see each other often."

"The cancer's getting worse. My time is drawing close." Audrey's breathing was raspy. Kristi could tell it was all she could do to keep her eyes open.

"You don't need to talk. I'll just sit here with you and hold your hand." Kristi struggled to keep from breaking down. It was difficult to see how quickly this sweet lady had gone downhill.

"I—I wish I could be up and around. I don't like being stuck in this bed. It makes me feel worthless."

Kristi gently patted Audrey's cold hand. "You are not worthless. Your comforting words and heartfelt prayers have been a big help to me." She glanced away briefly, blinking to keep tears from falling onto her cheeks. This was not a time to give in to her emotions. She wanted to be strong for Audrey's sake.

"Are you still praying for that young man—Joel, isn't that his name?"

"Yes, I've been praying." Kristi chose not to mention that Joel had called several times over the weekend and left messages. He'd sounded so desperate, it had been hard not to return his calls. But Kristi felt sure he'd only been trying to prey on her sympathy in hopes of getting her back. In one of his messages, Joel had said he'd changed and would never say or do anything to hurt her again. Words were cheap. Joel had done nothing to prove he'd changed. Even if he had, Kristi wasn't sure she could ever believe him. *A zebra doesn't change its stripes.* She brought her hand up to her chest. *If he really had changed, he wouldn't have quit coming to church.*

Turning her focus back to Audrey, Kristi said, "I've been praying for you, too."

"Thank you, dear." Audrey's eyelids fluttered, then closed.

Kristi could tell she had fallen asleep by the way her chest rose slowly and fell. Thinking the gentle woman needed her rest, she stood and slipped quietly out of the room. She would check on Audrey a little later. Right now, other patients needed her care.

CHAPTER 3

Millersburg

Elsie shivered, covering herself with her shawl as she hurried down the driveway to the phone shack. It had been a week since Doris got out of the hospital, and she still needed help. But Elsie noticed some improvement. Doris got around better on her crutches. Her color was back, too, and she appeared to be more rested. Of course, her broken leg and bumped head would mend, but it would take longer for Doris's heart to heal after the loss of her baby. She and Brian would continue to need their family for spiritual and moral support in the days ahead.

As soon as Elsie checked for messages, she'd head for Doris's house. Arlene would join her again, only this time instead of cleaning, they planned on baking. Christmas was less than three weeks away, so baking some things ahead and freezing them would jumpstart their holiday preparations.

She stepped into the phone shack, glancing quickly around for spiders lurking about, and turned on the answering machine. There was only one message—from Joel. Elsie suspected he'd called to ask if the will had been found. She brought her hand up to her cheek. *I should have called him before now.* Every time she'd thought to do it, something came up and it didn't get done.

As Elsie listened to the message, her jaw clenched. *Is that all he ever thinks about?* With a feeling of dread, she dialed Joel's number. Elsie was surprised when he picked up the phone. Quite often when she called, she would get his voice mail.

"Hi, Joel, it's Elsie."

"Oh, good. I'm glad you called. I've been lying around with a bad back and a cold, wondering if you've found the will." His voice sounded raspy, like he'd been coughing a lot.

"Are you okay?"

"I'm some better, but I was pretty much flat on my back for the better part of a week."

"I'm sorry to hear that."

"So, about Dad's will... Have you had any luck?"

Elsie shook her head over Joel's misplaced priorities. "Doris fell down the stairs on Thanksgiving, so the search for the will has been postponed until she's fully recovered."

Silence on the other end.

"Joel, did you hear what I said?"

"Yeah. Is Doris hurt bad?"

"She broke her leg. Worse than that, she lost her boppli."

"What baby?"

Elsie wrapped her finger around the phone cord and swallowed hard. It was difficult to talk about it—especially with Joel, whom she was sure wouldn't understand.

"I didn't know she was expecting a baby."

"Doris found out she was expecting a few weeks ago. Since she and Brian have been married over six years, they didn't think they could have any children." Her shoulders slumped as she continued to speak. "They were so excited about it, and now their hopes have been crushed."

"I'm sorry to hear this, but I'm also disappointed I wasn't notified of her pregnancy or told that she'd fallen and lost the baby." He coughed a couple of times and let out a heavy sigh.

Elsie heard the frustration in her brother's voice. "I'm sorry, Joel. I assumed Doris had told you when she found out she was pregnant." She paused for a breath. "It's no excuse, but things have been hectic since her accident. Arlene and I have been going over to help Doris every day, so I kept forgetting to call you."

Once more, the phone became silent on the other end.

"Joel, are you still there?"

"Yeah. Just trying to process all this. I'll try to stop by and see Doris as soon as I have some free time. Thanks to my back going out, I lost a week's worth of work, so there's some catching up to do. I need money coming in more than anything right now."

She gripped the phone so tightly her fingers throbbed. Hearing him reminded her of the funeral—the way Joel had disregarded their father's passing for the sake of getting his share of the inheritance. Even when he made an effort to be sympathetic, his own needs always came first. *If your family was important to you, you'd make the time to see Doris right away,* she thought with regret.

Joel cleared his throat. "About the missing will. . . Since you and Arlene are busy helping Doris right now, maybe I should go over to Dad's place and search for it again."

Elsie's jaw clenched. "So you don't have time to see Doris right now, but you could make time to search for the will?"

"Well, I—"

"How can you even be thinking about Dad's will when our sister is in pain and grieving the loss of her baby?" Elsie was ready to slam the receiver and end this conversation. She'd had enough of Joel being so self-centered, especially toward their family. But she drew in a slow, steady breath and allowed her brother to respond.

"Okay, you're right, but before we hang up, I was wondering what you would think about selling Dad's horses."

"What?" Her voice grew sharper. "Why are you bringing that up? *What is he thinking?*

"Because we could all use the money—especially Doris. I'm sure she's gonna have some hospital and doctor bills to pay." Joel's tone grew louder, too.

Elsie sighed in frustration. "Until Dad's will is found and we know how he wanted things divided up, we should not sell anything. I'm sure our sisters would agree with me on that."

He grunted. "Of course they would. You three have always sided against me."

She couldn't argue the point, but it was because Joel had made so many unwise decisions and given unreasonable demands. It would be easier for Elsie to side with him if he put others' needs ahead of his own.

"Listen, I need to bid on a job right now. I'll forget about Dad's will for the moment. Let me know when you're ready to start looking for it again." Joel hung up without saying goodbye.

Elsie pressed down on the receiver and got up from her chair. Her muscles were tight, and her toes felt numb when she stepped out of the phone shack. The conversation with Joel had been unnerving, but she didn't have time to dwell on it. Elsie wished she could count on her brother to go and see Doris. If she told her sister Joel might drop by for a visit, Doris would be disappointed if he didn't follow through. Elsie was hesitant to say anything, so she decided to remain silent on the subject. Right now, she needed to go to Doris's house and see how she was doing.

≋

Berlin

"Here's a cozy coverlet you can rest under while we're waiting for your husband to get here. Is there anything else I can do for you before I head home?" Arlene asked as she gathered up her things.

"No, you and Elsie did enough today with all the baking you got done." Doris placed the small covering next to her on the recliner. "Brian will be here soon, so you should both go home and tend to your families." Doris had spent part of the day in the kitchen, with her broken leg propped on a stool, so she could visit with her sisters. The rest of the time she'd rested in Brian's recliner. Sitting around so much got on her nerves. Doris had always been a doer, and watching others do all the work she should have been doing herself made her feel even worse.

Another thing that really bothered Doris was seeing Arlene's baby, Samuel, laughing and rolling about in his playpen. It was wrong to be jealous, but she couldn't help herself. She wanted nothing more than to have a child of her own and struggled with the thought that it might never happen.

Elsie stepped in front of Doris's chair. "Are you

sure you don't want one of us to stay until Brian gets home from work? I'd be happy to do that."

"No, you go ahead. I'll stay right here in the recliner until he arrives, so don't worry about me."

Both sisters hesitated but finally nodded. "We'll be back tomorrow, so don't try to do anything on your own," Arlene said.

She held up one hand. "I promise."

After Elsie and Arlene left, Doris leaned her head back and closed her eyes, feeling drowsy. She was almost to the point of dozing off, when a knock sounded on the door, jolting her upright. Needing to see who it was, she grabbed her crutches and stood. When she hobbled across the room and opened the door, she was surprised to see her friend Anna on the porch.

"I've wanted to come by and see how you're doing," Anna said breathlessly, "but things have been busy at the schoolhouse with the Christmas program coming up soon, and I couldn't get away."

"Well, you're here now, and I'm glad to see you." Doris gestured with her head toward the living room. "Come inside and we can sit and visit."

"Jah, we do need to sit, because you should get off your feet." Anna removed her outer garments and draped them over a chair. "How are you feeling? Is your leg still painful?"

"It hurts sometimes," Doris admitted. "It feels better when I keep it propped up." She took a seat in the recliner, and Anna seated herself on the couch across from her.

"How are things at school? Do all the scholars know their parts for the program?"

"Some do, but others are having a hard time

remembering their recitations." Anna smiled. "I'm sure everyone will do fine on the evening of the program though."

"I remember when I was nine years old I was given a poem to recite. When I looked out and saw my parents that evening, I became *naerfich* and forgot what I was supposed to say." Doris rubbed the bridge of her nose, as the embarrassment of the moment came back to her. She'd taken some teasing from Joel on the way home, and of course, he'd bragged about the fact that he'd done well with his part.

"I felt nervous during some of my Christmas programs when I was a girl, too." Anna sat quietly, as though pondering something. Then she looked at Doris and said, "I'm sorry you lost your boppli. I know how much you looked forward to becoming a mamm."

Tears welled in Doris's eyes, but she tilted her head up and blinked to prevent them from falling onto her cheeks. "It's hard to say this, but I guess it was not meant to be. Maybe Brian and I aren't supposed to have any kinner."

"Is that what you really think, or is it your way of accepting what happened?"

"I–I'm not sure. My desire to be a parent hasn't left, but I need to accept whatever God's will is for me and Brian."

Anna nodded slowly, as a flush of crimson color crept across her cheeks. "I understand. I've had to work through my feelings for Joel and accept the fact that he and I are not meant to be together. He's engaged to marry someone else now, so there's no hope of us ever being together."

"Actually, he's not engaged anymore." Feeling a sudden chill, Doris picked up the coverlet and placed it over her knees, appreciating the warmth it offered.

"Really?" Anna's eyes widened. "What happened?"

"It's not my place to give the details, but I don't think Joel and Kristi will be getting back together."

"Can you tell me this much—did he break up with her, the same way as he did me?"

"No, it was Kristi who ended their relationship."

Anna glanced out the window, then looked directly at Doris. "Do you think. . . ? Is there any chance Joel might return to the Amish faith?"

"I honestly doubt it." Doris wanted to say there was a possibility Joel might return and show an interest in Anna again, but he had given no signs of making such a change. Even if he had, she couldn't imagine him giving up his modern ways for the plain life—not after he'd been gone for more than seven years.

"I need to forget about Joel and move on with my life, don't I?" Anna's chin quivered.

"Jah, I believe you should. It's the right thing to do."

&

Akron

As Joel left the jobsite and headed for the bank, he felt thankful he was finally able to work again; although he still had to take it easy. The last thing he wanted to do was reinjure his back and end up out of commission once more. He'd been paid for the first half of a kitchen remodel and wanted to put the money in the bank.

I'll put it in our joint account, he decided. *If Kristi checks on the balance again, and discovers I've put some of the money back that I previously took out, maybe she'll decide I'm deserving of a second chance.*

A short time later, Joel pulled into a space in the bank's parking lot and walked into the building. When he reached the first available teller, he explained, "I'd like to deposit a check into the joint account I have with Kristi Palmer."

When the middle-aged woman gave him a blank stare, he realized she needed the account number. Having memorized it from previous deposits he had made, Joel gave her the information.

Peering at him through her metal-framed glasses, she let out a soft breath and turned to the computer, entering the necessary data. She looked back at Joel and squinted. "I'm sorry, sir, but that account's been closed."

"What?" His arm jerked, and he felt sweat bead on his forehead. "Are—are you sure?"

She gave a brief nod. "According to the statement on the computer, Miss Palmer closed the account several days ago."

That's just great. Joel rubbed the side of his neck. *Is she trying to send me a message?*

"Is there anything else I can do for you, Mr. Byler?"

"What?" Joel jerked his head.

She repeated herself.

"Uh, sure. I'll put this check in my business account." He gave her the number and rolled his shoulders in an attempt to shake away some of the tension he felt. *Maybe it's really over between me and Kristi. Is it time to move on with my life?*

CHAPTER 4

The second Sunday of December found Kristi at her parents' home, sharing a meal after church. Ever since she and Joel had broken up, Sunday dinners had become a regular occurrence. Last year during the holidays, Kristi and Joel had driven around, looking at Christmas lights. They'd picked out two trees—one to put in her condo and one for Joel's single-wide. She remembered how they'd stayed up late to ring in the New Year, making a toast with sparkling cider at midnight. Those times together had been fun, but Kristi needed to start fresh, without Joel in the picture.

She felt thankful her parents were Christians and had always been there when she had a need. Although the pain of losing Joel had lessened, at times she missed what they'd once had.

"You're not eating much today. Is the roast not tender enough?"

Mom's question scattered Kristi's thoughts, and she nearly lost her grip on the fork she held. "Uh, no, it's fine." She took a bite of meat and blotted her lips with her napkin. "Really good, in fact."

"Did you get a chance to greet our new youth pastor when church let out?" Mom asked. "His name is Darin Underwood, in case you didn't hear it when Pastor Anderson introduced him to the congregation."

"No, I didn't get to meet him today. Too many other people were talking to him, and it would have been awkward if I'd barged in." Kristi brought her glass to her lips and sipped some water.

"I spoke with Darin for a few minutes before church started." Dad picked up the salt shaker and sprinkled some on his meat. Then he glanced briefly at Mom, as though expecting her to say something. Dad's blood pressure had been running a little on the high side lately, and the doctor suggested he cut down on salt and get more exercise. He'd joined the fitness center where Kristi sometimes went, but giving up salt seemed to be hard for him.

Mom didn't say anything, but her narrowed eyes spoke volumes.

They ate in silence for a while, with only the sounds of utensils clinking against their plates. Then Mom looked at Kristi and said, "I've been thinking about inviting the new youth pastor over for a meal soon. It will give us a chance to get to know him better. I hope you'll be free to join us that evening." She nudged Kristi's arm. "Darin is single, you know."

"I hope you're not trying to play matchmaker, Mom." Kristi groaned. "As I've mentioned before, I'm not ready to pursue a relationship right now."

Mom's cheeks colored as she picked up her glass. "I'm not suggesting anything like that. I only thought—"

"Changing the subject," Kristi interrupted, "have you done much on your own with the quilted pillow slip you're making?"

"A little, but I'll work on it more when we go back to the quilting class this Saturday. Our Amish teacher is so patient and good at what she does." Mom chuckled. "I'll bet she could sew a quilt in her sleep."

Kristi smiled. "The quilt I'm making for my bed will take longer to make than our six-week class allows, so I've been working on it at home in the evenings."

Dad smiled. "I'm glad my two favorite ladies have found something they can enjoy doing together."

"It's been fun, and after each lesson Mom and I try out a different restaurant in Amish country." Kristi fiddled with her dress sleeve. They hadn't been back to Der Dutchman in Walnut Creek since they'd seen Doris, but she hoped they could go there again sometime.

༄

Berlin

"I'm glad you were able to make it to church today, but you must be tired." Arlene followed her sister to the couch. Once Doris was stretched out, she put a pillow under her leg.

Doris nodded. "The trip there was tiring, and sitting for three hours wore me out. That's why Brian and I didn't stay for the meal."

"Is there something I can fix for you now?"

"No, Brian heated some soup for us as soon as we got home. What about you? Did you have a chance to eat with your family before you came over here?" Doris asked.

"Jah. When I saw you leave, we decided not to stay for the meal either." Arlene leaned back in the rocking chair and started it moving slowly. "After we got home, I fixed sandwiches for everyone, fed and diapered Samuel, and then put him down for a nap. If he wakes up before I get back, Larry or one of the girls will keep him occupied until I get back."

Doris yawned and covered her mouth with her hand. "You really didn't have to come here today. Brian's with me. If I need anything, he'll take care of it."

"I know, but I wasn't sure if you'd eaten, so—"

"A van just pulled into the yard," Brian announced as he walked into the room. "It's your aunt," he said, looking out the living room window. "She's getting out of the vehicle."

Arlene hopped up. "I wonder what she's doing here." She turned to Doris. "Did you know Aunt Verna was coming?"

Doris shook her head.

"Guess we'll find out the reason for her visit soon enough." Brian opened the door and stepped outside.

Arlene grabbed her shawl and followed. Aunt Verna was walking toward the house with her suitcase, which Brian was quick to take from her.

"Are you surprised to see me?" Aunt Verna gave Arlene a hug.

"I certainly am. Neither Doris nor I knew you were coming. Does Elsie know?"

"Nope. When I heard about Doris's accident, I decided she could probably use some help, so I talked it over with Lester, and he said I could come for as long as I'm needed." She grinned. "I talked to him about joining me here for Christmas, and he agreed. He will be here on Christmas Eve. It'll be nice to spend the holiday with our three special nieces."

Arlene gently squeezed her aunt's hand. "Having you both here will be wunderbaar, and your help will certainly be appreciated."

As Joel drove through the town of Berlin, memories of the past flooded his mind. As a teenager, he and some of his buddies came here for pizza and to hang out together. *Those days were carefree,* he thought, turning onto the road that led to Doris's house. While he'd never had enough money to satisfy his wants, Joel had been better off than he was right now. At least back then he wasn't faced with a bunch of debts he couldn't pay. Life seemed much simpler when he was still Amish.

Joel slowed to turn onto Doris and Brian's driveway. Their place was small compared to most of the Amish homes he'd been in, but they didn't need much space since only the two of them lived there. *Too bad she lost her baby,* he thought. *I bet Brian would have happily added onto the house if they needed more room for a growing family.*

He pulled up next to the barn and turned off the ignition. Joel had driven his everyday car today, knowing better than to show his fancy Corvette to any of his family. He hoped his visit with Doris would go well and that he'd have the right words to say. Joel had never been good at communicating with Doris—at least not since they'd become adults. He always sensed her resentment of him for having left the Amish faith. It didn't help that his former girlfriend, Anna Detweiler, was Doris's best friend. *Doris probably hasn't forgiven me for turning my back on Anna and our relationship.*

Determined to make the best of this visit, Joel grabbed the "Get Well" balloon he'd bought and got out of the car. He knocked on the door and was startled when he was greeted by Aunt Verna.

"I'm surprised to see you here," they said in unison.

Joel's cheeks heated. Apparently his aunt was aware that he didn't come around very often. "I came to see how Doris is doing."

She tipped her head to one side. "What was that?"

"I said, 'I came to see how Doris is doing.'" Joel spoke a little louder this time. "Just didn't expect you to be here."

She smiled and gave him a hug. "I got here a short time ago. Came to help out so your sisters could have a break. With Christmas coming soon, they'll have lots to do at their own homes, so I'll take care of things here."

"I'm sure your help will be appreciated." Joel patted her back, continuing to speak loud enough for her to hear. "It's good to see you."

"Come inside and say hello to Doris. You just missed Arlene. She went home a few minutes ago." Aunt Verna led the way to the living room, where Joel found his sister on the couch, with Brian sitting on the end of it by her feet.

Joel moved over to stand beside Doris and handed her the balloon. "This is for you. I heard about your accident and wanted to come by and see how you're doing."

"Thank you. I'm getting along as well as can be expected." Clinging to the balloon, she clasped her hands tightly together in her lap.

"I'm sorry for your loss."

Doris gave a brief nod in response.

"Please, take a seat." Brian gestured to the recliner near the rocker, where Aunt Verna sat.

Scraping a hand through his hair, Joel did as his brother-in-law suggested. He'd been right to visit, but he felt strangely out of place. Sometimes when he was around his siblings and their spouses, things became heated. Other times, his tension and sense of being out of place dissipated.

"How have you been, Joel?" Aunt Verna asked.

"I'm gettin' by." *But things would be better if I had more money.*

"Did you say you're going to buy something?"

"No, I said I'm getting by."

She smiled at him. "Glad to hear it. How's that pretty young woman who was with you at my bruder's funeral? Kristi—isn't that her name?"

Joel winced at the mention of Kristi. "We broke up," he mumbled, hoping to keep his composure.

"What was that?" Aunt Verna cupped one hand around her ear.

"He said they broke up." Doris turned to Joel and frowned. "You seem to have a knack for messing things up with the people you're supposed to love."

As soon as the words were out of her mouth, a sharp pain hit Joel in the chest. His sister was right. There was no denying it. This whole time he'd been attempting to get Kristi back because he was lonely without her. He'd ruined the chance of marrying the woman he loved, all for the sake of having money. It was likely he would never hold Kristi in his arms again, and that pained him the most.

Doris gasped. "I—I'm sorry, Joel. I shouldn't have said that."

Shrugging, he stared at his shoes. "You only spoke what you feel is true. I don't have a good track record with women. Apparently you felt the need to remind me of that."

"Maybe we need to change the subject," Brian interjected.

"Or maybe it would be best if I go." Joel stood and looked at Doris. "I hope your leg heals as it should and that you'll feel better soon." He said a quick goodbye and hurried out the door.

"Probably shouldn't have come here," he muttered, while opening his car door. *I'm glad Doris is doing okay, but I'm tired of her putting me down for my mistakes. I never seem to say or do the right thing when I'm around any of my family. Don't know why I bother to try. Even after all this time, Doris is obviously still upset with me for breaking up with Anna.*

As Joel drove down the driveway, he met an Amish buggy heading toward him. He moved the car over as far as he could to let it pass. As the buggy went by, he recognized the driver. It was Anna. *What are the odds?* Joel's toes curled inside his shoes. Not knowing what else to do, he gave a wave and continued out onto the road.

As he traveled on, Joel thought about Anna and all the Sunday afternoons they'd spent together when they were courting. A lot of history lay between them, and every time he saw her, scenes from the past would rush through his head. They'd had some fun times back then, even after Joel became dissatisfied with his life. Before he left the Amish faith, he thought he could convince Anna to go English, too. They could have started a new life together. Anna's experience with children might have helped her get a job as a nanny or working at a daycare center. But Joel now recognized that she would never have agreed to leave. She was committed to the old ways.

He gripped the steering wheel and gritted his teeth. *I shouldn't be thinking about this right now. I'm not Amish anymore, and it's over between me and Anna. There's no going back.*

CHAPTER 5

Charm

The following day, when Elsie arrived at Dad's house to do more sorting, she was surprised to see Arlene's buggy parked by the barn. It was the first time since Doris's accident that they'd been able to continue searching for the will. Thanks to Aunt Verna showing up and offering to care for Doris, Elsie and Arlene felt free to spend time here again. They could only be at Dad's a few days a week however. With Christmas drawing closer, there was much to be done at home in preparation for the big day.

After Elsie put her horse away in the corral, she grabbed the basket of food she'd brought and went into the house. Arlene sat in the living room, going through a stack of magazines.

"Sorry I'm a little late." Elsie set the basket down, removed her jacket and bonnet, and hung them on a wall peg near the door. "I hope you haven't been working on your own for long."

"No—only fifteen minutes or so." Arlene held up one of the magazines. "Just when I think we've come to the end of catalogs and magazines, I find there are more."

"I don't suppose you've found Dad's will in any of them?"

"No will, but I did find this inside the first magazine I went through." Arlene pointed to the dollar bill lying on the coffee table in front of her.

Elsie pursed her lips. "I wonder why Dad would

put money inside a magazine."

"Maybe he was preoccupied and didn't realize he'd done it."

"Or perhaps he put it there for safekeeping. I need to put some food in the refrigerator that I brought for Glen, and then we should keep looking." Elsie picked up the basket and headed for the kitchen. After she'd put the food away, she returned to the living room.

"When we decide to take a break, I'll need to change Glen's sheets and make up his bed. He's been busy with work, not to mention taking care of Dad's horses and doing chores around this place, so I want to help out."

Arlene nodded. "That's understandable. I'd do the same if one of my kinner were staying here."

Elsie walked by the front window and looked out. "It will be nice having Aunt Verna and Uncle Lester for Christmas."

"Jah. I enjoy having all the family gathered together for the special holiday, celebrating Jesus' birth."

"Well, I guess we'd better get busy." Elsie grabbed a stack of magazines and took a seat beside her sister. Instead of turning each of the pages, she held the magazine by the bound edge and shook it. To her surprise, several bills fell out. "Wow! We may be on to something here."

She grabbed another magazine and gave it a good shake. Arlene did the same with the one she held. More money came out—mostly dollar bills, but a couple of fives were also included. As they continued going through the magazines, they discovered more, and then the money stopped.

"Guess maybe Dad only put money in those few magazines." Arlene picked up the bills and counted them out loud. "I can't believe it. Two hundred dollars. What should we do with it?"

Elsie shrugged. "I'm not sure. It would probably be best to set it aside for now. You never know. We might find more in the days ahead."

A knock sounded on the door, and Elsie went to answer it. She was surprised to see Ben Yoder, a local taxidermist, holding a pheasant of all things. It took her a few minutes to recognize it, but then she realized it was the same bird she'd found in her dad's freezer several months ago.

"Your daed asked me to taxidermy this for him a few months back." Ben held up the pheasant. "Business has been slow lately, so I got it done sooner than expected." He dipped his head slightly. "Unfortunately, not soon enough for Eustace to enjoy."

Elsie nodded. She would give nearly anything to have her dad back.

"Do you want the pheasant, or should I try to sell it to someone in the area?"

"One of the men or boys in our family might like it. What is the cost?"

"Normally, a bird like this can go for upwards to four hundred dollars, but since it's standing and not in a flying position, I didn't have to do quite as much work." Ben pulled a piece of paper out of his pocket. "This is how much I was planning to charge your daed."

Elsie stared at the paper and blinked. The bill was for two hundred dollars—exactly the amount she and Arlene had found in the magazines this morning. It seemed as if it were meant to be. "If you'll wait right here, I'll get the money."

He gave a nod and handed her the pheasant.

"I need the money we found in Dad's magazines to pay for this," Elsie announced when she returned to the living room. She placed the bird on the coffee table. "Ben Yoder did this up for Dad, and the bill is two hundred dollars—which is exactly how much money we have."

"The last thing we need is a pheasant." Arlene crossed her arms.

"It's a nice reminder of Dad, and maybe one of the men or boys in our family would like it."

Arlene sighed. "Since Ben did the work, I guess we should use the money we found to pay him." She handed Elsie the bills and glanced briefly at the bird. "It sure looks real, doesn't it?"

"Jah. Ben did a good job." Elsie moved toward the door, clutching the money in her hand. "I'd best not keep him waiting on the porch. As soon as I pay him, we can have lunch."

❧

"What should we do next?" Arlene asked when she finished drying their lunch dishes. "We've gone through most of the magazines on the first floor and taken a break. Well, I did anyway, while you took care of Glen's sheets."

Elsie wrung out the sponge and began wiping down the counter closest to the stove. "Guess we could do some more sorting upstairs."

"There're still things in the basement that haven't been gone through."

Elsie shivered. "I'm hoping we can talk the

men into cleaning down there because schpinne are bound to be lurking about."

Arlene waved the dish towel at Elsie. "You and your fear of spiders."

"I can't help it. They creep me out."

Rolling her eyes, Arlene reached for the last dish she'd dried and placed it in the cupboard. "Maybe we should take the magazines and catalogs we've already looked through out to the burn barrel. There's no point in keeping them."

"True." Elsie put the sponge away. "Let's put our jackets on and take care of those now. It's a chilly day, and it might feel good to stand around the barrel while the magazines burn."

Arlene chuckled. "Next thing you'll be suggesting we look for some marshmallows to roast."

"You know, that's not a bad idea." Elsie poked her sister's arm. "Just kidding."

After putting on their jackets, they stacked magazines in a cardboard box and carried it outside.

Arlene was about to light the fire when Henry Raber's tractor pulled in. He climbed down and headed their way, leaving his dog in her carrier fastened to the back of his rig.

"I was driving by and saw two buggies parked by your daed's barn, so I decided to stop and give you my news." Henry's smile stretched wide.

"What news is that?" Elsie asked.

"I've hired a driver, and me and Peaches will be heading to Florida next week."

"So you're really going to do it, huh?" Elsie remembered hearing Henry previously mention his desire to go there.

He bobbed his head enthusiastically. "I've rented

a small house in Pinecraft, and I plan to stay through the winter. Won't return to Ohio till the weather warms up." Henry stared at the ground and shuffled his feet. "I'd hoped your daed could make a trip to Florida with me, but since that's not gonna happen, at least I'll have my hund to keep me company."

"It sounds like a real adventure." Arlene smiled. "Someday, when Samuel's older, maybe my family will make it to Florida. I'm sure the kinner would love being able to run around in the sand and play in the waves."

Elsie thought about Doris, and how she and Brian had talked about going to Sarasota for a vacation. Once Doris's leg healed, it might do her some good to get away for a while—especially to someplace warm.

"I'm surprised to see you two here today," Henry commented. "I heard what happened to Doris and figured you'd be in Berlin taking care of her."

"We've been doing that," Elsie replied. "But Aunt Verna showed up yesterday to help out, so Arlene and I decided to take off for a few hours and get some more sorting done."

"Any luck finding your daed's will?"

Arlene shook her head. "It's like looking for a sewing needle in a bale of hay."

Henry laughed. "There's an awful lot here for you to go through. My good friend was quite the hoarder."

"How well we know," Elsie and Arlene said at the same time.

"Well, I won't keep ya. If I don't get goin' soon, Peaches will probably wake up and start howling."

Elsie leaned closer to Arlene and whispered in

her ear. When her sister nodded, she stepped up to Henry and said, "Ben Yoder came by earlier, with a pheasant he'd stuffed for Dad. How would you like to have it, in remembrance of him?"

"Are you sure? You already gave me his old straw *hut*."

"The hat won't hold up forever," Arlene said, "but you can put the pheasant somewhere in your house, and it should last a long time."

"Jah, probably a lot longer than me." Henry's eyes misted and he gave them both a hug. "I'd be happy to take the pheasant. Oh, and when I get to Florida, I'll remember to send you both a postcard."

❧

Berlin

"What would you like for supper this evening?" Aunt Verna asked when she entered the living room.

Doris turned the corner of the page down from the book she was reading. "I believe there's a package of ground beef in the refrigerator. Maybe you could make a meatloaf."

The older woman's gray eyebrows squished together. "You want me to fix ground peas?"

Exasperated, Doris heaved a sigh. For most of the day, her aunt had misinterpreted what she'd said. *Her hearing is probably getting worse. It would make things easier if she would get a hearing aid.* "Aunt Verna," Doris said loudly and as patiently as she could, "I suggested that you make a meatloaf for supper, using the ground beef in the refrigerator."

Aunt Verna moved her head slowly up and down. "Sure, I can do that. Should I get started on it now?"

"If you like." Doris made sure to speak loud enough. She felt worn out from repeating herself so many times throughout the day.

"All right then. Give a holler if you need anything." Aunt Verna turned and shuffled off toward the kitchen.

Even though Doris appreciated the extra help, she'd rather it be one of her sisters doing the cooking and cleaning for her. In addition to Aunt Verna's inability to hear things well, she often became sidetracked, like when she'd left the refrigerator door open after lunch. Doris discovered it when she'd hobbled out to the kitchen for a glass of water. Fortunately, she had caught it before anything spoiled.

Another time, Aunt Verna turned on the water in the kitchen sink and forgot to turn it off because she'd gone outside to fill the birdfeeders. Doris heard it running all the way from the living room.

She shut the book, placing it on her lap, and closed her eyes. *I wouldn't even be in this predicament right now if I hadn't fallen down the stairs.* Tears seeped from her eyes. *I can't do much of anything around the house. I have to rely on others to help me. Their support is appreciated, but I feel helpless and don't like being this way.* She sniffed and wiped the tears from her cheeks. *My clumsiness caused me to lose the child I so desperately wanted.*

Opening her eyes, Doris placed both hands on her stomach. "I'm sorry, so sorry," she sobbed. Even though the baby was gone, she spoke as though it was still there. "This is all my fault. I'm the reason you were never born."

Doris rubbed her nose, breathing slowly to calm herself. *Will I ever conceive again?*

CHAPTER 6

Charm

"There's a postcard and a couple of bills lying on the table. I went out and got them when the mail came earlier." Aunt Verna unwrapped a piece of peppermint candy and popped it in her mouth.

"Who's the postcard from?" Elsie questioned.

"Go ahead—take a look."

Elsie picked up the card and smiled. "It's from Dad's friend Henry Raber. He says he and Peaches are doing well, and enjoying the warm weather in Sarasota. They've been going to the beach quite a bit, and Henry often visits with other snowbirds staying in Pinecraft." Elsie placed the card back on the table. "I'm glad he was able to make this trip. It's hard to believe he's been there a week and a half already."

"Jah. Henry's a nice man, and I'm sure he's been lonely since your daed passed on. I'm glad he's having a good time down there." Aunt Verna crunched on her candy.

Elsie picked up the bills, setting them on her dad's rolltop desk to pay.

"You know, Elsie, I still don't understand why you want me to stay here." Aunt Verna put both hands on her hips and frowned, her upbeat countenance suddenly changing. "I was perfectly happy helping out at Doris's. Besides, I thought you and Arlene wanted to search for your daed's will."

"We do, but we thought it would be better if you were helping us since you said previously that

Dad told you where he'd put the will." Elsie made sure her explanation was loud enough for her aunt to hear. "Arlene and I will take turns helping out at Doris's, while the other one is here sorting things with you."

"Guess that makes sense, but as I've said, I don't remember where my bruder said he put it." Aunt Verna took a seat at the table and massaged her forehead. "That's the problem with getting older. You lose your thinker, and your ears don't work so good anymore. Makes me feel *nixnutzich* sometimes."

Elsie patted her aunt's shoulder. "You're not worthless. I appreciate you staying here and helping me sort things." She gestured to the refrigerator. "In addition to doing more sorting, I'd like to clean that, inside and out, as well as defrost the freezer section. The last time I put something in there for Glen, I noticed it was thick with ice."

"I could bake some peanut butter kichlin while you're doing that. I'll bet Glen would enjoy having some when he gets home from work this evening."

Elsie smiled. "I know he would. Peanut butter is my eldest son's favorite kind of cookie. After we're done in the kitchen we can do more sorting and searching."

Aunt Verna tipped her head. "What did you say?"

Elsie repeated herself.

"Oh, okay. I'll get started on the kichlin right away."

While Aunt Verna got out the baking supplies, Elsie set a pan of warm water in the freezer, hoping the ice would thaw while she cleaned the inside of the refrigerator.

By the time the first batch of cookies had been

taken from the oven, the ice in the freezer had melted enough so Elsie could begin chipping away what was left. Removing a bag of frozen peas, she was surprised to discover a gallon-size plastic bag behind it. At first, she thought it was empty, but on closer look, she realized there was large manila envelope inside. "How strange. I wonder what this could be."

Elsie opened the plastic bag and took out the envelope. After reading the words on the outside, written in black marking pen, she gasped. "It's Dad's will! I've found the will!"

Aunt Verna dropped her spatula on the counter and hurried over. "Did you say you found your daed's will?"

"Jah."

"Where was it?"

"In there." Elsie pointed to the freezer section. "It was behind a package of frozen peas."

Aunt Verna stood several seconds, blinking her eyes rapidly. Suddenly, her mouth opened wide and she screeched. "Ach, my! I remember now. How could I have been so *schlappich*?"

Elsie's forehead wrinkled. "What do you mean? How were you careless?"

Aunt Verna took a seat at the table and motioned for Elsie to do the same. "This is so unbelievable, I barely believe it myself."

Desperate to know more, Elsie clutched her aunt's arm. "Do you know why Dad's will was in the freezer? Did he put it there?"

"No, he did not." Aunt Verna's cheeks reddened. "I remember it all now, as though it happened yesterday." She sucked in a quick breath and continued. "When your daed told me he'd made out a will and had it notarized, he took it out of the rolltop desk. Then he showed me the manila envelope, which he kept in a plastic bag, so if something were spilled on it, no harm would be done." She paused and drew in another breath. "About that time, we heard a commotion going on outside with the horses. So Eustace handed me the bag and asked if I'd put the will back in the desk."

"But it wasn't in the desk, Aunt Verna. Arlene and I looked through every drawer and cubby."

"That's because it was in the freezer."

"But how'd it get there?"

"I don't actually remember doing it." Aunt Verna glanced around, as though searching for answers. "I realize now how it must have happened. I had a bag of peas in one hand, and the will in the other. I must have put them both in the freezer by mistake." She paused, rubbing her chin. "Then, anxious to know what was going on with the horses, I hurried outside and forgot that your daed had asked me to put the will away in his desk."

Elsie sat in stunned silence. The freezer was the last place she would have thought to look for Dad's will. Now that it had been found, she needed to notify her siblings and call everyone together so the will could be read.

⤳

Akron

Joel was about to stop working for the day when his cell phone rang. Seeing it was Elsie, he answered the call.

"Hi, Joel. I'm calling to let you know Dad's will's been found."

Joel released a throaty laugh. "Well, hallelujah! It's about time! Where'd ya find it?"

"In Dad's freezer."

His head jerked back. "Say what?"

"It was inside a plastic bag behind some frozen peas."

"I knew our dad was eccentric, but what in the world was he thinking, putting the will in the freezer? How did he think we'd ever find it there?"

Elsie cleared her throat. "Actually, it was Aunt Verna who put the will in the freezer, but she did it without thinking."

"I would say so. No one with half a brain would do something that stupid on purpose." Joel's face heated. "I—I didn't mean she was stupid. It just doesn't make sense that she would put Dad's will in the freezer."

"Dad had shown her the document, and when he went outside to check on the horses, Aunt Verna got sidetracked and accidently put it in the freezer along with the bag of peas." Elsie paused. "Would you be able to meet with us tomorrow evening for the reading of the will?"

"Why wait that long? I'm free tonight. Can't we do it then?"

"It wouldn't give me time to notify everyone and make plans to get together. I'll speak to Arlene and Doris, then call you as soon as we have a definite time and place."

"Okay, whatever." Joel released a noisy breath. *I should realize by now that we're operating on Amish time, not mine.*

Berlin

Joel's heart pounded as he neared Doris's house. He had been counting the minutes all day, anxious to get here this evening for the reading of Dad's will. He'd had a hard time sleeping last night, wondering what his share of the inheritance would be. The only thing that helped him get through this day was keeping busy on the job he'd begun yesterday.

When Joel started up his sister's driveway, he spotted three buggies parked near the barn. *I wonder who else is here besides Arlene and Elsie. Sure hope they didn't invite anyone outside the family to join us. This is no one's business but ours.*

He turned off the car and got out. Taking the steps two at a time, Joel knocked on the door. He was greeted by Brian, who invited him in. "Everyone's in the living room waiting for you."

Joel removed his jacket and hung it on a wall peg, then followed Brian into the next room. Doris sat in the recliner with her leg propped up, while Elsie, John, Arlene, and Larry were seated on the couch. Joel spotted Aunt Verna in the rocking chair. "Are you here for the reading of Dad's will?"

She tilted her head. "Excuse me. What was that?"

Joel repeated his question.

"Jah. Glen brought me over tonight. He's in the kitchen, eating a snack."

"Speaking of the will, where is it?" Joel asked.

"Right here." John held up a large manila envelope and stood. "Your sisters asked if I would read it." He motioned to the couch. "So you can take my seat there, if you like."

"Oh, okay." Joel took a seat beside Elsie and put both hands on his knees to keep his feet from tapping the floor. He couldn't remember the last time he'd felt so anxious.

"Would anyone like a cup of coffee before we get started?" Elsie asked. "I made a fresh pot awhile ago."

"No, I'm good. Let's get it on with it, shall we?" Joel's neck and shoulders tensed as he leaned slightly forward.

John opened the envelope and pulled out four smaller envelopes, along with a folded document. He placed the envelopes on the coffee table, unfolded the will, and began. "I, Eustace J. Byler, being of legal age and sound mind, do declare that this is my last will and testament. I hereby revoke, annul, and cancel all wills and codicils previously made by me, either jointly or separately. This last will expresses my wishes without undue influence or duress."

John paused and cleared his throat. Continuing to read the will, he stated the names of each of Eustace's children and their dates of birth. "I also appoint my sister, Verna Weaver, as the person responsible to ensure that this will is followed. Should she precede me in death, I appoint my son-in-law, John Troyer."

"The envelopes provided with this will for my children stipulate what each of them will receive. However, they are not to be opened until such time as my son, Joel Byler, performs a heartfelt, selfless act. The selfless act must be voted upon by all three sisters, with the final decision being made by Verna as to whether the stipulation has been met."

Heart thumping so hard he felt it might explode in his chest, Joel leaped to his feet. "That's not fair! How come Dad picked on me?" His hand shook as he pointed at all three of his sisters. "Why didn't Dad ask each of you to do something selfless? How come I have to jump through hoops in order to get my inheritance?"

"It's not only you, Joel," Elsie spoke up. "We all have to wait to open our envelopes until you've done a selfless act that's agreed upon by each of us."

Joel didn't understand how his oldest sister could sit there with such a calm look on her face. "What about you, Doris? How do you feel about this?"

"It doesn't matter how I feel. We have to abide by Dad's wishes," she responded.

Arlene nodded. "He must have had a reason for the four envelopes with our names on them, as well as the request he made of you."

Anger bubbled within Joel as he folded his arms and glared at the piece of paper in John's hands. Then he looked at Aunt Verna. She'd started rocking her chair really fast. "Did you know about this beforehand? Did Dad tell you what he was going to do?"

She looked at him strangely, while tipping her head. "Do about what?"

Joel clapped his hands together so hard, Aunt Verna nearly jumped out of her chair. "Didn't you hear a word John read?"

"Of course I did. He spoke plenty loud enough for me to hear." She left her seat and walked up to Joel. "My bruder wanted you, his only son, to do something meaningful for someone other than yourself."

Joel looked down at the envelopes lying on the coffee table. He was tempted to grab his and open it right now.

Aunt Verna touched Joel's arm. "Before your daed died, he and I talked quite a bit about you."

"Is that so? I'm sure whatever he had to say was negative."

Tears welled in her eyes. "Your selfish actions hurt him, Joel. I'm sure many of the things you've said and done have hurt your sisters, too."

Joel didn't bother to look at Doris, Elsie, or Arlene. He already knew what they thought of him.

"You need to give this some serious thought," Aunt Verna continued. "If you don't do as your daed said, then none of you will get your inheritance."

"Oh really? Who's gonna get it then? You? Old Henry?" Joel's voice rose even louder. "Or maybe all Dad's money will go to those horses no one wants to sell." Joel stomped across the room, grabbed his jacket, and stormed out the door. *If Dad thought he was going to make me knuckle under and do whatever he said in order to get my share of his money, he was sorely mistaken. I'm gonna get what's coming to me, but it won't be the way he planned.*

CHAPTER 7

Thursday morning of the following week, Doris sat at her kitchen table with Brian, drinking coffee while they waited for Arlene to arrive. Elsie had gone to Dad's house again, but this time she and Aunt Verna would be going through more magazines, catalogs, and newspapers in case they held money. Once they were done for the day, Elsie planned to do some Christmas shopping at a few stores in Charm and would take Aunt Verna along.

Doris added some cream and sugar to her coffee, swirling it together with her spoon, then leaned back in her chair. "Arlene said she'd be bringing some of her homemade cinnamon rolls with extra cream cheese frosting."

"That would be nice." Brian smacked his lips before sipping some coffee.

She stared out the window at the birdhouse that was once in her dad's tree house. The last few months had been depressing. It was hard losing Dad, and now trying to get through the loss of her baby.

I don't feel like celebrating Christmas this year, much less buying any presents, Doris thought. *Brian and I were so happy about my pregnancy. I wish we could skip Christmas and start the new year.* She swallowed some coffee and winced when it burned her throat.

"Are you all right, Doris?" Brian touched her arm. "Does your leg hurt this morning?"

"It's not my leg. It's my throat. I added a little

cream to my coffee, thinking it would cool off a bit, but the coffee was still quite hot when I swallowed it."

"Would you like a glass of cold water?" He started to rise from his chair.

"No, I'm okay." She glanced at the clock on the wall. "I don't want you to be late for work, so if you'd like to go now, I'll be fine until Arlene gets here."

He shook his head. "It's not that late. I can wait awhile longer."

Sighing, Doris drummed her fingers on the table. She wished she could clean her own house, or even go back to work so she could help with the hospital bills that would need to be paid. She had so much time to sit and think. Feeling melancholy wasn't making things better for them.

"Is something bothering you?"

"Jah. I've been thinking more about the stipulations of Dad's will. We have my hospital bill to pay, so we could sure use some extra money."

"True."

"It's not likely any of us will get our inheritance. What are the chances of Joel completing a selfless act?" Her forehead tightened as she frowned. "I can't imagine what our daed was thinking when he put that clause in his will."

Brian clasped Doris's hand. "I don't know, either, but I do know if we put our trust in the Lord, He will provide for our needs."

❧

Akron

Joel pounded his truck's steering wheel in frustration. He'd taken time off from his job to contact a lawyer about Dad's will, only to learn that his chances of contesting it were slim to none. Since the document had been notarized, with two witnesses present, it would be next to impossible to prove his father was incompetent when he'd made out the will. As far as the stipulation went, the lawyer said Joel's dad had been within his legal rights to disperse his assets as he saw fit. "Besides," he'd added before Joel left his office, "the Amish are inclined to do things a bit differently than we would."

"Yeah, well my dad liked to do everything different," Joel muttered as he sat in the parking lot of the lawyer's office, staring out the window while mulling things over. *Just what kind of a good deed am I supposed to do? I can't imagine what so-called selfless act would meet with my sisters' and Aunt Verna's approval. What in the world was Dad thinking? Did he do this on purpose to get even with me for leaving the Amish faith? Or was it because he didn't like me coming to him a few times and asking to borrow money?*

Joel sagged in his seat, rocking back and forth. *If I didn't need money so bad, I'd walk away from this and let my sisters have everything.* He frowned as the truth of the situation fully set in. If he walked away and refused to comply with his father's wishes, then Elsie, Arlene, and Doris wouldn't get their share of the inheritance either. It was a catch-22. He needed to talk to someone about this—someone who could help him sort things out and come up with a deed his sisters and Aunt Verna would agree was a selfless act. If he could do that, they would all get their money, and everyone would be happy.

Joel reached into his pocket and pulled out his phone. He'd try calling Tom first; maybe he'd have some good advice. If not, then he might try Kristi.

❦

Charm

"You seem quiet today," Aunt Verna commented as she and Elsie sat at the Chalet in the Valley restaurant, having lunch. "Are you umgerennt about your daed's will?"

"I'll admit I'm upset. It's an impossible situation."

"In Luke 18:27, Jesus said, 'The things which are impossible with men are possible with God.'" Aunt Verna placed her hand on Elsie's arm and gave it a few gentle pats. "You must have the faith to believe your bruder can change and become the man your daed wanted him to be."

Elsie sighed, toying with the napkin in front of her. "We all want Joel to change, but unless he gets right with God, he will never set his selfish desires aside and learn to truly care about others." She picked up her cup of tea and took a drink. "My other concern is that one of my sisters, or even me, will become so desperate for money we'll accept whatever deed Joel may decide to do as good enough, just so we can get our share of the inheritance."

"That will not happen because I will have the final word as to whether he has actually done a heartfelt, selfless act. Now let's commit this situation to God and enjoy the rest of our lunch." Aunt Verna smiled. "This meal is on me."

Elsie knew better than to argue. Her aunt was strong-willed, just like Dad. When she made up her mind on something, it was best to let it stand. She only hoped Joel would come to his senses and do a good deed they could all agree upon.

◆

Akron

Kristi sat beside Audrey's bed, silently praying while she held the elderly woman's hand. Audrey was going downhill so fast and was often unresponsive. It broke Kristi's heart when she thought how sad it was that no one other than herself and the other staff members visited Audrey.

Last week, knowing how much her patient loved flowers, Kristi had bought a Christmas cactus in full bloom and placed it on the table beside Audrey's bed. "Thank you," Audrey had whispered tearfully. "You're an angel, Miss Kristi."

Kristi would make sure to water the cactus as needed and hoped it would continue to bloom all the way past Christmas.

Audrey's eyes opened, and she offered Kristi a weak smile. "Oh, it's you—my angel of mercy. How long have you been sitting here?"

Kristi glanced at her watch. "Fifteen minutes or so. I haven't said anything because I didn't want to wake you."

Audrey lifted a shaky hand, letting it fall close to the edge of her bed. "You spend too much time with me. Don't you have other patients to tend to?"

"Yes, I do, and they are all taken care of." Kristi took Audrey's hand, holding it gently. "You slept most of the morning, and I've been worried about you."

"I'll be going home soon, and then you won't have to worry anymore," Audrey murmured. "I will be safe in the arms of my Lord."

In an attempt to hold back tears, Kristi pointed to the cactus. "It's doing well. I think it likes it here in your room."

Audrey gave a feeble nod. "I believe there will be lots of flowers in heaven."

Kristi swallowed hard, barely able to speak around the lump in her throat. "According to what I read in the Bible, there will be lots of beautiful things in heaven for us to enjoy."

"Yes." Audrey's eyelids closed, and Kristi could tell from her steady breathing that she had fallen asleep.

Slipping quietly from the room, she started down the hall. When she entered the break room a few minutes later, her cell phone vibrated in her pocket. She pulled it out to see who was calling. It was Joel, so she let it go to voice mail, as she had done since their breakup.

"How's Audrey?" Dorine asked, joining Kristi for their afternoon break.

"Not well. She's failing fast, but she did wake up and talk to me for a few minutes."

Dorine fixed herself a cup of coffee. "Audrey's your favorite patient here, isn't she?"

"It's not that she's my favorite, exactly, but she definitely needs me the most, and not just in a physical sense."

"I understand what you're saying. The poor woman has no family to sit beside her bed and offer comfort. You've done that for her, Kristi. And the cactus you bought is proof of how much you care."

"Audrey's a special lady, and she's ministered to me along the way, too." Kristi took an orange from the fruit bowl on the table and sat down. Before peeling it, she glanced at her cell phone and decided to listen to the message Joel had obviously left.

"Hey, Kristi, this is Joel. I hope you're doing well." There was a short pause. "I'm faced with an unusual situation right now and could really use some advice." Another pause—this one followed by a groan. "The thing is, my dad's will was finally located—in his freezer of all places. But I don't know how much my share of the inheritance is because Dad wrote a ridiculous stipulation. He expects me to do some kind of a good deed—he called it a selfless act. And until I do it and it's accepted by my sisters, as well as my aunt, neither me nor my siblings can open the envelopes he left us, which will let us know how much we are entitled to. So what I need to know is what kind of good deed would be considered a selfless act. Since you've done many good deeds working as a nurse, I figured you'd be the one to ask. When you get this message, I'd appreciate it if you'd give me a call."

Kristi sat, staring at her phone, trying to process all Joel had said. Could it be true, or was it just another attempt to get her to call so he could try to convince her to take him back?

If it is true, she thought, *Joel's father made a wise decision, for Joel surely needs to think of someone other than himself for a change. But if he does a good deed only to get the money he wants so badly, then nothing will have been gained.*

Kristi hoped for Joel's sake, as well as for his family, that he would come to realize the importance of putting other people's needs ahead of his own. But in order to do a true selfless act, he would need to first get right with God.

CHAPTER 8

Farmerstown

Joel had spent the last few days wracking his brain, trying to come up with something he could do to earn the right to open the envelope Dad left for him. This morning he'd come up with a plan, and as soon as he finished working for the day, he headed to the schoolhouse where Anna taught. Hopefully the scholars would be gone by the time he arrived. If things were as they had been when he was in school, the teacher would still be there.

When Joel pulled his truck into the schoolyard, he saw a few children milling about. It was a good indication that they'd been dismissed for the day. He popped a breath mint in his mouth and got out of the truck. As he walked toward the door, his nephew Scott stepped out, carrying a lunch box in one hand while adjusting his straw hat with the other.

"Hey, Uncle Joel! What are you doin' here?" Eyes wide, the boy looked up at Joel and grinned.

Joel raked his fingers through the back of his hair. "I. . .umm. . .came by to talk to your teacher."

Scott tipped his head, looking quizzically at Joel.

"It's just a little grown-up talk." No way was Joel about to explain the reason for his visit with Anna.

"Are ya comin' to the school Christmas program tomorrow evening? Me, my brother, and my sisters all have parts." The boy moved his head slowly up and down. "We've been practicin' for the last couple of weeks."

"I bet you have." Joel remembered how excited he used to get when he was a boy and the class would prepare for the program their parents and other family members would be invited to attend. He'd always tried to do his best so he wouldn't embarrass his folks.

Joel flinched when he thought about Christmas, only a few days away. He'd been invited to spend Christmas Eve with his buddy, Tom, but Christmas Day he would be by himself. He'd thought maybe one of his sisters would invite him to spend the holiday at her house, but after the scene he'd created when Dad's will was read, he wasn't surprised no one had asked. *I wonder what Kristi will be doing this year. I sure miss spending time with her. It seems odd not to have bought her a gift.* Joel was giving in to self-pity, but he couldn't seem to help himself. He felt like a ship without an anchor these days.

"So are ya comin' to the Christmas program?" Scott tugged on Joel's jacket.

"Maybe. If I get off work in time to drive down here."

"Sure hope you can make it." The boy continued to look at Joel. "Guess I'd better head out. Doug, Martha, and Lillian went home already. I stayed after to practice my part a bit longer."

Joel gave Scott's shoulder a squeeze. "I'll try to be there to see you perform."

"Okay! See you soon, Uncle Joel."

Joel watched his nephew head out on his bike, then turned and went into the schoolhouse. He found Anna at the front of the room, sitting behind her desk and going over paperwork. When Joel cleared his throat, she jumped.

"I—I'm surprised to see you, Joel. If you stopped by to see one of your nieces or nephews, they've already left." Anna's cheeks were bright pink, and her blue eyes as vivid as ever.

"Well, I. . .uh. . .was visiting with my nephew Scott outside, and he mentioned the Christmas program tomorrow evening. I told him I'd try to make it to the holiday performance, but I actually came here today to see you."

"Oh, what about?" Anna placed her pen beside the papers on her desk.

Joel leaned on her desk, hoping he wouldn't lose his nerve and would be able to say the right words. "See. . .the thing is. . .I came to apologize."

Fingering her paperwork, Anna murmured, "For what, Joel?"

"For hurting you when I broke things off and left the Amish faith." There, it was out. If she accepted his apology he'd stop by Dad's place and tell Aunt Verna what he'd done. Telling Anna he was sorry would surely be considered a selfless act.

She blinked a couple of times, and the color in her cheeks darkened. "What brought this on all of a sudden? Have you changed your mind about being English?"

He shook his head. "I'm happy living with modern things. I. . .I've been thinking about us, though, and wanted you to know that I feel bad about the way things ended." Joel leaned a bit closer. "Will you accept my apology?" Remembering how his dimpled smile used to temper Anna's mood whenever they got into a disagreement in the past, Joel thought he'd go that route and see if it would work on her now. So he gave Anna his deepest smile, gazing into her eyes. Hoping to ensure success in his endeavor, Joel placed his hand on hers and gave her fingers a tender squeeze.

Blushing further, Anna gave a slow nod. "I. . .I appreciate you coming by. It means a lot to me."

"Good." He moved away from her, shuffling his feet and feeling a bit guilty for coming here with an ulterior motive. He hoped she hadn't gotten the wrong impression.

Joel hadn't actually lied to Anna; he did feel bad for hurting her in the past. But if not for the stipulation in Dad's will, he probably never would have apologized.

"Guess I'd better go and let you get back to whatever you were doing. See you around, Anna." Joel turned from the desk.

"Remember, if you're not doing anything tomorrow evening, you're welcome to come to our Christmas program," Anna called sweetly.

He lifted his hand in a parting wave. "I will try to be there." *I'll only be coming for Scott.*

❧

Charm

Feeling rather pleased with himself, Joel whistled a tune he'd learned as a boy and turned onto the road leading to Dad's place. He felt good about his visit with Anna and was confident that when he told Aunt Verna, she'd be impressed. If she agreed what he'd done met the condition of the will, then surely his sisters would, too. Since Anna was Doris's friend, Doris would no doubt be pleased to learn of Joel's apology.

As Joel sat in his truck on the hill above Dad's house, he was tempted to get out and wander around, reflecting on his childhood a bit. He could sit on his old rock-seat and daydream awhile, but it was really too cold for that. Besides, Joel was anxious to speak with his aunt.

Turning the steering wheel, he drove down the driveway and parked his vehicle near the barn. When he stepped out and heard the horses whinny, he was tempted to lead them into the barn, as he'd done for a good many years while growing up. But it wasn't his job anymore. Glen was staying here, and he'd take care of the animals when he got home from work, if he wasn't here already.

Shaking his thoughts aside, Joel hurried up the front porch and knocked on the door. He waited several seconds, and when no one answered, he knocked again, a little louder this time. If Aunt Verna was here, she may not have heard him.

A few more seconds passed. Joel was about to try the door when it suddenly swung open. Aunt Verna, wearing a black scarf on her head, looked at him quizzically. "This is an unexpected surprise. Have you been working in the area today?"

"No, I. . ." Joel paused and moistened his lips. "Is it all right if I come in?"

She cupped her hand around one ear. "What was that?"

Joel repeated himself, a little louder this time.

"Of course you may." She opened the door wider, and Joel stepped inside. "Should we go in the kitchen? I was about to fix myself a glass of butter-milk. Would you like some?"

His lips puckered, thinking about the soured milk his dad used to drink. Apparently Aunt Verna liked it, too. "No thanks. I'll take a glass of water though."

"No problem."

He followed her to the kitchen and took two glasses from the cupboard. After handing one to her, he filled his glass with water and took a seat at the table. Once Aunt Verna had her buttermilk, she joined him. "To what do I owe the pleasure of your visit?" she asked.

Joel took a quick drink and set his glass on the table. "I just came from the schoolhouse in Farmerstown."

"Oh? Did you see your nieces and nephews there?"

"I talked to Scott for a few minutes, but I didn't see the others. I went there to speak with their teacher, Anna Detweiler."

Aunt Verna peered at Joel over the top of her glasses. "Are you two getting back together?"

Joel shook his head. "I went there to tell Anna I was sorry for the hurt I caused when I broke up with her seven years ago."

"Could you repeat that, please?"

"I went there to tell Anna I was sorry for the hurt I caused when I broke up with her seven years ago."

Aunt Verna took a sip of buttermilk. "Has it really been that long?"

"Yes, but that's not the point."

"What is the point?"

"I apologized, and she forgave me."

"I'm glad to hear that. It's always good when a

person realizes they've wronged someone and tries to make amends."

Smiling, Joel sagged in his chair with relief. Once Aunt Verna told Doris, Arlene, and Elsie what he'd done, he felt sure he would soon be opening the envelope Dad left for him.

He took another drink and cleared his throat. "So now that I've done my good deed, will you tell my sisters you approve and allow me to receive my inheritance?"

She pursed her lips, frowning deeply. "Apologizing to Anna was not a selfless act, Joel."

Perplexed and feeling a bit miffed, Joel rapped his knuckles on the table. "Then tell me what specifically I need to do."

"I can't. It's something you must find out for yourself." Aunt Verna left her seat and stepped up to Joel, placing her hand on his heart. "It must come from within. It needs to be heartfelt, not something you do only in the hope of getting your share of my brother's money."

Joel's hands curled into a fist as he inhaled a long breath. This was not going the way he'd planned.

"How is your spiritual life, Joel?" Aunt Verna spoke softly. "Have you prayed about this situation?"

He snorted. "I don't pray about anything anymore."

"Well, maybe it's time you start." She looked at him with squinted eyes.

Feeling uncomfortable, Joel pushed back his chair. "Sorry I bothered you, Aunt Verna. You obviously don't understand."

"I believe I do." She pointed a bony finger at him. "It's you who doesn't understand. Your daed knew that, and he tried to—"

Joel whirled around, turning his back on her. "I don't want to hear anything about my dad. He never treated me well after I left home, and the stupid thing he put in his will only proves he had no love for me!" Without waiting for his aunt's response, he jerked open the back door and dashed outside into the frigid air. He was not going to knuckle under and do a selfless act simply because his dad wanted him to. He would figure out some other way to make his fortune!

CHAPTER 9

Farmerstown

It was hard to believe Christmas was only two days away, but as Doris sat beside Brian at the back of the schoolhouse, the reality sank in. Four of her nephews and nieces took turns reciting their pieces. The story of Jesus' birth had been acted out in a Nativity scene, with Doug and Scott both playing the parts of shepherds, while Martha and Lillian were angels.

Doris was glad she'd felt up to coming, for she wouldn't have wanted to miss it. Her best friend was a talented teacher and had done a good job with the children in preparation for this evening's program.

Glancing around the room, she noticed several hand-drawn pictures of winter scenes. In addition to those, the scholars had made cutout snowflakes of various sizes and shapes to decorate the walls. It brought back memories from when she was a girl. But seeing the scholars and listening to their recitations was bittersweet. It was a harsh reminder that she might never have any children of her own.

She clutched her shawl around her shoulders. *I wonder if my sisters know how fortunate they are to have been given the chance to be mothers.* Her eyes watered, and she bit the inside of her cheek, hoping the tears wouldn't fall. *There's no point feeling sorry for myself. It won't change a thing. I need to accept what's happened to me and find a new purpose in life.*

Doris glanced at Brian and offered him a brief smile when he clasped her hand. He always seemed to be aware when she needed some reassurance or comfort during times of despair. *I feel blessed,* she thought, *to have found a good husband who loves and cares for me.*

Turning her attention to the front of the room, Doris couldn't help but smile when one of the smaller students recited a poem while holding his hand against his heart: "Christmas comes just once a year; but the love of God is always here."

Another child, holding a wrapped package, added, "Christmas is not about gifts or toys. God sent His Son to earth for moms, dads, girls, and boys."

Doris thought about the trials people sometimes faced and how keeping their focus on God helped them get through even the most difficult times. As the children emphasized through their recitations, poems, and skits, the true meaning of Christmas was God's love for His people.

She closed her eyes and offered a brief prayer. *Thank You, Lord, for the gift of Your Son. Help me love others as You have loved us.*

❦

"The program went well, don't you think?" Arlene said to Larry as they headed for home in their buggy.

"It sure did, and I'm glad the snow they've been forecasting held off so the roads are clear."

Scott groaned from his seat behind them.

"What's the matter, Son?" Arlene called. "Are you disappointed because your uncle Joel didn't come to the program?"

"It ain't that. I mean isn't. I've got a *bauchweh.* Sure hope I don't throw up."

"Hang on, Scott, we'll be home soon." Larry bumped Arlene's arm with his elbow. "It's no wonder our boy has a stomachache. Did you see all the popcorn he ate after the program?"

"He had some candy, too," Martha interjected. "Teacher Anna brought some for each of the scholars tonight."

Arlene turned and reached over the seat, patting her son's knee. "You'll feel better once we get home and you can go to bed. I have a homeopathic remedy for tummy aches, and that should help, too."

Scott's only response was a deep moan.

Poor little guy. Everything went so well at the program tonight, Arlene felt bad it had ended on a sour note for Scott.

"It was good to see Doris out tonight," Larry commented.

"Jah. I wasn't sure she'd be up to it, but I'm glad she came. She's been cooped up in the house too much since her accident." Arlene shifted under the blanket covering her lap. "Once she gets her cast off, she should do even better."

By the time they arrived home it had begun to snow, and the storm seemed to be getting stronger as the snow stuck to the ground.

"I'll get the snow shovel out before I come in for the evening, in case we get a good accumulation of this white stuff during the night." Larry pulled the buggy up near the house to let everyone out.

"Yippee! Can we make a big *schneeballe*?" Lillian asked when she jumped down from the buggy.

"No snowballs tonight," Larry said. "It's late and you kinner need to get ready for bed. School's out till after Christmas, so if it keeps snowing, you can all play in it tomorrow."

"I don't wanna play in the snow," Martha said. "It's too *kelt* for me."

"It won't be cold if you put on plenty of clothes." Doug ran ahead of his sisters, while Scott trailed behind.

Arlene could tell her boy wasn't feeling well, because normally Scott would have been excited about the snow.

As Larry helped her out of the buggy, he leaned close and said, "How about making some hot chocolate with marshmallows after the kinner go to bed? We can sit by the fire and enjoy each other's company for a while."

She smiled. "That sounds nice. I'll take care of making it as soon as the little ones are tucked in."

While Arlene and the children headed inside, Larry led the horse to the barn before he put their buggy away for the night.

After Arlene placed the baby in his crib, she sent Doug, Martha, and Lillian upstairs to wash and get ready for bed. Then she gave Scott a remedy for indigestion and took his temperature. He was running a slight fever, but she didn't think it was anything to worry about. By tomorrow morning he'd probably be his old self again, ready to romp and play in the snow.

∽

Akron

Joel entered his mobile home, slung his jacket over a chair, and glanced at the cell phone, noting it was nine o'clock—too late to head for Farmerstown. The school program had probably been over awhile already. He'd planned on going, but his day had been busy, and he'd worked longer than he expected. To make matters worse, it had started snowing about an hour ago, and the vehicles ahead of him had been crawling along. It didn't help that the snow was coming down heavier and sticking to everything. The temperature had dropped suddenly, and the roads could get slick.

Joel's thoughts went to Kristi. He hoped if she was coming home from work, or was on the road for any other reason, that she'd be careful out there. As Christmas drew near, he found himself missing her more than ever. *Sure wish she would have forgiven me and agreed to start over.*

He reached for the TV remote and found the local weather report to see what the forecast was for their area. Turning up the volume so he could hear it from the kitchen, he made himself a sandwich.

Maybe it's for the best I didn't go to the program, Joel thought when he returned to the living room with a ham and cheese sandwich. *With the tension between me and my sisters, I may have said or done the wrong thing.* Sometimes Joel felt as if his family looked for things they didn't like about him. If his sisters cared about his financial situation, they would have spoken up when John had read the will and admitted that Dad's demands were ridiculous. If they'd all stuck together on this, they could have opened their envelopes by now. But of course, they'd have to get Aunt Verna to agree to it as well. Joel had always liked and respected his aunt, but sometimes she could be downright stubborn, like his dad.

"She should have accepted my apology to Anna as a selfless act," he mumbled, leaning his head against the back of the couch. "Now I'm stuck trying to figure out what my next move should be."

When Joel had left his dad's place after his conversation with Aunt Verna, he'd decided to stop trying to come up with something everyone would see as heartfelt. But after he'd cooled down, and taken another look at his bank account, along with the few jobs he had lined up for the rest of the month, Joel realized he needed to keep trying to meet the stipulations of the will. There had to be something he could do that wouldn't be a big sacrifice for him but would still satisfy his sisters and Aunt Verna. He needed to figure out what it was.

❧

"I see you're working the evening shift again," Yvonne Patterson, one of the other nurses, said when she passed Kristi in the hall. "Are you filling in for Barbara?"

Kristi turned to face Yvonne. "Yes. Shortly before I was supposed to get off work, our supervisor let me know Barbara had called in sick. I volunteered to take her place."

"How come? I would think you'd be exhausted after working all day."

"I'll admit it's not easy working back-to-back shifts, but as the week's progressed, Audrey's gotten worse, and I wanted to be with her tonight." Kristi sighed. "She hardly recognizes me anymore, but I keep hoping she'll rally a bit."

Yvonne gave Kristi's arm a gentle pat. "You have a genuine heart for your patients, and everyone here speaks highly of you. I've heard some folks call you a saint."

Kristi felt the heat of a blush erupt on her

cheeks. "I'm definitely not that. I just try to treat everyone kindly and do what the Bible says."

"Your Christianity shows. You don't talk about it all over the place. You live it."

Kristi and Yvonne visited a few more minutes, then moved down the hall to check on patients. Unexpectedly, an image of Joel flashed across Kristi's mind. *I think I may have failed at being a Christian example to him,* she thought with regret. *If I'd been more Christlike, maybe he would have turned his life over to the Lord instead of putting himself first.*

I shouldn't be thinking about this right now, she told herself. *I can't undo the past, nor can I, or anyone else, make Joel become a Christian if he doesn't want to. He was raised in a Christian home and exposed to Bible teaching from the time he was a boy. Joel became selfish and self-centered of his own accord. All I can do is pray for him—pray that he will see the truth before it's too late.*

Pushing her thoughts aside, Kristi stepped into Audrey's room. The light beside her bed was still on, and Audrey's eyes were open. For a minute, Kristi thought the dear woman was staring at the ceiling, but taking a closer look, she realized Audrey wasn't moving.

Kristi's heart pounded as she checked for a pulse. Nothing. And no breath came from Audrey's slightly open mouth.

"You've gone home," Kristi murmured tearfully. "Your body is healed, and now you are in the presence of the Lord."

CHAPTER 10

I appreciate you having me over this evening."
Joel flopped into a chair in Tom's living room.
"Otherwise I'd have been alone on Christmas Eve."

Tom's dimples deepened as he took a seat on the
couch across from Joel. "You're welcome to stay the
night and spend Christmas Day here, too."

"Naw, that's okay. Your folks will be here tomorrow, and I wouldn't feel right about cutting in on
your family time."

"It's no big deal. I'm sure Mom and Dad
wouldn't be bothered if you joined us for dinner." Tom thumped his stomach. "Mom will be
cooking a juicy ham, baked potatoes, and a green
bean casserole. My contribution to the meal will be
the pumpkin and apple pies I bought at a local bakery the other day."

Tom's offer was tempting, but Joel declined. "My
aunt Verna called this morning and invited me to
join her at my sister Elsie's place for Christmas dinner. Things have been kind of tense between me and
my family since Dad's will was found, so I think I
ought to show up and try to be sociable. I'm taking
everyone gifts, so maybe they'll see it as a selfless act."

Tom's forehead wrinkled. "You think so?"

"Sure, why not?"

Before Tom could reply, his cell phone rang.
"I'd better take this call. It's my mom." He grabbed
the phone lying beside him and headed out to the
kitchen.

Joel leaned back in his chair, closed his eyes,

and tried to relax. Tom kept yakking like a magpie, carrying on a lengthy conversation with his mother, while Joel tried to ignore it. He'd told his buddy previously about the situation with his family and Dad's stipulation regarding the will. Now he wondered if he should have kept quiet. From the look on his friend's face before his phone rang, he didn't approve of Joel buying gifts for his family in the hope of getting the envelope Dad had left for him. It didn't matter what Tom thought. Joel had to try something to get his aunt's and sisters' approval.

❧

"I'm sorry our new youth pastor couldn't join us this evening," Kristi's mother said as the three of them sat at the dining room table, eating open-faced sandwiches and tomato soup. "I've tried on several occasions to schedule a time when he could come for a meal, but either he's been busy or you've had to work." She looked at Kristi with a hopeful expression. "But I'm not giving up. If I can't work something out before the end of the year, I'll try to set something up with Darin for the first or second week of January."

Kristi groaned inwardly. Mom meant well, but Kristi had no interest in developing a new relationship with anyone so soon after breaking up with Joel. While the pain from it was diminishing, at times like tonight, she missed what they'd once had. Then there was the sadness she felt over losing dear, sweet Audrey. A short memorial service would be held at the nursing home the day after Christmas. Since Audrey had no family members, only the staff and some of the patients would attend.

"Are you feeling okay, Kristi?" Dad asked, breaking into her thoughts. "You're not your usual talkative self this evening."

"I was thinking about the patient we lost at the nursing home last night. I'm going to miss my visits with her." Kristi took a bite of her sandwich. The slice of french bread was covered with lettuce, turkey lunchmeat, and Swiss cheese. Squiggles of mustard and mayonnaise traveled across the top. Normally she would have devoured the meal because it tasted so good, but tonight her appetite was diminished.

"Why don't you try to find another nursing job, Kristi?" Mom asked. "Something where you're not working with elderly patients."

"I enjoy my work there. I consider it a type of ministry." Kristi hoped her mother wouldn't go on and on about this. Sometimes Mom offered her opinions too freely, especially where Kristi was concerned.

"So what should we do after we're done eating?" Dad asked. "Should we open our gifts or play a game?"

"We can't open gifts, Paul." Mom nudged Dad's arm. "We've always waited till Christmas morning to do that. And since Kristi will be spending the night here, we can get up early if we want, eat the breakfast casserole I put together earlier today, and then open our Christmas presents to each other."

Leave it up to Mom to make sure we keep to our tradition. Kristi couldn't help smiling. Some things never changed.

"Okay, then," Dad conceded, "as soon as I'm done eating, I'll get out one of our favorite board games. We can play awhile and then have some hot chocolate and ginger cookies."

Mom swatted his hand playfully. "I'm surprised there are any left. You ate enough of those cookies when I baked them earlier this week."

He reached over and patted her cheek. "I never could resist snitching any of your baked goods. You're the queen of our kitchen."

Mom giggled. "So what does that make you?"

He puffed out his chest, grinning widely. "The king, of course. Whatever you bake, I eat. What a great arrangement."

Kristi loved to see the banter between her parents. They'd been sweethearts in high school and had gotten married soon after graduating from college. It warmed her heart that even after being married nearly thirty years Mom and Dad were still in love and enjoyed each other's company. Kristi hoped to have that kind of a relationship with a man someday.

◇

Farmerstown

"How is Scott feeling?" Aunt Verna asked soon after she, Uncle Lester, and Glen entered Arlene's house.

Arlene's brows raised. "How'd you know he wasn't feeling well? He didn't complain of a bauch-weh until we were on our way home from the schoolhouse last night."

"I'm the one who told her." Glen spoke up. "I heard about it from Uncle Larry when I came by here this morning to see if his driver could take me to work." He leaned against the doorframe. "My driver came down with the flu last night and couldn't pick me up."

"I see." Arlene took everyone's coats and hung

them up. "I'm glad you made it here today." She gave her uncle a hug.

He smiled, his hazel eyes twinkling. "I wouldn't have missed this special time with our family for all the money in the world."

Arlene invited them into the living room, where Elsie, John, Blaine, and Mary sat, along with Doris and Brian.

Arlene's aunt and uncle took a seat on either side of her. "What about Scott? Is he feeling better today?" Aunt Verna asked.

"Not much, but he doesn't seem to be any worse either. He's upstairs with Doug, Hope, Lillian, and Martha. I'll call them down as soon as supper is ready to be served."

"And how's this little fellow doing?" Aunt Verna moved over to where Elsie sat, holding Samuel.

"He's been content to have me hold him since we got here fifteen minutes ago." Elsie kissed the top of the baby's head. "I think he loves his aunt Elsie."

John began talking to Lester about how his trip went. Arlene liked to see the family all together. These were the special times that made life worth cherishing.

"While you all visit, I'm going to slip into the kitchen and check on the chicken soup simmering on the stove. Once it's thoroughly heated, we can set out the sandwiches Elsie brought and then call everyone to the table."

"Is there anything I can do to help?" Elsie asked.

"No, that's okay. You're helping by keeping my baby entertained."

Arlene went to the kitchen. When she lifted

the lid on the soup kettle, her mouth watered, and she inhaled deeply. Even when she was a girl, chicken noodle had been her favorite kind of soup. Her children liked it, too—especially Scott. Sometimes when she fixed it, he ate two or three bowls. *I'll bet the delicious aroma of this soup will bring his appetite back tonight.*

A short time later, everyone sat around the table. After their silent prayers, Arlene dished up the soup, and the sandwiches were passed around.

"I'm glad we kept our Christmas Eve meal simple," Elsie said. "Tomorrow at our place, we'll be eating a big meal, so I hope everyone comes hungry to help eat the large turkey John bought the other day."

"I'm looking forward to it." Brian smiled at Doris. "How about you?"

She nodded slowly. "I only wish I could do more to help with the meal."

"It'll be taken care of," Elsie said. "So don't even worry about it."

"Mama, can I be excused?" Scott set his spoon down. "I'm not hungerich."

"You need to eat your soup, Son," Larry said. "If you don't, there will be no cookies or candy for dessert."

"I don't care. My belly hurts, and I wanna go lie down."

Arlene looked at Larry, and when he nodded, she said, "Go on up, Scott. I'll check on you in a bit."

Holding his stomach, Scott got up. Walking slowly, he left the room.

"I'll bet that boy has the flu." Aunt Verna clicked her tongue and nudged her husband's arm.

"Sure hope the rest of us aren't exposed to it now."

Glen shrugged his shoulders. "If we are, there's nothing we can do about it. Let's try to enjoy the rest of our meal."

As they continued to eat, the conversation around the table went from talking about the Christmas program at the schoolhouse, to the snowy weather, which had stopped as suddenly as it started.

"Guess we won't get to make any more snowballs." Lillian's chin jutted out. "I only got to make a few this morning before my toes got too cold."

Doug bumped his sister's arm. "That's 'cause ya didn't wear heavy enough socks inside your boots."

Aunt Verna tilted her head in his direction. "Did you say something about a heavy box?"

Uncle Lester looked at her and raised his brows. The children all snickered, while Doug shook his head. "I said *heavy socks* not *box*."

"Will Uncle Joel be at your house on Christmas Day?" Martha asked, looking at Elsie.

"I don't know. Aunt Verna invited him to come, but he may have other plans."

"It would be nice if Joel made an effort to be here to celebrate with the family tomorrow," Uncle Lester said before taking a bite of his sandwich.

"I hope he comes, 'cause if he brings his harmonica, it might make Scott feel better." Martha paused for a drink of water. "He's been wantin' another lesson."

Arlene hoped for her nephew's sake that Joel would join them, too. With it being Christmas, maybe he would be in a good mood. She remembered how much her brother enjoyed Christmas when he was a boy. Of course, they all had, but Joel talked about it nonstop for several days before the big event. Arlene had always thought it was the gifts they received on Christmas morning that Joel liked most of all. He would jump up and down and clap his hands every time someone handed him a gift. Dad used to reprimand him, saying if he didn't calm down, he'd be the last one to get his presents.

After the meal and the dishes were done, the grownups sat at the table playing a new game John had brought along, while the children went back upstairs to play. The game was just getting interesting when Doug bounded down the stairs and raced up to his dad. "Scott's throwin' up, and his belly hurts so bad, he can't even walk."

Concerned, Arlene jumped up. "I think we ought to call one of our drivers and take Scott to the hospital. It may only be the flu, but I'd feel better if he got checked out."

"I agree with you." Larry pushed his chair aside, grabbed his jacket, and went out the door, while Arlene hurried upstairs to check on Scott. This was certainly not the way she'd planned their Christmas Eve gathering to end, but their son's health came first, and she felt sure the others would understand.

❧

Millersburg

"I wish we could have accompanied Larry, Arlene, and Scott to the hospital," Elsie told John as they and their family traveled home by horse and buggy. "I'm anxious to know what they find out and how he's doing."

"They said they would call as soon as they know

something." John touched her arm. "I'll go out to the phone shack and check for messages every couple of hours once we get home."

Elsie tried to relax, but she had a horrible feeling something might be seriously wrong with her nephew. It was an inner sense she sometimes got when things weren't as they should be. She hoped she was wrong this time, but she would feel much better once they heard something from Arlene.

"It was nice of your aunt and uncle to stay at Arlene's with the kinner," John said.

"Jah. I think Doris and Brian were going to stay awhile longer, too." She sighed deeply. "I believe Doris is doing a little better emotionally, but her old spark isn't back yet."

"It'll come. It's only been a month since she lost the boppli."

"True."

When they rounded the next bend, Elsie spotted flames shooting into the air. With trembling lips, she let out a gasp. "Ach, John! Our house—it's on fire!"

The
SELFLESS
Act

CHAPTER 1

Millersburg

Joel smiled, glancing at the box full of red and green wrapped packages on the passenger seat beside him. He'd bought these gifts for his sisters, their husbands, and Aunt Verna and Uncle Lester. More packages in the back of his truck waited for his nieces and nephews. He hoped his generosity in bringing Christmas presents would be well-received.

What could be more selfless than buying Christmas gifts for seventeen family members when I'm short on money? he thought. Thankfully, Joel had been able to borrow some money from his buddy Tom Hunter. But of course that meant one more obligation to pay. Joel still hadn't gotten all his subcontractors paid from jobs they'd done for him several months ago. He wondered if he'd ever be debt free.

"Should be doing more than fine if I ever get my share of Dad's will," he mumbled, turning in the direction of his sister Elsie's house, where he'd been invited for Christmas dinner. If Elsie, Arlene, Doris, and Aunt Verna thought the gifts he'd brought for everyone qualified as a selfless act, before the day was out, he might get to open the envelope Dad had left for him.

Guiding his truck onto the back country road leading to Elsie and John's place, Joel's hands began to sweat. *What if Aunt Verna thinks the gifts I bought are superficial and not a selfless act? She does have the final say. And until she's convinced I've committed a selfless act, I'm not getting any of Dad's money.*

When Joel had apologized to his ex-girlfriend Anna for hurting her during their breakup more than seven years ago, his aunt hadn't seen it as a heartfelt, much less selfless deed. Aunt Verna could be tough like Joel's dad—stubborn, too. When she made up her mind about something, there was no changing it. Joel needed to keep on her good side. If he said enough nice things to his aunt today and she liked the gifts he'd bought everyone, it might help his cause.

Pulling into Elsie's driveway, Joel slammed on the brakes and did a double-take. "Oh, no! What happened?"

Joel undid his seatbelt and hopped out of the truck. He almost pinched himself to see if he was in the middle of a nightmare. The smell of burned wood and ash made him cough. His sister's house was gone—burned to the ground.

Joel's heart hammered in his chest as he got back in his truck and turned it around. *I need to find Elsie—see if everyone's okay. Maybe they're at Arlene's. If not, then she may know why their house caught fire and where they're staying.*

⤜⤛

Farmerstown

After Joel pulled up to the barn by Arlene and Larry's house, he turned off the engine, hopped out, and raced up the porch steps. He'd only knocked once when the door opened and Doug stuck his head out.

"Where's your mother? I need to talk to her right away."

"She and my daed are at the hospital with Scott." Doug stared up at him with a curious expression.

Joel's mouth hung slightly open. "What's wrong with your brother?" He pushed his hands deep into his pockets.

Doug opened the door wider and stepped aside. "You look cold. You'd better come in, and we'll tell you about it."

The icy air cut through Joel's boots, so he stomped the snow off his feet and did as the boy suggested. Anxious to know why Scott and his parents were at the hospital, Joel also wanted to find out if anyone knew about the fire that had destroyed his eldest sister's house. It didn't take long for him to ask, because Elsie and John, along with Uncle Lester and Aunt Verna, were seated on the living room sofa. The children—Martha, Mary, Hope, and Lillian—sat on the floor near the fireplace, while Glen and Blaine occupied the two recliners. The somber expressions on what should have been a joyous Christmas afternoon revealed the depth of everyone's sorrow.

Joel stood in front of the couch, looking down at them. He opened his mouth, but at first, nothing came out. He wasn't sure what to say. "I. . . uh. . .just came from Millersburg and was stunned when I saw what little remains of your house. What happened, Elsie? Was anyone hurt?"

"No." John's shoulders slumped. "We were here last night, having supper with the rest of the family, and soon after Scott was taken to the hospital, we headed for home." He paused, rubbing his hand down one side of his bearded face. "When we got there and saw our house engulfed in flames, I ran to the phone shack and called for help."

"Unfortunately, by the time the fire trucks came, our house was gone." Elsie's chin trembled. "We have nothing left, Joel. Only the clothes on our backs." She dabbed at her tear-filled eyes with a tissue.

"And the barn," John added. "Fortunately, it's far enough from the house so it didn't catch fire from any sparks."

"Of course, we can't live in the barn." Elsie's voice sounded strained, and she sniffed, rubbing her nose with the tissue. "We don't know how long it'll be before we can afford to rebuild."

"You'd best wait till spring, when the weather is warmer," Uncle Lester interjected. "By then, maybe a benefit auction can take place to help with your expenses."

Aunt Verna nodded and clasped Elsie's hand. "We're thankful none of you were inside when the fire started. Material possessions can be replaced, but lives cannot."

Material possessions can't be replaced if you don't have money to replace them, Joel was tempted to retort. Knowing his sister and aunt wouldn't appreciate his thoughts, he kept them to himself. "I'm sorry for your loss." He shifted his weight from one foot to the other. "Do you know how the fire got started?"

John shook his head. "Elsie's sure she didn't leave the stove on, and we didn't have a fire in the fireplace. I thought all the gas lamps were out before we left to come here to celebrate Christmas Eve, but I may have carelessly forgotten to turn one off."

Joel rubbed the heel of his palm against his

chest as he tried to calm his nerves. His sister and brother-in-law's situation was tragic, but there was nothing he could do to help them out. Given his own financial issues, he didn't have any extra cash to give.

He sank into the rocking chair across from them, and Doug knelt on the floor beside him. "Do ya wanna hear about Scott now?" the boy asked, looking up at Joel.

"Yes, I do." Joel focused his attention on Doug.

"He complained of a bellyache last night and started throwin' up. So Dad called a driver, and they took him to the hospital."

"It sounds like the flu to me. Why would they take him to the hospital for that?"

"It wasn't the flu." Elsie's lips compressed. "Scott was in so much pain he couldn't even walk. When they got to the hospital, they found out his appendix had ruptured."

"Wow! Is he gonna be okay?" Joel rubbed the bridge of his nose.

"I spoke with Arlene on the phone after Scott came out of surgery. He seemed to be doing all right, but the doctor is worried about infection from the poison that was spread when it ruptured." Elsie sighed. "If I could be at the hospital right now, I'd know more. Sitting here, thinking about the fire and worrying about Scott is taking its toll on me." She paused to wipe the tears on her cheeks with another tissue. "This has not been a good Christmas for the kinner or us adults."

"Where's Doris? Does she know about all this?" Joel asked.

"I called and left a message on their answering

machine this morning," John replied. "I'm sure once they hear the news they'll come over right away. I left a message for you, too, Joel, but your mailbox was full."

"Yeah, sorry about that. I need to delete some messages." Joel stood up and tightened his fists. "I want to find out how Scott's doing." He looked at Elsie. "Do you know what hospital they took him to?"

"Union, in Dover." Elsie stood, too. "Would you mind if I go with you? I'm sure Arlene could use some support."

"That's fine. I have a box of Christmas presents for everyone out in the truck. I'll bring them inside, and as soon as you're ready to go, we can be on our way."

❦

Berlin

Using one crutch under her arm for support, Doris stood at the stove, scrambling eggs. She'd been able to do a few more things on her own lately and wanted to have breakfast ready for Brian when he came in from doing chores.

She finished the eggs and was about to put them in the oven to keep warm, when Brian entered the kitchen. His grim expression let Doris know something was amiss. "What's wrong? You look umgerennt."

"I am upset, and you will be too when you hear this news." He removed his knitted cap and hung it on a wall peg, then took a seat at the table, motioning for Doris to do the same.

"What is it, Brian? You're scaring me." She

hobbled across the room and lowered herself into the chair across from him.

"I stopped at the phone shack to check for messages and found one from John." Deep wrinkles formed across Brian's forehead. "Their house caught fire last night. They lost everything."

Doris's spine stiffened. She clutched the edge of the table. "Ach, that's baremlich! Was anyone hurt?"

"No, but there's nothing left of the house. John said they spent last night at Arlene and Larry's. I'm guessing that's where they still are."

"We ought to be with them. They need our support right now." Doris grabbed her crutch and started to stand.

"Let's eat breakfast first."

"I. . .I don't think I can." She felt as if a lump was stuck in her throat. "I feel sick about this."

"Same here." Brian drew in a deep breath. "There's more, Doris."

"Wh–what do you mean?"

"When Larry and Arlene took Scott to the hospital last night, they found out his appendix had ruptured."

"Oh, no!" She covered her mouth and fell back in her chair, dropping her crutch to the floor. *Lord, why are so many terrible things happening to our family?* she prayed. *How much more can we take?*

❦

Dover

Elsie stood in the hospital waiting room, sobbing as she hugged her sister. "What a horrible Christmas this has turned out to be for all of us."

Arlene's tears wet Elsie's dress as she gently

patted her back. "I'm so sorry to hear of your loss. I can't imagine how it must feel to have lost your home and everything in it."

"It's a small thing compared to the loss of a loved one. I hope and pray Scott's going to be okay."

"Same here." Joel stepped up to them. "The little guy doesn't deserve this."

"Loss and illness are hard," Larry said. "But with God's help and with support from each other, we'll all get through this."

"I brought him a gift, but it's at your house. Guess I can give it to him when he gets home." Joel glanced down the hall. "I don't suppose he's up to company yet."

Larry shook his head. "He's sleeping and needs his rest. Let's sit down and visit while we're waiting for him to wake up."

Arlene drew in her bottom lip. "I'll sit a few minutes, but then I'm going back to his room. I want to be there when he wakes up."

Elsie and Arlene sat beside each other while the men pulled up chairs facing them.

"You're welcome to stay at our house for as long as you like." Arlene lightly stroked Elsie's forearm as she spoke in a quiet tone. "But it might work better for your family if you moved into Dad's old place until you're able to rebuild. There's more room there, and you can all spread out."

"True, but Aunt Verna and Uncle Lester are staying there now, as well as Glen." Elsie massaged the back of her neck, contemplating things. "Once they return to their home in Burton, John and I can take the downstairs bedroom, which would free one of the upstairs rooms so Blaine and Glen wouldn't have to share." It was difficult to look at the positives right now, but bemoaning their situation wouldn't change a thing. They would have to make the best of their situation and be grateful they had a warm place to stay.

Joel glanced at his cell phone and scratched his jaw. "The Weather Channel has issued a warning for a snowstorm that will hit the area within the next hour." He turned to Elsie. "I think we should go now, before the roads get real bad, or we could end up stuck here overnight."

"You two go ahead. I'm not going anywhere until I'm sure Scott's out of danger," Arlene was quick to say. "Larry and I spent last night here, and we'll stay as long as needed."

"That's right," her husband agreed.

Arlene offered Elsie a tired-looking smile as she leaned her back against the chair. "Danki for bringing Larry and me a change of clothes."

"You're welcome. I feel bad you'll have to spend another night trying to sleep in a chair, when you ought to be home in your own bed."

"We'll be okay." Larry stood. "I'm going to the vending machine to get some coffee. Would anyone else like some?" He looked at Joel. "Maybe you'd like a cup for the road."

"No, that's okay. Vending machine coffee's not for me. I like mine fresh."

Elsie made no comment as she slipped on her outer garments. She wished she could stay at the hospital with Arlene, but John and the children were waiting for her. After the trauma they'd all been through on Christmas Eve, her place was with them.

CHAPTER 2

Charm

"*Hallich Neiyaahr*, Mama!" Hope stepped up to Elsie and gave her a hug.

"Happy New Year to you, too." Returning the hug, and forcing a smile, Elsie patted her youngest daughter's head. It was good for the children to be optimistic, but Elsie felt as though her world had been turned upside down. These were the times when being a parent and trying to hold things together could be daunting. She was thankful to be staying in Dad's old house but missed her own place, where she and John started their life together nearly twenty-two years ago. So many memories had been made there—all gone up in smoke. At least none of the animals had been affected by the fire. They'd been brought over to Dad's place, but with his horses taking up most of the stalls in the barn, they had to do a bit of shifting to make room.

"Are we gonna do anything special today?" Hope looked up at Elsie with expectancy.

"I don't think so." Elsie yawned and sat down in her dad's recliner. "I'm feeling kind of *mied* this morning."

"I know why you're tired," John said when he entered the living room. "You got up at the crack of dawn." He took a seat in the chair beside her as Hope scampered out of the room.

Elsie yawned a second time, stretching her arms over her head. "I'm used to our queen-size mattress and couldn't sleep any longer in that small bed."

"Lester and I can move upstairs and let you have your daed's old room." Aunt Verna spoke up from across the room, where she sat in the rocking chair near the fireplace.

Elsie shook her head. "It's better for you and Uncle Lester to sleep downstairs. With his arthritis, climbing the steps would be too hard."

"Well, it's only for a few more days." Aunt Verna smiled. "I read in the paper that there's no snow in the forecast for several days, and I called one of our drivers. He's coming to get us Monday afternoon, so we'll soon be out of your hair."

"You don't have to be in a hurry to leave." John spoke loudly, no doubt compensating for Aunt Verna's hearing loss. "We've enjoyed being with you over the holidays and appreciate all you've done to help out."

"We were glad to be here, but it's time to head home." Aunt Verna glanced toward the kitchen, where her husband had gone to refill his coffee cup a few minutes ago. "Lester is eager to get back to the comforts of our own home." Her voice lowered. "He's not used to so much activity. I think the kinner get on his *naerfe* sometimes."

Elsie didn't respond because she didn't want to hurt her aunt's feelings, but living under the same roof with Aunt Verna and Uncle Lester this past week had gotten on her nerves a few times, too. In addition to practically yelling so her aunt could hear, Elsie had kept busy following behind Aunt Verna to close the refrigerator and cupboard doors. Her aunt was easily sidetracked, and a few times when she'd been cooking something on the stove, she'd wandered off to do something else and nearly burned whatever had been in the pot. Then there was the matter of Uncle Lester trying to do things he shouldn't and having to listen to Aunt Verna get after him.

"It's good to know Scott's home from the hospital now and is doing quite well," Elsie said, deciding they needed a change of subject.

Aunt Verna cupped one hand around her ear. "Did you say something about Scott and a bell?"

Elsie cleared her throat as she resisted the urge to roll her eyes. "No, I said, 'It's good to know Scott's home from the hospital now and is doing quite well.'"

"Jah. That boy gave us all quite a scare."

Uncle Lester entered the living room empty-handed. "Where's the coffee you went after?" John asked.

"I sat at the kitchen table and drank it," he replied. "Wanted to read *The Budget* and see if any of the scribes from our home area had written anything interesting."

John quirked an eyebrow. "Did they?"

"Nope. At least nothin' I thought was interesting." Uncle Lester took a seat on the couch beside John. "It was mostly about the weather and who the visiting ministers were at their last church service."

The topic of church made Elsie realize that, as long as they lived in Dad's house, they'd go to every-other-week services in his district, rather than their own, since it was much closer. Once the weather improved, they would visit their own church district whenever possible.

"What did you say, Lester?" Aunt Verna called from across the room.

He flapped his hand. "Nothing, Verna. It's not worth mentioning."

"You must have thought whatever you said was worth mentioning, or you wouldn't have said it. I wish you'd speak a little louder and slower when you talk. Sometimes I can't keep up, because you talk too fast."

Uncle Lester glanced at Elsie and lifted his shoulders in a brief shrug. Then, speaking slow and loud, he repeated what he'd first said.

The knitting needles Aunt Verna held clicked noisily. "I always find it interesting to read about what other people are doing. Every little detail is fascinating to me."

"You would say that. Maybe you ought to see about becoming one of the scribes. Then you could write whatever you want."

Aunt Verna looked at Lester and wrinkled her nose. "I'm not a writer; I'm a reader."

Just then, Mary burst into the room. "Hope tripped and fell over something. Now she has a bloody nose."

Elsie groaned.

"It's okay. Stay where you are." John rose to his feet. "I'll take care of it."

Elsie leaned her head back and closed her eyes. She hoped things would go better in the coming year.

∽

Akron

"Happy New Year! It's so nice you could join us for dinner today," Kristi's mother said when their new youth pastor, Darin Underwood, entered the house.

He smiled and handed her a bottle of sparkling cider. "After last night's New Year's Eve party with the teens at church, it's nice to be someplace where it's a little quieter."

Mom motioned toward Kristi. "You remember my daughter, don't you?"

Darin nodded before stuffing his gray gloves into his coat pockets. "It's nice to see you again, Kristi."

"It's good to see you, too." Kristi blinked a few times and smiled. "Can I take your jacket?"

"Sure. Just give me a sec." He removed his jacket and gave it to Kristi.

After hanging it in the hall closet, she led the way to the living room, where Dad sat reading the newspaper.

"Glad you could make it." Dad rose from his seat and shook Darin's hand. "JoAnn and Kristi made pork and sauerkraut for dinner. Sure hope you like it."

"It's a recipe I got from an Amish cookbook I bought before Christmas," Kristi said.

Darin sniffed the air. "So that must be what I smell. It's hard to hide the tangy odor of sauerkraut."

"I hope you're not opposed to eating it." Dad gestured to the kitchen. "My wife should have asked ahead of time if your taste buds lean toward sauerkraut."

"I'm fine with it. Whenever I get a hot dog and sauerkraut's available, I always put some on." He wiggled his brows. "Think I could eat a good hot dog every day."

Kristi cringed. She preferred having variety in her diet. The idea of eating the same meal every day made her nauseous. If their new youth leader wasn't joking about being able to eat a hot dog every day, then his eating habits apparently didn't lean toward the healthy side of things. After Dad told Darin to take a seat, she excused herself to help Mom.

"Come here, Kristi," Mom whispered when she entered the kitchen. "Darin's cute, isn't he? Did you see how his blue eyes lit up when he first came in and saw you?"

Kristi lifted her chin toward the ceiling, gazing at a small strand of cobweb hanging over them that Mom must have missed the last time she cleaned. "He's probably glad to have been invited for a free meal. A healthier one than he normally eats, I might add." She lowered her voice. "I have a feeling Darin lives on junk food."

"What are you basing that on?"

"He told Dad he likes hot dogs and could eat one every day."

"I'm sure he was only kidding." Mom tapped Kristi's shoulder. "You really should get to know the man before you judge his eating habits."

Wanting to change the topic, Kristi gestured to the stove. "Should I start dishing things up so we can eat?"

"That would be good. While you're doing that, I'll light the candles on the dining room table." She smiled at Kristi. "Candlelight adds a little romance to any meal."

After her mother left the room, Kristi released a sigh. She hoped Mom hadn't set this dinner up in an effort to play matchmaker. From the few times Kristi had spoken with Darin, he seemed nice enough. But she wasn't sure about beginning a new relationship with any man. Besides, she didn't know if Darin was even interested in her.

As they sat around the table a short time later, eating pork roast, sauerkraut, mashed potatoes, green beans, and fruit salad, Kristi found herself comparing Darin to Joel. It wasn't a fair thing to do, since her relationship with Joel was over, but she couldn't seem to help it. Darin's hair was blond, and his eyes were deep blue. Joel's brown eyes matched his dark wavy hair. But it wasn't their appearances she reflected on. It was the difference in their personalities. Darin was a jokester and had already told more corny jokes since they'd sat down to eat than Kristi had heard in the last year from other sources. While being "Mr. Funnyman" may go over well with the youth at their church, Kristi found it a bit annoying. Joel had a sense of humor, too, but he'd never spouted off one joke after another and then laughed at his own wisecracks the way Darin had been doing today. Mom certainly thought he was funny. She'd chuckled after and even during every one of his jokes. Was she only being polite, or did she really think he was that funny?

Kristi glanced over at Dad. He seemed engrossed in eating and had left most of the chatting up to Mom and Darin during the meal. Kristi, too, had been rather quiet; but then, it was hard to get in a word with Darin monopolizing much of the conversation.

When they finished eating, Kristi excused herself to clear the table. Mom joined her in the kitchen a few minutes later. "Darin is sure humorous, isn't he?" Mom snickered. "The joke he told about the farmer who lost his chicken was so funny. I'm glad we invited him today. We all needed a good laugh."

Kristi silently opened the dishwasher and put the glasses inside.

Mom began rinsing the plates before handing them to Kristi. "I think Darin likes you, dear. Didn't you see the way he kept smiling in your direction?"

She shrugged.

"How do you feel about him?" Mom passed Kristi the bowl she'd rinsed.

"I don't know Darin well enough yet to say for sure, but so far I'm not feeling any chemistry between us."

"Give it some time. Once you get to know each other better, your feelings could change." Mom bumped Kristi's arm. "I wasn't immediately attracted to your father, either, but after we dated awhile, he sort of grew on me."

Kristi tapped her foot impatiently. "Darin and I are not dating, Mom."

"But you could be. Would you go out with him if he asked?"

"I don't know—maybe."

Mom's lips lifted at the corners as she rinsed some of the silverware. "I bet he will ask you soon."

"We'll see." Kristi continued loading the dishwasher. If Darin told more jokes while they ate dessert, she might look for an excuse to go home early.

⁂

Joel stared out the living room window at the snow still on the ground. Even though most of the roads had been cleared, he'd only been driving his work truck to get around. As much as he wanted to take the Corvette out for a spin, he wouldn't chance crashing it during the snowy season. Besides, if he took the car out on the roads, it would probably be filthy by the time he came home. Slush and mud seemed to be everywhere now that some of the snow had melted.

He looked up at the gray sky and wondered when the next snowstorm would arrive. From what he'd heard on a recent weather forecast, the next few days would be rain and clouds, but another snow-storm might follow.

Bored, Joel flopped onto the couch and turned on the TV. One of the channels was airing a show based on a romance novel. The male and female leads sat on a couch, kissing. The young woman had auburn hair, which reminded him of Kristi.

I wonder what she did to ring in the New Year. Has she found someone new and started dating again? He thought about last year and how much fun he'd had with Kristi as they celebrated the New Year. They'd talked about their hopes and dreams for the future and discussed wedding plans, even though they hadn't set a date.

Joel picked up his cell phone and scrolled down to her number, fighting the urge to call. *If I did, she'd probably ignore it, and I'd end up talking to her voice mail, like all the other times I've called since she broke up with me.* It didn't take a genius to know Kristi had made a clean break. However, a place in Joel's heart hoped she would change her mind and give him another chance. *Once I've done a selfless act that's acceptable to my sisters and Aunt Verna, maybe Kristi will see me in a different light.*

He closed his eyes, picturing her pretty face. *If I could only see her again, even from a distance, it might give me a ray of hope.*

Forcing his contemplations to go in a different direction, Joel thought about the Christmas presents he'd bought for his sisters and their families. He had left them with Aunt Verna before he and Elsie had gone to the hospital to see about Scott but never heard a word about whether anyone liked what he'd gotten them. *So much for my sisters and aunt seeing the gifts as a selfless act. I'm gonna have to come up with something better than that. My bank account's shrinking, and I need money soon.*

CHAPTER 3

Charm

"The house seems quiet, doesn't it?" John asked as he and Elsie sat on the living room sofa, eating popcorn and drinking hot cider Monday evening. The fire popped and danced behind the grate, giving off warm, welcoming heat and cozy light.

"Jah. During the holidays there's so much preparation and getting together with family and friends. Now we get to settle back and reflect on the moments, since most everything has calmed down." She took a sip from her mug. The cider was nice and tangy. For the first time since their house had caught fire, she felt herself relax a bit. It was good to sit with her husband and visit. The children were upstairs in bed—even Blaine and Glen, who both had to get up early for work tomorrow morning. Aunt Verna and Uncle Lester returned to their own home early this afternoon, so Elsie had moved her and John's things to the downstairs master bedroom. Their sons said earlier it would be nice they didn't have to share a room anymore. It wasn't that the young men didn't get along; they both needed their own space.

Elsie remembered when she and Arlene once shared a bedroom in this house. It had been all right when they were young girls, but after they'd become teenagers, a few conflicts arose, despite their closeness. When John built the house he and Elsie lived in after they were married, he'd made sure there were plenty of bedrooms. It had been nice for each of their children to have their own room. Here, with only three bedrooms upstairs, Hope and Mary had to share a room. So far they didn't seem to mind, but if they lived here much longer, the girls might start fussing with each other, the way Elsie and Arlene used to do.

"You're awfully quiet." John touched Elsie's arm. "Are you feeling mied tonight, or is something wrong?"

"I'm reflecting on the past, and wondering how long our girls will get along if they have to keep sharing a bedroom."

"We'll rebuild as soon as we can." He refilled his bowl with more popcorn from the larger bowl on the coffee table. "If we had your inheritance, we could begin as soon as the weather improves."

Elsie looked down at her hands. "There's nothing I can do about it, John."

"Maybe your aunt would concede and let you open your envelopes now. We could all use the money—even Joel."

Blinking rapidly, she turned to face him. "Do you think Dad would have put such a perplexing provision in his will if he didn't have a good reason for it?"

"I. . .I don't know, Elsie. Your daed wasn't like most people I know. He had some unusual habits and saw and did things a bit differently than most. I doubt he thought of the impact it will have on you, Arlene, and Doris if Joel doesn't come through."

"You're right, but Dad cared about his family and wanted the best for each of us. He must have believed Joel would eventually meet the requirements set forth in the will."

"I'm not sure he ever will." John laced his fingers together. "If your daed wanted the best for his daughters, then he would have allowed you to open your envelopes and acquire whatever he had in mind for you. By making you wait till Joel does an act of kindness..."

"A heartfelt, selfless act," she corrected.

"Jah, okay. Anyway, by making you wait till then, it's as though you, Arlene, and Doris are being punished for your bruder's selfishness." He crossed his arms. "If you want my opinion, only Joel should have to wait to open his envelope until he does the proper deed."

Elsie didn't admit it to John, but she'd thought the same thing numerous times since they'd discovered Dad's will in his freezer. Even so, it wouldn't be right to go against the stipulation he'd set forth so she could have her share of whatever Dad had left for her. She leaned her head on her husband's shoulder and closed her eyes. "It'll work out in God's time. We just need to be patient."

Farmerstown

Arlene pulled the pins from her bun and began brushing her long, silky hair. She glanced at the mirror hanging on the bedroom wall and noticed the dark circles under her eyes. After all the lost sleep she'd had during Scott's ordeal, she still didn't feel caught up on her rest, so she'd decided to go to bed earlier than usual tonight. An inspirational novel lay on her nightstand that she'd started to read but put on hold. It would be nice to do some leisure reading before drifting off to sleep this evening.

The children were already in bed, and Larry had gone out to the barn a short time ago to check on one of their cats that had been in a fight the other day and ended up with an abscess on its head. Her husband had always given their animals good care. Not like the person Arlene had read about in the paper the other day, who'd lost two of his horses because he'd neglected them.

Such a shame, she thought, remembering how well her dad had taken care of the horses he'd raised. *Dad may have been a bit eccentric, but he never neglected his animals or children.*

She moved over to stand by the window. It was a clear, starry night, with no snow in sight. Arlene sighed, twisting her fingers around the ends of her hair. The old year had ended on a frightening note, but a new year was beginning, and she hoped things would improve.

Thankfully, Scott was feeling better; although he wouldn't be allowed to return to school for at least another week. Arlene wasn't taking any chances with her son's life. Too many germs could be passed around at school, and Scott's immune system wasn't as strong as it should be yet.

In addition to her concern for his health, Arlene worried about the hospital bills that would soon be coming in. With only Larry working to provide for their needs, she wondered if she ought to seek employment. *Maybe I could get a job waitressing at one of the restaurants in Charm,* she thought. *I probably wouldn't make a lot, but at least it would be something to help out.*

"Didn't you say you were going to bed?" Larry asked, entering the room.

She turned from the window to face him. "I am."

"Then how come you're standing in front of the *fenschder?*"

"I was thinking."

He smiled, moving to stand beside her. "I hope they were good thoughts."

"Some were. Some not so good."

"Is it something we should talk about?"

Arlene nodded and lowered herself to the end of the bed. When Larry joined her there, she instinctively clasped his hand. "I'm grateful Scott's okay, but I'm worried about our finances."

"We've had money issues before and come through it." He pointed to the Bible lying on the table next to his side of the bed. "God has always provided for us."

"Jah, but maybe He expects us to do something, too."

"Like what?"

She released his hand, rocking back and forth with her arms folded. "What would you think of me getting a job? Maybe I could work at one of the nearby restaurants."

Shaking his head briskly, Larry pressed his thumb to his chest. "No way! I'm the bread winner in this family. Your place is here, taking care of the *kinner* as well as the house."

"But they're all in school most of the day. And if they came home after school let out and I wasn't home from work yet, I'm sure they could fend for themselves a short time."

"No." He rose from the bed and looked directly into her eyes. "It's better for them and you if you're not working outside the house." As if the matter were settled, Larry opened the closet door and took out his pajamas. Then he came to where she still sat, bent down, and kissed her forehead. "Try not to worry. Somehow, some way, the money to pay the hospital bills will be there when we need it."

Arlene wished she could be that certain. If she could open the envelope Dad had left her, their financial problems would most likely be solved.

⁂

Akron

Exhausted from a hard day at work on a job that wouldn't pay much, Joel crashed on the couch as soon as he'd eaten supper. He tried watching TV for a bit, but his eyes grew heavy, and soon he dozed off.

Sometime later, he was roused from a deep sleep by the rumble of a car. Feeling as though he was in a stupor, he rolled off the couch and stood. "Now who in the world could that be?"

Joel stumbled over to the window, pulled the curtain aside, and peered out. One of his outside lights was burned out, making it hard to tell what the vehicle looked like. Joel thought it might be a truck, but he couldn't be sure. He figured if it was someone he knew, they would turn off the ignition and come up to the house. Instead, the driver of the rig sat in the driveway a few minutes, then drove up to the garage, backed up, and headed for Joel's shop.

Oh, no! Warning bells went off in Joel's head. He quickly grabbed the brightest flashlight he owned and jerked the door open. Stepping onto the porch, Joel saw his own breath as he shined the light on the vehicle. Sure enough, it was a truck, but he didn't recognize it.

Who is that? He moved over to the steps to get

a better look. Suddenly, the door on the driver's side of the vehicle opened. A tall man with a scruffy beard stepped out.

"What do you want?" Joel called, holding the flashlight so he could see what the man was doing.

The bearded fellow didn't look in Joel's direction as he reached into the back of his truck, took out a cardboard box, and started walking unsteadily toward the shop. He was clearly drunk or maybe high on something.

"Stop where you are!" Joel hollered. "Get back in your truck or I'm calling the sheriff!"

The man hesitated, then started moving again in a zigzag pattern.

Joel's heart pounded as he squeezed tighter on the flashlight. His fingers were numb from the cold, but his body felt like it was overheating. *If I had a gun, I'd fire it over that guy's head. Maybe he'd be scared enough to hightail it outa here.* Joel shouted at the fellow once more, this time with a little more force. *I sure hope he doesn't have a gun. If he does, I could be in trouble.*

Even though Joel was concerned for his own welfare, he was more worried about his prized Corvette in the shop. "This is your last warning," he yelled at the top of his lungs. "The sheriff lives nearby. It won't take him long to get here."

The bearded man stopped walking and turned to face Joel. Then he wobbled back to his truck, placed the box he held inside, and got in. He sat behind the wheel several seconds, then turned the vehicle around, drove up the driveway, and headed out onto the main road.

Joel stood watching to be sure the man wasn't

coming back, then he ducked back inside and grabbed his cell phone. "As if I don't have enough to worry about," he muttered, before dialing 911. Joel gave the best description he could of the man and his vehicle. The lady on the phone, who worked for dispatch, told Joel she'd send a patrol car out to his address and they'd search the area to see if they could spot the trespasser's truck. If the vehicle returned, Joel was to call back right away.

He clicked off the phone and slid it into his pocket. When he brought his hands up to his face, he noticed they were shaking. Having an uninvited visitor on his property had unnerved him. *If I had a watchdog, it might have dissuaded the intruder—not to mention, given me a warning that someone was there.*

After pondering the idea further, Joel decided he would go to the local animal shelter in the morning to see about getting a dog. He also needed to fix the outside light that had burned out.

"Maybe I should get an alarm system, too—at least for the shop," he mumbled. With a car that expensive on his property, Joel couldn't afford to take any chances. He should have taken care of this when he'd first bought the Vette.

Joel peered out the living room window to be sure the strange man hadn't come back. He felt some relief knowing the sheriff would drive by his place and check around the area. There was no way he could get much sleep tonight. In fact, he probably wouldn't sleep well until he'd made sure his property was well protected.

CHAPTER 4

The next day before going to work, Joel replaced the yard light that had been out, then drove to the animal shelter to look for a dog. Before he left, the sheriff's office called to let him know the guy who'd come on his property had tried the same thing at a house a mile down the road. He'd been caught and taken to jail, so that was a relief. Even so, Joel needed to make sure his property was protected from intruders. He wanted a dog big enough to be intimidating but not so large it would cost Joel a lot of money to feed. A good strong bark was also a must.

He wandered up and down the aisles, peering into each of the dogs' cages. There weren't many to choose from. Joel figured they were probably picked over because people came here looking for dogs to give as Christmas gifts. One dog in particular caught Joel's attention—not for himself, because the critter was too small. The brown-and-white terrier mix reminded him of the one Doris had as a child. She'd named it Bristleface and taught the yappy critter all kinds of tricks. Joel would never forget how hard his sister cried when Bristleface ran into the road and got hit by a car. The dog had been killed on impact. After that, Doris had never asked for another dog.

"She might like one now though," Joel said aloud. It wouldn't replace the baby she'd lost, but it would be good company. Since the dog looked so much like the one she'd had before, Doris might be happy to have it. *It could even be the selfless act I'm supposed to do.* He smiled to himself. *Once Doris sees the mutt, I bet she'll put in a good word for me with Aunt Verna.*

He crouched down and stuck his fingers through the cage, letting the dog lick them. "What do you say, Bristleface Two? Would ya like a new home?"

Yip! Yip! The dog's tail wagged as it wiggled around. It was the answer Joel needed. Setting aside his idea of getting a watchdog for himself, Joel hurried to the front of the shelter to let the person in charge know he'd found the right dog for his sister. Maybe an alarm system for his shop and better lighting would be all he would need at this time.

❦

Joel climbed into his truck with the dog and scratched the side of his head. *Now what?* His original intent was to find a dog for himself, take it to his place, then head to the job he'd started yesterday. Now he had the yappy terrier to deal with, and he didn't have time to go all the way to Doris's house this morning. He could take the critter to his place and lock it in the house while he was at work, but the dog might not be housebroken, so that wasn't a good choice.

"Guess I'll have to be late for work whether I like it or not," he muttered, moving the dog off his lap and onto the passenger's seat. Sometimes Joel didn't think things through well enough; this was one of those times. *I should have waited till I finished working for the day to visit the animal shelter. Sure hope Doris is home when I get there, or I'll really be in a fix.*

He picked up his cell phone and called the owner of the house where he had been working, to let them know he'd be a few hours late. When that was done, he started up the truck and headed for the freeway, going south. The first few miles, the dog rode calmly, until it started throwing up.

"Are you kidding me?" Joel looked over at the poor mutt, while he brought his vehicle to a stop on the shoulder of the road. Then he grabbed a rag from under his seat to wipe up the stinky stuff. He opened his window, hoping to get rid of the putrid odor, but the icy-cold air blowing in wasn't pleasant. The trip to Doris's would be miserable.

$\sim$

Berlin

Because Brian was working, Doris had hired a driver to take her to an afternoon appointment to get her leg x-rayed. If it had healed as well as the doctor hoped, she'd get the cast off next week. After the appointment, she planned to meet her friend Anna for an early supper.

Doris was able to get around better now, with the aid of one crutch or a cane, so her sisters didn't come over as often as they had before to help out. When Elsie and her family moved into Dad's house, Doris had been worried Aunt Verna and Uncle Lester might come back here to her place to stay. She loved her aunt and uncle, but she was glad when they'd returned to their home in Burton. A few days of shouting in order to be heard by Aunt Verna was tolerable, but any longer became unbearable. Usually the shouting wouldn't bother her so much, but Doris was sensitive about everything these days. She was still trying to come to grips with having lost her baby, and seeing her sisters go through trials of their own on Christmas Eve had only worsened her depression.

What I need is to go back to work at the restaurant, where I'll be busy and around people, she thought. After her cast came off, she'd be faced with physical therapy, so it could be several weeks or even months before she was able to be on her feet long enough to complete a shift at Der Dutchman.

Hearing a car come up the driveway, Doris went to the living room window and looked out. At first, she thought her driver had mixed up the time and arrived early. She did a double-take when she saw Joel's truck pull up in front of the house and jerked her head when he got out of his vehicle with a scruffy-looking dog in his arms.

What is Joel doing here, and why does he have that hund with him? Doris hobbled to the door and opened it.

"Hey, look what I've got for you!" He was all smiles as he held the dog close to Doris's face.

She leaned her head back when it tried to lick her nose. "You bought this dog for me?" Doris couldn't imagine what would possess her brother to do such a thing. She'd never mentioned wanting a dog—to Joel or anyone else, for that matter.

Still grinning, he nodded. "I got it at the animal shelter in Akron this morning. It looks so much like the dog you had when we were kids, I couldn't resist buying it for you." Joel stroked the terrier's pointy little ears. "Thought maybe you could call it Bristleface Two."

Doris leaned against the doorframe for support

and warmth. "It was nice of you to think of me, Joel, but I can't take care of a dog."

"Oh, you mean because of your leg?" He gestured to her cast.

"It's not that. I'll be going back to work as soon as I'm able, and no one will be here to keep an eye on the dog." She sucked in her bottom lip. "Besides, I lost my desire to have a hund after Bristleface died."

Joel pressed one hand to his temple. "So you won't take the mutt?"

"No, sorry, I can't." She stepped back into the house.

"So what am I supposed to do with him?"

Doris shrugged. "You could keep him or see if someone else in the family would like a dog."

He moved his hand to the back of his neck. "I don't have time to run all over the place, trying to find a home for the critter. I have a job to do and need to head there now."

"Well, you can't leave him here. My driver will be coming this afternoon to take me to an appointment, and I'm meeting Anna for supper after that."

Joel glanced at the dog and frowned. "It's out of the way, but maybe I'll stop by Arlene's place and see if one of her kids would like the mutt."

"That's a good idea." Her body lacked tension and stress as she patted the dog's head. Doris had felt this way when she owned her own little terrier when she was a girl. The dog made her forget all the problems she'd had at school or with her siblings—at least for a little while. This dog might do the same, but she didn't want the extra responsibility.

Wait a minute, she thought. *I know who Joel should give the hund to.* "You know, Scott's still out of school, recuperating from his surgery. I'll bet he'd like a dog to play with."

"You could be right, Sis. Don't know why I didn't think of it." Joel turned to go. "Have a nice day. Oh, and tell Anna I said hello."

Doris stood in the doorway, watching him get in his truck and drive away. As the wind picked up, she quickly shut the door. Even though the sun shone brightly, the air was bitter cold. She should have put a jacket or her shawl on before answering the door.

❧

Farmerstown

Arlene stepped onto the porch and was about to shake some throw rugs when Joel's truck pulled into the yard. Scott must have seen it, too, for he poked his head out the door. "Look, Mom, Uncle Joel's here. Bet he came to see how I'm doin'."

Arlene hoped it was true, but her brother had only shown up once to see Scott since his surgery, using the excuse that he'd been busy with work. *No one should ever be too busy for family,* she thought.

"Go back inside, Son. It's icy cold out here. You can visit with your uncle when he comes inside." She remained in place, holding the rugs.

Scott's lower lip protruded, but he did as she asked. Watching Joel get out of his truck, Arlene was surprised to see that he was holding a dog.

Joel smiled when he stepped onto the porch. "How's Scott doing?"

"Better, but not quite ready to return to school."

"I'm glad he's doin' better. The kid's probably happy he gets to stay home awhile."

"He is, but he still has to do his schoolwork. Scott's brother has been bringing it home for him." She stared at the dog in Joel's arms. The critter had a shiny black nose, reminding her of a wet olive. "Aren't you going to introduce me to your new friend, Joel?"

"Oh, well. . .I actually thought maybe Scott might like to have this little fellow." Joel patted the terrier's head. "That is, if it's all right with you."

Arlene bit the inside of her cheek, wondering if this was her brother's attempt at doing another so-called selfless act. Giving the dog to her son might make Joel believe he had an easy chance at getting his portion of the will, but she wouldn't vote for it and didn't think her sisters or Aunt Verna would either. On the other hand, Scott had been bored since he'd come home from the hospital, so having a dog to fuss over could be a good thing.

"Come inside, and we'll see what Scott thinks." She draped the rugs over the porch railing and opened the door.

As soon as they entered the house, Scott greeted them, smiling from ear to ear. "What have ya got, Uncle Joel? Is that your cute little hund?"

"It's yours if you want it." Joel handed the dog to Scott.

"Wow, ya mean it? I get to keep him for my very own?"

"Yep. Every boy needs a good dog."

Scott held the terrier close and snickered when it licked his chin. "I think he likes me. What's his name?"

"That's up to you." Joel stroked the dog's head. "He reminds me of a dog your aunt Doris had when she was a girl, so if you can't come up with something better, you could call him Bristleface Two."

"Can I just name him 'Bristleface,' without the word 'two'?"

"Don't see why not." Joel looked at Arlene. "Sorry I can't stay, but I'm already late for work. I'll come by some other time to see how Scott and his new dog are doing." He paused and gave Scott's shoulder a pat. "Take care of Bristleface, ya hear?"

Scott's grin never left his face. "I will. You can be sure of it."

As Arlene watched Joel get in his truck and drive off, she couldn't help thinking her brother's heart had softened a bit.

∞

Berlin

As soon as Doris entered Boyd & Wurthmann Restaurant, she spotted Anna sitting at a table near the window. She headed that way and took a seat across from her.

"How'd your doctor's appointment go?" Anna asked.

"I didn't see the doctor today. Just had an X-ray of my leg taken. I'll see the doctor in a few days to get the results. Then he'll decide how soon the cast can come off."

"I bet you're anxious for that."

"Jah." Doris glanced down at her cast. "I'm tired of the cumbersome thing and will be glad when I'm able to go back to waitressing."

"Have you thought about looking for something

closer to home?" Anna tilted her body toward Doris. "Maybe they're hiring here."

Doris removed her shawl and placed it across her lap. "This would be a nice place to work, I suppose, but Der Dutchman is a bigger restaurant. More people seem to go there, which means more tips."

"I see what you mean." Anna gestured to her menu. "I already know what I want, but feel free to take your time deciding. Since school's out for the day, I don't have to rush."

"Me neither. Brian will be working late this evening, and I told my driver I'd call for a ride home after I had supper with you." Doris studied the menu, although she didn't know why. She planned to have her favorite turkey club sandwich, with a cup of chicken noodle soup.

When their waitress came, they told her what they wanted. Anna ordered a cold plate of cottage cheese, Jell-O, fruit, trail bologna, and swiss cheese. She also asked for a bowl of chili.

"How are things at school?" Doris asked, after taking a sip of water. "Have things settled down now that Christmas is over?"

"Jah. Everything's pretty much back to normal. But with Valentine's Day coming next month, the scholars will soon begin making cards to give each other. Of course when I bring heart-shaped cookies and fruit punch for a treat on Valentine's Day, they'll get pretty excited."

Doris smiled, remembering how much she'd enjoyed making Valentine cards for her classmates, as well as family members and friends from their church district. Even many of the boys, including

Joel, seemed to like exchanging Valentine's Day greetings.

Thinking about her brother, Doris remembered to tell Anna that she'd seen Joel earlier today and he'd said to say hello.

"That was nice of him." Anna cupped her chin in her hands. "I think I'm finally ready to let go of my feelings for Joel."

Doris blinked a couple of times. "Really? How did that happen?"

Anna's cheeks reddened. "Well, I've met someone."

"Is it someone I know?" Doris leaned in closer.

"I don't think so. He's new to our area. His name is Melvin Mast. I met him a few weeks ago when he came to the school Christmas program with his folks."

"I'm confused." Doris glanced down, realizing she was fumbling with her napkin, so she unfolded it and placed it on her lap. "If he's new to the area, why was he at the program?"

"His younger cousin attends my school."

"Have you seen Melvin since then?"

Anna nodded. "He's in our church district, so I've seen him at church a few times. He also dropped by the school the other day to pick up his cousin, and. . ." She paused to drink some water. "He asked if I'd like to go out to supper with him sometime."

Doris laughed. "My goodness, this new fellow didn't waste any time, did he?"

"Well, we're both in our late twenties and not getting any younger." Anna fiddled with her spoon. "I don't know yet if Melvin's the one, but I do think he's good-looking, and he seems very kind."

Doris reached across the table and touched her friend's hand. "I wish you all the best."

She felt relieved that Anna would no longer be pining for Joel. She'd done it far too long.

CHAPTER 5

North Canton

Kristi shivered against the cold as she entered the North Canton Skate Center with Darin and fifteen eager teens from their church youth group. It was the first Saturday of February, and after Darin had practically begged her to accompany him, she'd agreed to act as a chaperone. While Kristi wasn't by any means a professional on roller skates, it was good exercise and a chance to do something fun for a change. Last week she'd worked several back-to-back shifts at the nursing home and needed a little downtime.

As the teens chatted with each other and their new youth leader, Kristi sat on a bench by herself to put on her skates. She hadn't gone roller skating since she was a teenager and had forgotten how noisy it could be. Between the hum of voices, and the music blaring overhead, it was hard to think.

"Let's get something to eat before we start skating." Irv, a fifteen-year-old freckle-faced boy, pointed to the snack bar. "I need a few hot dogs to get me revved up."

Darin bobbed his head. "I'm with you on that. Anyone else want to eat now?"

Several hands went up, and then he turned to Kristi. "How about you? Should I order us both a hot dog with fries?"

"No thanks. Think I'll skate awhile, then see later on if they have anything healthier than hot dogs in the snack area."

Darin finished lacing up his skates and pushed a chunk of hair out of his face. "Okay, whatever you want to do is fine with me." He stood, did a few wobbly turns on his skates, and rolled off in the direction of the snack bar. Several of the teens followed, but a few went out on the rink.

Kristi watched the kids start skating. They seemed to get it right, without a problem. They made it look simple, in fact. Hopefully, it would be easy to skate out there, with the amount of bodies already filling up the ever-shrinking skating space.

There are a lot of people here tonight, she mused. *We'll be packed in tightly, like a tin of sardines wearing roller skates.*

A bit unsteady at first, Kristi inched her way along, until she, too, was on the rink. She would take it slow and easy until she felt more confident, because the last thing she needed was to fall and make a fool of herself.

She'd only been skating fifteen minutes when Darin, flailing his arms overhead, skated up to her with a big grin. "I'd forgotten how much fun skating could be. Haven't been at a rink in several years."

"Me neither. It took awhile to get my balance." She smiled as he nodded and did a few awkward-looking turns.

"You weren't in the snack bar very long. Did you get anything to eat?"

"Sure did." He grinned and smacked his lips. "The hot dog was so good I practically inhaled it."

Kristi resisted the urge to give Darin her thoughts on the importance of a healthy diet. Instead, she gave a small wave and sailed right past him.

Half an hour later, she headed for the snack

bar. The line was short, but she stood off to the side to figure out what to order. Her eyebrows drew in as she browsed the menu board. Kristi didn't care to eat most of the foods listed, since she preferred organic food with less sugar. Finally, she settled on a slice of pizza and a bottle of water. As she sat at one of the tables with her food, watching the skaters on the floor, she spotted a man who reminded her of Joel. He had the same thick, dark hair and short-cropped beard. However, this guy was skating with two small children, each holding his hand. He was obviously not Joel.

I shouldn't be thinking of Joel right now, Kristi berated herself. *What we once had is over, and it's time to move on.* How many times had she thought about him and given herself a mental shake? She picked up her slice of pizza and took a small bite. *If only things could have worked out differently between us.*

As Kristi got up from her seat to throw away her paper plate and napkin, she thought about Joel's family and wondered how they were all doing. She'd meant to go back to Der Dutchman Restaurant to see Doris again but hadn't made it. She'd been busy during the holidays, and now with the unpredictable weather, she didn't feel like driving down to Holmes County on roads that were often icy or covered in snow. Besides, it was hard to see Doris and not think about Joel.

"You coming back out to skate?" Darin skated up to her. "They just announced the next song is for couples only. Would you like to be my partner?"

Couples only? She nearly jumped. Her face, neck, and ears were impossibly hot. *Oh, my. Maybe Darin is interested in me.* Kristi hesitated but finally nodded. "Sure." She tossed the trash from her meal in the garbage, cleaned her hands with a disposable wipe, and followed him out to the skating floor.

Darin took her hand, and they skated easily along. *This is actually kind of fun.* Even though she doubted Darin would be a potential guy for her to go out with, she began to have second thoughts as she continued to skate with him. He seemed so gentle and kind. And the way his eyes sparkled when he talked to her made it feel almost like they were on a date. That thought was quickly dispelled, however, when two of the teens—Rick and Connie, skated up to them.

Connie's cheeks flushed pink, while her blue eyes danced merrily. "This is fun, isn't it, Darin?"

"Sure is." He grinned at Kristi. "We should do this again sometime."

Kristi couldn't believe Darin allowed the teens to call him by his first name. It seemed disrespectful. At the very least, Connie could have called him "Pastor Darin."

He acts like he's one of them, instead of their pastor, she thought when Darin let go of her hand and skated in circles around Rick and Connie. *He's just a big kid at heart.* Kristi guessed that wasn't all bad. Some people took life too seriously.

"Wanna see me skate backward?" Darin asked, returning to her side.

"Sure, if you want to." She looked at him and giggled nervously. *I hope neither of us falls.*

He turned and got in front of her, then reached out his hands. She was about to take hold of them when the guy who looked like he could be related to Joel came by, holding hands with the little girl

Kristi had seen him with earlier. Being this close to the man, she realized he didn't resemble Joel as much as she'd first thought. His eyes were blue, not brown, and there was a slight hump in the middle of his nose. *Guess everyone has someone who resembles them,* she thought, clasping Darin's hands.

They skated for a while, facing each other, until Darin started skating too fast. Suddenly, he stumbled, let go of her hand, and fell.

"Are you okay?" Kristi stopped skating and reached out her hand to help him up.

"I don't think anything's broken, but my knees sure hurt." He gave her a sheepish grin. "Guess that's what I get for showin' off."

Holding tightly to Darin's hand, Kristi guided him off the floor and over to a bench. "Should I go to the snack bar and get some ice for your knees?"

"Yeah, I'd appreciate it."

Being careful not to fall herself, she made her way to the snack bar. When she returned with two small bags of ice, she found Darin surrounded by several of the girls from their church, all wearing concerned expressions.

"Thanks, Kristi." He took the ice from her and placed it on his injured knees. "It hurts more now that I'm sitting than it did when I fell."

Kristi checked his knees to be sure nothing was broken. "I think they're both just badly bruised, but the ice should help."

"It's kinda handy to have a nurse along to take care of me. Maybe we can go out for supper sometime next week, and I'll reward you for your kindness."

Kristi's face heated, and she turned her head

away from him, hoping he wouldn't notice. "There's no need for that."

"Are you saying you don't want to go out for a meal?"

"No, of course not. I only meant—"

"Hey, Darin, my dad just called. He wants to know what time to pick me up at the church." Rick squatted in front of Darin, holding a cell phone. "What happened to you?"

Darin explained his accident, then told Rick to tell his dad he could pick him up in an hour. He looked up at Kristi. "Would you mind driving the van? I'm not going to do any more skating, and with my knees hurting, the idea of pressing either of my feet on the gas pedal or brake holds no appeal right now."

"I don't mind driving," she replied, relieved that he hadn't mentioned going out to dinner again. It could be construed as a date, and she wasn't ready for that.

ᕫ

Akron

When Kristi entered the church sanctuary the following morning, she spotted Darin sitting halfway down at one end of a pew. Several people stood in the aisle talking to him, so Kristi held back until they moved on.

"How are your knees?" she asked.

"Still a little tender this morning, and there's some swelling, but you were right—they are both bruised." He placed his hand on each knee and grimaced. "Ice helps some, but I wish there was something else I could put on the bruises."

"Actually, there is." Kristi reached into her purse and pulled out a tube of Arnica. "This is a homeopathic remedy available at most health food stores. Why don't you take it home and try it?" She handed the tube of medicine to him.

"Thanks, Kristi. I'll buy you a replacement as soon as I can."

"There's no need for that. I have another one at home." She removed her coat, draping it over one arm.

Darin slid over a ways. "Why don't you sit beside me? The service is about to start."

Kristi glanced at her parents, sitting in the row behind them, and couldn't help but notice Mom's giddy demeanor. *She was happy when I told her I'd gone skating with Darin and the teens last night, so she'd probably be thrilled if I sit with him now.*

The worship team had already started the first song, but other people were filing in, so Kristi could still take a seat with her parents. But she decided to sit beside Darin, so she slid in next to him.

Kristi set her purse on the floor by her feet and laid her coat over the back of the pew. She opened the bulletin and quickly scanned it to see what was on this week's agenda. Then she glanced around, feeling a little nervous. *Sure hope this doesn't start any rumors going around the church. The last thing I need is for people to think I'm making a play for our new youth pastor.*

⌘

Joel hadn't slept well—mostly because he'd had a dream about Kristi. She was still on his mind after he'd gotten dressed and eaten breakfast, and it bothered him a lot. *Why am I thinking about her all of a sudden? I haven't talked to Kristi for several months. Could the dream I had be a sign that I should contact her again?*

He squinted at his reflection in the hall mirror and released an impatient huff. *I wonder how she'd respond if I showed up at church today and tried talking to her. Would she listen? Would she consider giving me a second chance?*

Joel stepped into his bedroom, opened the closet door, and pulled out his nicest jacket. *If I hurry, I can probably make it to church before the service ends. Think I'll throw caution to the wind and give it a try.*

When Joel arrived at the church, his stomach quivered, and he began to have second thoughts. If Kristi was here today, she'd no doubt be sitting with her folks. Since neither of them cared that much for Joel, they might ask him to leave. For that matter, Kristi could just as easily tell him to get lost. But maybe with so many Christians around her, she'd be less apt to make an undesirable scene. *This could give me an edge,* he thought.

All those weeks after their breakup, Joel had tried to contact Kristi, and she'd never returned any of his calls. How much clearer could she make it?

He stepped into the entryway and hesitated. *It'd probably be best if I turn around now and head for home, but since I'm here, I may as well go through with it.*

Joel opened the door to the sanctuary and stepped inside, careful to shut it quietly. The worship team was on the platform, and some woman Joel had never met was reading scripture from the front of the room.

He stood there a few minutes, scanning the

pews, hoping Kristi would be somewhere near the back. About halfway down, he spotted her, sitting beside a man with blond hair. He wasn't her dad.

Joel's heart started to pound, and his nerves wavered. Kristi's folks sat in the pew behind them, and the blond-headed guy was leaning close to Kristi, as though he was whispering something in her ear.

I'm too late. Joel's jaw clenched so hard his teeth clicked together. *She's already found someone else.* He felt heat behind his eyes, and his shoulders slumped in defeat. *Kristi.* Clutching his arm toward his chest, Joel turned and hurried out the door. This would be the last time he'd ever set foot in this church. It would also be the final time he'd try to make contact with her. He definitely needed to move on.

Chapter 6

Farmerstown

It was nice having you and your family visit our church today," Arlene said as she and Elsie sat in the kitchen together, drinking tea. "And I'm glad you came here afterward so we'd have more time to chat." She reached down and patted Bristleface's head. He leaned against her chair, seeming to absorb the sweet attention.

"It's always good to visit with family." Elsie smiled, although there was no sparkle in her eyes. "I see Scott's new pet has taken a liking to you."

"Jah, this little terrier knows when he's got it made." Arlene wondered if her sister was trying to put on a brave front by talking about things other than what was actually on her mind. Elsie hadn't been the same since their house burned down. Arlene certainly understood how hard it could be to remain cheerful when tragedies occurred. Adding more tea to her near-empty cup, she said, "I wish Doris and Brian could have joined us, too."

"It would have been nice, but since Brian is down with the flu, I'm sure Doris didn't even go to their own church service today."

"It's understandable. She needs to take care of him. I hope for her sake she doesn't get sick, too." Arlene tapped the side of her mug.

Elsie added half a spoonful of sugar to her tea and stirred it around. "I'm glad her leg has finally healed and she's able to work at the restaurant again. I think she missed it, and with hospital and doctor bills to pay, they need the extra money coming in."

"How well I know." Arlene sighed. "I think we'll be paying on Scott's hospital bill till the end of this year."

"We all need money right now." Elsie bit her bottom lip. "I don't mean to sound greedy, but it would sure be nice if we could all open our envelopes to see how much Dad left us." She looked out the window, watching the birds eating from one of the feeders.

Arlene cleared her throat. "I'm sure he gave us equal shares of whatever his assets are, but if Joel doesn't do something we can all agree is a heartfelt, selfless act, we may never get whatever Dad wanted us to have."

Elsie drank some tea, then added a bit more sugar. "Have you heard anything from Joel lately?" she asked, looking back at her sister.

"No. Have you?"

"Huh-uh. Not since he came by a few weeks ago to see if we all liked our Christmas presents. I think he was hoping we'd say his gift-giving was a selfless act." Elsie pushed her chair back a ways to cross her legs.

Arlene folded her arms. "Same thing for when he gave Scott the dog. I heard from Aunt Verna a few weeks after that, and she said Joel had called and told her what he'd done."

"What'd she say in response?"

"Not a lot. Just said she told Joel she thought Scott would enjoy having the dog, but it wasn't a selfless act."

"Maybe our bruder isn't capable of doing something completely selfless. Whatever he's done so far has been with an ulterior motive." Elsie blew out a breath, rattling her lips. "He's trying too hard, and it's not heartfelt."

"What's not heartfelt?" Scott asked when he entered the room and squatted beside his dog.

"Nothing, Son." Arlene pointed at the terrier, still lying beside her feet. "I don't really like having your dog in the kitchen, but he has a persuasive way about him."

"I showed Uncle John and my cousins the tricks I've taught my hund, and I want Aunt Elsie to see what he can do."

Elsie rose from her chair. "I'll go out to the living room, and you can show me in there."

Scott's face lit up. "Okay! After that, I'm gonna play a song I learned on the harmonica Uncle Joel gave me." He looked up at Arlene. "Are ya comin', Mom?"

She nodded. "I'll be there as soon as I put our tea cups in the sink."

Scott headed for the living room with the dog at his heels, and Elsie followed.

Arlene smiled as she cleared the dishes from the table and placed them in the sink. Joel had done a good thing by giving Scott the mutt, but it really wasn't enough. He needed to do something sacrificial without trying to get anything in return. Unless her brother had a complete change of heart, it wasn't likely he'd ever do a good deed for anyone without expecting something back.

✂

Elsie had felt uptight most of the day, but after laughing at Bristleface's antics as he did several tricks, she relaxed a bit. Laughter was good medicine. She remembered her mother had often quoted Proverbs 17:22: *"A merry heart doeth good like a medicine: but a broken spirit drieth the bones."* Her bones had certainly felt dry since they'd lost their house. She'd struggled to find any joy at all, but she still tried to hide her frustrations and despondency from the children. If they knew how disheartened their mother felt, it would upset them. Even John didn't know the extent of her depression. She'd shared a few of her thoughts with him, but most things she kept hidden in her heart. There was nothing her husband could do about their situation, so what was the point in saying anything? Truth was, John probably held in his thoughts and feelings, too. Some days Elsie wondered if anything in their lives would ever feel right again.

Thunder sounded in the distance, causing Elsie to rise from her seat in the rocking chair. She went to the living room window and looked out. "It's snowing—really hard!"

Arlene and both of the men joined her at the window.

"You don't hear dunner when it's snowing very often," Larry commented. "I have a feeling we might be in for another storm."

"Could turn into a blizzard." John's brows furrowed. "I can hear the horses out in the barn, whinnying something awful."

Arlene slipped her arm around Elsie's waist. "I think it would be safer if you spent the night here."

Larry nodded. "I agree with my fraa. Sure wouldn't advise going home with a spooky horse in this kind of weather, even though Charm's not that far from here."

Elsie looked at John to get his reaction.

"I believe you're right, Larry," he replied. "If you're sure you don't mind, we'll crash here tonight. If things look better in the morning, we'll head back to Charm."

"What about *schul*?" Hope spoke up. "If we spend the night here, how am I gonna get to school on time tomorrow?"

"I'll take you there with my horse and buggy." John gave her shoulder a squeeze. "Try not to worry about it, okay? If the storm is too bad, school will probably be cancelled tomorrow anyway."

Elsie shivered as another clap of thunder sounded. This one seemed a little closer than the last. The snow was falling harder. She was pretty sure they were in for a blizzard.

Hearing the thunder made her think about Dad and how lightning and thunder had struck the night he'd been killed in his tree house. She closed her eyes. *I miss you, Dad. I'd rather we had you here with us right now than be waiting to see how much of your money we were going to get.*

❦

Akron

Joel had developed a headache soon after he'd left the church, but even though he'd taken something for it, the pounding pain remained.

It's probably from the stress of knowing I've lost Kristi for good, he told himself as he lay down on his bed. Joel had spent most of the day in bed, hoping some rest would help the headache go away, and he'd only gotten up once to get a bite to eat.

A clap of thunder brought his head off the

pillow. "Dunner this time of the year?" Joel didn't know why, but the German-Dutch word rolled off his tongue. He got up and looked out the window. It was snowing hard, and the wind blew furiously. Another boom sounded, and a vision of his dad came to mind. *What must it have been like for him, up in the tree house when the lightning struck?* He shuddered at the thought.

For the first time since his father's death, Joel teared up. A knot formed in his stomach, and a gut-wrenching sob tore from his throat. "Oh Dad, I have so many regrets." It grieved him to know he hadn't had a chance to say goodbye or make amends with Dad before he died. But it was too late to do anything about it now.

Blurry-eyed, Joel's gaze came to rest on the black book with golden embossed letters along the spine lying on his dresser. It was the NIV Bible Kristi had given him last year at Christmas. He'd taken it to church with him a few times, hoping to impress her, but had never opened it when he was at home. But now Joel felt a strong need to open it.

He picked up the Bible and sat on the end of his bed. A green ribbon stuck out, so he opened it to that section. After reading several verses, Joel paused at 1 John 3:17: "If anyone has material possessions and sees a brother or sister in need but has no pity on them, how can the love of God be in that person?"

He continued to read verses 18, 19, and 20: "Dear children, let us not love with words or speech but with actions and in truth. This is how we know that we belong to the truth and how we set our hearts at rest in his presence: If our hearts condemn us, we know that God is greater than our hearts, and he knows everything."

Tears stinging his eyes, Joel read on, until he came to verse 23: "And this is his command: to believe in the name of his Son, Jesus Christ, and to love one another as he commanded us."

As the words from the passage pierced his heart, Joel fell to his knees beside his bed. The truth of his transgressions hit him with the force of a strong wind. His self-centeredness and deceitfulness had caused him to lose Kristi, and they had put a wedge between him and his family for years. He hadn't been a good son and had brought shame to his father. *No wonder Dad was so hard on me. He wanted me to see the error of my ways and become the man I should be.*

"Father in heaven," Joel prayed tearfully, "I've been so selfish, always thinking of myself instead of others. I believe in the name of Jesus and ask Your forgiveness. Let Your love flow into my heart, and help me to be a better person. I commit my life to You."

When his prayer was finished, Joel stood, holding the Bible against his chest. The seed that had been planted when he'd attended the Amish church with his parents and siblings as a child had finally taken root.

A deep ache pressed against Joel's heart. He felt the pain of what his sisters had recently gone through as though it were his own. Joel sank to his bed as a realization hit him. He knew what he had to do. The only problem was, it might take some time to make it happen.

CHAPTER 7

Berlin

It was the third Saturday of March, and Doris had been back to work for over a month. While she found her job enjoyable, it didn't fulfill her deepest desire to raise a family. The extra money she made helped pay some of their bills, but many expenses from her hospital stay hadn't yet been covered.

Doris had been enjoying a day off and was about to begin washing the breakfast dishes when she glanced out the kitchen window. She was surprised to see her brother's truck pull in. She hadn't heard from Joel in several weeks, and he'd even quit doing things to try and win the right to open his envelope. She hadn't been able to figure that out because, until then, he'd been so open about how much he needed money.

We all need money, Doris thought as she dried her hands on a clean towel. *Arlene and Larry have expenses, and John and Elsie need to build a new house. There is no doubt in my mind that a large sum of money is in Dad's bank account. But thanks to Joel, none of us can touch a penny of it.*

She waited until Joel got out of his truck, then went to the door to greet him. The minute he stepped onto the porch, Doris knew there was something different about her brother. Gone were the worry lines on his forehead and dark circles beneath his eyes. There was no grim twist to his mouth, nor the determined swagger he normally had. Instead, Joel's countenance was serene, as he smiled and took Doris's hand. Speaking in a gentle, sincere tone, he said, "I have something for you. It should help your current financial situation." He reached into his jacket pocket, pulled out an envelope, and handed it to her.

"What's this?" she questioned.

"Open it and see."

Doris did as he asked. Staring at the certified check inside, all she could do at first was manage a little squeak. "One hundred thousand dollars? Where did you get this kind of money, Joel, and why are you giving it to me?"

He gestured to the door. "Let's go inside, and I'll explain."

When they entered the living room, Doris called for Brian, who'd been in the bathroom, brushing his teeth. After he joined them, they all took a seat, and Doris showed him the check Joel had given her.

Brian's eyes narrowed as he looked at Joel with disbelief. "What's this all about?"

"I sold a very expensive classic car I got at an auction several months ago," Joel explained. "I was able to get top dollar for it, and this is one-third of the money. Arlene and Elsie will each get a third as well. I'll be going to see them after I leave here."

Doris sat on the sofa with her hands folded in her lap, unable to take it all in. "But why, Joel? What made you sell the car?" She scooted to the edge of her seat.

Joel's eyes watered, and his chin quivered slightly as he began speaking. "On a cold night in February, when thunder sounded during a snowstorm, I thought about Dad and all the things I'd done to hurt him, as well as the rest of my family."

His voice cracked, and he paused to pull a hankie from his pocket. "I read some verses in the Bible Kristi had given me last Christmas, and it opened my eyes to the truth. I've been selfish and arrogant. Because of it, I've lost Kristi—the love of my life. Dad died without ever knowing that I loved him." He looked at Doris with pleading eyes. "Can you forgive me for being so self-centered?"

Doris's heart went out to her brother. She knew without reservation that his apology was heartfelt. She was certain he hadn't sold his car and given her the check so he could receive his share of Dad's estate. Joel's trembling shoulders and the sadness in his eyes let her know he was truly repentant.

She went over to him quickly and gave him a hug. "I forgive you, Joel. And if Dad were here right now, he would forgive you, too. He only wanted the best for you and all his children."

"I believe you're right." Joel swiped at the tears that had escaped his eyes.

Doris looked at Brian, hoping he would say something, but he sat quietly, staring at the floor. After several seconds, he turned to Joel and said, "We appreciate your gesture, and it's good that you've seen the error of your ways. However, we can't take the check."

The color drained from Joel's face. "Why not? It's a gift—no strings attached."

Brian tipped his head. "Seriously? You don't expect anything in return?"

Joel shook his head briskly, making a sweeping movement with his hand. "Nothing at all. I don't care about Dad's money anymore."

Shocked by this admission, Doris hugged him

again. "You really have changed, haven't you? It was all in the Lord's timing."

"Yes, and my eyes have been opened. I have a lot of things to make up for, and this is only the beginning."

She smiled. "If you need our help in any way, don't hesitate to ask."

Joel nodded. "I need to finish saying what's on my heart."

"Certainly. Go ahead."

"In addition to giving you, Elsie, and Arlene the money from the sale of my car, I plan to help build a new home for Elsie and John." Joel drew in a deep breath and exhaled slowly. "I'm also going to start spending more time with my family and be there whenever they need me."

Doris's eyes filled with joyful tears. Joel might not be living among them anymore, but she felt as if he'd truly come home.

❦

Farmerstown

When Joel pulled into Arlene's yard and got out of his truck, he was greeted by Scott playing in the yard with his dog.

"Hey, Uncle Joel, I'm glad you're here. Would ya like to see some of the tricks I've taught Bristleface?"

Joel ruffled the boy's hair. "Maybe in a little bit. Right now, I need to speak to your mamm and daed. Are they both here?"

"Mom is, but my dad took Doug to the Shoe and Boot store in Charm. My bruder's *fiess* have grown so much his toes are about to poke through his shoes."

"Maybe he'll have big feet like mine." Smiling, Joel lifted one foot. "When I was a teenager, my daed used to say I had clodhoppers."

Scott snickered. "Never heard that expression before."

Joel glanced toward the house, then back at his nephew. "I'm going inside to talk to your mamm right now, but I'll be back soon. Then you can show me all the tricks you've taught your hund."

"Okay!" Scott gave the edge of Joel's jacket a tug. "Oh, and guess what else?"

"What?"

"I've been practicin' the harmonica every chance I get. I can play a couple of tunes pretty good."

"That's great. I'll be anxious to hear what you've learned." Joel bent down to give the dog's head a quick pat. "After you've shown me what this scruffy little terrier can do, we'll sit on the porch awhile, and you can play your tunes."

"Ya mean you don't have to rush off?" Scott knelt, and Bristleface plopped down next to him.

"Not today, Scott. For that matter, I plan to come around here more often and get to know you and my other nephews and nieces a lot better."

The boy's eyes widened, and a big grin spread across his face. "Really, Uncle Joel?"

"Jah, that's right." As Joel turned and stepped onto the porch, he smiled. He'd missed so much by not spending time with his family, but that was all behind him now.

～

When Joel walked into Arlene's kitchen and handed her a check for her portion of the car sale, she was so surprised she had to sit down at the table. "Where did you come up with this much money, and why are you giving it to me?"

"It's one-third of what I made selling the fancy Corvette I bought some time ago." He took a seat in the chair beside her. "I've always wanted a car like that, and until recently, I had no intention of ever letting it go. I kept it a secret—from my family, as well as Kristi, which was wrong."

"What changed your mind? Was it because you needed money and haven't been able to get your hands on Dad's?" Arlene's tone was bitter, and she bit her tongue to keep from saying more.

"The money's not for me. I divided it three ways between you, Doris, and Elsie."

She stared at the check. "Do my sisters know about this?"

"Only Doris so far. I'll be going to see Elsie next, to give her—"

"Give me what?" Elsie asked, entering the room.

Arlene's eyes widened as she turned to look at her sister. "I knew you were coming over today to help me do some cleaning but didn't realize you were here already."

"I just arrived." Elsie moved closer to the table. "What is it you planned to give me, Joel—another gift to try and sway me to say you've done something selfless?" She removed her sweater and hung it over the back of the chair next to her.

"It's nothing like that." He motioned for her to sit down, then reached into his pocket and handed her a check.

Elsie's mouth formed an *O*. "One hundred thousand dollars? What's this all about, Joel?"

Speaking calmly, he explained about the fancy car he'd sold and how he'd divided the money three ways.

Elsie glanced at Arlene, then back at Joel. "Is this another attempt at getting your share of the inheritance?"

He shook his head. "Through the reading of some scripture, plus a lot of soul-searching and praying, I've committed my life to the Lord. I realize how selfish I've been all these years, and I want to make amends." Joel paused and clasped his sisters' hands. "I can't begin to tell you both how sorry I am for all the hurtful things I've done in the past. But it's going to be different from now on, starting with this money I'm giving you. I expect nothing in return—no strings attached, like I said to Doris and Brian awhile ago. I don't care anymore about whatever Dad wanted me to have."

"Are you *anscht*?" Arlene could hardly believe the things Joel said. He'd been living for himself so long, with no regard for any of them, it was hard to accept that he could have changed. But the Bible was true, and lives were transformed when people accepted it and put God's principles into practice. If Joel truly had surrendered his life to Christ, then the slate was wiped clean, and he could begin anew.

"I'm very serious." Joel's eyes filled with tears. "Will you both forgive me?"

Arlene looked at Elsie, and when she nodded, they spoke at the same time. "I forgive you, Joel."

"My change of heart and repentance goes beyond the money I gave you both," he said. "Elsie, as you know, I make my living building and remodeling, and I plan to help as much as I can with rebuilding a house for you and your family."

Elsie's eyes clouded as she squeezed Joel's hand. "Danki. Your help will be most appreciated."

He looked at Arlene and smiled. "From now on, I want to spend more time with everyone in my family. Will that be all right with you?"

"It's more than all right." A sob caught in her throat. *Thank You, God. Joel's become the brother I've always longed for, and I feel sure he's truly had a change of heart.*

CHAPTER 8

Charm

The next Monday, Arlene and her sisters got together in the evening to talk about Joel.

"I think our bruder was sincere when he gave us those checks," Arlene said as the three of them sat at the kitchen table in Dad's old house. "He seemed genuinely repentant for neglecting all of us, too."

"I agree. I've never seen Joel with such a peaceful expression as he had when he visited us on Saturday." Elsie went to the refrigerator and took out the Millionaire Pie she'd made. After slicing it and placing the pan on the table, she passed some plates to her sisters.

Doris smiled and took a piece. "Yum. This is one of my favorite pies."

"Mine, too," Arlene agreed.

"Getting back to Joel, when he came by to see me and Brian, I noticed right away how different he looked. He even spoke in a softer tone," Doris said. "I think we should call Aunt Verna and let her know what's happened. It's time for us to take a vote."

Arlene nodded. "I already know what my vote will be."

Elsie pushed her chair aside and stood. "I'll go out to the phone shack right now and give her a call. The sooner we get this settled, the better it will be for all of us."

༄

The following day, Elsie was dusting the living room furniture when she heard a car pull into the yard. Going to the door, she was surprised to see Aunt Verna getting out of a van. The lady driver got out, opened the back hatch, and lifted out a suitcase, placing it on the ground.

Aunt Verna reached for the handle and began to tug the suitcase along the ground.

Elsie wrapped her woolen shawl around her shoulders and rushed outside. Walking carefully around the piles of snow still in the yard, she saw Aunt Verna let go of the handle, then she greeted her with a hug. "I'm surprised to see you so soon. When we spoke yesterday, you said you'd try to be here by the end of the week."

The elderly woman tipped her head. "What was that?"

Speaking louder, Elsie repeated what she'd said.

Aunt Verna smiled and patted Elsie's shoulder. "My driver has other plans for the end of the week. Since she was only available today and tomorrow, I decided I'd better come now. I would have called first, but I wasn't sure when you would check your messages, so I decided to just come ahead."

"Well, I'm glad you're here. I'll try calling Doris and Arlene, but I don't know if I can reach them today."

"That's okay. I can stay till tomorrow evening. That's when my driver will be back to pick me up."

While Aunt Verna said goodbye to her driver, Elsie bent down and picked up her small suitcase. *No sense trying to pull this travel bag through piles of snow.* Out of consideration for her aunt, she would put her things in the downstairs bedroom, and she and John would sleep upstairs. That meant Glen and Blaine would have to share a room again, but it was only for one night, so it shouldn't be a problem.

Once inside, Elsie took her aunt's coat and other outer garments and hung them up. "Have you had lunch yet?"

"Do I have a hunch about what?"

"No, I asked if you've had lunch yet. I've eaten already, but there's some leftover *schplitt–aerbs supp* I can reheat if you want."

Aunt Verna's nose wrinkled. "I've never cared much for split-pea soup. Your daed always liked it, but not me."

"Oh, I see. Can I fix you a sandwich then?"

"No, it's okay. I developed a *koppweh* on the drive here and would really like to lie down awhile." She rubbed her temples.

"I'm sorry you have a headache. I'll put your things in mine and John's room, and you can rest there on our bed." Elsie made sure to speak slowly and loud enough for her aunt to hear.

"Are you sure? I can take one of the bedrooms upstairs."

"The downstairs bedroom will be best. It'll be easier if you don't have to climb the stairs."

"Okay, if you insist. Elsie, could you please bring me a cold washcloth for my forehead?" Aunt Verna questioned before starting down the hall in the direction of the bedroom.

"Sure, no problem. I'll bring you a cup of chamomile tea and some aspirin, too," Elsie called.

Apparently her aunt didn't hear what she said, for she continued down the hall without a response.

I'll take it to her anyway, Elsie thought as she started for the kitchen. *Then I'll go out to the phone shack and call Doris, Arlene, and Joel. Maybe we can*

*all meet to talk about opening those envelopes before we
sit down to a nice meal at the get-together this evening.*

❧

Akron

As Joel headed down the freeway, he glanced in the
rearview mirror and smiled. He didn't know why
Elsie had invited him to join her family for supper
this evening, but he'd gladly accepted the invitation.
Besides enjoying a delicious home-cooked meal, he
looked forward to spending time with her family.

He glanced at the satchel on the seat beside
him, where he'd put his harmonica, then looked
quickly back at the road. After they ate, he looked
forward to playing a few tunes for the family. *Sure
wish Arlene and her family could be there. I'll bet Scott
would enjoy playing his harmonica with me.* The boy
reminded Joel of himself at that age—full of curios-
ity and eager to try new things. *Sure hope he doesn't
rebel like I did when he starts his running-around
years. If he does, I'll speak up and try to guide him in
the right direction.*

Joel winced, feeling a stab of regret. His parents
and sisters—especially Doris—had tried to make
him see the error of his ways, but he'd ignored them
and done his own thing.

*I wonder how things would be for me now if I
hadn't rebelled.* He gripped the steering wheel as a
car passed him, going much too fast. *If I'd stayed
Amish, I wouldn't have met Kristi. Maybe I was meant
to be with Anna, but of course, I botched that up, too.*

Joel thought about the choices people made and
how one simple act or decision could change the
course of a person's life. His decision to go English

had certainly set his life on a different path. If he'd remained Amish, he wouldn't have been so desperate to make money so he could acquire worldly things. It wasn't that modern things were all bad, but putting material possessions ahead of family and always striving for more made people selfish and greedy. He wondered if his desire to own the Corvette had been purely to make him feel good about himself. When Joel had been out driving the car and people admired it, he'd felt proud of himself for owning something so nice—something the average person couldn't afford.

He didn't care about that anymore. He wanted to live a normal life, make a decent living, and someday find a sweet, Christian wife. *I almost did,* he reminded himself. *But she's out of my life now, and I need to quit dwelling on it. God's given me another chance, so I have to keep my focus on living a life pleasing to Him.*

Charm

Joel stepped onto his dad's porch and was surprised when Aunt Verna opened the door. "I sure didn't expect to see you here this evening." He gave her a hug.

"I arrived this afternoon." She opened the door wider and let him in. "After you hang up your jacket, join me in the living room, where your sisters are waiting." She patted his shoulder.

Joel was even more surprised. When he'd received Elsie's invitation for supper, he'd assumed it would only be him and her family. Having the rest of his family together this evening would be even nicer though. He looked forward to more gatherings like this.

Coming into his father's house and looking around, he felt different on the inside—better. *I'm sure my daed would be pleased to know that the stipulation he put in his will helped me pull out of a downward spiral.*

Bringing his thoughts to a halt, Joel placed his jacket on a wall peg and entered the living room, where Arlene, Doris, and Elsie sat on the couch. They were talking about Aunt Verna getting some new hearing aids. His sisters sounded thrilled, and his aunt said she couldn't wait to use them so she could hear like a kid again. There was no sign of his sisters' husbands, though, or any of their children.

"I'm glad you could make it, Joel. We'll eat supper after we've had our meeting." Elsie pointed to the recliner where Dad used to sit. "Please, take a seat."

He did as she'd requested, and Aunt Verna took a seat in the rocking chair.

"Where's everyone else?" Joel asked, looking around.

"The kinner are upstairs, and the men, including Glen and Blaine, are in the barn. They'll come inside as soon as we call them," Arlene replied.

Aunt Verna cleared her throat, before looking at Joel. "Your sisters have told me about the money you gave them from the sale of your fancy car."

He nodded.

"They also said you've had a change of heart and apologized for all the hurts you have caused your family." She kept her gaze steadily on him.

Joel rubbed the bridge of his nose, hoping he

wouldn't break down. He still felt deep remorse for all the things he'd done in the past. "I made my peace with God, Aunt Verna. I've committed my life to Him and want to do things better from now on." He glanced at his sisters, all looking intently at him. "When I gave out those checks, I didn't expect anything in return. And if I don't get anything from Dad's estate, that's okay, too."

"Did I hear you right, Joel?" Aunt Verna tipped her head, peering at him over the top of her glasses. "Did you just say if you didn't get anything from your daed's estate, it would be okay?"

"That's right." Joel dropped his gaze to the floor. "I treated Dad badly and don't deserve a single thing."

"But he wanted all of you to have something." Aunt Verna picked up four envelopes that had been lying on the small table to her left. "Your sisters and I have agreed that by selling your prized car and giving all the money to them, you've done a heartfelt, selfless act. Therefore, it's time for all of you to open your envelopes." She rose from her chair and handed each of them an envelope.

Joel looked at the one with his name on it, and his eyes filled with tears. All these months he'd been desperate to receive his inheritance, and now he hesitated to open the envelope. Maybe Dad hadn't left him anything at all. Or perhaps he'd given him equal shares in the money he'd made from the oil wells on his land. Whatever he got of monetary value, Joel didn't feel deserving of it.

With trembling fingers, he opened the envelope and read the note inside: "To my son, Joel, I leave my house, the barn, and the three acres the two buildings sit on." Joel was fully aware that the rest of Dad's acreage was where the oil wells sat, so he wouldn't get any profit from those. And there had been no mention of Joel getting any of the money in Dad's bank account, which meant, with the exception of the horses in the barn, and the house he'd grown up in, Joel hadn't been given anything of real value.

Joel clasped his hands together in his lap. *Guess I'm getting exactly what I deserve. Sure don't know what I'm gonna do with the barn or house.*

CHAPTER 9

Berlin

On the first Saturday of April, another day off for Doris, she'd gone to town to run a few errands. It was nice to know their financial burdens would be lifted soon. Now they wouldn't have to be stressed out, trying to make ends meet. Doris needed to consider whether she wanted to continue working or stay home and keep house.

Her last stop before heading home was the pharmacy inside the German Village complex. As she approached the cashier with her purchases, she glanced to the left and saw Kristi Palmer heading her way.

"It's so nice to see you, Doris." Kristi smiled, toting some bottles of vitamins. "It's been awhile since we talked, and I've been wondering how you and your family are doing."

"A lot has happened since we last spoke. If you have a few minutes, maybe we can sit on a bench outside the store and visit."

"I have plenty of time. I just came from the quilt shop where I went to buy material for the queen-sized quilt I'm making." Kristi set her purchases on the counter and opened the satchel she'd been carrying over her shoulder. "Here, let me show you the color of materials I picked for my quilt." She opened the bag and pulled up the fabric.

"Oh, those shades of purple are so pretty." Doris paused until Kristi put the material back in place. "I didn't realize you knew how to quilt."

"I didn't—not until I took some classes from the Amish lady at the quilt shop on Main Street." Kristi picked up her vitamins and got in line behind Doris. "When you gave me that beautiful wall hanging I became inspired."

"Do you still have it?" Doris turned and looked at her intently.

"Definitely. It's hanging on my bedroom wall. I think it looks great there, and it has a special meaning for me."

Doris was pleased to hear this. She half-expected Kristi to get rid of the quilted piece after her breakup with Joel.

When they'd paid for their purchases, Doris led the way out of the store, where she found an empty bench near the Christian bookstore. After they'd both taken a seat, she filled Kristi in on all that had happened since their last visit, including the fire that destroyed Elsie and John's house, as well as what Joel had done with the money from the sale of his classic car.

Kristi looked at Doris in disbelief. "Did he do it so he could get his inheritance?"

"No. In fact, Joel said he didn't care about the money anymore. He just wanted—"

An elderly Amish woman came up to Doris and rested her hand on the back of the bench. "Do you know whether your sister Elsie is home today?"

"I'm not sure," Doris replied. "Is there something you need to ask her?"

The woman smiled. "I wanted to let her know that my son Harold is available to help when they're ready to move into their new house."

"It's nice of him to offer, Ada. They'll be moving

out of Dad's old place the last Saturday of this month, so I'm sure they'll appreciate all the help they can get."

"I'll let Harold know." Ada said goodbye and headed into the market across the way.

Doris turned to face Kristi. "I'm sorry. I should have introduced you. Ada's been a friend of our family for years. In fact, she used to go to school with my dad."

"It's all right. I wasn't offended." Kristi held her purse in her lap, twisting the strap around her fingers. "I'm really sorry to hear about Elsie losing her house. Is there anything they need?"

"Furniture, mostly, but now that my sisters and I will get our share of Dad's estate, Elsie will be able to afford whatever she needs."

"That's wonderful news." Kristi stood. "I need to get going. It was nice seeing you, Doris. Please tell your sisters I said hello."

Doris rose from the bench and gave Kristi a hug. Then she picked up her things and headed toward her horse and buggy, which were secured at one of the hitching rails in the parking lot. She'd hoped Kristi might ask her to say hello to Joel, too. Apparently she didn't care about him anymore.

How sad, she thought when she turned and saw Kristi walk away. *She didn't even seem that interested when I tried to tell her Joel has changed. Maybe the relationship between Kristi and my brother was never meant to be.*

⁓

When Kristi entered the Farmstead Restaurant and saw the long line that went almost out the door, she realized she'd probably have to wait awhile before being seated at a table. Since she wasn't in a hurry to get home, she didn't really mind the wait. Besides, it would give her a chance to digest all that Doris had told her. Was it possible Joel had actually changed? Could he really have sold his Corvette and given his sisters the money? For his family's sake, she hoped it was true.

It's a shame he couldn't have changed when we were still dating, Kristi thought. *It's been quite awhile since I last heard from Joel. If he loved me, the way he said he did, I would think he'd have let me know he'd made things right with his family.* She shifted her purse to the other shoulder. *But then, I chose not to respond to any of the messages he did leave, so I guess it makes sense that he didn't call later.*

Kristi assumed that, more than six months after their breakup, Joel had moved on with his life. For her, though, it had been hard to move on—at least when it came to dating. She was actually thankful Darin hadn't pursued a relationship with her. She was content to be his friend.

*It's still hard for me to fathom that Joel could have changed. I wonder what all he said to make Doris believe him. Could he have only said it to get his inheritance, or is it possible that—*Kristi's thoughts halted when the person behind her nudged her arm gently. "Excuse me, Miss, but the people ahead of you have moved to the front of the line."

"Oh, sorry." Kristi's cheeks warmed as she quickly stepped forward. She was almost to the hostess's desk and could see into part of the restaurant, including the all-you-can-eat buffet. She watched the young Amish waitress clear a table, wiping the area clean as soon as the customers rose and headed for the desk to pay for their meal. Several other workers moved quickly about, trying to cater to many hungry patrons.

Her mouth watered, smelling the delicious aromas. She could hardly wait until it was her turn to be seated at a table. Kristi had eaten at this restaurant before and remembered how good the baked chicken on the buffet had tasted. Another thing Kristi had enjoyed were the pickled red beets. *After I'm seated and it's time to place my order, I'm definitely going to do the buffet.*

Kristi didn't normally eat much for lunch, but today she'd make an exception and would probably be full the rest of the day. *I may not have to eat any supper tonight, but if I get hungry later, I'll fix a light snack. I probably should go for a run as soon as I get home, to burn off all the calories I'll be eating today.*

The man and woman in front of Kristi were being seated, so it was her turn next. Her stomach growled, and she placed her hand over it, hoping no one had heard. In a short while she'd be choosing whatever she wanted from the delicious array of foods on the buffet.

Looking to the right, where a man and woman sat in a booth, Kristi's breath caught in her throat. It was Joel, with the pretty Amish woman she'd seen him talking to the day of his father's funeral. When she'd asked Joel about it later, he'd said the woman's name was Anna, and that he'd been engaged to marry her before he left the Amish faith. Apparently they were back together, for Joel reached across the table and placed his hand on Anna's.

I can't believe it. Unbidden tears sprang to

Kristi's eyes. *I should have expected he would even- tually give up on me. No wonder Joel hasn't called or left any messages for so long. He's obviously back with his old girlfriend.* A lump lodged in her throat. *I bet he's planning to return to the Amish faith again, too. Or maybe Joel's convinced Anna to become part of the English world with him.*

The hostess returned from seating the other people, but before she could say anything, Kristi turned, nearly bumping into the gentleman behind her, and rushed out the door. She'd waited all that time to be seated, but now her appetite was gone.

∽

Joel smiled as Anna told him about Melvin Mast, who had recently started courting her. He couldn't remember ever seeing her face glow like this—not even when the two of them had been courting. Anna deserved to be happy, and he wished her well, reaching across the table and placing his hand over hers.

Joel hadn't made plans to meet Anna here for lunch. They'd both arrived around the same time, and after learning she was alone, he'd invited her to sit with him. He was anxious to see how she was doing and tell her that he'd committed his life to the Lord. Anna seemed as happy for Joel as he was for her starting a relationship with Melvin. They'd laughed and talked when they began eating, and Joel couldn't remember the last time he'd felt so relaxed in her presence. Of course, he felt better around everyone these days—especially his family members.

Joel thought about the inheritance he'd received

from his father and bit back a chuckle. There would have been a day he'd have been hopping mad at Dad for leaving him so little and at his sisters for getting much more than him. Not that it was their fault. None of them knew what Dad had designated in his will. To Joel's surprise, shortly after Doris, Arlene, and Elsie opened their envelopes, they'd each offered to give him part of the money they'd been left. He'd said no. He didn't deserve one penny of what Dad wanted his daughters to have. All three of them had been dutiful to Dad—especially after Mom died and he'd needed their help. Joel's sisters had always been kind and loving to their parents; unlike him, who'd given Mom and Dad nothing but trouble and heartache.

Once more, Joel wished he could turn back the hands of time and begin again. Knowing what he did now, if he could start over, he'd be a better son and brother. Well, he couldn't undo the past, but he'd spend the rest of his days trying to make it up to his sisters and their families.

"Joel, did you hear what I said?"

Anna's question drove his thoughts aside, and he blinked a couple of times. "Sorry, I was spacing—kind of lost in my thoughts."

"There's a young woman out by the hostess's desk, and she looks a lot like the woman you brought to your daed's funeral." Anna pointed in that direction.

He turned his head sharply, but only caught a glimpse of the back of a woman's auburn head as she hurried from the restaurant. "That couldn't have been Kristi," he murmured. "What would she be doing here?"

CHAPTER 10

Charm

"We need some more boxes to load up the last of your food items," Joel called to Elsie as he emptied one of the kitchen cupboards.

"I think there are some more in the barn." She smiled. "Thank you for taking the day off to help us move. We also appreciate all the work you've done on our new home."

"I was happy to do it, Elsie." Joel glanced around the kitchen. "Now I need to figure out what to do with Dad's house."

She placed her hand on his arm. "It belongs to you now. For whatever reason, Dad wanted you to have it."

"I realize that, but I have my own place in Akron."

"You said it's a mobile home, right?"

He nodded.

Elsie made a sweeping gesture of the kitchen. "This isn't fancy, but it's a solidly built home. With the three acres it sits on, there'd be room for you to build a shop for all the tools and supplies you need for your construction business."

Joel massaged the back of his neck. "Are you suggesting I sell my place and move here?"

"It'd be nice for all of us if you did. Keeping the home we grew up in would be meaningful, and living closer would give us opportunities to see you more often."

He tilted his head, weighing his choices. He

could either sell Dad's place and use the money to build a new house on the property he owned now, or sell his land and mobile home and move here. If he did the latter, he'd have to update the house, connect to the power lines, and get an Internet provider, because he needed that for his business and computer. Since the jobs Joel often did were in various locations, he didn't need to live in Akron. He could commute to most anywhere in this part of Ohio within a few hours' drive. Still, what would he do in this rambling old house all alone? If he had a wife and children, it would be a nice place to live and raise a family. But by himself, all he'd have were the memories from growing up here as a child.

"Are you thinking about my suggestion?" Elsie tugged on his shirtsleeve.

"I am, and as nice as it would be to live closer to you and the rest of our family, it may not be the sensible thing to do."

"Well, give it some thought before you make a final decision." Elsie looked at the open cupboard they'd just emptied of food.

"I will. And I'll be praying about it, too." Joel turned toward the back door. "I'll head out to the barn now and look for those boxes."

Elsie grabbed a sponge and rinsed it in the sink; then she stepped over to the cupboard and started wiping the shelves. "Okay. If you see Aunt Verna, would you let her know I could use her help in here? She went outside some time ago to hang a few dishtowels on the line, and I haven't seen her since."

He chuckled. "You know our dear aunt. She can easily become distracted."

"You're right about that. It was nice of her

and Uncle Lester to come down to help with the move." Elsie grinned. "I think she's looking forward to spending the next few nights in our new home. Since it has two bedrooms on the main floor, she and Uncle Lester can have a cozy room on the first floor, and John and I won't have to give up our room."

"They could stay here, you know."

"Right, but since Glen will be staying here until you decide what to do with the place, I thought he would enjoy having some peace and quiet without any visitors."

Joel gave his sister a hug. "You're a thoughtful *mudder*." He opened the back door and stepped out.

Grinning, Aunt Verna waved at him from where she was rocking back and forth on the porch swing.

He smiled in response. "I can see you're enjoying yourself. But when you get tired of swinging, Elsie could you use your help in the kitchen."

Her forehead wrinkled. "Elsie has a kitten?"

Joel resisted the urge to laugh. *She must not have her new hearing aids turned on.* "No, she said she needs your help in the kitchen."

"Oh of course." She rose from the swing, pausing for a minute to watch some robins searching for worms in the grass, before going into the house.

Joel headed for the barn. He'd barely set foot inside when Dad's spirited horse started acting up, kicking at the back wall in his stall. *I wonder what's got him so worked up.*

Speaking softly to the horse, Joel entered the stall. "Whoa, boy. Settle down."

With an ear-piercing whinny, the horse reared

up, then kicked again—this time putting a hole in the wall.

Joel figured a cat, or even a mouse, may have spooked the horse. He grabbed a rope, put it around the animal's neck, and tied him to the other side of the stall. Then he knelt in front of the wall to examine the damage. When Joel peered into the gaping hole, he was surprised to see something shiny. It looked like a piece of chrome, but it wasn't close enough for him to reach. The horse's stall was at the back of the barn, where outside, dirt was built up along the whole side and stretched out into the hillside. Dad had called it a "bank barn." Joel used to climb up on the mound of dirt when he was a boy and pretend he was standing on a mountain. He remembered once, Dad had caught him playing up there and told him in no uncertain terms to get off and never go up there again. When Joel asked why, Dad said, "Because you could fall and get hurt." Joel never understood what the big deal was. The mound of dirt wasn't that high. But he'd done as Dad asked and never went near it again. For that matter, Dad had been fussy about Joel or anyone else coming into this particular stall. Joel always figured it was because Dad had been so finicky about his own horse.

Gazing back at the hole, Joel decided to investigate further. He was curious about what was behind the wall. "Better get a flashlight," he mumbled.

After moving the horse to another stall, Joel was about to head out to his truck when he spotted a flashlight on the shelf halfway up the wall. Several shelves made the wall inside the stall look like a huge, built-in bookcase that went from top to bottom and all the way from one side to the other along the back wall.

Reaching up to get the flashlight, Joel touched something cold. It felt like a knob. Twisting it to the left, he was stunned when the bookcase-like structure swung open, revealing another room, apparently hidden under all the dirt behind the barn.

"What in the world?" Joel turned the flashlight on and shined the beam of light into the room. His nose twitched when he stepped inside. The room had a different smell. Dust, mixed with fuel and rubber, tainted the air.

He rested his hands on his hips. "What did Dad keep secret in here?"

Seeing a lot of things covered with tarps, he moved to the closest one and pulled it back. A beautiful old car came into view.

"Oh, wow!" Like a kid in a candy store, Joel went to each tarp, pulling them off. It seemed like a dream, but he'd just discovered not one, but ten antique classic cars hidden under all those dusty tarps.

Joel's breath caught in his throat. "I'll bet these beauties are worth millions!"

Yelling for Elsie, he dashed out of the barn.

Humming to the tune of the song playing on her car radio, Kristi turned off the freeway in the direction of Charm. She wasn't sure if Elsie and her family still lived in Eustace's old house, but she had something for them and hoped to deliver it today. If they had already moved to their new home, then

Kristi didn't know what to do, because she did not have their new address.

"I should have thought to ask Doris," Kristi muttered. She would have liked to have brought this love gift sooner, but it had taken a few weeks for donations to come in after she'd gotten the word out to church members about the fire that had destroyed the home of Joel's sister. Even though Doris had said she and her siblings would receive an inheritance from their father, Kristi didn't know how much it was or whether they'd gotten the money yet. She wanted to do something to help out. In addition to several boxes of food, the church had collected over a thousand dollars in cash. It wasn't an enormous amount of money, but it would help with some of their expenses. Kristi felt grateful for the congregation's generosity to a family they'd never met.

That's what all churches should do, she thought, turning on the road that led to Eustace Byler's house. *Helping people in need, regardless of whether we know them or not, is the Christian thing to do, and it's a testimony of Christ's love for us.*

When she pulled into the yard a few minutes later, Kristi noticed a teenage Amish boy wearing a straw hat, carrying a cardboard box over to a truck parked near the house. Her heart began to pound—it was the truck Joel used for work, which meant he must be here. From the looks of the boxes stacked on the front porch, this must be moving day for Elsie's family. As much as she dreaded facing Joel, Kristi wasn't leaving here until she'd seen Elsie and given her the church's gifts.

Turning off the engine, she stepped out of the

car. When she approached the young man, she asked if Elsie was there.

He pointed to the barn. "Joel's there, too—looking at the new cars he just got. He says they're worth a whole lot of money, so now Uncle Joel has a big collection of cars." The boy bobbed his head, grinning widely. "My uncle is rich!"

Kristi's spine stiffened. Apparently Joel had not changed at all. His emphasis was still on money, and now he'd bought more cars. *Won't he ever get his priorities right?*

"Would you please get your mother?" she asked. "I have some things in the car I want to give her." With any luck, only Elsie would come out, and she'd avoid seeing Joel at all.

The boy nodded and headed for the barn. A few minutes later, Elsie appeared. . .and Joel was with her.

Joel halted when he stepped out of the barn and saw Kristi standing beside her car. He had no idea what she was doing here, but the sight of her beautiful face and auburn hair made his heart race. If he hadn't known she had a new boyfriend, he would have dashed over to her, explained that he'd become a Christian, and begged her once again to take him back. He'd never loved another woman the way he did her. Even though he didn't deserve a second chance, if Kristi would forgive Joel for his past mistakes and agree to become his wife, he'd spend the rest of his life trying to make her happy.

Heart thumping so hard blood pulsated in his head, Joel approached Kristi. Before he had a chance to say anything, she smiled at Elsie and said, "Doris told me about your house burning down, and I've brought you a little something from my church." She opened her trunk and pointed to several boxes full of food. Then she reached into her purse, pulled out an envelope, and handed it to Elsie. "Please accept this love gift and use it in any way you need for your new home."

"I. . .I don't know what to say." Elsie's eyes filled with tears. "Thanks to the inheritance I've received from my dad, my husband and I have all the money we need, so I don't feel right about taking this."

Kristi glanced briefly at Joel, then looked quickly back at Elsie. "I would like you to have it. I'm sure you can use the extra food, and if you don't need the money, feel free to pass it along to someone else in need."

"That's called 'paying it forward,'" Joel spoke up.

Without looking at him, Kristi nodded.

Elsie hugged Kristi. "Please tell your church people I said thank you." She gave Joel's arm a little nudge. "I'll leave you two alone so you can talk. I believe you have some catching up to do." Without another word, she hurried into the house. Joel's nephew removed one of the boxes from Kristi's truck and followed his mother inside.

Palms sweaty and heart still beating hard, Joel cleared his throat. "Umm. . .there's something I'd like you to know, Kristi."

"Don't tell me. Let me guess. You've gotten a huge inheritance from your dad, so you've purchased several more cars, which you are keeping in his barn."

He shook his head vigorously. "No, it's not like that."

Her eyes narrowed. "How is it then?"

Joel quickly explained how he'd accidentally found the secret room in his dad's barn, and was surprised to find the old cars. "At first I couldn't figure out why they were there or how they even got in the hidden room behind the barn." He paused and drew in a quick breath. "Then my aunt came out, and after I showed her what I'd found, she informed me that a long time ago, when Dad was a teenager, he'd had his own car. It was during his running-around years, when he'd been allowed to experience some things outside the Amish world."

Kristi stared at him with an uncertain expression.

"Anyway," Joel continued, "Aunt Verna said even after Dad sold his car and joined the church, he often talked about his interest in classic cars. Nobody had any idea his interest went further than merely talking about cars." He motioned to the barn, slowly shaking his head. "Apparently over the years, Dad bought several old cars and snuck them in a room behind a secret door. So now. . ."

"I know—your nephew told me—you're rich."

Joel pulled his fingers through his thick hair. "If I sell them, I probably will get a lot of money, but I won't keep it all. I'll give a good chunk of it to someone in need." He took a step closer to her. "You see, Kristi, after committing my life to God, I've come to realize how selfish I was, and I've changed."

"He's telling you the truth," Aunt Verna said when she came out of the barn.

Joel was surprised his aunt had even heard what he'd said, but then he remembered her new hearing aids and figured she'd finally turned them on.

Aunt Verna stepped up to them and placed

both hands on Kristi's shoulders. "My nephew is not the same person he was before. He sold his first classic car to help his family, and now, thanks to my brother's will stating that Joel should have the house, barn, and everything in it, he has more cars to sell so he can help others."

Joel gave his aunt a quick wink. "If no one has any objections, I may keep one of the cars. It'll be fun to fix it up. Then every time I drive it, I'll think of Dad."

"I think that would be fine, Joel." Aunt Verna slipped her arm around his waist. "Your daed was a bit eccentric, which is probably why he bought all those vehicles when he knew it went against our church rules for a member to own a car. But given that he kept them in the secret room for his own amusement and didn't drive them, I'm sure if anyone outside our family hears of this, they'll understand."

"I hope so, but even if they don't, what's done is done. We can't go back and change the past."

"No, but we can make the best of the here and now and plan well for our future." Aunt Verna stepped aside and gave Joel a gentle push toward Kristi. "You two are obviously in love with each other. Don't you think you ought to talk things through and begin again?"

Before either Joel or Kristi could respond, his aunt turned and headed for the house.

Trembling for fear of her rejection, Joel looked directly at Kristi. "Aunt Verna's right. I do still love you, but I won't try to get in the way of your new relationship."

Her forehead wrinkled. "What new relationship?"

Joel explained about the day he'd shown up at church and seen her sitting beside a blond-haired man.

"That was Darin, our new youth pastor." Kristi shook her head. "We're not in a relationship. We're just friends."

Joel heaved a sigh of relief.

"But aren't you in a relationship, Joel?"

"What makes you think that?"

"I saw you at the Farmstead Restaurant in Berlin a few weeks ago with the young woman you used to date. You were holding her hand."

So it was Kristi I saw leaving the restaurant that day. Laughter bubbled in Joel's chest and spilled over.

She tipped her head. "What's so funny?"

"Anna and I aren't back together. We ran into each other by accident that day and decided to share a table. I wasn't holding her hand either. I only touched it when I was telling her I was glad to hear she's being courted by a new man in her church district."

Kristi's cheeks flamed a bright pink. "So we both assumed the other was seeing someone else, when neither of us has ever gotten over the other."

He reached for her hand and was glad when she didn't pull it away. "Does that mean you still love me?"

She nodded slowly. "I've tried to fight it and denied my feelings so many times I began to believe it was true. But the day I saw you with Anna, I knew the love I felt for you had never really died."

Joel smiled with relief. "Can you ever forgive me for all the hurt I caused? Would you be willing to give me another chance?"

"Yes," she murmured, tears shimmering in her eyes.

Barely able to speak around the lump lodged in his throat, Joel dropped to his knees. "Kristi Palmer, would you do me the honor of becoming my wife?"

"I will."

Joel stood and pulled Kristi into his arms. Hoping no one was watching their display of affection, he kissed her gently on the lips. When the kiss ended, he smoothed Kristi's hair back from her face and whispered, "When I finally realized that true compassion is feeling someone else's pain and doing something about it, I wanted to do a heartfelt, selfless act and didn't care about getting anything in return. When we raise our own children someday, I hope we can teach them that."

Kristi pressed her head against his chest. "We will, Joel. That's a promise."

EPILOGUE

One Year Later

Kristi stood at the kitchen window, looking out at the flowers and trees in full bloom. After being married to Joel these past six months, and living here in his father's old house, she still felt as though she were living a dream. Residing in Amish country and becoming part of her husband's wonderful family had filled a place in Kristi's heart she'd always felt was missing. To add to her joy, she'd been taking classes to become a midwife to the Amish and other women in the area. A week ago, she'd had the privilege of assisting the midwife when her sister-in-law's baby boy was born. What a miracle it was that the Lord had given Doris a healthy pregnancy and a strong infant. She and Brian named their son Andrew Joel. He was a sweet little guy, and seeing him sleeping in Doris's arms made Kristi eager to start her own family with Joel.

She glanced around the spacious kitchen Joel had remodeled to suit their needs. It wasn't fancy by English standards, but he'd installed electricity and given Kristi two oversized ovens. She looked forward to entertaining here for years to come. This evening, Arlene, Elsie, Doris, and their families would be coming over for a potluck dinner. Since Akron wasn't far away, her folks had been invited, too.

Turning her gaze back to the window, Kristi spotted Joel filling one of their bird feeders. These days, when he wasn't working at some jobsite for his business, his energies were spent on getting things done around here. Tonight, as most evenings, they would leave their television set off and enjoy a delightful time with their families.

Joel might not be a member of the Amish church, but the love he'd shown for his family and, most of all, for God proved that he was Amish in his heart.

She smiled, thinking about her husband's identity here in this community. Joel had become known as the Amish millionaire's son, who cared about people more than himself, and whose generosity had helped many.

Kristi closed her eyes and whispered a prayer. "Thank You, Lord, for teaching us by Your example to look for ways to perform selfless acts."

MILLIONAIRE PIE

Ingredients:

2 (9 inch) baked pie shells

2 cups powdered sugar, not sifted

1 stick butter, softened

1 egg

¼ teaspoon salt

¼ teaspoon vanilla

1 cup whipping cream

1 cup crushed pineapple, well-drained

½ cup pecans

Cream powdered sugar and butter in mixing bowl. Add egg, salt, and vanilla. Mix until fluffy. Spread mixture in baked pie shells. In another bowl, whip cream until it forms stiff peaks. Blend in well-drained pineapple and nuts. Spoon whipped-cream mixture on top of pies and chill until ready to serve.